T BEHOLDERS

HESTER MUSSON

June, 1878. The body of a boy is pulled from the depths of the River Thames, suspected to be the beloved missing child of the widely admired Liberal MP Ralph Gethin.

Four months earlier. Harriet is a young maid newly employed at Finton Hall. Fleeing the drudgery of an unwanted engagement in the small village where she grew up, Harriet is entranced by the grand country hall; she is entranced, too, by her glamorous mistress Clara Gethin, whose unearthly singing voice floats through the house. But Clara, though captivating, is erratic. The master of the house is a much-lauded politician, but he is strangely absent. And some of their beautiful belongings seem to tell terrible stories.

Unable to ignore her growing unease, Harriet sets out to discover their secrets. When she uncovers a shocking truth, a chain of events is set in motion that could cost Harriet everything, even her freedom …

———————◦

HESTER MUSSON studied at Bristol University and the RCS in Glasgow. She worked as an actress and autocue operator before writing full time, and now lives in Scotland.

The Beholders

Hester Musson

4th ESTATE · London

For my parents

4th Estate
An imprint of HarperCollins*Publishers*
1 London Bridge Street
London SE1 9GF

www.4thestate.co.uk

HarperCollins*Publishers*
Macken House
39/40 Mayor Street Upper
Dublin 1
D01 C9W8, Ireland

First published in Great Britain in 2024 by 4th Estate

1

Typeset in Goudy Oldstyle Std
by Palimpsest Book Production Ltd, Falkirk, Stirlingshire

Printed and bound in the UK
using 100% renewable electricity at CPI Group (UK) Ltd

'Some say a good eye is necessary; but I think any eye that can see at all can see whether the plaits lie straight by the threads, or whether they stretch awry.'

The Lady's Maid; her duties and
how to perform them (1878) p.25

'. . . behold the Throne Of Chaos'
Paradise Lost, Book II (2.959-960) John Milton (1674)

London Evening Standard

THE GETHIN CHILD MURDER

Tuesday 25th June, 1878

Proceedings at the Old Bailey were disrupted today as chaotic scenes followed a momentous turn in the Gethin trial. Mrs Clara Gethin, the wife of Mr Ralph Gethin MP, was indicted yesterday for the wilful murder of their child and the disposal of his body in the River Thames in London.

At the time of the disturbance, a former housemaid employed by the Gethins at Finton Hall, Hertfordshire, was being questioned by the prosecution. The court was hearing a most distressing account of Mrs Gethin's treatment of her son, when an outburst from the public gallery caused Mrs Gethin to turn towards the source of the intrusion. A young woman was incoherently shouting the name of the murdered infant. It was as the woman was escorted from the gallery by two constables that Mrs Gethin turned back to the court and chose to break her silence for the first time.

FINTON HALL

FEBRUARY

Wednesday, 27th February

Letter from Mother. As expected.

Dear Harriet,

Thank you for the money you sent us last week – how much better for us all if you had brought it home with you yourself. Your letter has put me about, I won't pretend otherwise, and you know the reason. What am I to tell your father and sisters?

You must know that your father is no better. The doctor took me to one side yesterday to say his lungs are so weak, he may not be able to work for months, if at all. These last years in the quarry have told on him – I always said it would come to no good, digging up farmland for stones, and now they are after building an ironworks too, I'm told. Much good it will do your family. Your youngest sister is to be scullery maid at Beechwood, but you know how little we can expect from that. Your money will at least pay for the aprons and caps she needs. The rest will have to be put by for the doctor – James Stanworth, who was always so good to us, is leaving for America, and we cannot trust on Lady Stanworth's kindness forever.

If there wasn't William waiting, I would give thanks that you had found such a good place. I asked the new butler at Beechwood if he knew of Mr and Mrs Gethin (I pretended I was asking for your father's cousin's child – that is the wretched position you have put me in), and he said there is much talk in London of Mr Gethin doing great things for the country and for workers with his modern ideas. But there is no reason for you to stay in service now, Harriet. William, as you surely know, is to be made head gardener and have the Mill Lane cottage. You could ensure your father's comfort and put all our minds at rest. I only hope you have not lost sight of yourself. William is still most kind and loving to us all – that is something else we cannot trust on forever.

With love,
Mother

MARCH

Friday, 1st March

I'm on the floor in the pantry, so I'll be out of sight if someone comes into the kitchen. There's a drawer in the dresser there where I keep this book, but I'll be finding a new place for it now there's something in it to read. It's so perfect and weighty in its green cover, so expecting of a better hand, I've been half afraid of it. I've been waiting for a minute's quietness or for something to happen that's worthy of disturbing the lovely blankness of the page, but there's neither peace nor interest to be had at Finton Hall. So this is how I'm starting in earnest, hurriedly scratching out in pencil whatever comes to mind, sitting between a sack of beetroot and an old milk churn. Mrs B gave me the book in Gloucester Square, about a month before she died. She said I'd get better at writing if I kept a diary to show her. I thought she just wanted to hear servants' gossip first-hand, but maybe I should've listened – my letters are so cramped and uneven, they look ashamed of themselves.

I'm supposed to be washing up, but when I came down there was no one here. Mrs Clarkson has a rest about now and Mary's cleaning the upstairs rooms, as far as she cleans anything. Laurence slinks off somewhere – probably to lord it over the stable lad – when he should be ready to open the door to visitors. Not that anyone ever comes. He'll be back before Mrs Clarkson shows her big round face again, that's certain. She says her name in this voice – *Meesis Clockson*. It's supposed to be from when she worked in France, but it made me smile first time she said it, especially as her face *is* so round, like a

7

handsome clockface. I shouldn't have done that. She said, 'Something amusing you, Harriet?' Though it sounded like, 'Something amoosin oo, Arriet?' which didn't help.

———

Someone's come into the kitchen, and I didn't get up right away – my feet ache so, it's as if they've been walloped – so now I can't. I don't know who it is. They are so quiet, I keep thinking they've gone, but then there's a sigh or a shuffle again.

If I'm caught, there will be trouble. Mrs Clarkson doesn't just look like a clock – all our timings are set by her. Somehow, she eats up the minutes like she's always running fast. However hard I work, I'm behind time. Duncan, the coachman, says it's her job to pick the household servants, and her nose is out of joint because the missus employed me without telling her. I can believe it. She loves telling us all what a wonderful housekeeper she is, and how the master hired her on the spot when he overheard her giving a knife-cleaner the scolding of his life in her last place. Whatever the reason, she doesn't like me. She came tick-tocking around when I was scrubbing the floor in the morning room earlier and used her foot to point out where I needed to go over a bit, then gave me a sharp kick on the leg to hurry me up. I turned and looked at her, which she didn't like.

'Don't slant your eyes at me like that' – then something in French – 'there is a deal of work to be done before the master gets home.'

All high horse. I told her I found it a deal easier to do my work quickly when I wasn't being kicked. She narrowed her eyes at me then and gave a nasty, secret smile.

'We won't have to worry about you when the master's home. You'll find he won't want your sort upstairs.'

She leered at me strangely and piled on three more jobs before I could ask what she meant. It's not the first time she's said something like that

8

about the master. I don't know what it is about me that he's going to find so dreadful, but it casts a shadow over my time here. What always lifts my day and makes it all right is cleaning the nursery and taking up meals for the wet nurse, Lizzie. She's friendlier than the others, and I get to see the baby, who has won my heart twenty times over—

They've just tried to open one of the sticky drawers in the dresser. Silence again.

The job itself is almost as hard as it was back at the Henshaws', though a much grander place, of course, and I'd rather clean lovely things than their nasty dark old rooms. The things upstairs *are* lovely – every room has a different colour that rules all the others, so when I'm in the morning room I believe I could never live happily without yellow, and when I'm in the drawing room I can't think there's anything more beautiful to look at than blue – that blue that comes at dusk, deep and rich, but with light still in it. It covers the walls and sort of flows into ornaments and paintings. There's a scene at sea with lusty blue waves crashing against rocks – 'First Sight of America', it says – and every time I look at it, I'm stumped by how easy it is for the likes of James Stanworth to set off and see such a place for himself while I'm stuck wiping the dust from a picture. I'm as likely to get to the moon.

At the moment we're turning everything upside down, taking up carpets, taking down pictures and all that to clean properly, so I've been close enough to kiss some of the portraits – there's a little black boy in blue livery with a silver circlet around his neck, and a gentleman with eyes nearly the same blue that I'd like to see in a real face. Only the missus' portrait looks out of place – smaller, and she's dressed in green—

It was her in the kitchen! The missus, Mrs Gethin. God knows what she was doing poking about in there. She started humming to herself – just as I started writing about her – a velvety sound, and I leaned forward enough to see a slice of her skirts. Dark brown silk, certainly not a servant. I felt like a mouse peeking out of a hole at a waiting cat. Heart going like a tiny hammer. She's gone now.

I wrote before there is nothing of interest, but that's not true, it's just that I haven't met her since I arrived, not since she visited Mrs B's. The master's away in London being a member of parliament, so there's only the missus at home. I'm scared to death she's forgotten all about me and I might never see her again – upstairs and downstairs are like two different worlds in this house – and I'll only have her portrait to stare at like before. It used to hang in the drawing room at Gloucester Square, and I couldn't take my eyes off it – in it she's about sixteen, dressed in a green, gauzy thing and sitting in the corner of a garden in sunshine so lovely it warmed my skin just looking at it. But it was her expression that fixed me, looking a bit off to the side, behind my shoulder as it were, as if she was expecting to see something impossibly wonderful – like the end of a rainbow, or an elephant. I actually looked behind me once – not that I'd tell anyone – and was disappointed to see only the dullness of who-cares-o'clock and the sconces in need of a rub.

It was painted in Italy, which is why the light is so warm. Mrs B told me how the missus comes from a very old, noble family, who had to move abroad because they lost all their money, and when her parents died she went to live with Mrs B at Gloucester Square – they're related somehow. It clutched at my heart a bit that the girl in green had ended up there. I didn't want to picture her in the same rooms, looking out of the same windows as me. Not even ordinary rainbows to be seen. I think she might have felt the same way. Annie was cook there before I arrived, and she told me how the missus and Mrs B had a falling out because Mrs B didn't think she should marry Mr Gethin. All I know is she never came back to visit after her marriage. Not until she wrote last summer and asked herself to tea.

Later

Someone else came into the kitchen, so I was sure to jump up quick and hide my writing things behind a trencher at the back of a shelf. I knocked a jug as I did it though, which rocked itself onto the floor. It didn't break (thank God), but I couldn't keep hiding. Mary – she straight away asked what I was doing, and I said I was looking for where the sand was for the big pans. She said there wasn't any big pans to wash, which was true – so I said I'd just had the thought and was having a look so I'd be prepared – trying to get familiar.

Mary's face is like a rat's but very pretty – if that doesn't sound too strange. Brown hair and a delicate, pointy nose with bright little eyes. Not a freckle on her, unlike me. I could almost see her snout and whiskers snuffling the air trying to work out what I was really about. She's a bit younger than me – seventeen, I think – though head housemaid now I'm here, and always staring. It was her that showed me around last week. 'Here's the scullery,' or, 'Here's the boot room,' she'd say and look at me like she was saying something else. That's been the way ever since – it's like she can't believe I'm here, which might be the case as she's Mrs Clarkson's niece.

It feels strange to be writing about her in this book when I've got to go up and share a room. Risky, like I'm telling these things to someone I know can't keep a secret. I don't even know whom I'm writing it for, now Mrs B is gone. This was my first chance to get it back – I've been creeping around in the dark with my candle, trying not to upturn anything. Everyone else has gone to bed, so it's just me at the servants' table in an unsteady pool of light – same as every other night as Mrs Clarkson always gives me extra jobs straight after dinner and then won't let me leave the washing up until the morning. She says that any girl she had trained would have had it all done by nine, and the reason I'm so slow is because I'm clumsy. Truth is, I'm more like a general servant here than a housemaid. My hands are nearly as cracked and raw as they

11

were at the Henshaws'. I'd be ashamed to button Mrs Gethin's cuff now, though even at Gloucester Square, I noticed how red my fingers were against the white skin and blue veins of her wrist. I'd never been so close to a lady before and remember feeling as awed as when I was handed a doll as a child. To be allowed to touch the trim of its perfect dress and straighten its bonnet at will filled my little heart with almost religious fervour and a ferocious desire to protect.

Any visitor at Mrs B's was a rarity. I think Annie believed actually having one – and twice, no less – was an injustice. There was a lot of huffing as she dragged down a recipe book for the fancy biscuits (I swear I saw cobwebs). Her outrage made me laugh, which was good because I was on edge about meeting the girl in the painting. I'd only worked in the boarding house before and had never served a lady (except Mrs B, who was mad as a twig so didn't count).

It turned out all right; I didn't drop anything or kick the furniture. Mrs Gethin as she'd become wasn't sixteen anymore, of course. Nearer twenty-six and in a plain, loose, grey dress that almost hid her condition – I only noticed because, being shy, I kept dropping my gaze to her middle and eventually saw the slight roundness. What I did see of her face told me it was still striking and youthful, but there was worry in it. She was telling Mrs B about her lady's maid when I brought the tea in – I didn't hear what the trouble was exactly, but there had clearly been some misunderstanding, and the missus had come to London looking for her. I thought that was touching – that she should take such trouble.

When I went back in to clear the plates, Mrs B was plinking away unevenly on the piano, something forlorn – the story of the maid had moved her (though she later told me Mrs Gethin had been vexingly vague about what happened). Mrs Gethin herself had her eyes fixed on the rug. She looked quite pinched, but that might have been Mrs B's playing. My own gaze flicked from her face to the painting; it was too much not to compare the same features in such different lights and years. She was so still, it seemed she wasn't aware of me at all, but glancing back, I found her eyes were on my face. It flustered me so, I froze, half bent over the table to pick up the tray, and the words just fell out.

'I've often wondered, ma'am . . .'

Her expression didn't change.

'I've often wondered what you were looking at in that painting.'

She turned her gaze to the portrait and looked at it so long I thought she'd forgotten me. When her eyes found mine again, something had changed in them, like black pools after a pebble's been dropped in.

'I don't remember. What do you imagine I'm looking at?'

That made me even more flustered. My head filled up with just one awful word until it was either say that or say nothing. I mumbled it.

'An elephant maybe.'

Her laughter – sudden and fiercely impish – jolted Mrs B out of her playing; the old lady looked over and giggled without understanding. I felt my face flush.

'I mean something *like* that. Something you wouldn't think of.'

I could hear my voice turning sulky.

'I just . . . I'd like to see whatever it was, what made you look that way, that was all. Ma'am.'

I seized the tray as Mrs B began tottering towards us and escaped to the kitchen. Later, at the front door when she was leaving, Mrs Gethin shocked me by putting a hand on my arm.

'Thank you for taking notice of my old portrait.'

Her face was less pinched, and her eyes still had that shimmer.

'I feel I've had a friend all this time and not known it. As if I'm still . . .'

She didn't finish, only smiled a little, as if at her own silliness. I studied the portrait even more closely after she'd gone. It bothered me that she couldn't remember what she was looking at, but the idea that we were somehow friends unfurled inside me like a tiny rose, sweet and delicate.

A few days later she returned. Her missing lady's maid was not to be found, and she looked worn out. By then I was out of sorts myself. William had written to say he was to have the head gardener position when Mr Noakes retires in the spring. It means we can marry much earlier than expected. Annie plundered Mrs B's store of brandy to celebrate (I was sick in the wash basin next morning), but I couldn't tell her his letter had come as a shock and not of the right kind – I was too surprised by it myself. Lying in bed at night, I turned all my thoughts over, trying to find out which one was at fault. At Easter I had felt no different – he was as he always has been: big, blunt, tender sometimes. I don't remember a time without him. Like an older brother at first, and later – I don't know when the change came about. It feels as if we have had an understanding all my life. One day, when he can support us, we will be married and have children. One day.

It was the girl in green, I think, that forced me to admit how unready I am to go home and marry. That expression in her face. I found myself for the first time unwilling to look at her. William's letter should have brought the same bright hope into my eyes, but it didn't, and for that I felt guilty. Still do, like I've failed at something important. When Mrs Gethin returned, I peered at her as much as I could, as if I might find an answer in the older version, something to explain my feelings or guidance as to what to do. Her careworn face didn't offer much comfort, but it made me more curious as to what lay behind it. Seemed to me her burdens would be worth the trouble; they'd carry a greater weight and meaning than anything life in the Mill Lane cottage with William might bring. Mrs B was in bed when she arrived – she was ailing even then – and when I brought in the tea, Mrs Gethin was pacing the room and fumbling at the buttons of her left sleeve. I was bolder than I had been before.

'Can I help you, ma'am?'

She stopped and looked my way. I gestured.

'Oh.'

Abruptly, she sat down on the sofa and held her arm out. I had to sit too, perching on the edge, and was seized by that fierce, other-worldly feeling I'd had with the doll. The loop was stiff and tight, and needed working over the button. Looking after Mrs B was a pleasure, keeping her warm and clearing the crumbs she couldn't help dropping down herself, but this was different. The quality of Mrs Gethin's person – her smooth skin and warm scents – seemed to agitate the air around her with hidden music. Tending to this tiny part of her wardrobe, I felt more like I was handmaid to a goddess.

'Are you happy here?'

The question came out of nowhere. Now I think perhaps it was only because her mind had been so much on the troubles of her own servant.

'Yes, ma'am, very much.'

I was too shy to look at her, but I could feel her eyes on me.

'What will you do when Lady Berrington is no longer with us?'

No one had spoken openly about Mrs B's death before. It shocked me a little.

'I should go home, ma'am . . .'

I had been going to say 'and marry' but the words died in my throat.

'Should?'

Her attention seemed to sharpen.

'Is there a special reason?'

I took a breath and said it.

'I am to be married, ma'am.'

The loop finally secured itself over the button, but I didn't let go. Most people when I tell them burst into smiles and rain down good wishes. Mrs Gethin did none of that. She leaned forward slightly.

'Do you not wish it?'

'Oh, I do, ma'am!'

I let go of her cuff instantly and looked up. A sort of panic had seized me.

'No, I do! It's been a long engagement, and I . . . I just . . .'

My eyes, by some will of their own, turned to the girl in green. Mrs Gethin looked at the portrait too and back to me again. I was horrified to feel tears brimming. Next thing I knew she had taken my hand – hers felt as soft as silk – and moved closer along the sofa. After a moment, she spoke quietly.

'Consider. Your life is yours. You must do with it as you wish. If something . . .'

She looked back at the portrait as if for inspiration. I held my breath, scared she might let go of my hand.

'If you find yourself in a situation . . . painted, say, by others, and something beyond the frame calls you . . .'

She lifted her fingers to my chin and gently turned my face towards her.

'For heaven's sake, you must go to it.'

She looked at me with such tender earnestness, I think I should have sobbed and told her about William's letter and my strange reluctance if Mrs B hadn't chosen that moment to enter.

Mrs Gethin returned to Finton Hall after that, and I didn't see her again. Her words buried themselves in my heart like treasure. I take them out sometimes to turn them over and wonder at their meaning, though I know I shall never spend them. My world is different from hers. I wrote to William that I couldn't leave Mrs B in what was most likely her last illness and went to great lengths to keep the old lady alive – for her sake, of course, but also mine. Hours I spent reading Milton and relaying gossip by her bedside to keep her old mind from dimming. Annie thought I was angling for something in her will.

Then at around the same time she gave me this diary, Mrs B told me there was a housemaid's place at Finton Hall. I remember smiling to myself – even dying, she wanted a part in other people's lives. But when I perched on her bed and took her hand to talk to her, to remind her of William, I found there was none of the usual twinkle in her eye. She was looking at me with a directness that knocked my words flat.

'She'll be safe with you. You'll look after her. You'll make her better and bring her back to herself.'

It was an odd thing to say, even for her. I nodded as I always did, but she gripped my hand tightly; the strength of it was startling. Her eyes seemed not her own, they regarded me so strangely.

'Promise me, Harriet.'

I nodded again. What else could I do? Her urgency sent a shiver of something like fear through me. I've thought about it often since. How can a lady like Mrs Gethin, living in Finton Hall, not be safe? And if she's ill, how am I supposed to help her? Scrub the floors harder? But at the time, I was pulled into Mrs B's spell. It brought back that sense of grace and purpose I had felt simply buttoning Mrs Gethin's cuff, as if something had beckoned me that needed protection. I did nothing about it until shortly after Mrs B died when Mrs Gethin wrote herself with orders to send the portrait ahead – as if I'd accepted the position. She wrote that she'd be pleased to see both me and the painting again. A picture and an old lady's whimsy are absurd reasons to take a place, I know. Going home to William is a matter of when, not whether, but the thought of packing up that face and not following it to the real woman at Finton Hall made the air turn ashy.

So here I am, and here the portrait is – in a much grander drawing room – and I haven't seen a whisker of the missus before today. I begin to wonder if I imagined her kindness. If she's not out in the carriage or walking, she usually keeps to her rooms. Mary says she's difficult, always changing her mind and making up rules that have no reason – scrape this candle in her bedroom but never that one, don't touch the books in the library, and so on. She looked like she was going to say more, something worse about the missus, but stopped herself. I didn't bother asking more – waiting to see Mrs Gethin again has made me short with the other servants – they don't interest me – and impatient with the work, as if I'd been promised more than a housemaid's lot. I know how foolish that sounds. William's bewildered letters only serve to make me stick to the place more stubbornly.

I can't find the will to go to bed. It's so quiet. At Mrs B's there was always someone walking past or a carriage any time of night. And there'd be rattlings and clunks from next door. Here the silence presses in. It's almost as if the world has hushed so I can hear my own thoughts. I have a fancy the silence has turned up just to listen.

I must be tired thinking that. These hours of writing will cost me. It's the walk to the top I'm putting off – I'm still not used to the corners and stairs and long passages. From the outside Finton Hall looks like something out of a fairy tale. When I was driven here in the dogcart from the station, after miles and miles of nothing but small farms and humble cottages, I couldn't take my eyes off all the turrets and chimneys and creeping ivy. It feels strange to be in a place so far from anywhere else. So still. Walking up to bed at night, I think my own movement could set something off – disturbing the darkness like it's a riverbed. Makes me think of all the silt rising up and clouding the water while slimy mud creatures rush out of their hiding places. I'd rather curl up down here where there's still warmth. So long as I can stay sitting down, I don't care if ten monsters and a dozen lunatics jump out of the oven.

Sunday, 3rd March

Mrs B said if you give something beautiful your attention, it might just show you a secret – I don't think she meant a secret that would give you a bloodied finger. There's a cabinet of curiosities in the hall that I spend too long staring at when I'm cleaning. It even has a tiny elephant in it, carved in ivory, which made me splutter when I first saw it, thinking of what I'd said to the missus in Gloucester Square. There's also an eerie miniature portrait, just of someone's left eye and the area around it – Mary says it's called a lover's eye. The expression is unreadable without seeing the whole face, but I'm sure the eye follows me about in an unfriendly way. I've tucked it behind a glass paperweight with a real butterfly trapped inside and hope no one notices. And ever since I arrived, I've been wondering over a little lozenge-shaped thing which is beautifully jewelled but seems to serve no purpose. Today while I was cleaning it, I must have pressed something because a blade suddenly shot out, making me shriek and slicing my hand. Mary helped clean me up. She said it's the master who collects all the things in the house – they're from all over the world – and it was also him that made the house so pretty, long before he was married (he was in coal mining before he went into politics, and in Mary's words – which always sound borrowed – had to buy himself a society wife). He must have chosen the pictures too, which, though beautiful, aren't always pleasant up close. I don't know why he would want to look so often at volcanoes burying people in hot ash, or bloody battle scenes, or hell itself with its tortured souls. All those faces screaming silently from the walls.

The master isn't the only mystery. I asked about the lady's maid at dinner tonight, the one the missus was looking for in London. Mrs Clarkson told me to mind my own business, and Mary put her knife into her meat so hard it screeched the plate.

Tuesday, 5th March

I hate it. The work, the people, the house even, with its miles of quiet corridors and wild, staring eyes. Sculptures of rearing horses or captured nymphs seem positioned on purpose to make me jump. The master's got fine tastes, but he didn't make it friendly for the servants who have to carry coal and water up and down all day. There are times I'd swear the steps inch higher as I'm walking up them. I've come up to write about it as there's no one to talk to who'd care. If Mrs Clarkson sees the mess first, she can do what she likes. I was hauling a load of coal up to the morning room when I heard squealing and laughing, and Mary ran down past me. She should have been sweeping out the breakfast and dining rooms, which – strangely for a grand house like this – I've never seen used, but I notice she only really works when her aunt is watching.

It was on the corner of the back stairs and I'd turned in surprise when Laurence bounded around as well and knocked the scuttle with his leg. Cracked his shin – and I hope it hurt. Coal bounced and tumbled everywhere. The scuttle smashed and clanged its way to the bottom, so I was sure Clockface would come in a rage and accuse me of being clumsy again. Laurence swore and carried on chasing after Mary, who shrieked and ran off down the passage. I was so tired, I had to sit down and cry.

Clearing up is going to take an age. I picked up the coal – the stairs, walls and myself are all covered in black dust – and took the scuttle into the kitchen. They were there, making faces at each other behind my back, I could feel it. I don't know how I hadn't noticed before. No wonder Mary's always staring and twitching at me, jealous as a cat. And Laurence – well, he's the same as any other footman. Tall and handsome, like the fancy fire irons that are a devil to clean in the drawing room, but a lot less use. He looked me up and down when I first arrived, taking me all in – his brows and lashes are so fair they're almost white, it's quite startling when he looks at you – and I was reminded of the under footman at Beechwood; William said he'd tup anything that moved, given a chance. Laurence is a dressed-up puppet compared to William. His green handkerchief soaked in cologne isn't part of his livery, nor is the large ring he's always swivelling on his little finger. And I know from Mary that the master scooped him out of some hovel when he was a child to train him up as a pageboy. I wish he hadn't bothered.

Now I've got coal dust on the pillowcase. Another bloody thing to clean.

Later

Perhaps a good thing I don't have anyone to speak my mind to. I'd be eating my words now. Still in a mood, I stomped down to start cleaning up the dropped coal and turned the corner to find Laurence already on his hands and knees halfway up the steps with buckets and brushes all around him. He was swathed from top to toe in white aprons and lengths of old linen to protect his livery from the coal dust – a besmirched angel.

'Oh.'

I stopped. He sat back on his heels and raised an eyebrow.

'A mighty mess you've made.'

'*Me?*'

My blood was up, and I saw his smile too late.

'Oh.'

It's never been just him and me before. His handsomeness, even in such ridiculous clothes, is difficult to ignore. He has very fair, curly hair, and the way his brows and lashes almost fade into the paleness of his skin, he looks carved in marble like one of the statues. I felt my face flush and said the first thing to cover it.

'I can help.'

He watched me make my reluctant way down the steps and wagged a brush at me.

'Clean yourself up, you look like you've been tumbled by a miner.'

I hesitated, unsure what to say to that, and he swiped at my waist.

'Look, he squeezed you there . . . And he pinched you fine there . . .'

Sounding – God help me – like Mary, I squeaked and flailed my hands about.

'Stop it.'

Another stab with the brush.

'There's a tickle . . .'

'I said stop it. I'm going.'

He laughed and turned back to the job. I trudged back to the attic, half-annoyed at myself for smiling.

Saturday, 9th March

I might not have fully seen the missus again, but I've *heard* her now. It's Mary's evening off and she's gone somewhere with Laurence, though she didn't say that. I don't know why she can't talk straight. Too used to hiding it from Clockface, I suppose – I've seen how careful they are in the kitchen, barely looking at each other when the cat's about. I've not been so quick to dismiss Laurence since he took care of the coal spill. For all his swagger, I've seen him warm a shawl for Mary when she comes in with freezing hands from scrubbing the steps, and he snatched a bone from the joint when Clockface wasn't watching to throw to the old yard dog. Perhaps Mary has something to feel jealous over after all, other than fine features.

She was in the drawing room when I went to fasten the windows, putting rouge on herself in the big mirror. When she saw who it was, she went back to dabbing at her face and turning it this way and that like an artist admiring her work. The rouge was too thick, I thought, but she looked nice all the same – like a picture, one of the pretty ones with creamy-cheeked, pink-lipped ladies lolling about on daybeds or grassy banks. She said she had an appointment to keep, smiling all secretively. After she'd gone, I looked at my own complexion in the glass – more off-milk than cream, and freckled – and felt dull. I remember William stroking the line of my jaw once and saying it was a shame that between us we'd make square-shaped babies. It's true, probably. My face is a built thing, not a painting – something to be put to use rather than admired. I don't think rouge would help. Odd to feel I'm the only plain one for miles around. Usually, it's the pretty servants that stand out. Perhaps that's what Clockface meant by my 'sort', and the master prefers handsome servants to go with his handsome furnishings. I'll bet money the lady's maid no one will talk about was fair-faced too.

Mary being away meant I had to take the supper things up to the missus. Clockface took them in, which disappointed me sorely, but she made me carry the tray. As we came nearer, I heard singing and was so surprised I stopped on the stairs. Clockface huffed and hurried me along – she's quicker to temper than Mother. There wasn't any point in staying anyway as the song cut off as soon as Clockface knocked. I don't know what it was – the words weren't English – but the warmth of it slipped under my skin. It was like seeing the sun after months of gloom. There was so much feeling in it – sadness and sweetness at once – it threw beauty into all the dark corners of my day, like her portrait used to. Even this little attic room looks less bleak. I'm sitting on my bed – and with Mary out it doesn't matter how much it squeaks – with a blanket around me and the candle on a chair. The cracked jug and tin bowl on the washstand and scrap of faded rug are not so miserable tonight. And it doesn't matter that my hands are so stiff from cold that my letters are even worse. At least I can write this without Mary's staring – she's curious about what I'm writing, or that I'm writing at all. I don't tell her what Mrs B said – that I should try and notice everything and write it all down, so no precious thing slips me by. Our small window doesn't have much of a view because of other gabled parts of the house, but tonight there's a moon glinting in. I'm glinting back.

Sunday, 10th March

Met her! Met her at last, and I've been half giddy for the rest of the day. I was dusting the drawing room except I wasn't because I was looking out at the view. The rooms at the front of the house have huge windows and it's a relief to look outside and see some distance. It's been drizzling for days, and mists shroud the house, so it feels as if we're lost in an eternity of fog. But today the rain clouds moving across the valley were like veils trailing over the green, and between them – golden light. Gilded patches of land. It all moved, light and dark dancing and turning together across a huge floor.

'Good morning.'

I jerked like a hen. Think I might have squawked too. I never heard her come in, she was just there like a ghost watching me I don't know how long. I forgot to curtsy and stared at her with my mouth open until I could bring up a 'sorry, ma'am'. For a long moment, she didn't say anything. I thought, she must think me simple as well as idle – and what was I expecting? Her hand on mine? More talk of me being like a friend and breaking out of picture frames? That was almost nine months ago.

After a moment's study of my face, she asked what I was looking at and walked right up to me to peer out of the window. Prattling on about gilded shadows and dancing colours while standing in an apron with a duster in my hands was impossible, but I could hardly claim to be doing anything useful.

'The weather's changed, ma'am. I was looking at the light.'

'The light?'

She seemed struck by the idea, then nodded.

'Yes, it's a stirring sort of weather.'

I tried to take her all in again sideways. She's about my height, though her hat added a foot, and was all feathers and flounce, everything black. Black silk dress with a black lace shawl around her shoulders. She was paler and thinner than before, but her features were still unsettlingly familiar from the portrait. The light caught on the very fine, very light hairs on her face, she was that close, and I thought – poetically, I think – how she was all dark and light shades like the weather. Her scent was of blossom and something else sweet but sweet in a minor key. She smelled fit to eat.

'How long were you with Lady Berrington?'

'Nearly two years, ma'am.'

'And before?'

I paused, trying to think how to describe the Henshaws' boarding house. How to say anything that wouldn't sound stupid to her.

'With another family in London, ma'am.'

She nodded faintly and – thankfully – didn't ask anything more. I thought of the dank little room next to the kitchen where I had slept and the soot-coated cobwebs clogging the corners. They were the first thing I saw when I lit my candle each morning. Every day I promised myself I'd find a moment to clear them, and then didn't think about it again until I crawled into bed at night. The spacious drawing room of Finton Hall with its clean air and gorgeous furnishings grew bright around me. I breathed in sharply as if my lungs had been clogged by the memory.

'It looks well there, does it not?'

She had turned towards the wall with the portrait. I felt a surge of happiness – Gloucester Square was not forgotten then. But I paused. Agreeing with her would have been a lie. Her portrait is out of place in all the rich blue and gilt of the room, and it's taken the hook of a larger painting so looks marooned. She didn't seem to notice my silence.

'There was music playing. Beyond the garden wall. Some street musicians had stopped in the road.'

She turned and smiled at me.

'You asked what I was looking at, do you remember? And I couldn't recall.'

I was flooded by her smile – my own face must have lit up. She turned back to the painting.

'I was listening. It was music.'

I wanted more – I wanted to know how well she remembered Mrs B's.

'Not an elephant then, ma'am?'

Her laughter came instantly; she didn't need to think about it. My fingers squeezed and worked the duster as if they could wring pleasure out of it.

'No, I'm afraid not an elephant. The music coming so suddenly though . . .'

She closed her eyes, as if it was playing still. I took my chance to study her face openly, looking for any sign of the trouble Mrs B had hinted at. There was only yearning – for youth or Italy perhaps. Her eyes opened again directly onto mine, and I had the strangest feeling they had been watching me all the while through their closed lids. It made me forget myself.

'Why did you not have the portrait sent here before, ma'am? It must remind you of Italy.'

THE BEHOLDERS

She gave the picture a more considering look.

'Lady Berrington liked it. And as I couldn't stay with her myself . . .'

Her expression clouded, her mind gone elsewhere. I remembered what Annie had said about Mrs B wanting the missus to remain at Gloucester Square as her companion and the falling out that that had caused. The missus murmured to herself.

'I believe it did me good to think of it hanging somewhere it would be taken care of and enjoyed.'

She smiled at me then.

'I am very glad you have come to Finton Hall.'

The way she looked at me, I was sure she was remembering our last conversation about my going home to marry William. I felt confused and almost ashamed, as if my unbroken engagement might disappoint her. She told me I could continue, and I bobbed – up and down I went today. I wished she'd say more about the portrait – why it wouldn't be enjoyed here – but didn't dare ask. Also, I didn't fancy the idea of working with her in the room. There's a hoard of busts and vases above the fireplace, and I was industrious over them, not missing the dent of a nostril or curve of a handle. I didn't stop for what felt like an hour, trying not to flinch as I usually do when wiping the duster over the blank, white eyes of the sculptures. All the while I hoped she'd start talking again, but when I did look around she was gone. As noiselessly as she came. If it wasn't for the clear memory of her standing next to me so I could feel the warmth of the living off her, I'd think I'd seen an apparition.

Behind with the rooms again – short words from Ding Dong. She can tell it to the bedbugs as far as I care.

Monday, 11th March

I've found out about the man with the blue eyes in the picture in the drawing room. Laurence was collecting music for the missus when I

26

went in there gathering up brass to clean. I wanted him to tease me like before, so asked about the picture. He barely glanced at it.

'That's the old devil that pays our wages.'

'The master?'

It gave me a jolt, as if I'd found out he'd been watching me all this time. In the portrait he's seated and there's no background to speak of, so his face takes all the attention. There's a delicacy to his features, which seems almost at odds with the steady blue of his gaze. Laurence tucked music sheets under his arm.

'The honourable *member* himself.'

My stomach plunged.

'Isn't he . . . kind?'

He gave a sour sort of laugh.

'Oh, he's kind all right. A saint.'

He stopped abruptly, as if he'd been punctured, and left quickly after barely a nod. I don't understand why he should be so bitter. It reminds me of Clockface's threats about the master and makes me a little afraid.

Tuesday, 12th March

Letters from William and Mother on the same day. I had a job getting them off Clockface – she seems to think I'm obliged to tell her who they're from. When she finally handed them over, she dropped them on purpose and tutted.

'Clumsy girl.'

William's first.

Dear Harriet,

I think it is time we spoke plain. I am sorry Lady Berrington passed away – I didn't mention that before. She sounded from your letters a very nice lady even if I didn't understand all of her ways like I told you. I hope you are not too cut up about it.

But I am more sorry that you didn't come home to see us when you could and that you have taken a new place, particularly as it is outside of London and I thought seeing London was the big thing with you. I believed you when you said you couldn't leave your mistress as she was ill and that was what kept you from coming back home. We have an understanding, Harriet. When I wrote to tell you about my new position and what I've saved, you knew what I was saying. I don't think it is asking too much that you give your notice in a new place where you don't even know anyone. I shall expect to hear from you that you are coming home by Easter.

Yours as ever,

William

PS you know you're more to me than anyone else, and you know I'd be the happiest man in the county if you'd let me be the one to take care of you. Who else will say that, Harriet?

Strange writing out his words in my hand. Strangest of all writing my own name, as if it's been stolen somehow. Here's the other.

Dear Harriet,

As your mother, I am writing to tell you that you are very close to losing William, and it would be nothing less than you deserve. I don't know what you were thinking, taking another situation when you know he is waiting. I have never felt more embarrassed. How can you risk displeasing him? Dorcas Harding is pretty and knows what's good for her. Unless you're foolish enough to want to spend the rest of your life in service – and you can expect nothing more from your father and me if you do – you will come home now and make amends before it is too late.

With love,

Mother

PS I expect it was that Berrington woman putting ideas into your head – you know Mr Bridges told Mr Noakes who told William that he had heard Lord S say that she was considered quite mad and a liability in society, especially since her husband died and failed to leave anyone in charge of her. See sense, Harriet. It would grieve me to see you ruin your chances.

PPS I enclose a newspaper cutting about the Quarrymen's Association. They have won the right to work fewer hours, and the sick and injured are to be helped. It all comes too late for your poor dear father. If he weren't so ill from that blessed quarry, he would fetch you home himself. You are breaking his heart, Harriet.

I know Father would never stir himself so much – he'd grunt and go back to his whittling. And what she means by not expecting more from *them* when I've been sending nearly all my wages home, I don't know. At least now I know what William meant by 'anyone else'. Dorcas *is* pretty and was always more well liked than me.

Sunday, 17th March

My half day off and it's hammering rain. Torrential. Water is pouring off the gables and turrets and overflowing the gutters too, so it sounds like the second flood coming. The walk I planned is lost. Seems looking forward to something is a sure way to have it snatched from me. I've been no further than the yard yet. The most green I've seen so far is the baize on the servants' side of the doors and the missus' dress in the portrait – I was closer to trees in London.

I've not talked with the missus since last Sunday, though I've tried hard enough, finding reasons to go up and down that staircase. Twice I've heard her singing – worth the toll on my legs. I'd like to sink into her voice and be swayed about by it like seaweed under water. The work doesn't feel so hard, knowing I'm doing it for her. There's no reason for me to be near her though unless she wishes it. The most I do is curtsy or nod if she passes while I'm wiping stair rods or whatnot.

If I had Mary's job, I'd have to talk to her every day, but I usually see her from a distance when I'm rubbing windows or airing the guest bedrooms. She leans on Laurence sometimes when he helps her out of the carriage and says a few words to him as if they're old friends. Mary says it's the vicarage she goes to so often – they are very musical there, and the missus goes to sing. She made it sound shameful somehow. I've also seen the missus walking towards the woods at the back in her dark dresses. Any weather. That's when I feel the distance between us most. I can't imagine anymore what that's like, stepping out into the fresh air whenever I feel like it. Clockface thinks if I'm not on my hands and knees scouring something, the sky will fall in.

As I couldn't go out, I wandered towards the missus' room again, hoping to hear her voice, but at the bottom of the stairs were Mary and Laurence, tucked into the corner beside the big dresser. They were pressed against each other and deep in a kiss so long and searching, it seemed bottomless. I stepped back before they knew I was there and stood in my own confusion, heart beating, aware of a sense of wanting and of loss. Me and William never kiss like that. It's not that he lacks passion as such, but his eager lips and rough fumblings under my petticoat have always felt more to do with him than me. I was wondering what that meant – if I am destined never to know what Mary knows – when I heard them taking their leave of each other and had to flee down the passageway.

I took the east stairs instead, all the way up to the nursery and asked Lizzie if I could help with the baby. If I can't see the missus herself, I thought, maybe I can find out more about her. Lizzie's different from the others – always pleased to see me and so comfortable and patient, it's soothing just to be near her. There's nothing for her to do but nurse the little one and she's glad of any company she can get, I think. She must miss her own child. The nursery is on the third floor, the other side of the house from the missus' rooms, which I thought was odd, but Lizzie says the missus has shown scant interest in Edward since his birth. The nursery is always ready for when she's supposed to visit in the afternoon – she won't allow him to be brought to her – but she hardly ever comes and when she does, she rarely holds the child. Other times she turns up without warning and spends an age staring at him.

'Does she sing to him?'

Lizzie shook out a linen with a snap and folded it deftly.

'Oh yes, she does. Nothing you'd normally sing to a child. It's . . . mournful.'

'Is she kind to you?'

She considered.

'She's nothing at all to me, really. Or, I should say, I'm nothing to her.'

I laughed with her – that's the way it is – but inside I felt a secret satisfaction that the missus had remembered me. Her treatment of Edward is a puzzle though. I leaned over the cot to watch his intent little face. Babies' eyelashes make me tingle; I don't know how a mother could resist him. Perhaps Mrs B knew. I remember how hard she had gripped my hand when she asked me to make the missus better. Maybe there was trouble already about the coming child, and she knew it. Edward frowned in his sleep and clenched his tiny fist. I had the fiercest urge to scoop him up and cuddle him against me. As that was out of the question, I walked to the window and stared at the drenching.

'How far is the church?'

'About four miles, in the village.'

I hadn't realised we were so far off. The hall pressed in on me suddenly.

'Is that why no one goes?'

Lizzie shrugged.

'Mr Gethin takes the household when he's here. He likes things done properly. It's a credit to him.'

I was silent. Any mention of the master makes me uneasy. His arrival is an unknown, shapeless thing coming my way that can't be put off, like an operation. If it's my face he takes objection to, I can hardly help it. But Duncan is no picture either, and his leg is twisted from a mining accident. The master employed him here when he couldn't work in the mine anymore, which doesn't sound like a man who would dismiss a housemaid for having a square jaw. The more I handle and clean the lovely things in the house, the more I want to make a good impression when he arrives. Silly as it is, I find myself being most particular when working in sight of his portrait. His eyes follow me around like the lover's eye in the cabinet used to before I hid it, but I don't find the master's gaze unfriendly. Lizzie took my silence otherwise.

'You must go to church if you want to, Harriet. They can't stop you.'

I wasn't sure about that, but I nodded. Truth is, I've been too tired to think about it. Mrs B always said prayers and took us to St James'. Perhaps I'm sliding into bad ways, being here – though if I keep turning the other cheek to old Ding Dong, I'll be black and blue. Just then I was thinking more that it would be a chance to see other people. Finton Hall seems cut off from the rest of the world. No wonder the missus escapes to the vicarage so much – I'd go a little odd sitting up here with nothing to do. But then I would spend all day with the baby. There's Hill Court I've heard talked about as a neighbour, but it doesn't sound close. The master must have wanted a house fit for a recluse when he bought it.

'What's he like? Mr Gethin?'

Lizzie shook her head.

'I only saw him a few times when he came to look at the baby before going to London. He was interested at least.'

'But he hasn't come back to visit?'

'It's the war business keeping him in town.'

She sounded as weary of it as I am. There are battles in the kitchen about it. Laurence says we shouldn't get involved and the politicians aren't to be trusted. Clockface gave him an earful for that, seeing as the master's an MP and in favour. She talks as if Russian troops were marching on Finton Hall itself, though I doubt she has any real scruples about what's happening in other countries. She would go to war with her own shadow if the master said it was a good idea. All I know is, I'm glad if it keeps him in London a bit longer.

Thursday, 21st March

Letter from Annie.

Dearest Har,

I am married! It really happened, can you believe it? We're in Margate and it's as damp and soggy as that awful cake I used to make for Mrs B – do you remember? What a month for weather! But we don't mind as we don't care to leave our room very often. Please hurry up and marry William and we can compare EVERYTHING.

The wedding was a bore – you didn't miss very much, except for the wine afterwards. Robert paid for it even though he's so serious – you remember him – the constable with the birthmark who came to the kitchen a few times at Gloucester Sq? (He's detective sergeant now and the darling of Scotland Yard.) Andrew has found us rooms in Lambeth with a yard so I can take in washing for the boys in his section house. No more working for loony old ladies for me.

You have to write and tell me everything. I still don't know why you bolted off to Hertfordshire instead of going home – has William done something? I hope not – you made him sound like a prince.

What's it like there? How are the other servants? Most importantly, when can you come and see us in London? WHEN?

Your ever affectionate MARRIED friend,

Annie

I've sat down to write to her twice, but I don't know what to say. Did I make William sound like a prince? I suppose I must have. When that under footman from Beechwood clicked his tongue at us once and said,

'Never mind, eh?' – meaning me – William knocked him down. At the time, I thought one might call that chivalrous, but now I think he did it out of shame on his own account, not to defend me. I wish I could have an hour with Annie in the kitchen in Gloucester Square; I'd tell her everything then, and she'd sort out the wheat from the chaff and tell it back to me in a way that makes sense. Somehow, it's so much harder to put it down on paper when she's miles away.

I keep starting to answer William's letter too, but each time my pen grinds to a halt and bleeds ink all over the paper. Seems I can't write to anyone except myself. I know I should give him a date and be done with it, but there's my promise to Mrs B, and I've barely seen the missus yet. I want the feeling of making my own choices a little while longer. We'll be married long enough, and from what I've seen, the choice of a husband is the last real choice any woman makes.

I don't count Annie in that. Poor Andrew never had a chance. She lured him down the steps into the kitchen at Gloucester Square with delicacies that poor Mrs B certainly paid for but never got a taste of. Annie gets what she wants and doesn't mind how. Her marrying a policeman makes me snort.

Monday, 25th March

Seems to me the missus is more ghost than mistress, appearing suddenly at awkward times the way she does – always full of secrets and sadness. I'd been working hard on the grate in the library this morning, blackening it. The master uses the library as his study, and there's a rumour he's coming back, war or not. I heard Laurence tell one of the garden hands he's expected in time for the Easter holiday. He kicked a clod of earth as he said it, which exploded instantly, nearly knocking him off balance and dirtying his boot. The news made my stomach turn over. I was out in the yard beating a carpet as it wasn't raining – only time I can get into the fresh air, so I don't mind it – and the lad had wandered in to get something from the stables. Laurence never misses a chance to strut about in front of the outdoor servants. He gave him trouble for coming so close to the house in his dirt, but the stable boy's hardly in livery and all the mucky work of the house happens out there, me and my red face and rolled-up sleeves to show it. The lad knew it – seemed to be enjoying himself. He's the one as has the same slow gait as William.

The library is a good room to work in. All those books are like very polite, very quiet company that don't mind at all if you give them the time of day or not. I worked up another sweat blackening the grate and did it well. When I stood up, I saw in the mirror I'd got a smudge on my face but was loath to trudge downstairs just to wash. The books weren't going to mind. Then I dusted and waxed as if the master was watching – brought up a tremendous shine on a table in the middle of the room. In the centre of that there's a curious thing. It looks out of place and ugly amongst the other objects in the house. I felt a kind of kinship with it. There are two upright metal rings overlapping, one with teeth, and a wooden handle. I didn't dare turn it, but once polished and reflected in the table, it began to look strangely beautiful. I sometimes wonder if it's only housemaids who notice these things.

We're not turning the room out completely, taking all the books off the shelves. In fact, we're forbidden from shifting a single volume. It's a strange rule. Clockface was particularly pointed about it.

'They're not for the likes of you, whatever airs you give yourself.'

Mary must have been talking about me writing. I dusted every ledge properly – gave the books' bottoms a good pat. Then I ran my fingers along the back of the shelves to feel if anything was hidden behind the books, but nothing answered.

There's a stepladder to reach the higher volumes. I was halfway up it, rubbing the spine of an ancient guide to breeding pigs, when I glanced at the next one and saw a volume of Milton's poetry. It gave me a jolt, like when you meet a friend in town unexpected. The house on Gloucester Square and Mrs B came back to me – the evenings after prayers when she'd open up the Milton like it was the Bible itself and read us something or sing it. She was always turning poems into songs.

I only hesitated a second. My own fingers were just itching to flout Clockface. They tugged the book from its place, and I opened it with one arm around the upright of the stepladder. It fell open on 'When I consider how my light is spent' as chance would have it. That one always moved Mrs B to tears, especially the last line. I remember her singing voice – frail, but with sudden robust moments as if it had fallen through to a younger self. That line seemed to throw her in and out of it: 'They also serve who only stand and wait'. In truth, it wasn't pleasant to listen to, but I'd give anything to hear that cracked old voice again.

I remember the poem well. Milton has just gone blind, and he's fretting that God will punish him for not being able to serve Him anymore. It mentions the parable of the talents from the real Bible – Mrs B liked to read that straight after – where the servant who looks after his master's money by burying it in the ground is punished for not using it to make *more* money. I thought that seemed mean. Servants are always expected to do more than they're paid for and given tasks that should be no one's business but their master's. In the poem, Milton thinks his blindness has buried his talent, which for him means not being able to write anymore. (Mrs B said, as it turned out, he kept working just as much and made his daughters write everything down.) The tune came back, and I started humming it as I read over the words. Then tried to sing them a little. It was so comforting I forgot where I was until another voice joined mine, picking up the song beautifully as if I'd summoned Mrs B back to earth as an angel.

I slammed the book shut without looking around, as if I could still hide what I was doing, and shoved it back in its place. There she was again, out of nowhere – dark grey dress in the softer, flowing style, hair simply done. She was standing by the table with the odd metal thing, I don't know how long.

'A pretty tune. Where is it from?'

She moved across to the fireplace, then turned and ran a finger over some of the spines I'd just dusted. I peered through the steps at her.

'Sorry, ma'am.'

My apology didn't seem to reach her. As she'd ignored everything else about me except the song, it didn't sound reasonable either.

'Mrs B made it up, ma'am. She used to sing it.'

She made a half turn towards me.

'Lady Berrington composed it for the Milton?'

'Yes, ma'am.'

She looked as if she was considering an unexpected piece of news – something challenging. She began reciting.

When I consider how my light is spent,
Ere half my days . . .

Then fell silent. After a moment, her expression hardened, and she jumped to the end of the poem.

Thousands at his bidding speed
And post o'er Land and Ocean without rest:
They also serve who only stand and wait.

'Do you think that is true?'

There was a catch in her voice. She wasn't looking my way, but the silence itself seemed to turn on me.

'I don't know, ma'am.'

Her head made a small, impatient movement.

'Of course you don't *know*. I asked what you *think*. Is it possible to do nothing and still serve God?'

I was stung. After the smiles and confidences of before, her tone was like a slap. I felt my nose go warm and tears prick the back of my eyes.

'Doing nothing isn't something I know much about, ma'am.'

I regretted it immediately. My hands gripped the rail of the steps as if the whole room was about to flip on its head. She looked up quickly, only meeting my eyes for a second, and away again. Her head lowered a little, shoulders rounded. I felt as if I'd done something terrible, ripped pages from a book or the hair from a doll. There are two chairs near the middle table, and she went and collapsed into one. It's struck me since that she could have accused me well enough of doing nothing – or nothing I was supposed to be doing – reading a book I'd been forbidden to touch and singing. I don't suppose God would be best pleased either – idle hands and the rest. But then I don't know how dusting shelves is serving *Him*.

The ladder creaked as I climbed down, but she didn't look up. I walked towards her, planning I don't know what. It nearly burst from my mouth that I wanted to help her, if she would only tell me how, that that was why Mrs B had sent me here. But she spoke first.

'Even when you have been given something – a talent – but are forced to bury it?'

She was still thinking about the poem. There was such unhappiness in her face, I drew nearer.

'A talent, ma'am?'

'Yes . . .'

I thought confusedly about Edward – could he be the thing she meant? She was looking at me with an odd mixture of appeal and distrust, as if she couldn't bring herself to say more. I cast about for something that would help, and my eye fell on the metal thing with the handle – I remembered what Mrs B had said about beauty.

'I think, ma'am, it might be true.'

She looked at me doubtfully, but there was also a sort of hunger in her eyes. I gestured at the object.

'This does nothing. But it's out for all to see, and I just spent several minutes cleaning it, and it looks – well, I think it looks lovely the way the light comes off it.'

The missus dropped her gaze to it.

'It's only a lifeless thing.'

For some reason, I felt I must convince her.

'I don't know what it is, ma'am, but it had a use once, didn't it? Before it was put there?'

She nodded slowly. Her eyes darkened.

'Yes, it had a terrible use. And now it's here, polished and prized and useless.'

Her face seemed to sag. She made to speak again but stopped.

'Never mind.'

She stared into space as if I was no longer there – like other servants are never really there. I had said the wrong thing – fallen through the floor and out of sight. With effort, she stood up and moved slowly towards the door. My mind raced, trying to think how to make it right, what to say to bring her back, but she left the room, and I was alone again. So much more alone than before. I knew she had meant far more than her words had carried, and I had missed it. It was as if she had come to the edge of the divide between us and called across, but I hadn't understood, so she went away. She won't seek me out again.

A sense of desolation spread around me. I saw myself from the outside, a housemaid wanting to play a part in the lives of her betters, blackening other people's grates and enduring bad tempers, while a different life – respectable and comfortable – lies abandoned, growing more fragile by the day. Mother was right – Mrs B had been in a world of her own thinking I could help the missus. There is no point in my being here. I should go home. Out of these thoughts came another truth, too large to ignore.

I don't want to marry William.

The clear fact of it fell at my feet, as if exhausted from running after me for so long. At the same time, a different thought formed, equally clear and certain.

I shall have to marry William.

A small sigh, almost a gasp, escaped me, a lonely sound in the quiet of the room. It's true most people would think themselves lucky to have a comfortable bed, enough to eat and a plot in the same graveyard they walk through every Sunday. Any other girl would be overjoyed to be married and living in the Mill Lane cottage. Even I know only a fool would trade a husband for a life as a housemaid.

I wandered towards the fire – dusting shelves was now too awful to think of – and turned as she had done to put my finger to a book spine. *The British Farmer; or, Sketches Of a Country Life*. I was about to pluck it out, for no better reason than that she had touched it, when I heard someone else coming. Clockface doesn't have the missus' ability to appear out of thin air. I had time to grasp the duster and flick it towards the book trough.

She tutted when she saw me and let out a string of French words, none of them flattering by the sound of it. Mary's in bed, claiming some malady, so I should have known I'd be a target. She looked wolfishly around the room and then peered at me again. Before I knew what she was about, she had put a clammy hand around the back of my neck and forced me in front of the mirror. I'd forgotten about the smudge on my cheek.

'You're not fit to be seen in a respectable house. What will Mr Gethin think of me for allowing you upstairs?'

She put her face so close to mine I could smell her breath, the breakfast of best bacon that none of the rest of us get a look at. I thought I was going to hear the story of the poor knife-cleaner again, but what she said was worse.

'Don't think I haven't written to him and told him all about the nasty blot dirtying his house.'

She smiled at me in the mirror.

'You think you're special, don't you? Wait until the master's home. You'll find out just how special you are then.'

She pushed a finger gently into the nape of my neck as she let me go, which made my skin crawl. I ran all the way up here and washed my face. For once, I am glad the mirror is so small – I don't want to see my reflection. I don't want to see what the missus saw. Now this page is smudged too with these useless, idiot tears. I shall write the letter to William.

Wednesday, 27th March

I didn't tell Lizzie about what happened – I didn't want to – but the nursery is always soothing, as if it's in a different house, a house with pleasant people and normal pictures on the walls. I picked Edward up today – he'd brought up some of his feed, so Lizzie was busy cleaning herself, and he was wailing for comfort. She's doing a good job – he's as plump and soft as a cushion and smells as good as a pudding still warm from the oven.

'He likes you.'

I think he did – he quietened right down and looked up at me with his blue eyes like he was pleased to make my acquaintance. Then she said a strange thing.

'She never calls him by his name.'

I looked up at her.

'The missus?'

She nodded.

'She always asks about "the baby", never Edward, and when she does find the time to talk to him, it's like she's speaking to someone else's child.'

Edward started making baby noises – not crying, just finding his voice the same way he might find a toy that's been put in his way or his own foot. Lizzie put her head on one side, watching.

'I thought nothing of it at first. But then one day I asked her if she wanted to hold Edward – when I still asked those things – and she said . . . well, I didn't think she was going to give me any answer at all to start with, but then she said, "Who?" in a quiet voice. It was so odd, I had to pretend I hadn't heard.'

Edward produced a funny burble that made his eyes go wide in surprise. Neither of us smiled.

'Why would she say that?'

She shook her head.

'Never known anything like it before.'

I held the little boy close to me as if to protect him from something. It makes me shudder to think how helpless little ones are. It's a wonder any of us survive long enough to find ourselves grown. At least he has Lizzie for a nurse. He's lucky in that, and I said so.

'Well, he's an easy baby.'

She smiled and held out her arms, but I held him closer.

'No, I want to keep him forever.'

She laughed, and I had to turn to the window, so she wouldn't see the tears coming. They seem to rise in me for no reason at all. I whispered into his warmth.

'Where shall we go, little one? Over the hills and far away?'

For comfort, I told myself that one day soon I'd have my own little pudding just like him.

Writing that stopped my pencil. My letter to William is still in my pocket – my fingers reached to feel for it, and I've found they've bent a crease in it. I haven't given notice yet.

The nursery window looks out onto the front. It's one of my favourite views as it's possible to see across the countryside – meadows and woods. My heart tumbles out and rolls around the hedgerows. A tree-lined driveway comes straight at the house from a road that's out of sight and then sweeps around a dry fountain. As I stood pointing out to Edward a crow that was crossing our view with determined flaps, a horse and cab trotted out from under the trees. My heart fled back into my body with a thump, though it was straight away clear it couldn't be the master. Lizzie came over to look. An arrival of any sort at this house is an event.

'It must be a delivery.'

The cab didn't go around the back though. A boy jumped down from the box, opened the door and after a moment of grappling with something inside, brought out a large, domed object, covered in a green cloth. He carried it out of sight towards the front door. I thought it looked like a birdcage, and Lizzie agreed.

'A new pet maybe.'

'New?'

'She had a little dog before. It died right after Edward was born. I've never seen a soul so out of her mind over an animal. There used to be a little china spaniel in here – a gift for the baby – and she threw it right across the room at the wall.'

'Here in the nursery?'

She nodded, lifting her eyebrows meaningfully. After a moment, she seemed to relent.

'But then the timing was a shame. New mothers can have funny heads . . .' She trailed off, looking at Edward. 'She's got you though, hasn't she? If she wants a pretty little poppet to play with.'

She waggled her finger in his face, which astonished him.

'Lizzie . . .'

I had another thought.

'Do you know about the lady's maid that was here? The missus went looking for her in London.'

She yawned and shook her head.

'I never met a lady's maid. It was before my time.'

'It's only . . . The others are . . . strange about it. They won't tell me what happened.'

Her expression dropped into a knowing look, and she rolled her eyes.

'Lady's maids are always at the sharp end of kitchen gossip. Most likely that's why she left. Anyway, servants are always looking for better places.'

I nodded, as if I agreed. The boy reappeared and the cab set off at a trot back to the big wide world. I watched them go. Edward twisted his head to look at me as if jealous. I blew air through my lips, and he drooled and gurgled and turned back to Lizzie. We were still making fools of ourselves, competing for baby smiles, when there was movement on the drive below again. It was the missus. She marched straight across to the fountain, holding the birdcage (we were right) at arm's-length. Resting it on the ledge, she sat next to it, apparently watching the little yellow thing I could just make out inside. Then she opened the cage door. Lizzie peered closer and clutched my arm.

'She can't want to let it out, surely?'

Turned out she did. She reached in and caught it, held it up to her face for a moment and then threw it into the air. It fluttered about in an urgent, scattered way before making a dash for the top of the fountain. Next thing, she had pushed the birdcage over into the fountain and was striding back towards the house. The bird took fright at the movement and became an unsteady speck, disappearing into the trees.

Me and Lizzie looked at each other, almost as wide-eyed as Edward. She whistled.

'Well, we won't be seeing that poor creature again.'

I agreed, feeling truly sorry for the little thing, lost and alone outside the safety of the hall. But turned out we were wrong about that too. I was rushing to get the fire lit in the drawing room a little later when I saw Laurence through the window. He was wandering around with the birdcage dangling from one hand, looking up into the trees. Come dinner, he was still out there. Clockface was taking her time with something in the pantry, but Mary was nearly in flames with the need to tell someone. I noticed there was no trace left of her mysterious 'illness'. She even helped me lay the table and carry things from the kitchen so she could stick by me with her snout in my ear. It was a canary – a gift from the master. When the missus saw it and read his letter, she'd picked it up and taken it straight out as Lizzie and me saw. But soon after, she repented on account of the little thing not having much of a chance by itself outside.

'What made her throw it out to start with?'

Mary rolled her eyes and shook her head in that way she has that looks not her own. Then she glanced at me like she was full of something big that I wasn't supposed to know. Before I could ask, Laurence was in the room. He held up the birdcage like a trophy before dropping it onto the table. The canary fluttered and twittered. Clapping her hands, Mary asked how he'd done it, and he threw himself into a chair, sticking his legs out.

'Cabbage. The little bugger likes cabbage.'

'Mind your tongue at my table.'

Clockface was as cheerful as I've ever seen her, even humming a few notes as she kicked Laurence's feet out of the way and put a jug on the table. She straightened and with hands on hips considered the canary.

'I thought we were in for another fight when that turned up.'

Laurence made a smacking sound in his cheek.

'It wasn't that bad.'

Clockface bridled at him.

'You weren't there. She had the same look in her eye as when she saw her own portrait.'

He tore off a chunk of bread with his hands, which I know annoys her, and didn't answer. I didn't understand what they meant about the portrait – the missus seemed so pleased with it – and looked at Mary. She started to say something, but Clockface turned on her and barked a French word. She shrank back and didn't meet my eye again.

'Did she say where she wanted it?'

Clockface gestured at the bird. Laurence sniffed.

'In a pie if it was up to me.'

'Well, I don't want it making a mess in here. Where is she?'

Mary found her voice again.

'The drawing room.'

I set the last plate down with a thump.

'I'll take it to her.'

They all looked at me in silence. Then Clockface smiled almost sweetly.

'May as well make yourself useful. While you're still here.'

Leaving the room with dignity was challenging – the birdcage is heavier than it looks. I hobbled into the passage with it, trying not to upset its little inmate, and once I was out of sight, lowered it to the ground. I had told myself it would be better if I didn't see the missus again. The canary gave a little chirrup, and I looked down.

'Do you think she'll let me back in from the cold too?'

It didn't reply.

When I hauled the cage into the drawing room, the missus was sitting with sheets of music in her lap, but she wasn't looking at them. She was staring at nothing, it seemed, quite still, as if she'd been there a hundred years. Glancing uneasily at the portrait of the girl in green, I cleared my throat.

'Laurence found the canary, ma'am.'

Her head turned slowly my way, but her eyes remained blank and didn't find me for a moment, as if she was blind. It made me feel quite queer. Then with a start she was back. She sprang up like a young girl.

'I am glad. Now where shall we put you?'

She whirled around and settled on the table by the window, rushing over to remove a figurine I enjoy dusting and shoving it carelessly on the edge of the mantelshelf.

'Here, here.'

She kept her eyes on the bird, hands clasped, as I made the awkward journey across the room. No trace of the woman who had pushed the birdcage into the fountain, no hint of how she had been in the library. Lifting the cage onto the table, I felt the muscles in my upper arms and back shout in disbelief after all the taking down and putting up of pictures recently.

'Wonderful.'

She shifted it slightly from how I'd placed it and leaned down to look in at the canary with all the tenderness of a mother.

'Hello, little one. Shall we sing together, you and I?'

She might have been talking to a small child. I stared at the side of her head, wishing I could break into it and rummage through her brain. How can a bird inspire such affection and not her own baby son? I was anxious not to disappoint her again, but I couldn't leave without trying to understand about Edward. Even if it meant forgetting my place.

'I'm sure the baby would enjoy seeing it, ma'am.'

She stopped murmuring into the cage. My heart beat faster. I remembered what Lizzie had said about her throwing a china dog across the room, and my voice went up a notch.

'I could carry it up to the nursery for you . . .'

'Did you know that little birds are sometimes used by miners, as a warning?'

She straightened and looked at me.

'They take them down into the tunnels with them. If the bird can't breathe, they know there are dangerous gases. They have more chance of escaping before an explosion.'

Her expression was expectant.

'I didn't know that, ma'am.'

She nodded.

'Strange, isn't it? A creature designed for the skies and for singing . . .'

The thought was left unfinished, though I took her meaning. It was hard to imagine the little feathered thing deep underground, to think of roughened miners relying on the beating of its tiny breast for survival.

'You at least will have fresh air and freedom enough to fly, my pet.'

She was talking to the canary again, of course. I have thought since about what she meant by 'freedom enough'; can a bigger cage be called 'freedom' at all? But too much freedom, at least for the canary, would mean death. At the time, I was merely relieved she had not ordered me out of the room or grown angry at my impertinence, only gently shouldered aside my question with one of her own. She spoke again.

'Thank you for taking care of me.'

I looked up in surprise. Her face was turned to mine, serious. I became conscious – as if a bell had been rung – that she had returned to the edge of the divide between us and was signalling across. This time I met her gaze. We were like two question marks mirroring each other, I thought, though I couldn't say exactly what the question was. Her eyes had the same shimmer as at Mrs B's. I nodded, and she nodded back, as if something had been decided.

The two portraits caught my eye as I turned, and I felt a powerful urge to ask her why the master giving her the canary had upset her so much and what had provoked her about the girl in green, as Clockface said. Safe on the servants' stairs again, I gave myself another moment to breathe. Some errands leave just enough room for pockets of peace, time to float in a space without words if only for a few heartbeats. Annie would have flapped her apron at me and told me I had fallen in love, but it's not that. It's more like meeting someone I recognise, as if we're on the same path, though I don't know how I imagine that can be with her being a lady and everything. Whatever it is, I don't want to leave her.

I feel caught between two lives, each in its own way as impossible as the other.

APRIL

Monday, 1st April

Something has happened. I don't trust it, but I'm not going to tell my lucky stars that. I'm nervous even of writing it down. My letters look as skittish and unsteady as I feel. Where to start? The worst row yet with Clockface. I was in the scullery – she'd gone for her rest – and washing up the nursery lunch things. A few days of cold hands, rough-ened knees and aching arms had made me feel the smallness of my life again. I hadn't seen the missus since I took her the canary – the bright flashes I have of her are like the flame of a guttering candle, always on the point of going out. Even so, I'd still not fished the letter to William out of my pocket.

Mary's been ill in bed with something vague again, so I had all her rough work to do as well, but when I came back through to the kitchen, the door had been left open and light was spilling down the steps and making a square on the matting. It had been dull when I was cleaning in the morning, grey and wintry. There's a lovely blossom on the drive you can see from the nursery, and the sky loomed over it like a horrible old man leading a child away. So when I saw the patch of sunlight, I went and stood in it and lifted my skirt to warm my ankles. It was like stepping into a bath. I thought, what harm in going up into the yard for a few minutes to let it warm my face too?

The first swallows were overhead, and the air had that soft touch you don't think about all winter. It was like exploring a new world, walking from the kitchen door and across the yard. Freedom. To stride out as if I was going somewhere, anywhere, that wasn't another room to clean or another thing to fetch. Even the different feel of the ground under my feet. The old dog was warming herself against the wall, as free as any lord, and I stopped to give her a scratch.

There are formal gardens behind the house, which I would never dare set foot in, but the kitchen garden is walled off just beyond the yard. It's lovely in there with fruit trees blossoming along one wall and everything in order and smelling richly of earth and mulch. Hens were clucking somewhere out of sight. The garden lad nodded at me and went back to hoeing. I felt emboldened. A gate leads through to another walled space, now used more for storing implements, with weeds allowed to grow in the corners. I closed my eyes and was breathing in the fulsome green of nettles, when there was a commotion out of nowhere, a rapid beating noise I couldn't locate – it seemed to come from all sides. A voice hooted, and I was hit in the neck by something the size of a marrow, soft and sharp at once. It scored the skin under my ear and thudded to the ground.

A chicken. A chicken without a head, just a bloody mess above its breast, its feathers clumped with crimson. It jerked, wings beating rapidly again and leapt at me. I screamed sharply and twisted out of its way. Revulsion made me slap all around where it had touched; I didn't know if the blood on my neck was mine or the bird's. A bark of a laugh reached me.

'Frightened of a little blood, are we?'

Clockface. Not at her rest after all. She came through a doorway, wiping her hands on her apron, and looked at the top of the wall with interest.

'Never had one fly that high before.'

The coolness of her observation, the mild satisfaction in it, turned my stomach, I don't know why. It was only a dead chicken, a routine household task, but it felt as if something dark and sinister had broken through the sweetness of the day. The corpse came to a rest finally, twitching and weeping blood amongst the nettles. Clockface reached down and caught it up by the legs. It danced grotesquely by her side as she turned to me. I knew what was coming: a deal of trouble for being out of the house. I walked quickly towards the door that led out of the walled gardens as if I was on some urgent errand.

'Where do you think you're going?'

I knew I would have to pay for it, but I couldn't bear to look at her just then and pretended I hadn't heard. Once through the wall, I ran. The estate opens out on that side, and there's a large pasture with oak trees dotted about and woods all around the edge. I chose a tree and sat down. Why couldn't she just break their necks neatly and without fuss like they do at home? But then I remembered William had ripped a hen's head right off doing that, just to show he could. Tears stung the back of my eyes, and I pressed my hand to my scratched neck.

Narrow paths disappear into the dark of the woods. They beckon, like invitations. I wondered what would happen if I just picked one and walked down it without looking back. It's not a new fancy. I used to think the same thing at home, staring down the lane. Seemed to me that lane could go anywhere – over new lands, across seas; it was a path to freedom. Perhaps that's why I was so drawn to the girl in green, so eager to know what she is seeing beyond the picture – perhaps it was myself I was seeing in her and not the missus at all. But my life is different from hers. Drudgery and butchered chickens, I thought, that's where all my paths lead, all of them – there is no 'freedom enough' for me.

I don't think much would have made me get up. All the same, I didn't mean to fall asleep. I've no memory of drifting off. Just one moment feeling the relief of getting off my feet – and thinking how strange that the body can still feel its own joys even while the mind is wishing itself dead – and the next moment believing I was drowning. I took water up my nose, which *hurts*. Clockface must have come looking for me after she washed her hands and changed her apron and then gone back for a mug of water to throw in my face. The bitch.

Odd that words – just writing them down – can make my heart bump about like I've screamed them in her face. She loomed over me, watching me splutter, and then bullied me to my feet and followed me back to the house. I was insulted in both English and French – the gardeners heard every word. When we got to the steps, I tripped head over heels down them in my haste and landed on my knees at the bottom. My cap had come off and my hair fell loose and was plastered to my face. I must have looked a sight. Clockface was coming down the steps behind me, in full flow about all the work I was going to do to make up for the time I'd wasted. I was trying to get out of the way on all fours when all of a sudden she stopped dead. In the same moment I found myself looking at the toes of two spotless satin slippers, poking out from beneath a dark blue skirt.

'What is happening here, Mrs Clarkson?'

For some reason, I didn't get up. I don't know, why – I'm not one to beg, but something told me to keep small and wait. It was a strange moment. Clockface must have thought so too because she didn't answer straight off. The missus had to prompt her again before she spoke.

'I found her asleep outside, ma'am. She's been shirking, and not for the first time.'

'Asleep?'

'Yes, ma'am. Fast asleep for anyone to see in the middle of the day.'

There was a silence. A drop of water found its way around the back of my ear and swooped down my neck. It itched.

'I see.'

And then . . .

'Is this not usually the time you have your rest, Mrs Clarkson?'

It was so pointed, it made hope lurch in my chest. I didn't look at Clockface, but I could feel the sting of it in the tightness of her voice. Fury snapped in every word as she made a twisted little speech about believing it her duty to keep an eye on new servants at all hours. The missus gave a small smile.

'Your thoroughness is admirable, Mrs Clarkson.'

Clockface bowed her head.

'It is my duty to provide Mr Gethin and yourself with the best servants, ma'am, and leaving their appointment to myself and Mr Barrett will ensure the smoothest running of the household. I am confident my visit to London will result in an excellent new house-maid for you.'

I felt as if she'd kicked me in the chest. It was the first I'd heard of another housemaid. I remembered she had written to the master about me – Mr Barrett is his valet – and felt my heart stop. The missus was staring at Clockface too, her expression unreadable.

'Your visit to London?'

'Yes, ma'am.'

Clockface tilted her head.

'As Mr Gethin requested, ma'am? I'm to hire a girl from one of his charitable societies.'

The kitchen seemed filled with shrieking though no one spoke. After a moment, the missus straightened.

'Well, I am sure you will make an excellent choice, Mrs Clarkson.'

They both smiled – Clockface gloatingly – and I realised then that these two women loathe each other. I was simply the latest thing to get caught between their jaws. My face went blood hot. I felt I had let the missus down as much as myself – now I know we have a common enemy – and rose to my feet to protest, but she cut across.

'Harriet, sit down, I want to speak with you.'

She's never used my name before, and it was like the girl in the painting had stepped out of it and started talking to me – that's how unexpected it was.

'You can return to your rest now, thank you, Mrs Clarkson.'

Clockface looked just as taken aback.

'There's no need, thank you, ma'am. I'd just as soon get on with some work, as we're behind.' Looking at me.

'As you wish. With Mary unwell would you make sure there's a fire in the drawing room.'

Clockface baulked.

'Laurence . . .'

'Laurence is occupied.'

Another day I might have enjoyed seeing Clockface thrown out of 'her' kitchen and made to work on her knees, but I had no stomach for it in the midst of my own humiliation. She managed to leave without saying anything. I realised the missus had sat herself down and was watching me. She sits very straight – neat and still like a cat. It made me aware I was hunched over – a bedraggled heron – and I pulled my shoulders back a bit. She smiled slightly, in approval, I think, and I felt that sense again of two question marks facing each other.

'Were you asleep, Harriet?'

'Yes, ma'am.'

'Do you not sleep well here?'

'It's not that, ma'am.'

She looked at me very intently, and then dropped her gaze to my hands, which I realised were clutching the edge of the table. I hid them in my lap and didn't meet her eye.

'Why were you outside?'

'Why do *you* go outside?'

I don't know what it is about her that makes me say what's at the top of my mind, but I couldn't help it – the words lashed out of me before I could think, leaving an angry welt on the silence. It was as if I was suffocating again – everything I'd been thinking was rushing up my throat, but it was all coming out as fat, choking sobs. I couldn't see – for tears this time. Her chair scraped back, and I heard footsteps. I thought she'd gone to fetch Mrs Clarkson, but she returned at once and I found she was offering me a cloth. It was what the ham had been wrapped in and still damp, so I just held it in my lap.

'I don't want to go home.'

It came out in croaks and juddery breaths. I felt her hand gently squeeze my shoulder, and we both waited for my breath to stop jumping about.

When I could look at her again, her head was turned to the window, so I had the full show of her profile. She was an exotic thing in the kitchen – larger than life and shocking, like a lion in a stable. Even if we swapped clothes she wouldn't look right. She felt my stare and turned. Instead of giving me my notice though or asking more questions, she shocked me by answering mine.

'I go outside so I can imagine . . .'

She stopped, searched for it.

'So I can imagine what it would be like to keep walking or riding and never come back.'

It was so like what I'd been thinking myself, I stared at her with my mouth open. At the same time, I felt a sort of fear brushing along my arms and the back of my neck. She herself didn't look disturbed at all and even smiled a little as if pleased at finding the right words.

'Lady Berrington spoke very highly of you. She wrote that you're a gifted needlewoman.'

I don't think the missus has said anything to me yet that wasn't odd or unexpected. She turns like the weather – I remember thinking she *looked* like the light and shadow of moving clouds. I said something about Mrs B always being kind to me and explained about my mother doing the fine work for Lady Stanworth at Beechwood, how she taught me, hardly knowing whether I was going to get a sermon or more confidences. Neither, as it turned out. She began speaking again almost before I'd finished.

'Well, I don't think you can continue as housemaid here, Harriet, and I don't believe you wish to.'

I was silent and quickly lowered my eyes. The thought that she was about to dismiss me – never mind what I'd decided about William – fair cleaved me in two.

'However, I require the services of a lady's maid. Do you think you would like that?'

I watched my rough hands with their black nails fiddling with the ham cloth. A faint whiff of vinegar came off it. She might as well have asked if I'd like to be a horse.

'Harriet?'

I couldn't speak or move. She started talking again, saying I'd have a room to myself next to hers and even that I could use the library and read all the books I want. Her voice had gone higher, and she spoke faster. I looked up, not quite believing it, but she really did seem nervous. She placed a hand on the table – I don't know if a gesture towards me or to steady herself as she stood up.

'Will you think about it? If I let you go to your room and dry yourself . . .' (she looked with some puzzlement at the abandoned ham cloth). 'I'll send for you later.'

Her appeal sounded so earnest, I could only reply with a 'yes, ma'am' and stood up also. She lingered.

'Why do you refer to Lady Berrington as Mrs B?'

I hadn't even noticed, it comes so natural, so I just told her the truth.

'That's what she wanted, ma'am. She wouldn't let us call her anything else usually.'

I hesitated, not sure if I should explain how strange Mrs B was as a mistress.

'She liked to talk to us, ma'am, not like other employers talk to servants. But then . . .'

She raised her eyebrows, waiting.

'Well, I don't know if you ever noticed, ma'am, but she talked to the furniture too. Especially Lord Berrington's portrait. That got a scolding most days.'

The missus looked startled, then thoughtful, then strangest of all, she laughed out loud. It wasn't a laugh I'd ever have put with the

singing voice. That belonged to the heavens and butterflies and mountaintops – I don't know what I mean – that sort of thing – this was
stones and dirt and ditch water. But mirthful, like she had been at Mrs
B's about my elephant. She put a hand to her mouth as if she knew
she'd let out an imp. Then she looked at me and took it away, letting
me have a full wide grin. And there we were again at the edge, this
time with a rope thrown across.

'I hope you accept my offer, Harriet. Hurry and change your dress
now before you catch cold.'

As I went along the passage, I heard her singing again, full voiced,
something jaunty and joyful without words. I couldn't help myself – I
started laughing. The impossible had walked right into the kitchen
and tried to wipe my tears with a ham cloth. I must have looked mad
to Laurence, who lurched out of the boot room just then as if he'd
been lying in wait. There was something defiant in his face, which
was at odds with – but also explained by – the small posy of spring
flowers he brandished at me. I stared at them and then at him, thinking
the whole house had turned gate over chimney pot. He tossed his head
like a horse.

'Take them to Mary for me?'

Of course. I collapsed into laughter again, and the wounded look he
gave me is still making me giggle.

Nook

It took me an age to write that out. I wanted to get it all down while
I remembered, so I just dabbed at myself and wrote it sitting on the
bed, trying not to let the frame squeak and wake Mary. When I
finished, I found she was watching me anyway from her pillow.
Naturally, she wanted to know what I was laughing at and why I was
wet and – always – what I was writing about. I told her what had
happened with Clockface while I got changed into my print dress and

re-pinned my hair. Her little rat eyes grew as wide as nature'd let them, and she raised herself onto an elbow.

'Are you going to be dismissed?'

She was enjoying the drama.

'No.'

I spoke abruptly and then, emboldened by the missus' offer, poured out everything I have ever thought about Clockface, every resentment and spiteful feeling. It was a little cruel, seeing as Mary's her niece, but perhaps that's why I did it. It felt good to speak my mind. I said I doubted whether she had ever even set foot in France.

'Oh, no, she has!'

Mary was shocked. Words tumbled out of her in a rush.

'For ages. She ran away with a man – he was the son of the *mayor*, so it was a terrible scandal.'

Her face gleamed briefly with the thrill of it.

'But he deserted her there, and she had no one to turn to – she had to find work when she couldn't understand a word anyone said to her.'

I stared at her, my mouth stopped, and tried to match her words with the housekeeper of Finton Hall. It was like trying to make a shirt out of cloth that has been cut for trousers.

'Why didn't she go home?'

Mary shook her head, eyes wide.

'She and my grandad wouldn't speak to each other. She came over once but only on a trip with the French family she worked for – and that's when the master saw her hauling a knife-cleaner over the coals. Once she was settled here at the hall, she sent for me, but my da still won't see her. He says she thinks she's better than the rest of us. I have to leave her out of my letters.'

She looked truly sorry for a moment, but then a look of terror passed over her face, and she clutched my arm.

'Aunt Sarah will beat me to *death* if you say I told you.'

I thought of her and Laurence having to sneak about for fear of what

Clockface might say and wanted to run down to the kitchen and twist Aunt Sarah's ears.

'Of course, I won't tell her.'

I picked up the posy and held it out.

'From Laurence.'

I didn't wait for her reaction but pulled my box out from under the bed to put this away. The letters from William and Mother were poking out from under my Bible. Two things struck me – that the course of the rest of my life was about to be decided, as surely as Clockface's had been when she ran away with the mayor's son, and secondly, that something wasn't right with the letters. They looked like they had been taken out and put back again in a hurry, not hidden as I had left them. I took them, shut the box and came out to the little window seat at the end of the passageway.

I've been here half an hour now, and my belly is full of frogs. They jump between equal terrors, and I have to stop writing out of confusion. I keep looking at Mother's and William's letters. Even their handwriting seems to talk – homely and practical, good enough to be useful. My letters look different now, but what's the use of pretty handwriting when the hand that makes it is red and cracked? It is still not good enough to write for a mistress and, apart from my needle, I don't have the skills. Likely she'd never keep me on for all I think she likes me. And even if she does, what will the master do? He's already hired a different housemaid after Clockface's letter about me – surely, he'll never tolerate me as an upper servant. And there's still the other lady's maid the missus went searching for – what happened to her?

Later

I marched back into the bedroom and plumped myself down on Mary's bed.

'Tell me what happened to the maid who left, or I'll tell Laurence where he can shove his flowers next time.'

She quivered like a flower herself.

'Helene?'

'If that's her name, yes.'

I was sitting on her leg and leaned so she couldn't move it.

'She got into trouble.'

'With child?'

A nod. I felt strangely relieved it was something so ordinary.

'Why did the missus go after her?'

A shrug.

'Well, who was it? Who got her that way?'

She avoided my gaze, looking to the window as if she might escape through it. My eye fell on the posy that was still clutched in her hands. I remembered her jealousy and the reputation of footmen.

'Was it Laurence, Mary?'

It was as if I'd poked a snake. She grew rigid, drew herself up and all but hissed.

'No, it wasn't.'

She wrenched her leg free from under me and curled her body away.

'Ask Mr Barrett if you want to know.'

I've heard the master's valet mentioned before and some griping about the money he earns, but little else.

'Why? Was it him?'

She huffed and shook her head. I thought suddenly of the missus throwing the canary out of the house – a gift from the master – and how he hired only the prettiest servants. I looked closely at Mary.

'Not . . . the master . . .?'

A look of disbelief crossed her face, and she shook her head again. I almost shouted at her.

'Why won't you tell me?'

But I had cut her too deep by accusing Laurence. She turned from me, her whole body rigid. Changing my tone, I looked for a way back.

'They're very pretty flowers.'

She glanced at them and away again, but I saw her soften. I kept my voice light.

'My William never gives me flowers.'

I have rarely spoken about him, and I felt her interest sharpen.

'But I'm not pretty like you. It's funny, isn't it? How everyone here is so fair?'

She looked sideways at me. I smiled as if it didn't bother me.

'Was Helene pretty?'

I could tell by the way she blinked that she was. Leaning in, I lowered my voice.

'Do you think the master will mind, Mary? That I'm not? I'm worried he won't like me when he sees me.'

I didn't have to do any pretending about that and watched her closely. She frowned as if she'd never thought about it, and to do her justice, tried to say I was also fair. I only hope she never has to lie to save herself. Before I could change the subject and ask about the missus' portrait, heavy footsteps sounded in the passage. It was Clockface sent to fetch me – the missus means to humiliate her at every turn, I think. I wasn't going to betray Mary for telling me about the mayor's son, but I didn't mind giving her aunt a brazen look. She returned it powerfully.

I was reluctant to leave my letters and diary out when I was sure Mary had helped herself to a rummage through my box, so had to carry them with me to the drawing room. The missus looked at them – curious – but only asked me to sit down and told Clockface to fetch us some tea. It was strange sitting with her like that. In her dark blue dress, she looked a natural part of the room, like the whole thing was a picture. I would have liked to have been able to sit and stare at it all, unseen myself, and study how it all fitted together, but I kept my eyes down. If she was a lion in a stable, I was a monkey at a tea party.

'Have you considered my offer?'

The words I wanted to say rushed up my throat – or rather just the one word, Yes! but at the last moment it faltered and grew shy and disbelieving of itself. Other words came.

'It's difficult, ma'am.'

'Difficult?'

'You see, I still have someone . . . waiting for me . . .'

'Oh.'

Her voice dropped down into the ditch again, but without the mirth. It was only a small sound, but it carried both surprise and disappointment.

'I wouldn't want to let you down, ma'am. He's getting impatient.'

It was strangely weak as an argument and I was conscious of it falling short. There was a pause – while she waited for it to flutter to the ground is what it felt like.

'I thought you didn't want to go home.'

She sounded confused. I couldn't say otherwise. I couldn't say I'd stay. Eventually, she nodded.

'Well, Harriet. I wish you all happiness.'

'Thank you, ma'am.'

I was aware of a terrible disappointment. A door slamming shut in my face. Had I expected her to fight for me, to beg me? She had closed up tightly like a clam. Neither of us moved.

'You have been writing to him?'

She smiled faintly, looking at the materials I was holding. I looked at them too, barely understanding.

'Oh, no, I wasn't. I . . . It's a diary.'

She paused.

'I keep a diary.'

It came out quite fiercely as if I'd accused her of something.

'Well, *keep* is not the word. I burn each page as soon as I've written it. That way I can write anything I like, and no one will ever see it.'

Her eyes shone briefly with some burned-up secret. I wanted to ask why write at all – but remembered how writing down 'bitch' had made my very insides churn. Making words brings them into the world in a way just thinking can't. Perhaps even burning them can't get rid of them then. I realised I was clutching my diary to my body. Could I burn this? I knew I should, but the thought made me feel sick.

'Have you always kept a diary?'

The missus had come back from her own thoughts.

'No, ma'am. Mrs B – I mean Lady Berrington – said it would help me get better at my letters.'

She nodded.

'Is that the reason you still do it?'

'Yes, and . . .'

I had been going to say it was like having someone to talk to but stopped myself.

'I have never known a maid to keep one.'

'There's not often the time, ma'am.'

She nodded again and looked beyond me out of the window.

'I remember you saying.'

I felt my heart plunge, recalling how I had spoken to her in the library.

'Well, it's a shame. You could have helped me with notes and messages and had plenty of time to write for yourself. But of course, you will have far more interesting things to do with your time when you are married.'

I couldn't tell if the bitterness had been in her voice or if it was how I heard it in my head because a doleful chime seemed to ring in the room. Just then Clockface came in with the tea things. My face must have shown my distress because she smiled in her gloating way before fairly slamming the tray down on the table. The missus rose to her feet.

'Thank you, Mrs Clarkson, you can leave that with me.'

Clockface turned and looked her up and down. Her voice carried that tone of knowing better how a mistress should behave than the mistress herself.

'Very well, ma'am.'

With another more interested glance at me, she left the room. I thought I should get up to serve but felt glued to my chair. The missus busied herself with pouring tea and chatted away about weddings, I think, and the fine summer we would be having. It was all at a light musical trot I imagine she uses on guests – if she ever has any – no more needing an answer than the tinkling of the spoon against china – a thousand miles from what I've come to think of as her real voice. I couldn't listen properly anyway. *More interesting things to do with your time.* I looked about me as if I might find some relief or answer in the fine things in the room. The staring, blank eyes of the busts repelled me, and I looked quickly away from the master's piercing gaze. My eyes turned instead to the missus' portrait, the girl in green. She was still misplaced amidst all the grandeur, but her expression was as fresh and captivated as ever.

The missus was handing me a cup of tea. I had to balance my things in my lap to take it, hands shaking, cup and saucer rattling. She was still talking – a bride she had seen last year at a country wedding. I took a sip. The portrait glowed at the edge of my vision like a green island in the middle of a sea. I remembered the missus holding my hand in Gloucester Square and imploring me not to live my life for others; I remembered buttoning her cuff and feeling a kind of grace in the act; I thought of the strange distance between her and her baby son and remembered my promise to Mrs B.

There was a silence. She was standing between the table and her own chair, staring down at her cup. I looked at mine and realised all at once it was ordinary black tea that the servants drink – not the special kind reserved for upstairs. I don't know how Clockface dared.

She drank it very slowly – deliberately, as if it was a wine she was tasting. I expected her to ring the bell or fly down to the kitchen, but she seemed to come back to herself and sat down with that smile turned on me. *She'll be safe with you*, is what Mrs B had said.

I don't suppose she meant safe from inferior tea, but somehow this tiny, poisoned arrow from Clockface threw the woman in front of me, my mistress, into stark relief. I seemed to see her clearly for the first time. The fine silks, japanned cabinets and expensive wallpaper grew gaudy and florid against such loneliness. She seemed as fragile as the china cup I was holding. I stood up.

'Ma'am.'

She waited. I waited. Honestly, I think I'd be standing there still if I hadn't been holding the diary and everything so awkwardly with one hand that they finally swivelled away like they'd turned to soap and fell to the floor. I tried to stop it all by clutching at the falling book but only managed to spill the tea in my other hand, which slopped over the rug and the letter from William. The ink blurred, held the shape of the letters for a moment, and then dissolved away. They ended up a sort of shoreline at the edge of the tea stain. It didn't matter that I'd just proved myself too hopelessly clumsy to be any kind of servant – the washing away of William's handwriting was too much.

'I'll be your lady's maid.'

Everything was very still. She seemed fixed back into a painting. I looked down at the mess on the floor – and heard myself. My cheeks burned.

'If you'll still have me.'

A bubble of mirth popped from her. She glanced at the diary, which had landed open and face down, and at the tea soaking into the rug.

'Yes, I'll still have you, Harriet.'

She rose then, stepped across, and alarmed me very much by holding out her hand for me to shake. It was so soft I could hardly feel it in my roughened fingers. I don't know how on earth I'm to be a lady's maid. My hands make me feel I'm no maid at all.

Tuesday, 2nd April

Here I am. In my own room, and it has a view, same as the missus' next door and the nursery upstairs, out the front with the drive sweeping around in a circle and then miles of woods and farmland with chimney smoke pointing out invisible dwellings. It makes me take a great breath in every time I look at it, as if I've been shut in a tiny room and someone's just opened the door. My letter to William is written and sent, and I don't feel as guilty as perhaps I should. I have a little desk where I'm writing this – much easier than in the nook or in bed – and my own comfortable chair, a prettily patterned washstand with daisies running around the bowl and jug (not cracked). The rug looks new – pink and yellow flowers that match the curtains.

Mary saw me packing my things into the box and thought I was being thrown out without notice. When I told her, her face went quite white and her mouth fell open. Even her whiskers went still. She wanted to know what Clockface had said about it, as if Clockface is mistress here. At Beechwood, Lady Stanworth's maid eats with Mrs Hyatt in her room instead of the servants' hall – thank goodness that isn't the custom with Finton Hall's housekeeper. At dinner last night, she was an angry swarm of bees all on her own; when Mary dropped a spoon, she lunged for it herself and whacked the girl on her arm. She couldn't look at me, never mind speak. There was something almost fearful in the way she avoided me. But this morning she was smiling that nasty smile again as if she knows something I don't. She left for London straight after breakfast – I think to interview housemaids – but made a point of calling me Miss Watkins in a mocking voice a dozen times before she went. I wish I could eat with Lizzie in the nursery. At least I can see her more often now and help with the baby whenever she needs it. To think I'll be able to hold his sweet little body whenever I like almost and watch him grow up into his own little person. I can hardly believe it. And I shall find out what's come between the missus and her son. I can feel it now, like a calling. Mrs B must have been some kind of fortune teller.

The missus called me after breakfast – any time she rings the bell, it's me that's to go to her. She went through what's expected of me, and it's all the nicest bits of working for Mrs B. A cup of tea to her room first thing, then breakfast for myself in the kitchen. When she's ready, I'm to help her dress. She didn't mention hair, and I hope she won't. Mary will help me make the bed, and she even empties the slops. I'm in charge of the wardrobe, including the mending, which is one thing I can feel sure of doing properly. We made an inventory of every article, from her finest gown to her plainest hatpin, and she declared herself ready to throw it all out. I noticed there was only one drawer she didn't touch, at the bottom of the cabinet, but I didn't like to ask.

When we opened her wardrobe, she looked me up and down as if I was a joint of meat and fetched out what she called one of her old dresses. It's nothing like the dark, sombre gowns I've seen her wear. This one's lovely – rich blue velvet and lilac satin with ruffles all over the place and buttons down the front – and hardly looks worn. She held it up to me.

'I think it will fit well with little work.'

I was too surprised to answer. She didn't stop there but frowned hard at my head.

'I don't like caps on ladies' maids. Tie your hair with a ribbon, that will suffice.'

I don't know where I'm supposed to get ribbon from. She didn't offer any. I wish I hadn't spent the money on new aprons now, though I suppose I can send them home for my sisters at Beechwood. The missus pointed out a large basket of mending, saying how pleased she was that she'd finally have some items back she'd been missing. All for the want of a decent needlewoman. Ladies are as trapped by their situation as servants in some ways. Surrounded by lovely things but unable to help themselves if anything goes amiss. I remembered that the missus' family had lost all their money and felt grateful I can at least make my own living.

I wanted to say something to thank her. No other lady would have picked me out for her particular servant, especially after I'd been found asleep under a tree.

'I'll do my very best for you, ma'am. I hope you'll find me useful.'

She was still picking out the items I was to mend first, but when I spoke, she straightened and looked at me.

'Useful? You don't know how happy I feel already, knowing you are next door. But I hope we will enjoy ourselves as well.'

She stepped towards me and took hold of my hand again.

'I will do my best for you too. A lady's maid should be more than a servant.'

A glint came into her eye, and I think from what she said next, she was thinking about the scene with Clockface.

'We all need a little freedom. I won't tell you how to use yours.'

I smiled back, laughed even. Truth is I could have kissed her. Her gaze fell on the blue gown laid out on the bed, and her expression darkened a little.

'Take that with you. Be sure to alter it to your liking.'

'Yes, ma'am.'

She turned away abruptly and waved her hand towards the door. It was a sudden end to our time together, but perhaps that is how ladies are with their maids. I shall have to get used to it.

Thursday, 4th April

She sings to me. Just to me, and it seems to gladden her heart almost as much as it does mine. Performing to people, even one, makes all the difference, she says, and she dreams of singing operas on a real stage, like the theatres she was taken to in Italy as a girl. My cheers and clapping delight her like a child. Yesterday she sent me to fetch

68

the book of Milton's poetry from the library and then sat me down next to her at the piano to sing Mrs B's version of 'When I consider how my light is spent'. I couldn't have been more dumbstruck if she'd pushed me onto a stage in front of a crowd. She put one cool hand on the back of my neck and the other on my middle.

'Drop your shoulders and breathe from here. Breathe with me.'

Her touching me like that made me curl up, but then she started making the most ungodly sounds to show me how to place the voice. Great belting 'hoos' and 'hahs'. Laughter burst out of me; I couldn't help it.

'There. See?'

She beamed and patted my middle.

'Now, sing for me, Harriet Watkins!'

She roared it – but using my voice. It was my way of speaking exactly, coming from her mouth. I stared at her in astonishment. She returned my gaze and, still in my voice, asked innocently what the trouble was. It made me snort as loudly as if I'd been in Gloucester Square with Annie and Mrs B's brandy. Somehow, I got the tune out. The missus picked out the notes on the piano and wrote them down. Then we sang it together, and it was like floating on a river with her voice in full sail, pulling mine along.

I wonder if the talent she told me is buried is just that – her singing voice – and nothing to do with Edward after all. Perhaps she is angry at the master for keeping her in this remote house with almost no one to sing for and that is the reason she dreams of walking away. Certainly, something is amiss; she seems not herself at times, as Mrs B said. It's as if a different, darker mistress takes over. Her moods can turn on a sixpence, from laughing and teasing to ill humour and impatience. She had the canary brought to her room yesterday and was whistling to it, holding it on her finger and feeding it morsels, but today she just stared at it through the bars.

'It always returns to its cage.'

She sounded scornful.

'Always.' In the same mood, she turned on me. 'Where is the dress?'

I was sorting out some items for the laundry at the time and jumped as if I'd been pricked by a stray pin. It's true I've been putting off the alterations – the dress has been watching me from my mending chair, flaunting its richness and detail as if daring me to try on anything so fine. The missus' frown deepened.

'And I told you to put a ribbon in your hair.'

I began stammering about going to town (though how that will help when I haven't been paid yet), but she turned to the window with another flick of her hand, batting me away. I suppose it is only natural for ladies to be annoyed sometimes, and not always fairly, especially if they have troubles. It doesn't mean she will dismiss me. Lizzie agreed. (I ran up to the nursery first chance I had.) She said servants are convenient for masters to kick now and then, like a stool. No one then throws out the stool. She had just fed Edward and was putting him down. I spoke quietly.

'But what about Mr Gethin?'

I didn't look at her as I said it. My fears about the master are like spiders in a matchbox – I'm scared even to peek at them.

'What if he doesn't like it that I've been made lady's maid? When I don't have any experience and I don't look . . . right?'

'Harriet.'

Lizzie waited until I had met her eye. I was taken aback to see amusement playing with pity in her face.

'The master won't *notice* you.'

Later

Dinner was awful. I knew it would be with me wearing this dress, but it's not as if I have a choice. It didn't take much to make it fit as the missus had said, though I'm more angular than her. I could hardly meet my own eyes in the mirror – I look, not like a lady, but not like myself either. Some strange new creature that could do I don't know what. It took long minutes outside the kitchen door before I found the courage to enter; I had to remember not to wipe my palms on the expensive fabric.

If I'd walked in naked, it couldn't have caused more trouble. Clockface was in high spirits, but she dropped the smile when she saw me – nearly dropped the basin she was holding too.

'What do you think you're doing in *that*?'

I told her. Mary appeared in the pantry doorway, whiskers bristling.

'She never gave it you?'

They both looked amazed.

'Well, I didn't walk in and help myself to it, did I?'

That brought Clockface's smile back, and more than that – she put the basin down and hooted with laughter.

'Enjoy it while you can, (something in French that was certainly rude). You won't be in it for long. Or in this house.'

I looked at Mary, but she turned away. There was a long high whistle from Laurence, who'd just walked in behind me (I felt Mary go sharp). He came up short though and looked questioningly at the others. Something passed between them, I don't know what. Finally, Clockface spoke.

'Master's coming home in time for Easter. Told me so on Tuesday.'

She was looking at me as she said it, but it was as if she was really speaking to someone else, saying something more. My insides went cold. I stuck out my chin.

'And he's going to box my ears and throw me out, isn't that right, Mrs Clarkson?'

There was a stung moment, and then her lip curled.

'Oh ho, seems being lady's maid has lent your tongue an edge. Well, *Miss Watkins*, we'll have to mind our manners around you, I can see that.'

And then she was at it for the rest of the meal. Curtsying and calling me m'lady and trying to get the others to laugh with her. She spoke about all the fine maids she'd talked French with and then pretended to be baffled when I couldn't understand her.

'But I thought you were a lady's maid!'

The worst was the way she watched me eating. Everything I did with my hands, dipping bread in the stew, picking up a spoon – she raised her eyebrows as if to say it wasn't her place to comment. I gave it up after barely having anything, and she feigned dismay at my leaving. She's not the queen she thinks though. There was a knock on my door a while later, and outside I found a plate of stew and bread. Laurence. He nearly ruined it by tugging his forelock and calling me 'ma'am' as he disappeared down the stairs.

Friday, 5th April

Dearest Har,

Not a peep? Not even to congratulate me? What, I've been asking myself – and that poor dear husband of mine at least three times a day – is wrong with the girl? Have you got married without telling me? Have you fallen down a hole? Andrew can't tell me however often I ask. Please save him from a nagging wife and write!

He sends his love – or he would do if he wasn't sprawled on the rug fast asleep with his boots on. He's been helping Robert with his baby farmer investigations as well as working his usual beat, so the poor lamb doesn't know which way his head's on most of the time. Robert wants him to leave his division altogether and become a detective constable – the whole department is about to change and become all shiny and correct and ripe for good, hard-working men to make their names apparently – like Robert's doing. It's what I'd do, but Andrew says he'd rather deal with drunks and pickpockets all day long than baby killers, and I can see how that could wear a lad down. The stories I could tell you, Har, it would turn your hair white. Poor mothers paying some nurse to look after their babies while they scrape a living together, and then finding the woman's disappeared and their babes dead in a ditch. You'll remember Robert was a dour soul already, so it suits him well enough, and besides he lives for his work.

If I didn't have a kitchen stacked to the rafters with reeking police collars and shirts myself, I'd be marching up to Hertfordshire, you can be sure, to find out what's buttoned your lip. WRITE, Har – as God's my witness, you're giving me the collywobbles.

You're ever affectionate, bit cross friend,
Annie

Poor Annie. I'll write and tell her I'm a lady's maid now, she'll enjoy that. And first chance I get, I'll go to London and see her.

As I was putting her letter away with the others, I had an idea and untied the red ribbon binding them all. Mother gave it to me years ago. She couldn't use it for her Lady Stanworth work because of a small oil stain that won't come out. It doesn't really match the dress, but at least the missus can see I've tried. It's important that she sees I've tried.

Monday, 8th April

An arrival this morning. I had just finished dressing the missus and was on my knees pulling her skirt and petticoats straight. Waiting on her is beginning to feel more natural now and even wearing her dress no longer shocks me in the mirror. She was saying how quick-fingered I have become in only a few days, when the sound of wheels and hooves made us both start and turn towards the window, alert as squirrels. The master. I was so convinced of it I nearly pulled her forward by gripping the petticoat too tightly. She shooed me away.

'Who is it? Quickly.'

I scrambled up in time to see Duncan driving the dogcart towards the yard. Behind him, half hidden by a box, was a girl. Relief made me breathless.

'Oh! It's the new housemaid, ma'am.'

I looked back with a smile, thinking it would mean little to her, but a shadow fell over her face – sudden, like a grief remembered. Her head turned as if I'd said something ugly.

'What sort of girl is she?'

'What sort . . .?'

I glanced back at the now empty drive, unsure of what she meant or how I was supposed to know.

'Quite . . . small, I think, ma'am.'

'*Small?*'

Her eyes were black again. I felt the same helplessness as before, of being found wanting.

'From what I could see, ma'am.'

She stared at me a moment longer and then seated herself at her dressing table.

'I shall go out. Dress my hair – something different, but don't take all morning.'

I stared at her, shocked, and felt panic rising. Until today, she had only ever asked me to brush her hair and pass pins while she caught it back. I didn't dare tell her I had no experience and tried to think back to what Mrs B had me do. Her hair was so thin though, it was more about sticking in great switches all over her head. I think she just wanted to be touched more than anything.

I let the missus' hair down. It's very thick. She looks quite different with it all around her face – half wild. I always think that brushing her hair and seeing her head jerk back a little with each stroke is such a liberty. Today, I became aware of how much damage I could do as well. My fingers turned clumsy.

74

There was a hair rat on the dressing table. I decided to try and make some height at the front and draw up the hair from the back, as I'd seen on other ladies. She didn't say a word. When I glanced in the mirror, she was looking at me. No expression. Whatever thoughts she had were deep down those black wells. I didn't look again.

The hair wouldn't come right. I couldn't get the shape to stay and kept dropping sections. It wasn't going to work, not by a long march. My hands started to shake.

'Leave, Harriet.'

She said it so quietly, I felt my heart catch – there was such dismissal in it. It bothers me that she calls me Harriet still – as if she doesn't take me seriously enough as a lady's maid to use my surname. But the way she spoke, I felt as if she was offering me advice. As if she was urging me to leave Finton Hall altogether, for my own sake. *Leave*, Harriet. I put the pins I was holding down on the dressing table and met her eye briefly. Her expression was cold and feverish at the same time. I can't stop thinking about her other maid. Helene.

Back in my room, I looked at myself in the mirror and no longer felt like a strange creature that might do anything; certainly nothing that could help the missus. I saw myself as others see me – absurd. The red ribbon caught my eye, the bow knocked askew, and I snatched at it, pulling it out along with several strands of hair, which brought tears to my eyes. Sobs followed. I was sure Clockface was about to walk in and dismiss me for good. That housemaid had been hired to replace me entirely – I was supposed to have been driven out of the house, not made lady's maid. I threw the ribbon on the floor and gave myself over to misery. But there was no use hiding. When Clockface didn't appear, I dried my eyes and smoothed my hair, trying to conjure a less tortured face in the mirror. Better to 'sally forth and meet my adversary' as Mrs B used to say.

I took the servants' stairs down to the kitchen. Clockface was standing by the range looking very pleased with herself and, shrinking behind her box, was the child. My heart sank at how pretty she is. Her clear complexion and little waist feel like personal rebukes. Before anyone could speak, Laurence crashed into the kitchen, shirt and jacket open at the neck, half soaked and grinning. He took an exaggerated step back on seeing the girl.

'Well, what have we here?'

The child looked as if a bear had charged in and spoken to her. She dropped into a curtsy with a squeak. I think she called him sir. Clockface roared with laughter.

'There you are, Laurence, master to a (something French) at least.'

She threw a cloth at him and leered grossly.

'But not if you get yourself caught half dressed. *Your* master will be back any day now. Don't worry, dear.'

She turned to the girl, drawing her to the table and, before my disbelieving eyes, serving her a slice of lemon cake.

'Don't you take any notice.'

Laurence curled his lip but wiped the cloth over his face and neck while watching the girl with a thoughtful expression. Tup anything that moves, I thought, and felt sorry for Mary.

'Are you deaf, *Watkins*?'

Clockface barked it so suddenly at me I jumped and realised a bell had rung and was ringing again. It was the missus' room. Clockface peered at me, no doubt taking in the red eyes and blotchy cheeks.

'Or is it that the mighty have fallen?'

I turned and walked quickly out of the room and back to the stairs. By the second floor, I could hear hurried footsteps following. Laurence bounded up behind me. He looked worried.

'Does she know the housemaid's here?'

I nodded.

'We heard the cart.'

My voice was shaky, I realised, and it made him study me as Clockface had done.

'What's wrong?'

76

I was reluctant to tell him, but the simple fact of being asked made the words spill out of my mouth like a pot boiling over.

'She's different, the missus. Angry. I think she might dismiss me. I don't know how to do hair.'

I expected him to laugh and wouldn't have blamed him, but if anything, he looked relieved. He shook his head.

'She won't. She has her ways, that's all. You shouldn't worry about her.'

He made it sound as if there was someone else I should be worrying about. I swallowed.

'Mrs Clarkson says the master will throw me out when he comes. Is it because I'm not so . . . so . . . fetching as the other servants?'

I blushed to be telling him to his face that he was handsome. He did laugh then and tapped my cheek.

'A smile now and then would help nature along.'

I wanted a real answer and raised my voice.

'Why am I the only one? Everything in this house is so beautiful or grand, even the people.'

'Is it?'

He raised his eyebrows at me.

'Come here.'

Taking my arm, he pulled me through to the second-floor passageway. The doors to the missus' room and mine were yards away, but he turned his back on them and looked up. I followed his gaze to the corner of the ceiling and started back. There was a face. A tongue arched out of its grimacing mouth, and its eyes were greedy with hate. A stone gargoyle, from a church most likely. I shivered. Me and the missus had been walking under its evil gaze every time we went in and out of our rooms. It's so high up, I'd missed it even while cleaning. Laurence dropped my arm.

'I wouldn't call that beautiful.'

'What's it for? Did the master put it there?'

Fear made me shrill.

'Just do your work and look after the missus.'

'But I don't know what her trouble is – why won't she see her son?'
I lowered my voice.

'Is it something to do with the master, Laurence? I don't know how
I can help her.'

He seemed to regret showing me.

'You can stop asking questions.'

'Laurence . . .'

He drew himself up to his full height as if to put himself out of reach.
The muffled ringing of a bell reached us.

'You'd better go to her.'

Before I could answer, he had slipped back through the servants' door,
and I was left alone with the gargoyle. It made me think of the creepy
lover's eye, still hidden behind the butterfly paperweight in the hall
cabinet, and I knew I would never be able to walk to my room again
without glancing at it. The missus must surely do the same. She rang
the bell once more, and I hurried to her door, barging straight in as if
I expected to find her in some peril.

'Harriet, where have you been? I've been ringing for *days*.'

She was sitting in the window seat. Her cheerfulness sounded forced,
but I was flooded with relief all the same. I smiled, as if my failure
earlier had never happened. Her hair was as she usually wore it. With
a sudden movement, she was up and laughing.

'I shall go straight out. I don't want breakfast. Tell Duncan I want
the carriage. And have this sent to the vicarage.'

A letter was swept from the desk and appeared in my hands.

'Tomorrow afternoon, you will accompany me on a visit. But wait . . .'

She hurried to the cabinet and opened one of the small drawers
which held spare laces and ribbons. After a moment's thought, she
pulled out a length of dark blue ribbon and held it out to me.

'For your hair.'

I took it and thanked her. She lingered, watching me.

'I want you to be happy here.'

I nodded.

'Thank you, ma'am. I am. And ma'am . . .'

We both paused.

'I would like to help you in any way I can.'

Our smiles tried to meet each other like before, and almost did.

'I shall be in the morning room.'

She was gone. I sat on the bed and let myself lie back flat on the muddle of soft sheets – I felt I deserved the liberty. Staring at the drapes of the four-poster, folding themselves in and out of darkness, I thought about gargoyles. I believe they are meant to ward off evil spirits, but the presence of one inside the house is unnerving. I propped myself on my elbows and looked around the missus' room for anything sinister lurking in the corners.

Her room is as lovely in its way as any of the others in the house, but it's so crammed with red plush and floral patterns, working in it feels smothering at times. I feel I'm wading through an overgrown garden, as if the patterns don't stay flat but curl around my ankles and waist. It hadn't struck me 'til today that there's not much of her in it at all. Her perfume on the dressing table, her night things I was to put away – nothing else. She's invisible here, disconnected, like a ghost moving amongst furniture it doesn't recognise. The paintings are all of royalty. Some of the ornaments might be personal to her, but I think not. Mrs B had a story for every trinket, likeness, and stick of furniture in the house – even if I didn't believe half of them.

'*This* necklace a gift from a foreign count, *that* portrait a roguish ancestor who ran off with a baroness, *those* fire irons used by one servant to *murder* another!'

She even talked to things, especially the portrait of her late husband. I found a blob of marmalade stuck to the canvas once, as if she'd hurled a teacake.

I rose and went to the cabinet. The contents of the upper drawers were already familiar to me: belts and gloves, smaller items, then petticoats and chemises, all the undergarments. I knelt to open the bottom drawer, the one she hadn't shown me, and felt a tiny shock when it didn't budge. Locked. And no key that I could find.

Tuesday, 9th April

I've been at the hall for more than six weeks, and today was the first time I truly made it outside the grounds. The missus didn't offer much in the way of explanation – I had no warning of where we were going or why she wanted me until we were nearly there. Though I suppose, as a lady, she'd no more tell her shawl why she had brought it. After the last few days, it was a relief to be going anywhere. The carriage is a huge, ornate thing – it looks a hundred years old – with big windows the missus ordered to be opened. I couldn't take my eyes off the countryside. The air was warm, everything green was awake and fresh, the hedgerows alive with little birds and so many blooms. It made me realise how miserable the weather has been and that I've only watched the spring coming through moments at windows and feeling the air change as I worked in the yard. To be *in* it made me giddy. I was almost sorry the missus wanted me in the carriage with her and I wasn't sat at the back with Laurence. She kept watching me with that deep look of hers. I couldn't stop my face opening up and beaming like I was a flower myself.

After a short while, out of nowhere, she burst into song. A sweet note that fell away into a tune about someone making trees with his lute, and plants and flowers springing to life. She leaned forward to sing it out of the window, flinging magic over the hawthorn and hogweed. When we passed an astonished labourer on the side of the road with a hunk of bread frozen halfway to his mouth, she collapsed into laughter. I had to remember to breathe.

'That's a lovely song, ma'am.'

'Thank you, Harriet. Do you know it? "Orpheus with his lute"?'

She sang the first line again and smiled, eyes shining.

'I heard Jenny Lind sing it when I was fourteen. Have you heard her?'

As if that was likely – I'd never heard *of* her. The missus took a big breath in and closed her eyes as if hearing the Lind lady in her mind again.

'She is the greatest singer that ever lived.'

I don't know how she could know that, but watching her face, I believed it.

'She sang all over Europe. Oh, Italy! I wish I had seen her there. She went to America too.'

I tried to imagine that, touring the world, and couldn't. With effort, I can imagine finding my way to Italy, perhaps, but the idea of reaching anywhere like America through simple, earthly means has always seemed preposterous.

When the missus blinked her eyes open, there were tears in them. I remembered how she had spoken in the library of having a gift.

'I've never heard a voice like yours, ma'am. I heard you singing in the house when I first arrived, and it made me . . .'

I didn't know the right word as usual.

'It made me happy, even though the song was sad.'

She held my eye.

'I'm glad you agreed to be my maid, Harriet.'

'Me too, ma'am.'

I meant it. She was still looking at me.

'Harriet Watkins. The greatest lady's maid in the world.'

I jerked backwards. She had used my voice again, but this time she took more care over it, as if she had made it her study and wanted to get it right. I blinked at her stupidly. She laughed and put her hand briefly on mine.

'I like your voice too, Harriet. You mustn't mind me playing.'

She waited until I had returned her smile.

'Now you are my lady's maid, you must remember the rules are different for you. I trust you to use your time well, which means striving not to waste the advantages of your situation. A maid dulled by too much work doesn't please me. As I said, you must enjoy your freedom. There is the library to make use of, of course – you must read as many books as you wish. And the grounds to explore. My last girl, Helene, liked to walk.'

She sat back then and hummed the tune to herself. Her mention of Helene stumped me. I wanted to ask more, but what could I say, knowing what I know? The missus cared enough to follow her to London herself – they must have been close.

After half an hour or so we turned into the drive of a fairly modest house – I only say modest because I had been scared we were going to Hill Court, which is more like a palace if you listen to Mary. I was dreading meeting other servants and having them look at me, but the vicarage is smaller than the hall.

'Before her marriage, Mrs Trevelyan was a lady's maid and has kindly agreed to teach you hairdressing.'

I didn't have time to think about that before Laurence had opened the carriage door and we were being invited into the house by a freckle-faced parlourmaid. Mrs Trevelyan appeared and kissed the missus like an old friend. Turning to me, she held both my hands and called herself delighted. I don't think anyone's looked at me with such uncomplicated kindness since Mrs B in one of her more whimsical moods. The vicar is a much more sombre figure with a long beard, quite a lot younger than his wife. Younger, but not so youthful. He looked at both the missus and me, I thought, with disapproval.

To my surprise it was decided to 'start' straight away, and we separated – me and Mrs Trevelyan to her bedroom and the missus and the vicar into a room downstairs. I thought – stupidly – I'd be practising on the missus herself, but the freckly maid Tabitha was to be the model. She went up ahead of me, and I had a shock when I noticed the sleeve of her right arm ended too soon. Her hand and a few inches of her forearm are gone.

Mrs Trevelyan is the kindest teacher, and Tabitha the most patient model even though she can't be more than fifteen. She didn't mind my first disasters on her head. I kept dropping the brush and scattering pins, but Mrs T laughed so much, Tabitha and I caught each other's eye in the mirror and laughed too. Mrs T has very fine lines around her eyes which suit her, especially when she's smiling, and fair hair which hardly shows the grey. She's a gently ageing elf. I wonder about her and the vicar. He seems so mirthless in comparison. I felt a shot of guilt when he looked at me for never going to church.

I learned a little more about him – and the missus – once I'd managed to do something halfway sensible with Tabitha's hair and Mrs T decided it was enough for one lesson. Their doors are big heavy things that shut out the rest of the house very well. I could hear music as soon as it was opened, and it grew clearer as we came down the stairs. It was without doubt the missus, but not just her – a man's voice and a piano. We stopped in the hallway to listen. His voice – the vicar's – was like a glorious river running beneath, and hers was the sunlight glittering on top. Mrs T listened intently. Then the music broke off and there was muffled talking, quite passionate it sounded, and a quick flurry of notes on the piano. Mrs T nodded.

'Yes, that last refrain was a little heavy-handed.'

She turned to me, and the creases were back, making stars of her eyes.

'I think we had better not disturb them. I am sure you would like some tea after all your hard work. Tabby will show you where the kitchen is.'

I thanked her warmly and Tabitha too as she took me down. She seemed as kind as her mistress, but I was still nervous of being seen in the servants' quarters in this dress. I needn't have worried – they were as curious about the missus as I was about their master and, if anything, I think my fine clothes awed them a little. The cook, Gertrude – she doesn't like being called Mrs Gray despite her position and age – pushed tea and bread with jam in front of me, and the three of them – the housemaid Selina was suddenly there too – huddled around as if it was a council of war.

What was the missus like to work for? Had I met *him*? How was the baby? Why were the indoor servants so aloof? Duncan sometimes came in for a cup of tea, but Laurence never showed himself. Selina sighed and licked her lips.

'The more's the pity.'

Gertrude seared her with a look.

'If that man puts one foot in this kitchen, I'll set a hot iron on him.'

I eyed her, surprised, but the girls were running on. They saw the others at church sometimes or at servants' balls at Hill Court, but they didn't mix much. I told them how hard the work had been and how I came to be lady's maid. Selina nudged Tabitha.

'Same as when you were there then.'

I stopped pushing bread and jam into my mouth to stare at Tabitha. She shrugged.

'Only for a few weeks, over a year ago now. Mrs Trev offered me a place here . . .'

She lowered her voice.

'I was glad enough to say yes.'

'Fair stole you away, didn't she?'

Gertrude gave her a motherly look, then shook her head.

'They get through housemaids and boys quicker than I do hairpins. It's a bad lot when upper servants are worse even than their masters can be.'

I was still staring at Tabitha, thinking she must have known Helene. Gertrude patted my arm.

'Now you're a lady's maid, you can use the position you've been raised up to by God's grace to bring His love and goodness to the other servants.'

Her eyes shone with joy. *For* me, I think. I've never considered I might now have some sway in the house. The thought of bringing any kind of goodness to Clockface! But it has made me think I could be a friend to Lily, the new girl. She cowers in the kitchen close to Clockface, staring sullenly, as if the rest of us are all grinning goblins.

Gertrude hadn't finished, and I could see what was coming.

'I hope we'll see you in church when Mr Gethin is back. I'm sure things will be much easier at the hall then. He sets a wonderful example. Such a kind man.'

I stared at her. She smiled encouragingly and lowered her voice.

'And very patient.'

She threw a meaningful look upwards, in the direction of the missus. I thought of the missus' dark moods I'd seen or heard about and wondered if she was spoken of in that way all over the county. A flash of loyalty made me bristle. Gertrude's eyes shone more brightly talking about the master than when she was talking about God. I wonder what she'd make of the gargoyle. Changing the subject, I was bold enough to say it seemed strange that the missus doesn't go to church but comes and sings at the vicarage as often as she does. Selina spoke in a whisper, which was hardly necessary.

'Shut up together for *hours* sometimes.'

Her eyebrows made it obvious what she thought of that. I recalled the grim-faced man I had glimpsed and nearly choked on a piece of bread. Gertrude told her to mind her mouth, but it was clear the conversation had become as worn as old cloth between them. She sniffed.

'God moves in mysterious ways. Music is a path to the soul and our good parson knows that.'

She took my plate away to make an end of the subject, and I watched it go with sadness – the jam had been very sweet. A bell rang then anyway. Tabitha jumped and beckoned me.

'That will be for you too.'

I was sorry to leave. The vicarage was so ordinary after the hall – it seemed easier to breathe there somehow – and the servants so cheery and normal. It was a relief I hadn't expected – to be amongst faces as unremarkable as my own. Only Tabitha has a truly sweet face, even with her freckles, which are much more becoming on her than on my spattered face.

I was wondering if I had time to ask about Helene when she turned suddenly halfway up the stairs and took hold of my arm. She stared at me as if she was searching out something invisible.

'You're all right at the hall?'

I didn't know how to answer, so I nodded. She leaned in closer.

'There's something wrong there.'

'Wrong?'

She nodded.

'Something didn't feel right, which is why I was glad to come here. Servants keep leaving. I think it's more than Mrs Clarkson's bullying.'

My chest tightened.

'Is it the master?'

She frowned and looked down at her right arm.

'I don't think so. He hired me after my accident and brought me down here. He was kind.'

She rubbed below the elbow with her one hand and saw me looking.

'Caught it in a spinning machine, trying to fix a spindle when I was twelve.'

I felt my own right hand bunch into a fist. She shrugged.

'I don't notice it now. But if it wasn't for Mr Gethin, I'd be in the workhouse.'

I took a step closer and whispered.

'Do you know what happened to Helene, Tabitha? The lady's maid? Mary won't tell me.'

She glanced up and down the stairs before speaking.

'Not everything. She got into trouble, but it wasn't like her. She went to church even when none of the others did, which is how the vicarage lot came to know her – Mrs Trev was especially fond. They spoke French together.'

She frowned again.

'I didn't know her very well. I had only just started at the hall when the Gethins took her to London with them. They took a boot boy too, a little Indian lad, but he didn't come back. Helene said he ran away while they were in town, but she wouldn't say anything else. She was nervous all the time, and then, when her condition was known, she left. Everyone said it was Laurence – you must have seen what he's like?'

I nodded reluctantly.

'Duncan says he confessed, but Mr Barrett kept it quiet and forced Helene to go. Since then, servants have been leaving more quickly than makes sense. Though it's true most of them are dismissed almost as soon as they arrive. I don't know that I might have been thrown out too, but Mrs Trev got to me first.'

The bell rang again down in the kitchen. Tabitha made an impatient noise.

'Just mind yourself. Especially around Laurence.'

She turned and was at the top of the stairs quick as a hare, leaving me with a queasy feeling, as if the ground had become unstable. In the hallway, the vicar was looking as dour as before, but the missus was shining like a beacon, talking to Mrs Trevelyan almost as if she hadn't stopped singing. Words poured out of her like notes up and down a scale. They are planning a gathering at the hall for when the master is back, a musical evening. She was flushed and looked younger. Mrs T kept nodding and smiling in a motherly way, guiding her towards the door with the smallest shifts in her body and graceful turns of her wrist that the missus didn't notice. At the carriage, Laurence shut the door just as I was going to step up.

'You're at the back with me.'

After what Tabitha had just said, I shrank from the idea.

'No, I'm not.'

I feel hot just writing that down. He gave me the look it deserved and lowered his voice.

'Who do you think gave the order?'

I had no choice but to walk around, hoping the missus hadn't heard. There's not much room at the back, and we had to sit close. I was aware of the warmth and pressure of his arm against mine.

'You're a ray of sunshine today.'

I glanced at him. Strange to be so close, so private together on the carriage. Knowing what was being said at the vicarage, that he had even confessed to Barrett, I became aware of him in ways I didn't want to. But Mary had said Barrett knew it wasn't Laurence. I wanted to be alone to think clearly.

'Cat got your tongue?'

I tried to sound unconcerned.

'I'm tired. Don't have to talk, do I?'

There was a silence. He blew air through his lips.

'Plenty of talk in the vicarage kitchen, I don't doubt.'

Something in his tone made me feel ashamed. He knew what had been said or could guess it. I glanced up again and was shocked by the directness of his look – he was watching me as if to see what a small animal might do. For all the pale nakedness of his stare, I couldn't tell what lay behind it and turned away, flustered. He gave one of his bitter laughs.

It's odd how a place can change without looking any different. Finton Hall seemed darker and more troubling. Mary was waiting. I hardly knew how to meet her eye. She handed me a letter on the sly – William's handwriting on the envelope. It was kind of her. Clockface might have kept it from me for days. I returned her quick smile and hid it under the missus' cloak as I followed her up to help her change. Afterwards, she sent me straight back down for the wine and biscuits. I could hear Clockface talking in the kitchen as I drew near. She was speaking in urgent tones, and I stopped outside the door.

'. . . had to restrain her. If they hadn't, the portrait would have been ripped to shreds, and who knows what else? It makes me shudder to think of it.'

'But why did she want to cut up her own picture?'

I caught Lily's voice, low and worried. There was a splat as Clockface threw something fleshy onto a board.

'Sensible questions like that won't get you far with the likes of her. Frightful the look on her face when she saw it, and with that knife in her hand! (Something abrupt in French). If I were the master, I wouldn't feel safe in my own bed. It's no wonder he stays away.'

Lily said something else that I couldn't hear, and there was a huff.

'The rest of us have to put up with it and hope she's not taken any worse. There'll be blood shed one of these days.'

It sounded to me as if Clockface was enjoying the idea, but when I walked in, Lily was as white as a sheet. She turned her large eyes on me with distaste, as if I was as mad as the world believes the missus to be. I can see Clockface has her claws in her, as deep as in the fish she was gutting. I greeted them both cheerfully enough and earned myself a sneer. As I left, I could hear the silence behind me thrumming with all the unkind words waiting to be said.

I took another look at the portrait before taking the wine up. It is still in its awkward place on the drawing room wall, and the missus hasn't mentioned it again. I can't understand why its arrival should have upset her so much. The girl in green looks so fresh and happy, it's hard to imagine such pretty hands wielding a knife. But if it ever comes to it, I shall be ready. I have decided there is nothing she can do that will shock me.

Later

I won't copy out William's letter. He said he's glad, and now he's free to marry someone he feels proud to be seen with. Then he sent me greetings from my mother – my *own* mother – because, he explained, she's too upset to write herself yet. I crumpled the letter, threw it on the floor and stamped on it. I shall recommend that he marry my mother instead – they do think so very much of each other.

Wednesday, 10th April

My red ribbon has disappeared! I wanted to tie up my letters again when I put William's away in the box (after uncrumpling it). The ribbon should be on the floor where I threw it, but I don't remember seeing it. There's no crack it could fall down. While that's vanished, something else has appeared – a little pot of cold cream on my wash-stand. It's made with rose oil, I think – I can't stop lifting my knuckles to my nose to breathe in the smell. I had a moment's shame that the missus must have put it there because of my hands, but she's said nothing. All she can talk about is the musical evening – what food to order, what to wear, what to sing. The idea of having guests and music at the hall beats inside her like a second heart. We have been to the vicarage again, and I think my hairdressing skills are improving. Clockface makes lewd comments in the kitchen about the missus and the vicar, but I take no notice.

Friday, 12th April

She's gone to London, some business at Gloucester Square. Mrs B left the house to her, which is another thing keeping the master in town. He's making it into their London home and no doubt stuffing it full of paintings and statues and whatnot like he has here. I knew nothing of her leaving until yesterday when she said I was to pack for her and that I could have the whole weekend to myself. She's taken Laurence. My heart sank when I heard that. Why him and not her lady's maid? I worry the separation from me will not be good for her. Finton Hall seems further from the world than ever. It's flat and stale without her. I wander around her room, needlessly dusting and rearranging items and searching fruitlessly for the key to the bottom drawer.

Saturday, 13th April

First my ribbon, now my print dress has been taken, and I don't know when. I wanted to change into it to go for a walk, but the drawer is plain empty. Mary was washing the front steps when I went looking. She was so uninterested in my missing dress, I couldn't believe it was her that took it. When I turned to go, she asked me what London was like. I'm amazed she's never been.

'Busy, dirty. Big.'

She nodded.

'But all the people, the places . . .'

I knew what she was thinking of. Or whom.

'Laurence will be too busy with errands for the missus to see any of it.'

She glanced at me sharply but didn't take offence. I wanted to ask her about what Tabitha had said but knew she would shut me out if I did that. She looked troubled.

'I don't know why she took him with her.'

I offered her the feeble reason I'd found for myself.

'Muscle, I expect. There will be things to carry back she won't want to trust to a porter.'

She thought about it, wanting to believe it too. I wondered how far her jealousy reached.

'She hit him once.'

I stared at her.

'What?'

'She thought Helene was his fault, everyone did.'

Her voice went hard.

'She went for him, wild as anything. Called him horrible names.'

I studied her face.

'Why wasn't he dismissed?'

She shrugged and stared back down the drive.

'She changed her mind. She can't do enough for him now, treats him like a pet.'

'But I don't understand – why would she change her mind when everyone says it was him?'

It was the wrong choice of words. She stiffened, and I got a sense of bared teeth. I quickly changed my tone.

'Well, he doesn't give her flowers, does he?'

Her eyes brightened in spite of herself. I could feel her whiskers twitching as she tried not to smile.

'I found bluebells in my workbox on Friday.'

We hadn't shared confidences before. I was trying to think how to ask her more about the missus when she made a swift, deft movement with her hand at her neckline and pulled free a necklace. It was a small ring threaded onto a thin strip of leather. She showed it to me with the same half-defiant look Laurence gave when he offered his posy. It's a strange, skittish courtship they're having. I suppose I'm the best she has as a witness.

'It was his grandmother's.'

I looked more closely. It's a split ring from a charm bracelet, prettily engraved, and looks like gold. Expensive. I felt a flash of suspicion – hadn't the master rescued Laurence from a life of poverty? It seems unlikely he would be in possession of an heirloom. Mary held the ring in her palm as if it was a little bird she feared might fly away. I told her it was beautiful – it was – and she tucked it back inside her dress, looking happy for once. She was starting to tell me another story about Laurence, unable to stop herself now she had an audience, when Clockface appeared in the doorway like a witch in a fairy tale and that was that.

I asked Lily about my missing dress. She looked at me as if I was speaking in tongues and didn't bother with an answer. I think she is beginning to understand her position as Clockface's favourite.

Sunday, 14th April

I thought I had taken leave of my senses completely this afternoon. Opening the door of my room, I saw the girl in green gliding up the stairs. She was looking over my shoulder still, even as she moved straight towards me, and I nearly cried out. For a moment, I watched helplessly as she floated closer, convinced that in some shadowy way she was coming for me. Fear squeezed my throat shut. Which was lucky. She took a sharp turn at the top of the stairs, and there was Laurence – of course – carrying the portrait. The sight of him made my heart lurch in a different direction – he was supposed to be in London, so where was the missus? My face must have turned white because he paused when he saw me. I collected my wits and asked if the missus was back. No. She'd sent him home alone with orders for the portrait to be hung in her room.

'Why?'

I followed him in. It made me uncomfortable that the girl in green was being moved around. Laurence leaned her against a small table and squared up to an earl hanging near the door.

'Damned if I know. The housemaids should be doing this, not me.'

I was in no mood for glib replies.

'Why was the missus upset when her portrait arrived? She told me to send it from London herself, but Mrs Clarkson said she had a knife ready for it. I don't understand why.'

He turned his head to look at me as if I'd said something strange, then briefly back at the portrait. I carried on.

'And when the canary came – why did she throw it out? Is she angry at the master?'

He didn't answer for a moment.

'I told you. Just do your work.'

I wanted to kick him.

'Tell me.'

Shaking out his shoulders, he took hold of the earl.

'Laurence.'

He lifted down the painting, then picked up the girl in green. I felt my blood surge higher with every second he ignored me.

'I'll tell Mary what they said at the vicarage. That you confessed about Helene.'

He went very still for a moment. Horribly so. I was afraid suddenly of the thoughts going through his mind, of how his hands clenched the sides of the picture. Tabby had told me to be careful, but I saw I had set something building in him that I could not take back. Without speaking, he positioned the painting in the gap and reached behind to hook it by the chain. It wouldn't catch. He tried several times, handling it roughly until I worried for the painting itself. The final time, he must have caught some skin because he cried out loudly, holding one hand up and letting the portrait slide perilously to the floor. I saw pain set fire to his anger. It rushed up his body like molten iron and, with a roar that set my hair on end, he punched the wall. I stumbled backwards into one of the chairs, hands lifting feebly. He turned, breathing heavily, and I thought of the fire irons, if I had time to reach them. His face was full of rage and something else too, a private, anguished look. He glared at me.

'Tell her. See where it gets you.'

The skin on his knuckles was broken. He uncurled his fingers painfully and seemed on the point of saying more. Nothing came, and he turned abruptly, snatching up the painting of the earl on his way out. I rushed over to make sure the painting of the girl in green was undamaged and, though my hands were shaking, managed to hang it without trouble. After that, I retreated to my own room and haven't left it, even to eat. The hours are filled with sewing. And praying that the missus will return soon.

Monday, 15th April

It happened like a clap of thunder on a still day – nothing to warn of what was coming. I feel struck by lightning. I was in the library as the missus says I can use it whenever I like, but I wasn't there for the books. I still can't believe I'm allowed to touch them and, apart from the Milton, I don't know that I want to. I'm no reader except for letters – and I like tidying up the missus' papers in the morning room, if only because I now know how to spell words like 'soirée'. The thought of all the serious words on all the pages in the library makes me bone tired. But I was restless this afternoon, worried about the missus being in London without me and still unsettled by Laurence. My stitching went awry on a petticoat, and I gave it up. I searched through her room for the hundredth time and the desk in the morning room, looking for the key to the bottom drawer or a clue about her portrait, or Helene, or *anything*. Nothing. So, I tried the library instead for something more about the master, peering at books and behind them and tugging at anything with a handle. The only odd thing I found was a lump of flint in the drawer of the middle table.

I slammed the drawer shut again, and my eye fell on the strange machine. It had dulled since I cleaned it three weeks ago. Mary's lazy, and I doubt Lily has the strength to apply a duster with any spirit, she's so doll-like. I don't know why she was hired for a house like this. Perhaps it's no wonder they lose staff so quickly. I've tried talking to her again, but I can see she's reluctant to have anything to do with me. What I do know is she's an orphan with even bleaker choices than me outside this position. I keep thinking of Gertrude's words at the vicarage. I should try harder.

I considered the wheeled thing a moment more, then picked it up and gave it a good buff with my pocket handkerchief. The shine came back and with it somehow the shine to my day. It started me thinking how housemaids should really be held in higher esteem. We're priest-esses, perfecting the beauty of common, ordinary things. The fancy made me laugh. Perhaps dusting really is a way of serving God.

I heard a man's tread and felt my insides clench – Laurence on some errand or sloping off to his room, which is quickest by the backstairs at the library end of the house. He sleeps in the same place the silver's locked up in for safety (though I doubt it's any safer with him). My pulse quickened as the footsteps grew louder. I waited for them to fade again – no part of me knows what to do with itself when he is near – but instead of walking by, he turned into the doorway. My heart lurched and then seemed to cease altogether. He took two strides into the room before we were both stock-still like two dogs catching each other's scent. Not Laurence. The master. Without doubt. As if the man in the drawing room portrait had escaped but in doing so aged instantly. Everything Clockface and Laurence had said or hinted at roared into my head, and I had a dreadful urge to bolt for the door.

'Excuse me, sir.'

It was a whisper. I could hardly hear myself with the clamouring in my ears. His gaze travelled all over me.

'Ah.'

And he walked towards me.

I will try and get him down as Mrs B said I should. First impression is that he's a gentleman, of course. His face has that soft look – no whiskers. It's heavier than in the painting. There's not much hair on his head, and he's not overly tall. If anything, I was surprised by how ordinary he looks – except for his eyes. They are faded, with age perhaps, but alive in a way I've not met with before. I've never felt so looked at. And Lizzie had said he wouldn't notice me. I swallowed and spoke quickly as if talking would fend him off in some way.

'Harriet Watkins, sir, the new lady's maid.'

I felt as if I'd told him I was the butler. He raised his eyebrows, and his smile widened as if he was in on a joke I wasn't. After what Clockface had said, I was waiting for him to start speaking French. Instead, he touched my chin with his soft fingers, which gave me a start – I was mostly looking at the floor except for quick glances up. It was like the missus had once touched me, only he lifted my head up and a little to the side as if he was inspecting me for purchase or judging an ornament or I don't know.

'Harriet Watkins.'

He said my name slowly as if it was some sort of secret between us, and with a jolt I remembered Clockface had written to him complaining about me.

'May I?'

He looked at the metal thing in my hands.

'Oh!'

I thrust it at him and started talking quickly again about how I'd just picked it up to dust. I became aware of my hands and tried to hold them out of sight, which he saw – he saw everything – and then I was telling him how I had been a housemaid and was used to cleaning. Clockface could not have done worse for me herself.

He slowly drew his sleeve across the wheels, like a caress. His hands are smooth and soft like his face. Then he held it up, so it caught the light.

'Do you know what this is, Watkins?'

'No, sir.'

With great care, he placed it back in the centre of the table. I was expecting something more, but he only stood there admiring it. The silence was unbearable.

'I think it's lovely, sir.'

He looked at me with that searching expression.

'Hm?'

'Yes, sir. Well, I mean interesting. I think almost not knowing what it is makes it beautiful, sir.'

He seemed to take the idea seriously.

'If you knew what it was, it would stop being lovely?'

I hadn't thought that far on, and with him waiting for an answer like that – looking at *me* like I was something interesting – I found my thoughts wouldn't keep on a clear path but kept skittering off into the undergrowth.

'Oh . . . I don't know, sir. No . . .'

I leaned forward to peer at it, mind a frightened blank, when Mrs B came to my rescue.

'My last mistress, sir, said if you give your attention to something beautiful, it will tell you a secret. I think if you're used to seeing something and know what it is, you might forget that it's beautiful – not see it at all.'

I chanced a look at his face. His attention was all on me. I thought I shouldn't be talking this freely, even if he did ask the question. He answered just as if it was normal to be speaking with a maid like this.

'Perhaps its secret is that it *is* beautiful. If you give your attention to an object or person, however outwardly plain, then its beauty will be revealed.'

I could tell he was still looking at me and burned up hotter than before. The gargoyle flashed into my mind. Did he think that beautiful?

'Take this.'

He broke off gazing and wafted a hand at the machine.

'It's a steel and flint mill, used by miners in the last century to provide a light while they worked. The naked flame of a candle was too dangerous with the gases below ground.'

He opened the shallow drawer in the table and took out the lump of flint.

'Let me show you. Close those curtains.'

There are windows either end of the library. He walked briskly towards one and, bewildered, I hurried to pull the drapes opposite. The library was plunged into gloom.

'Now, come closer.'

We met in the middle, either side of the table. He picked up the mill and held it with one end pressed against his body. I could make out the handle on the wheel closest to him. He turned it, and immediately sparks flew up in the air, blasting the area between us with light. There was a frantic, grating sound, and I saw that his other hand was holding the piece of flint against the turning disc. His face, lit up and floating behind the streaming sparks, made me think of a line from *Paradise Lost* that Mrs B read to us – *with head up-lift above the wave, and eyes that sparkling blazed.* He was grinning like a schoolboy, his lips and teeth strangely magnified in the burning light. I found my own face rigidly drawing itself up into a smile too, as if some bolt of energy had passed from him to me. He let out a shout of a laugh, and the mill whirred to a stop which, after the bright light, cloaked us in almost total darkness. I blinked. The sudden blindness and silence made the hairs on my arms stand on end. Something moved in the dark, I thought, and I stumbled back towards the window, groping for the curtains. Daylight rushed in.

'Very effective, you see.'

The master tossed the flint back into its drawer.

'But still not very safe. This particular flint mill caused an explosion that killed a miner.'

He placed it carefully, almost lovingly, back on the table.

'But the man operating the mill itself survived. Interesting, isn't it?'

He seemed really to want me to agree with him. I moved slowly back into the room as he continued.

'They say the sparks change colour as the methane levels rise. He would have seen what was coming for a brief moment. I expect it was rather beautiful.'

I looked at the thing. It was awful now, like the beautiful paintings of death and horror. But also – it was true – interesting. He cleared his throat.

'You will no doubt have seen many items from my collection – handled them, of course. I am delighted you observe so closely. Nothing in this house lacks beauty, whether its purpose is ornamental or useful – that is of utmost importance to me.'

I remembered Clockface saying I was a dirty blot and felt my shoulders hunch, but he was looking at me quite seriously.

'Even the humblest-seeming thing can surprise one with its beauty. One simply needs to learn how to look.'

Still looking at me, he pointed at the flint mill.

'Behold! This funny little contraption was never designed to be beautiful, but it so fascinated lady's maid Harriet Watkins, she couldn't refrain from soiling her pretty white handkerchief to bring it up.'

I couldn't tell what his tone was – the hint of mockery made me look at him more boldly, but he was now smiling. I laughed – again as if my features were being moulded to his will.

'Of course, we use lamps in the mines now – much safer, much less lovely.'

His smile waned as if he was thinking something new.

'And what happy hearth have we deprived of the observant Harriet? You are from north of here, I think?'

I told him about home, and he wanted to know all about my parents and sisters and the Stanworths, and how often I wrote or visited, as if any of it could mean anything to him. Finally, he clapped his hands together and turned towards the desk.

'Well, we must be sure to take good care of you.'

It was my cue to leave, and I took it with a mixture of reluctance and relief. I was anxious to tend to the missus but came to my room first to look in the mirror – partly to see if there was any red left in my face but also to see what he was looking at. If I stared at myself for long enough, I wondered if I'd see beauty hidden in my humble features. Not really. Same solid jaw and long face. But not so tired now I'm not doing the rough work. My skin's clearer, and there's something – not in the features but in my expression I like. I don't think it was there earlier.

The missus was in her room, still in her travelling cloak, staring out of the window. I was very pleased to see her.

'I'm sorry, ma'am, I never knew to expect you.'

She turned her head, and I saw she was down those black wells again as I had feared. While I changed her out of her dress, she stared at her portrait, and I waited nervously for her reaction. The girl in green looks much more at home in the bedroom with the lush green wallpaper around her. I see more of the missus in her since last week. Or her in the missus, I suppose. It's as if they're moving towards each other.

'I remember how tedious it was to sit for that portrait.'

Her voice had a dreamy quality.

'He was a surly old man, the artist, resentful I think of having to paint spoilt aristocrats for a living. And I was a terrible subject, very impatient. He painted me in the garden itself only one time, and when the musicians started playing, I remember wanting to run through the gate and join them – so much so that I stood up. He swore terribly at me, and tore off his necktie in a rage, so I sat down again. I wish I had not. I wish I had run.'

I finished arranging her collar, thinking (after my talk with the master) how an ugly scene and bitter artist had still created something beautiful.

'Then you would not have had such a lovely portrait, ma'am.'

She shook her head, still staring at her former self.

'I wish I had. I wish *she* had. Then I would never have forgotten that day or the musicians for so long.'

Perhaps that's why she had wanted to attack it when it arrived at the hall. I imagined the girl in green jumping up and running out of sight beyond the frame, leaving still sunlight on an empty seat. The image was a happy one, but I didn't give it very much thought. My heart was still beating with a kind of excitement that the master had finally returned and, if anything, seemed to like me.

Tuesday, 16th April

Dear Harriet,

I know there is no earthly use in telling you the shock you have given your father. The damage is done, and I am not sure he will ever recover completely. God knows I have tried to guide all my children with a fair and loving hand; He alone sees the trials I have suffered without help and without complaint. The first banns were read for William and Dorcas at church on Sunday, and it won't have crossed your mind to think of the looks I had to endure from neighbours and friends. Not to mention from Prudence Harding who has always thought her family above the rest of us. If it wasn't for all the work to do and looking after your father and no one but me to do it, I would take to my bed myself.

I only hope you don't live to regret the course you have taken, Harriet. But that is a mother's vain hope, I fear. You have made your bed and you will have to lie in it. A man of Mr Gethin's liberal and compassionate nature only invites trouble into his home by his charity, I believe. I have heard rumours that I would not think to repeat from a parlour maid at Beechwood who knew a laundry maid in her last place whose brother's sister-in-law worked for the Gethins in London. I am sure it is only the vengeful tittle-tattle of a dismissed servant, one who was no doubt underserving of the Gethins' kindness in the first place, telling stories to undermine Mr Gethin's good name. It troubles me that they have chosen such an unfinished girl as yourself to serve as lady's maid and I pray daily that you do not give me cause to feel ashamed. You have chosen to disregard the loving guidance of

102

your mother, Harriet, but I entreat you, above all else, to be honest with yourself.

With love,

Mother

PS Sam Jessop was crushed to death in the quarry last week by a barrow that slipped off a plank. His widow, poor soul, will receive some relief through the Association in her time of sorrow. Not everyone can claim to be so fortunate.

I doubt I shall ever open a letter again, if only for the sake of my nerves.

Wednesday, 17th April

The house has jumped to attention. Everyone is busier, smarter, more serious about their work, as if it was all not quite real before. Even the furniture and paintings – the walls themselves – look more alive. The blank eyes of the statues seem luminous, as if something behind them has awoken. Laurence is up and down stairs as much as I used to be. Meals are served properly – the kitchen thrums like a machine with a red and sweating Clockface in the middle shouting orders and insults equally at the kitchen maid. She's from the village and comes in for the day. There was a different girl to start with, but she only lasted one morning before running home in tears according to Mary. This one is built like a ram. Clockface's tirades don't seem to have any effect at all. Perhaps it's because if she chose to, Bridie could knock Clockface flat with her forehead alone. I like her very much.

Servants' meals are different too. Mr Barrett sits at the head. He looks like someone who spends money on himself – Mary says he has a small fortune squirrelled away from all the years with the master, and Mr Gethin gives him advice on investments. He's short but well-fed, and sleek. Blinks slowly. No one knows what he's thinking. He stared long and hard at me when we met and hasn't looked at me since. I can't stop watching him, thinking about Helene, but I don't dare ask him what he knows. He says very little, which keeps everyone else quiet, so for now I like him too.

Clockface has to make do with murderous looks. I feel foolish now for ever believing her spiteful words about the master – I think she was just trying to frighten me. The man I met in the library would never throw a servant out without just cause. In truth, I wish they'd all heard how he spoke to me. Every time I enter the kitchen, I catch Mary and Laurence studying me as if they're expecting me to sprout a second head.

The master's been busy with visitors asking for charitable donations since his return – Mary says they descend like a blizzard the moment he's home. From what I've seen, they go away beaming. It seems Laurence was right – he really is a saint. I was in the hall when one rosy-looking gentleman came out of the library, talking nineteen to the dozen and spluttering with gratitude. They shook hands, and as the master clapped him on the back, he threw me a fleeting look of amusement, as if we were in the habit of sharing jokes about his visitors. Taken by surprise, I smiled back. This morning I saw him again from my window; he was getting into the carriage when Francis – a black servant boy they've brought back with them – tripped over the blanket he was carrying and landed flat on it. The master roared with laughter and threw him a coin once he was upright. Finton Hall feels lighter with him in it, less remote, and it's shaken off the heavy solitude.

I love Francis already. He's a sort of under footman or pageboy in lovely green livery like Laurence, only just turned ten years old – he proudly showed me the little clay pipe the master gave him for his birthday last week. No one has blinked at his colour – I think the master often hires servants with foreign forebears. The boot boy that Tabby said ran away was half-Bengali, not Indian, according to Duncan (he scratched a map in the dirt to show me) – his father was a sailor who married a Cardiff girl but then died, and the master found the little boy shoeless on the streets. He seems especially keen on helping the helpless. Several ladies have visited from societies that train friendless girls for service like the one Clockface hired Lily from.

Francis is not another stray like Lily though, or Laurence, or Tabby; his father's a writer and temperance lecturer, and his older brothers are apprenticed or clerks. The master talked to his mother at some political rally after she asked him a question from the crowd, and according to Francis, his whole family is pleased as Punch that he's been given this chance in such a grand house. He loves paintings and sculpture – especially anything shiny, I've noticed – and wants to study art one day. The master told his mother he'd be sure to show him some of his treasures. My mouth fell open at that. Francis has already had a letter from his father, which he read out to me with great care and huge breaths every three words or so. I wish I had letters from home like it. It urges him to work hard and take pride in his service and to learn everything he can. I've promised to help him write a letter back. He's a burst of sunshine, full of wonder, gazing at all the treasures in the same way I did. I saw him staring in amazement at the painting of the little black child. The artist has been particularly clever at making the light shine off the silver neck circlet – Francis nearly butted the painting with his forehead trying to study how it was done. He even lifted a finger to touch the paint but caught himself in time, before I suffered a small fit. His other great love seems to be Laurence. He follows him about like a smitten duckling, but Laurence looks angry and shakes him off with unkind words, or tries to. Duncan said he had been very fond of Joe, the boot boy who went missing. Neither had family of their own, and Joe looked up to him. Whatever the reason, Laurence has lost his swagger since the master's return. At dinner, he's sullen and doesn't look at anyone.

The missus is different too. Glassy. Looking at her, there's only a smooth, hard surface reflecting back, showing nothing of what's underneath. The master being home and the new bustle in the house have made her no happier. But she's no worse than her dark days before either. I don't know how to explain it. Sometimes she's so still, you'd think her spirit had slipped away, and I think of everything I've heard about her, the rages and sudden turns of mood. I keep watch. Planning the musical evening is the only thing that brings her to life, so I talk of it often, trying to draw her out. More trips to the vicarage are planned. Next time, I'm to learn a hairstyle for the soirée. With Barrett and the master here, I'm more aware of my supposed standing in the house and my lack of experience. An 'unfinished girl' as my mother put it, as if I'm missing an organ.

Thursday, 18th April

My dress has been returned, no damage to it that I can see, and placed back in the drawer. The thought of someone going through my things again, and now playing games – I growled like a bear. It was just before lunch yesterday, and I marched downstairs meaning to say what I thought of it for everyone to hear in the kitchen, never mind Barrett. I'm an upper servant – I suppose I must act like one to be respected. Only I was stopped in the hall by the sound of the piano being played in the drawing room and voices. The missus for certain – the first I've heard her sing since the master returned – but also another high voice, clear as a bell. No song really, but flurries of notes they were repeating to each other, the missus leading. The drawing room door was open, and as I tiptoed near, I heard a giggle – I couldn't believe it. Peering in, I saw Francis standing next to the piano and the missus turned to him with her face lit up like it is in the portrait. There was no danger of being noticed.

I got a shock though, looking beyond them. Something in me must have sensed the figure in the doorway at the other end of the room, mirroring me. The master was spying on them too, though I don't suppose I can say that of a man in his own house. But it's what it looked like. He'd seen me, and when my eyes met his, he smiled slowly with that hint of mischief. His face glimmered at me, if that's the right word, until I thought I would fall forward into the room. I coloured and curtsied, then thanked my stars all the way down to the kitchen – another master would have had my hide for eavesdropping.

I was filled with hope for the missus and spent most of lunch wondering how I might keep her in such good spirits, forgetting about the dress and ribbon until Barrett rose from the table. I cleared my throat and stood up too, knocking cutlery off my plate. The clatter at least caught their attention, and I set forth my complaint about my missing garments, directing most of it at Barrett's top button so I wouldn't lose my nerve. It was met with silence and confused stares. Clockface stood and pushed her chair under the table, so it shrieked horribly against the floor. She raised her eyebrows at Barrett.

'Something's missing from the girl's head, more likely.'

He sniffed and nodded without changing his expression. But none of that's the strangest thing that happened today. I took my moment as usual this afternoon to run up to the nursery and see Edward for a few minutes – and there was the missus again, *holding* him. She'd said she was going for a walk around the garden. I stood in the doorway like a statue and exchanged a look with Lizzie. The missus was walking slowly past the windows, humming, but stopped when she saw me. I tried to smile the surprise from my face.

'You look very comfortable, ma'am.'

She nodded faintly, suddenly not looking comfortable at all. Edward sensed the shift in her and started to squirm, leaning his head back. He let out a whimper. She shushed and jigged him as anyone would, humming softly again, lips almost touching his skin. For a moment, it seemed she had soothed him; he relaxed against her, eyes closing. Lizzie leaned forward to say something – a kind word no doubt – then changed her mind. I understand why. She knows Edward better than his own mother but showing it in any way would be an impertinence. I enjoyed watching the missus – she looked like the girl in the green dress again. A smile had crept over her face. I thought, this is Francis's doing; he's unlocked her heart.

Edward had the fidgets though. Some unknown want jerked him out of his slumber, and his little face went to creases. He arched himself backwards, pulled his mouth into a cavern of distress, and screamed at the top of his voice. It cut us all like a whip. The missus grew rigid and gripped him too tightly. She made soothing noises, or tried to, but he turned his face from her, bawling. I saw her own face shift from distress to anger. She began walking up and down with hurried, jerky movements that upset him more. Lizzie was telling her it was to be expected at this time of day, but I don't think she heard. In a sudden movement, she turned and thrust Edward at me. I had no choice but to gather him into my arms. He let out a piercing wail, but then slumber cloaked him again just as quickly and his cries quietened. His little hand found a pleat in my dress and his body curled into mine.

The missus stared at us in a way I didn't like. Lizzie said something again about him always being crotchety at this time. She was kind as could be, but the missus lifted her chin as if she'd received an insult. Next moment, she'd stalked out of the room. Lizzie sank back in her chair.

'Well, there's a shame.'

I knew it would be better to wait a bit before running after her. She'd be unreachable. Readjusting Edward, I pressed my lips against his hot little head, and we sat ourselves down on a rocking chair.

'What's she so scared of?'

Lizzie shrugged.

'I should never have told her the master had been up here with him.'

'The master?'

'Oh yes.'

She smiled brightly.

'The gifts he brought. Books, toys – too old for him yet, but so handsome. That's from him . . .'

I looked to where she'd nodded and saw a prettily decorated zoetrope sitting on the small chest next to me.

'He carried him about showing him everything, proud as any father I've seen.'

I rocked forward and gave the cylinder a push with my finger. Through the gaps, two seals bounced a ball back and forth off their noses. It was lovely – gave my heart a pang somehow to see such a pretty, childish thing and be holding a baby so close.

'Why would she mind the master being here?'

Lizzie shrugged again.

'I don't know, but it was as if I'd said a bear had been in.'

The missus was back under glass when I dressed her later. Not a ripple or shadow to hint at her feelings. I tended to her with all the kindness and care I know how to give. It's times like these she needs me most, I think. Though I can't help feeling a precious chance has been lost with Edward, that we've taken a backwards step. I miss how it was between us before she went to London.

Friday, 19th April

I was tidying her toilet when I heard her coming back to her room this morning – not her usual habit. She said she would rehearse a song for the musical evening – the one she sang in the carriage on my first trip to the vicarage. Delighted, I suggested the drawing room and piano, but she shook her head.

'We must imagine this room is a grand theatre filled with people, and you are a fine lady, sitting in the best box.'

She gestured that I sit on the bed and curtsied to me gravely, which made me smile.

'I dream of this.'

She closed her eyes.

'Whenever I sing on my own, I imagine there is only the little distance of the stage between myself and the audience. The silence is only the people holding their breath while they wait for me to begin.'

As she prepared herself, the quiet of the room really did begin to feel like the hush before a performance. The first note peeled away from her, and I felt my skin prickling all over. She sang quietly, as if not wishing to be heard, but I knew that in her mind the bedroom had disappeared completely, and she was standing before an audience of hundreds. The door was at my back, and her eyes remained closed, so neither of us noticed it swing open. We were, in our different ways, caught up in the performance, far away from Finton Hall. As she paused for a breath, a different voice intruded.

'Ah! Sullivan's Orpheus.'

I jumped from my seat, but the master didn't spare me a glance. He was leaning against the door frame, not even over the threshold, smiling in at the missus. She blinked rapidly like a sleepwalker who has been roughly awakened.

'I hope you will be singing it at the soirée?'

She stared as if not understanding. Her eyes seemed uncertain even of sight. The master pressed a hand to his chest and laughed lightly.

'Forgive me, I interrupted. I was only thinking that Garston will appreciate it, as a Gilbert and Sullivan admirer, you know?'

He was turning to leave when the missus spoke in a thin, high voice.

'Garston?'

'Yes.'

He swung back around, eyebrows raised.

'I've invited a few fellows from London.'

When she didn't respond, he gestured appealingly.

'We should be generous with our gifts, not hide them away for ourselves. And your voice, my dear, is a rare talent. We both know you're wasted at church and on servants. You deserve an audience that truly appreciates you.'

I was standing almost directly between them, but neither of them showed even a flicker of awareness that I existed. The missus was looking at him as if he had stopped short or spoken in an unfamiliar language. Two spots of red slowly bloomed across the top of her cheeks. I confess I do not know what happened in that silence. I was simply beneath notice as servants are. Finally, he smiled again and bowed to her.

'I look forward to hearing it in full at the party.'

The moment he was gone, the missus sat on the bed and pulled me back down with her.

'Harriet, listen to me.'

She took my hand but didn't meet my eye. Her ungloved fingers – cool and white – slid over my thickened skin and circled my paw.

'I need your help.'

I waited.

'At the musical evening.'

Her grip tightened as if what she wanted to say was finding its way out through her hands instead of her mouth. I didn't move, but whatever it is that lies inside just under my ribs closed up tight like a prodded hedgehog. The last thing I want is to be in sight of all the ladies and gentlemen at the party. I think she got a sense of spikes because she suddenly let go and clasped her own fingers. She changed into the remote lady, issuing orders.

'There will be more guests than I thought. We will arrange extra help, of course, but I would be so grateful if you would . . .'

She didn't finish and dropped her voice.

'I shall depend on you.'

I nodded reluctantly.

'Of course, ma'am.'

She squeezed my hand again, relieved, but said nothing about what she expects me to do. I wish I knew what she had been going to say.

Saturday, 20th April

Visitors. I'd been tidying the morning room, and when I came out into the passage there was a gentleman standing there. Face like a half-rotten apple. He glanced at me once and then again quickly, as if I was an unpleasant surprise, a dirty yard dog somehow got into the house. I thought he must be another one come begging for some cause, but when the missus rang for me later in the drawing room, he was there again with his grey and bony wife and the master.

The missus was talking brightly in a cold way, much like the chilly white sky that's been glaring down at us all week. She sent me off to fetch a newspaper from her desk. There was an advertisement in it by a lady's maid she wanted to show Mrs Murray. When I returned, she asked me to wait and walked over to a side table to find the page, talking all the while to Mrs Murray about the problem with servants and then – louder, I thought – about how fortunate she was to have such a clever, kind maid herself. I blinked. Odd to be spoken of as if I wasn't in the room, but my heart gave a little leap. The master was speaking quietly to Mr Murray, adjusting the position of objects on the mantelshelf from how the housemaids had left them as he did so. Mr Murray listened with his eyes turned to rest on my face. I felt hot. The fire was making a roaring sound in the chimney as if it was a winter's night. Then the missus strode back and handed me the dishevelled paper.

'Cut out this part for Mrs Murray and return with it.'

There are scissors in her bureau in the morning room. I read the maid's hopeful words once I'd snipped around them and felt sorry for her, being offered up to the Murrays. As I refolded the paper, I noticed a pen had been used to roughly circle a column. Looking more closely, I saw it was part of an article about the possible war and what had been debated in and out of parliament. The writer had sharpened his claws for those in favour, especially Liberal MPs like the master.

Mr Gethin famously fills his servants' quarters with the needy, the injured and the friendless in the name of Christian charity and social progress; will he make room for the maimed soldiers, fatherless children and destitute widows which his impassioned words (met with grim silence on his side of the house) will most certainly help create? There is a deplorable inconsistency in the character of some Englishmen, who conduct themselves with quiet dignity at home but call for excessive violence and unnecessary bloodspilling abroad.

I don't know much about the reasons for war, but it seems harsh to turn the master's goodness against him. 'Famous' goodness, it said. Funny, I felt my own chest swell with pride. To know I am lady's maid in a household written about in print. Finton Hall is not so cut off from the world then as, living in it, one might suppose. I walked a little taller back through the hall and found Francis, handsome in his new post. He is being trained to answer the door to visitors, now such things are known to exist. I've never seen anyone wait with such expectation. He looked ready to spring at the handle.

In the drawing room, the missus was busy handing out cups of tea from the tray that Laurence had just set down. As she served, she talked about the musical evening and how the ladies from Hill Court had agreed to play and sing. There was no sign of the anxiety she had shown when she asked for my help. She was extravagantly praising the elder Miss Spencer's voice when a shriek from Mrs Murray cut her off. We all turned and saw Francis in the doorway. He hadn't been able to resist following me to peek in at the party. The cry seemed to have rooted him to the spot, and one fist was bunching up the cloth of his coat. Mrs Murray put a hand to her throat and muttered something. I saw Laurence straighten slowly from the tea tray and turn his eyes to her.

'Of course, we have no need to look beyond our own walls for delightful voices.'

The master picked up the conversation again as if nothing had happened and strode over to Francis. He put a hand on the boy's shoulder and beamed at Mrs Murray.

'Sings like an angel. You must hear him.'

His enthusiasm didn't find its fellow in the room. I caught Mr Murray staring at Francis in a way that made me want to stand between them. The master didn't seem to notice; he was taken with the same boyish excitement as when showing me the flint mill.

'Come. Clara was teaching him yesterday. Show us, my dear.'

He led Francis stiff-legged towards the piano. The missus put down the sugar spoon.

'Ralph, I don't think . . .'

'Oh, come now. Just for us. What were you playing, hm?'

He gestured to the piano stool. She didn't move. The master flapped his hand at her before sitting down himself.

'Why shouldn't we *all* enjoy ourselves? Now . . .'

He played a few notes, looking at Francis encouragingly.

'Don't be afraid. I know at least three people in this room who have enjoyed hearing you sing already.'

He glanced at the missus and then at me. The missus gave me a confused look.

'Da-da-da-da . . .'

His voice was rich and loud.

'Now you.'

Francis looked as if he might faint from breathing too fast. His chin lifted and his mouth opened. A sort of gasp escaped and a hiccup. We all waited in painful silence. Then the corners of his mouth turned down and his eyes filled.

'Oh!'

Mrs Murray flicked a fan in front of her face.

'Must we really suffer this?'

Almost at the same moment, the missus dropped her cup and saucer.

They crashed onto the tea tray, drowning the sugar and breaking into pieces.

'How careless of me.'

I rushed forward to help, but she waved me away, turning to say something to Mr Murray. Laurence shook his head at me too and snatched up the tray. I looked at Francis, who had at least been startled out of his tears. The master was watching the little drama with an air of studied patience. He turned to Francis and smiled, squeezing his arm.

'There now, good lad. Never mind.'

He pressed another coin into his hand and nodded at Laurence, the smile dropping again. Laurence jerked his head towards the door, and Francis set off like clockwork. I wanted to leave too and held out the newspaper cutting to Mrs Murray.

'The advertisement, ma'am.'

She was still fanning herself like a belle at a ball about to swoon. I'd put her at fifty-five, face hard and sharp as slate. I'm every bit as tall and square-jawed as she is and my voice isn't weak, but she acted as if I wasn't there. I've heard of it before, servants being ignored by their betters just to confound them. She has strangely pale eyes, as if the colour has been leached from them. I watched them looking at anything but me and wondered if the master had been trying to show her how little he cared for her shrieks and comments. I put the clipping down next to her teacup.

'I'll leave it there, ma'am.'

'No.'

She tutted and pointed at a different place. The blood thumped in my cheeks. As I turned, I ripped off the address at the bottom of the advert. I hope she ends up with a girl like Bridie.

Francis was back at his post in the hall. I wanted to console him, but Laurence was there, yanking the boy's coat straight and slapping down the material where it had been creased in his fist. When

Francis's chin started quivering again, Laurence pinched it between finger and thumb.

'Stop that.'

He thrust his face close.

'Never let them see you beaten. Never show them. Especially him.'

I stepped towards them.

'Let go. You're hurting him.'

He turned his head and glared at me. I was shocked again by how naked his eyes look with their pale lashes, as if the violence in them might spill out unchecked.

'Of course, Miss Watkins. You know best. You know everything there is to know, don't you? A great pet with master and mistress alike.'

He straightened and walked right up to me, close enough so I could feel his heat and nearness. From the outside it would have looked like something else. My damned blood stirred.

'I'll tell you what you are, Harriet Watkins. You're a starved little mouse that's found some cheese.'

The back of my neck turned gooseflesh.

'Too pleased with itself to notice the trap's shut behind it.'

He snapped his fingers in my face and then mercifully picked up the tray and left. I felt myself trembling as I went to comfort Francis. He had his face turned to the front door, mouth twitching with the effort not to cry. I told him not to mind Laurence nor the master and mistress's guests, but I made a poor job of it, too distracted by my own smarting. He set his face into a scowl and wouldn't look at me. This is how it starts, I thought. All the meanness, all the secrets amongst servants. As I turned, my eye happened to fall on the cabinet and, with a start, I saw that the lover's eye had been moved from behind the paperweight and was staring at me with even greater malevolence than I remembered. Laurence's words are as empty as Clockface's, I keep telling myself, meant only to frighten me. It's the missus that is trapped here, not me. But I fancy I can feel all the eyes in this place watching – in pictures, on statues, carved into the gargoyle – and I think about Helene. She must have sat at this very table in this very room and thought herself well settled. Thought herself safe.

Easter Day, Sunday, 21st April

I slept fitfully and dreamt of dark, doorless corridors. An uneasy feeling has followed me since yesterday, and it was only made worse in church this morning. Lizzie was right that the whole household is made to go. There were all the neighbours I never meet, young and old faces seeking out ours, curious about the recluses at Finton Hall. I had been looking forward to seeing other people, but when it came to it, I felt like a creature in a zoo. The master moved amongst them all, clapping shoulders and shaking hands, greeting everyone like an old friend.

Laurence was also a welcome return, at least for some of the parish's daughters. He knew it too, firing glances and smiles about until I could have dried my stockings on all the flaming cheeks. Mary glared at them, stony as the font. I saw him slip a feather into her hand as we came out of the church. Cunning devil. It looked as if it had come off some lady's hat.

My place was in a pew with Barrett and Clockface, and I sat between them as stiffly as something stuffed. From the corner of my eye, I watched Barrett's hands making precise little movements, turning pages of the prayer book, straightening his immaculate cuffs, pinching a crease in his trousers to kneel. Mary says he's the reason Laurence is so rough with Francis. I pulled her under my umbrella while we were waiting to go in and made her talk to me. Barrett claims Laurence will be taken out of livery and made to work in the yard once Francis is trained – that he's here to replace him. Laurence also told her it was Barrett's fault that Joe left, the boot boy he was so fond of. I pointed out it's the master pays our wages, not his valet, but Mary shook her head and whispered,

'He can make anything happen he likes downstairs. He'll pretend a reason to make the master turn against him.'

In church, I kept glancing sideways at him, trying to learn more, but nothing seems to come off him – no scent, no emotion, no hint at his thoughts. There was only the sound of him breathing through his nose – a soughing noise, like waves breaking in the distance. I hated listening to it, hated sitting between him and Clockface. I think of them now as two parts of a grim machine, joined together like the wheels on the flint mill, but grinding out darkness instead of light.

The only really happy thing about church was hearing the missus sing again. Her voice rose above the rest of us like a blackbird amongst magpies, none of the hushed tones she's been using at the hall lately. I'm sure now that's what she meant by her talent being buried. The master is right that her gift is wasted; ladies have so few chances to perform. Invitations to charitable concerts spill over her desk; she pointed one out to me last week, a children's hospital that attracts great singers and artists, very respectable. Perhaps she has hopes.

I couldn't hear Francis singing, though he was in the pew behind me. No one spoke to him that I heard, but the stares were loud enough. His own gaze somehow rested on nothing and no one, even as dozens of pairs of eyes searched him all over. I hope he hasn't been frightened into silence. He should have a half day now the lunch has been cleared – I'll go and find him. I think I know what will cheer us both up.

Later

I thought I wanted to know all the secrets of this house. It would have been better to walk around with my eyes covered and ears stopped. I took some sheets of paper from the missus' desk and went to find Francis. He wasn't anywhere. Not in the room where he sleeps, nor the boot room where he goes to blow soap bubbles out of the clay pipe the master gave him, nor the pantry where I came across him once drawing the big, round bottles of oil from Italy. (I was amazed at how he managed to show the light glinting off them, but found him almost in tears about it, having only slate and slate pencil to work with.) He wasn't in the yard either, where he pats and talks to the old dog. I didn't believe he'd go any further, being so used to the crush of London streets and so unused to woods and fields and quiet spaces. Then I remembered with some loss of heart that if I wanted to find Francis, it was Laurence I should be looking for, and the quickest way to find him was through Mary.

She was in the hall, toying with the feather he'd given her at church. She hid it in her skirt until she saw it was me coming and then brought it out with a shy smile, wanting me to notice. I wish she had someone else to share it with. For once, she couldn't say where he was, or Francis. I left her sliding the tip of the feather under her chin and slowly down her neck, lost in a fancy, I imagine, where she knew exactly where Laurence was.

Bridie was in the kitchen when I passed through again and said she'd seen them go outside. I remembered how Laurence likes to preen in front of the stable lads and wandered down the block, breathing in the dark, sweet smell of dung and hay and horse sweat, sensing the heavy warmth of the bodies inside. Horses scare me a little, all that muscle and opinion in an animal.

There's another yard behind the stables with barns for feed and tack, and the carriage house. I'd given up looking and was standing by the wall, making the most of the fresh air on my face before the next raincloud burst. One of the big doors of the carriage house was open a man's width, and in the quiet I thought I heard a clunk. I've never been inside before and walked over to stick my head in. It was very dim, there being no windows, and the air colder. As my eyes got used to it, I made out the big carriage more clearly. I could just see that the door furthest from me was open. There was a voice, and the garden lad who reminds me of William loped around to the front, looking back over his shoulder. The carriage rocked as someone jumped out, the door slammed, and there was Laurence. He dropped his handkerchief and ducked for it, which drew a jeering comment from the boy. They both laughed, and Laurence slapped him on the arm as he passed. He looked as if he was going to jog straight on towards the doors and me – I opened my mouth to say his name – but he doubled back suddenly, put his hand around the boy's neck and kissed him.

Their lips were together for perhaps three astonished beats of my heart. There was only the firmness of Laurence's grip, the creases in their brows as their eyes shut tight, the fierceness of it. When it was done, they stayed face to face, foreheads touching, mouths smiling into each other. I remembered the scent of Laurence when he'd stood almost as close to me, and the blood swooped through my body.

Some part of me jerked, I don't know what or how exactly, but the big door creaked. Two heads whipped around, and I stumbled backwards into the light before turning to run across the yard. The door rattled again as someone followed. At the corner of the stable block, I glanced back. Laurence was coming for me, his expression set with a purpose that frightened me out of my wits. I fled again into the yard by the house and stopped in the middle, not knowing where I was going, where was safe. He slowed to a halt and glanced about at the house and stables. My feet had planted me in the safest place after all, within hearing of the kitchen and gardens and in sight of all those windows this side of the house – it was as if the hall itself had flicked open a hundred eyes to watch. We were both caught on invisible hooks and could only look at each other. But such a look. I had a more honest conversation with Laurence Triggs in those few moments of silence than we have ever had in words. He wanted to stop my mouth for good, and I believed he would do it. But there was a question too, a beseeching even – his naked eyes were raw with it. I didn't know how to answer – I thought of Mary and couldn't order my thoughts. He saw my hesitation and hated me for it. Even stronger than his hate though was his fear; I could taste it, like the sweat of the horses.

A clattering of hooves interrupted us. It sounded like fresh trouble bearing down, but it was the master, trotting through the archway on his grey mare. He yanked hard on the reins, hollering for the stable boy, and swung himself out of the saddle.

'She's cast a damned shoe.'

Seeing Laurence seemed to put him in a blacker mood.

'Never where you're paid to be.'

He bent to inspect the hoof, giving the mare a vicious jab in the ribs while he carried on talking. Laurence's gaze didn't shift from mine – it pinned me to the spot.

'I should put you to work out here, on your knees in the filth, as you like it so much. Help me with my boots then, man.'

Rising, the master caught sight of me and paused. I was forced to turn my eyes away from Laurence; it was like turning my back on a bull. I curtsied. The master stared for longer than was comfortable, none of his usual smiles, then strode off towards the house while the stable boy led the mare away. Laurence didn't move. His face was dreadful – full of desperation and threat.

'Do you know what could happen to me?'

His eyes bored into mine.

'Do you know what you could do?'

I stared back, unable to answer, and watched his jaw clench.

'Why did you have to go into the damned carriage house? You're meant to stay in the . . .'

He stopped, defeated suddenly, and his head dropped forward.

'This fucking house.'

I have never felt any advantage over Laurence before. The fear began to leave me.

'Why do you stay then?'

He looked up sharply.

'You think I can leave?'

'Why not?'

His eyes narrowed.

'You think they'd let me walk away and find another position, when I could . . .?'

The words failed him again.

'Could what?'

He hesitated, fear and distrust working his face. In another moment, he bit his lip so hard I thought it would bleed, and he shook away whatever he might have said.

'They know what I am; they can make me do anything they want.'

'They?'

I frowned.

'You mean Barrett?'

He looked at the ground, not answering. I thought of what the master had just said.

'Is it the master as well, Laurence? Does he know everything about you?'

Still no reply, but he made a movement like a horse trying to unbridle itself. I took a risk.

'Does he know about you and Helene?'

It was a mistake. He turned on me, and there was all the anger in him I had felt when he punched the wall. I lifted a hand.

'I won't . . .'

He waited.

'I won't say anything.'

I watched him struggling to believe it. Common sense told me to offer more, to make promises, but the question pounding in my head burst out instead.

'How could you do this to Mary?'

His eyes widened. The fingers of his right hand splayed themselves as if to grasp something, and light flashed off his signet ring. When he spoke, it was with great care, as if the words he was offering me were fragile and might break.

'I love her.'

I simply stared at him.

'Then *why?*'

'He bit his lip again. I could see him searching for an explanation I might understand and failing.

'It's . . . a different part of me, that's all. Telling Mary won't help her.'

Desperation showed in his face, rising fear and anger, and I grasped at an idea.

'All right. But you must be kinder to Francis. In return, if you like. Teach him properly. It's not his fault he was hired to replace you, or that Barrett got rid of the boot boy.'

Mary's words about Barrett had come back to me from outside the church. Surprise flashed across Laurence's face – I had knocked him off balance. I stepped closer.

'What happened to the boot boy, anyway? Why did he run away?'

An angry shout came from the house. Laurence wiped a hand roughly over his eyes. He turned and was halfway across the yard before spinning around again in sudden fury.

'Keep your bloody mouth shut. Or, damn your eyes, I'll make you pay.'

The door slammed shut behind him. I watched it as if expecting it to explode open again. Nothing moved except for one of the horses shifting about, bored in its stable. A single drop of rain hit my cheek, and I flinched. I took what felt to be my first breath since I had witnessed the kiss inside the carriage house. There was, after all, little to wonder at there, I realised – besides my own slowness. Annie would have seen it at once – his teasing and peacocking around the stable and garden boys, Clockface's leers. In London, she was always nudging my arm to look at certain men or pointing out streets and public places, eyebrows raised, while I would have strolled by without a glance. Now, to my surprise, the garden hand was no surprise at all. Tup anything that moves indeed – and why not out here as well as in the alleys and parks of London? But Mary. I remembered their kiss too, so full of need for each other. Perhaps it really is something different for him; I had never thought love could be divided up in that way, like different cuts of meat. But to let her believe she has the whole of him? Is that love? She would break in pieces, if she knew. She would never trust him again – even about Helene.

The house loomed darkly. I walked away from it, out of the yard and past the kitchen gardens. Turning the corner of the wall, I saw Francis in the pasture sitting under an oak tree. It seemed a hundred years ago that I had gone looking for him. He was slumped with his legs out, head sunk to his chest, pulling up clots of grass in his fingers. I watched for a while, tempted to go another way as my head was ringing so. But I had sat in the same place myself once, feeling as lonely and hopeless as he looked. The tears of a thousand servants must have watered that tree. I remembered the paper and pencil in my pocket and walked towards him. He lifted his head, and I saw his face was flickering with hurt again. As I knelt down, he turned away, and I reached out to stroke his cheek. He was still child enough to let me.

'What's wrong?'

He tucked his chin further into his chest and spoke so I could barely hear him. It was something about the stables and wanting Laurence to show him the horses. Laurence had made fun of him in front of the stable hand, mocking his big smile and asking if he was after stealing some hay as he had the teeth of a horse. I shifted my legs from under me, so I was sitting next to him.

'Let's think of all the happy things to tell your parents.'

He didn't answer, only fiddled with a bit of wire he had wrapped around his little finger to copy Laurence's signet ring. I started listing things aloud myself – the old dog, his smart livery, the clay pipe. His nature is too sunny to resist such a game for long. He soon piped up with riding on the dogcart, sleeping in his own room (that's a pallet in a crowded storeroom), and most of all, the master giving him a sketch-book for Easter and saying he could draw a glass paperweight with a real butterfly encased inside. I thought Francis would want to write about the missus too and how he'd sung with her, but maybe that memory's been marred forever by the Murrays and Laurence. Instead, he turned bashful and impish at once.

'And you, miss.'

I heard myself laugh out loud and then just as suddenly wanted to cry. Putting the pencil into his hand, I spoke briskly to hide it.

'Let's begin with the date.'

His letters came out slowly and at drunken angles. They looked as if they'd fallen onto the page from a height. Silly comparing myself to a child, but I had a moment of pride at how far my own writing has come, and how grateful I am to the missus – since we were counting blessings – for making me lady's maid. When Francis had finished, I asked if I might write something to his parents too. I wrote who I was and that they could be very proud of their boy, and I also promised that I would be his friend and take good care of him. Laurence will do as I ask, I think, despite his final threat. But not if I tell Mary his secret. I wish I could unknow it or lay it aside; I feel she will see it in my every move, as if his betrayal is now mine too. The sky finally opened again to pelt us with showers, and we ran inside to seal Francis's letter and add his family's address in Stepney.

Tuesday, 23rd April

I have been pleading ill health to take dinner in my room and skipping breakfast, so as not to face anyone, Mary especially. I couldn't avoid her forever though. The missus sent me away this morning, while she pored over printed programmes for the musical evening, and I crept down to the kitchen for some food. Mary was in the servant's passageway, blocking the way with two cans of water. She looked tired and had put them down for a moment to rest. My heart went out to her a bit. I asked if she wanted help, which made her whiskers stand on end for several seconds.

'They're for the master's rooms.'

'All right.'

She hesitated, looking me up and down. Not wanting to meet her eye, I picked up a can and set off. We were halfway up the stairs when a timid question came from behind.

'Has he said anything to you?'

I slowed, immediately regretting my offer to help.

'No?'

I didn't look around, but I don't think I'm any better at lying than she is.

'Nothing at all?'

'No.'

There was a silence. I've seen little of Laurence downstairs since Sunday and wondered if he was avoiding her too. We climbed a few more stairs, and then my feet came to a stop. My brain heaved. Why should I keep his secrets for him? He had probably already ruined Helene's life, so why was I letting him hurt Mary? If I was her, I should want to know, however painful the truth might be. I turned to look at her unhappy face; it peered up at mine, searching.

'All right. I'll tell you.'

I put my can down.

'Laurence has been keeping something from you.'

Her eyes widened.

'I know how much you care for him, Mary, but you need to know.'

A hardness came into her face, and she began climbing past me. I sighed.

'Mary, you don't understand. He—'

'No, you don't understand.'

She stopped a step above me and turned, shaking.

'Everyone thinks they know everything about him, but they don't. It wasn't his fault. If he hadn't said it was him, he'd have lost his place.'

I opened my mouth and shut it again. She glared at me.

'No one would have believed her anyway. She would have had to leave.'

I caught what she was talking about slowly enough. My mind groped blindly about until it smacked into the middle of it.

'Helene?'

Angry tears appeared in Mary's eyes.

'She was going to accuse . . .'

She dropped her voice and looked nervously up and down the stairs.

'She was saying it was a gentleman that got her with child, a friend of the master's in London. That he gave her something to make her sleepy and forced her. When she knew she was done for, she was going to go to the master himself with it and the police. Mr Barrett stopped her. He made Laurence say it was him, so no one would believe her if she ever did go to the police. They'd think she was trying to get more for herself.'

The fierceness returned.

'That's what Mr Barrett does. He said he'd get Laurence thrown out if he didn't say the baby was his. He said he'd make sure everyone thought it was him anyway and he'd be friendless and with no character. Nowhere would hire him after that, he'd have nowhere to go. He didn't have a choice.'

I heard Laurence's words again, that they could make him do anything they wanted, that he couldn't leave. He was trapped by Barrett, even more than Mary knew, and my resolve to tell her about the garden hand began to melt away. Besides, I had pressing questions of my own.

'Did the master know?'

Mary's lip curled.

'Barrett protects him; the master believes whatever he says.'

'But couldn't Laurence tell the missus?'

She scoffed and shook her head as if that was the last place anyone would look for help.

'She was vicious to him, and then she went so mad when she saw the portrait, the doctors had to lock her in her room for a week.'

'They . . . *what* . . .?'

Her face screwed itself up with contempt.

'Laurence hasn't done anything wrong. It's Barrett and *her* . . .' She jerked her head at wherever the missus might be. 'They cause all the trouble.'

She stomped on ahead, leaving me with my mouth open. My cheeks grew warm, thinking of how I had goaded Laurence about Helene in the yard. I had been more than ready to believe he was to blame, wanting to trust Tabby over Mary. But it was Barrett again. The master's valet swelled in my mind, a monstrous sponge, soaking up all the dirty swill before it could reach his employers. Was it possible he had acted to save Mr Gethin's reputation, to bury the scandal of his friend, without the master's knowledge? Gertrude had said upper servants can be worse than their superiors. I looked up. Mary was stomping back down towards me, fresh anger in her face.

'And I wasn't asking you about Laurence anyway. I was asking if the master had said anything about *that*.'

She prodded me painfully in the shoulder. I must have looked as blank as a sheet as her fury subsided slightly. She watched me a moment, and I could see her coming to a decision of her own.

'Come with me.'

She abandoned her can of water and pulled me up the stairs and onto the third floor. The master's rooms are at the back of the house, with Barrett's across the hall. I've never been in before – keeping them in order while he was in London was Mary's job, and I was never told to go in there when she was ill. She took me straight into his private sitting room. Gorgeous – all kinds of pretty armchairs, side tables, footrests and screens – and on every surface dozens of beautiful ornaments and curiosities. I could have spent hours looking at it all. There were many things I didn't recognise, strange objects like the flint mill.

Mary stood in the middle of it, waiting for my eyes to become accustomed, as it were. She looked quickly above the fireplace and back, directing my attention. There was a large painting – a portrait of a woman. For one delirious moment, I thought it was me. She sits on a stone balcony with her elbow resting on the ledge and her fingers raised to her throat as if to play with a pear-shaped pendant there. Beyond her a vast and beautiful landscape sweeps away with a colliery in the distance – heaps of coal merge gleamingly with the green hills, so they seem a harmonious part of the scene. The balcony is full of lovely things that speak of comfort and happy pastimes – a dog sleeps at her feet, music sheets rest near to hand, an empty birdcage with its door open is half-draped with green cloth, but then one sees the canary fluttering prettily in the air. It's like a painting from another era. Mary moved closer.

'This is the portrait that caused all the trouble. Not the one downstairs of her in the green dress.'

I tried to swallow and failed. It is the missus, of course. She looks out into the room, very serious; the painter's caught a bit of her wild look. But it was the dress that made me start, that made me see myself up there. The very same I'm wearing still. Blue and lilac with ruffles and pleated trims, buttons down the front. On her, in the picture, it looks even finer – whoever designed the dress knew exactly the effect it would have, brightening her brown eyes and showing off her lovely skin. Standing there, looking at it, I felt as if the real dress could see it too and rebelled at being stuck on such a poor substitute. It grew tighter around my chest, making it difficult to breathe; the cuffs chafed, and the weight of the skirt grew heavier.

'He had the dress made specially for the portrait, aunt says. It was an anniversary gift.'

Mary's shine was back, her love of scandal.

'But she refused to wear it again and wouldn't have the picture downstairs.'

'Why not?'

She shrugged.

'She threatened to rip it with a knife, so he had it brought up here. But turns out she was already carrying the baby. The doctor said it was because of that. Something not natural in her. That's when they locked her up to stop her stabbing anything else. She's only ever worn dark colours since then. We never saw the dress, 'til you showed up in it.'

I didn't answer. I couldn't. All the breath seemed to have left my body. This was the portrait all the gossip had been about, not the girl in green at all. I remembered how the master had looked me over when he first walked into the library, and the long look Barrett had given me. And the missus – I felt suffocated. A horrible sinking feeling plunged down and down. What had made her act that way? It is the master she fears – or hates – there can no longer be any doubt about that. But why? I stared hard at the portrait, looking for anything at all that could upset her, that could make her want to rip it to pieces. It was simply a beautiful gift, like the dress.

A clock somewhere in amongst all the treasures sounded a death knell, seemed to me. It put Mary in a sudden fuss.

'They'll be back soon – I haven't finished. Quick.'

'Mary.'

I touched her arm before she could flee.

'Thank you. For showing me.'

Her shoulders lifted slightly in a shrug.

'And I'm sorry. About Helene . . . for thinking it was Laurence.'

She looked sideways at me, reluctant to forgive so soon, but then nodded. After she had gone, I gazed up at the missus staring out of the portrait. Did she know the truth about Helene? Perhaps she had told the master, and he didn't believe her. My stomach churned with dread.

She had gone so mad – turned so violent – they had locked her up. I felt the dress tightening around me again, a symbol of something awful that I couldn't name. The idea of the master finding me there was unbearable. He must think I knew about the portrait and conspired with the missus to wear the dress. No wonder Clockface laughed the way she did when I walked into the kitchen the first time – she saw me for the puppet I am. They all did. A mouse in a trap, Laurence said.

I hurried up to the nursery and found Lizzie sorting out baby clothes. She made me sit down when she saw my face, but my worries about the portrait didn't impress her.

'There's nothing wrong with her giving you a dress she doesn't want.'

'But this one? It's too much for a servant, and now I know it means something between her and the master.'

She rubbed the lace at the cuff between two fingers.

'It is very fine.'

I could feel tears coming to my eyes.

'What if she only made me a lady's maid so she could dress me up in this? I'm a housemaid really, and I'm not even pretty like Mary and Lily.'

Lizzie leaned down so we were eye to eye.

'You forget, Harriet. Whatever they're about, it's not your fault or your business.'

It wasn't the comfort I'd come for. She straightened and walked to Edward's cot as he had started to cry.

'All the same, I'm glad I won't have her for a mistress much longer.'

She was walking away from me, so I only just caught it. My heart felt the first rumblings of a second calamity.

'What do you mean?'

She picked up Edward and kissed his scrunched little face.

'She was in here earlier. She wants him weaned.'

'*Weaned?*'

It seemed to me I couldn't have heard her right over Edward's wail. She gestured to wait a minute, sat down on the nursing chair and undid the front of her dress. Silence returned to the room. She shook her head.

'I don't know what's put her in such a hurry. The doctor won't be pleased. It's far too early.'

I didn't know what to say. Everything that feels safe and good about the hall is falling to pieces in my hands. The idea of losing Lizzie makes me feel orphaned. It makes no sense that the missus would let her go so early. A dark chasm has opened between me and my mistress. She doesn't know it, and I won't tell her yet; I shall tread carefully at the edge. I stared at my lap and the lovely folds of the dress, which now feels like a cage. It's as if the missus' troubles have taken a physical form and trapped me too. Mrs B had said she would be safe with me. She can't have thought at all about the other question – if I would be safe with her.

Friday, 26th April

What do I do? God, I can't even keep my writing even. I keep thinking it's my fault – I should never have asked poor Lily. I should have kept to my place and let her keep to hers.

It's because I wanted to get the hair right. My last lesson with Mrs T and Tabby was yesterday, and there will be so many people in the house tomorrow, I'm terrified of not doing it well. I thought of Lily because her hair is thick and a mass of curls when she lets it down, which meant I wouldn't have to worry about heating tongs. And I also thought it would be a way to be more friendly to her – show her I'm not a monster, whatever she hears in the kitchen. I asked her on the stairs after lunch. She stared at me for a moment as if I was a dog that might bite, but then put a hand up to the back of her head and smiled, a little slyly, I thought. Perhaps just at the thought of shedding the plain cap and servant's bun for a while.

She wasn't as patient a model as Tabby. We took the mirror off the wall in the attic room, so she could hold it, but she kept lifting it up and twisting her head. In the end, I took it from her and put it face down on the bed until I needed it. The style started to come together in spite of her restlessness and my impatience – her hair was easy to shape and the plaits didn't slip. Finally, I stood back and told her to stand up and face me.

'Lily!'

I'd been so concerned with the details, I hadn't noticed the effect. The pretty little housemaid had vanished – before me was a child princess of the fairy kingdom. She should have been in a ball gown, not a plain cotton dress in a cramped attic room.

'Show me!'

Her voice is surprisingly strong and low for someone who looks like they're made of porcelain. The London in it has hard edges. I held the mirror up for her and watched her eyes go wide. She stared in amazement, tilting her head different ways, as if she couldn't find herself in her own reflection. There was a sound outside in the passage – someone on the stairs – and then pounding footsteps. Mary flung the door open and stood panting and urgent. When she saw Lily, she seemed to stop breathing altogether.

'What are you doing?'

I felt myself stand a little straighter and my lips creep into a smile.

'I'm practising a new hairstyle for the missus.'

I'd have liked to parade Lily around the house and village – is what I felt right then. Mary blinked quickly, whiskers on end. I could see her thinking it should have been her that was asked to model. She looked Lily up and down.

'One of the guests has arrived a day early and the room's not done. You're needed. Now.'

There was a battalion of pins in Lily's head as well as the combs and ribbons I'd taken from the missus' room. I reached out, but she shied away.

133

'Lily, you can't go down like that.'

Mary looked cross.

'She has to. And the missus has been ringing for you. Come now.'

I scooped up Lily's cap.

'Take this. Try and get the rat out on your way down so it will fit on top.'

I didn't fancy her chances – the rat was also skewered with pins – but no one should have been about. No one would have been either. I found the missus with a familiar grey face in the drawing room, having tea. Mrs Murray had snagged her gown getting into the carriage in London and wanted it mended once she'd had her refreshment. There was plenty of time for Lily to have carried up coal and water and made herself scarce, but her reflection in the big mirror transfixed her. She couldn't tear herself away. When the missus showed Mrs Murray up to the room herself with me in tow, Lily finally turned, caught between the bed and the washstand like a startled deer. She hadn't taken out one pin. The missus was as calm and icy as a frozen pond.

'Leave the room at once and wait outside.'

As Lily scuttled out, I took a step forward.

'Ma'am . . .'

'Not now.' She didn't even look at me and turned to Mrs Murray. 'Please excuse me a moment, Victoria. Watkins will take your gown.' There was a determination to her that was somehow grimly cheerful.

'Ma'am, I asked Lily to model . . .'

I had to say something, explain for Lily, but she cut me off again.

'Thank you, Harriet.'

She stalked out and shut the door. Mrs Murray shook her head slightly, disapproving.

'Well.'

I imagine smiling for her would be equal to hitching up her skirts.

'There should be no difficulty in making this as good as new.'

It took me a moment to realise she was showing me the tear in her dress. I looked at the rent and the grease stains and wanted to laugh in her face. She was looking at me with her leached eyes as if daring me to contradict her.

'Ma'am.'

I helped her change – it was like getting clothes on a scarecrow, she made it so difficult. The missus returned as I was gathering up the damaged dress, full of charming apologies. She wouldn't meet my eye as she drifted past.

I ran to my room and dumped the dress next to my mending chair, then hurried up to the maids' room. Lily was sitting on the bed, hunched over, her hair a mess of pulled-out plaits and loose pins. I knelt in front of her and took her hands.

'Lily, what happened? What did Mrs Gethin say?'

She pulled away from me and drew the back of a hand across her nose, sniffing.

'She's throwing me out. Today.'

'Didn't you tell her what happened?'

'I tried.'

'She can't dismiss you without notice.'

She gave me a sour look and turned, crouching, to pull her box from under the bed. With her wild hair, she looked from the back like a scrawny witch intent on some wickedness. I had an idea.

'I can write home – there's a big house there . . .'

She turned and bawled at me.

'I don't want your help. You're bad luck. Leave me alone.'

Her face was set grimly, chasing away the doll look. The features of an older, more vital woman – the witch – were trying to push through. I backed off and went straight to find the missus, but Mary told me she had gone for a ride with the master and Mr Murray. Thinking of anything else is impossible until I have spoken to her. Oh poor Lily. I should have been ready for this.

Later

There was nothing to do in the end but take up Mrs Murray's dress and wait for the missus to return. Sewing is like writing. Stitches are words – placed one after another, bringing together pieces of cloth but also fragmented thoughts. I grew calmer as I worked. It took an age to remove the grease – the stain was stuck as fast as all the blackness of the day. At one point I heard the dogcart and ran to the window to see Lily being carried off with her box – I can only think to the station. Her hair was back under her cap and her head hung down. Lord knows what was going through her mind. She looked up at the house just as the cart passed under the trees, too far away to see her expression.

The missus was out all afternoon and came straight up to dress for dinner. I didn't go in immediately though as I could hear the master with her. Their voices were muffled, and I tiptoed quickly across the room to put my ear to the wall. I caught enough to know it was about Lily. The missus sounded brittle, saying she was glad to have her out of this house and that she'd do it again, a hundred times over if need be. There was a weariness to the master's voice.

'And what do you think will happen to her now? You've sent her back to London alone.'

The missus said something about finding a new place, but the master cut across her.

'After this? She'll be selling herself on the streets by the middle of the week.'

There was silence. The missus' voice, when it came, was low and hoarse.

'She should never have been brought here by that woman.'

He sighed, exasperated.

'That woman is my housekeeper, and loyal.'

'Oh, yes.'

A bitter laugh followed.

'No one can doubt her loyalty, not with the sums you pay her. And Barrett.'

She spat the name out.

'But, of course, they are more than servants to you, aren't they? More like abominable kin. There is blood between you.'

'This must stop, Clara.'

He must have turned because his voice was suddenly much louder, making me jump.

'All these servants leaving the hall so quickly – what does it say about you, do you think? It is only your reputation, my dear, that is suffering.'

Steps, and the door closed. I let a good ten minutes pass before going in myself. She was sitting at her dressing table in her hat and cloak, staring at nothing.

'Ma'am.'

I spoke gently. She didn't look at me or move.

'Ma'am, Lily only had her hair dressed like that because I wanted to practise. And there wasn't time to take it out with Mr and Mrs Murray arriving so early.'

She looked at the floor as if chastened, but her words were cold.

'Are you a party to my decisions regarding servants, Harriet?'

'No, ma'am.'

'Yet you believe you know all the reasons for Lily's dismissal?'

She met my eyes briefly. It seemed to me that behind her question was a different one. I couldn't make it out.

'She has no family, ma'am, nowhere to go. You gave her no notice.'

The missus turned again, more sharply.

'You forget yourself, Harriet.'

So I had. But I couldn't believe Lily had done anything worse than what I'd seen, and clearly the master thought so too.

'Do you think I must answer to you every time I hire or dismiss a servant?'

'No, ma'am, but it wasn't Lily's fault. It was mine.'

'No, Harriet.'

The anger left her suddenly.

'It is not your fault.'

She leaned her arms on the back of the chair and dropped her head to dig her fingers into the loosening coils.

'She was a thief.'

The words were swallowed, so I nearly didn't hear them.

'A *thief*, ma'am?'

It came out as disbelief, but at the same time the idea rang in my head as possible enough. Barely a child, coming from who knows what hardship and suddenly put in the way of treasures and luxury she can't ever have imagined. I'd noticed a slyness in her manner more than once. The missus, of course, hadn't followed my thoughts. She straightened, still without meeting my eye.

'Who do you think took your ribbon?'

My ribbon. It had disappeared shortly after Lily arrived, but . . . something inside me snapped to attention.

'I never said my ribbon was stolen.'

She stared at me.

'You stopped wearing it. Is it not lost?'

'It . . .'

I faltered, not wanting to say I had thrown it on the floor.

'It looked wrong with this dress.'

Neither of us was making any sense. She ran her eyes over the dress, much like the master had. Then she looked at me with an expression I've never seen before. It was as if she was holding in her hand something very important to both of us and was slowly, questioningly moving her arm out over a very long drop.

'Do you not like the dress, Harriet?'

I saw at once that she knew I had seen the painting. At the same time, with a horrible turn of my stomach, I understood how she knew.

My own words had told her. The blood drained from my face and then rushed back with force. I had thought it was Mary going through my things. The missus watched as I worked it out. It was how she knew my ribbon was missing; it explained the pot of cold cream for my hands; it's why she made a point of saying I could go outside for walks when I liked. She had read my diary. This diary.

As we faced each other, doors were flying open one behind the other. Waves of humiliation broke over me as I remembered what I had written – about wanting to be her handmaid, about Helene.

She didn't attempt to deny what we were both thinking.

'You should have burned every page, Harriet, as I do.'

I couldn't speak. Eventually she rose.

'We'll find you something more suitable.'

Walking towards the wardrobe, she stopped again.

'Harriet. That dress . . .'

'You wanted the master to see it.'

'Yes.'

She turned.

'Yes, I did. I wanted to show him . . .'

Her face became agitated, as if it were attached to a hundred tiny threads all being yanked at cross purposes. She made an effort to gain control.

'I wasn't thinking of you. It was cruel. Allow me . . . please, allow me to make amends.'

I turned to one side to gather my thoughts, to recover a little – I was remembering my promise to myself not to let her shock me – but she misread the movement. She darted forward and took hold of my hands.

'Don't leave, Harriet.'

Her eyes hungered at me. She talked quickly, urgently in my face.

'That painting. It isn't how it looks. Did you see the dog?'

Her grip tightened.

'The little dog, George Frederick? He looks asleep in the painting, but he isn't. He was hanged. He had him hanged. The canary is falling not flying – it's already dead. And the music . . . all the pages are torn or blowing away. There's a choker around my neck . . . did you see it, a pear?'

Something mad happened to her eyes. They loomed wide and then narrowed again.

'He wants to destroy me. And he can do it. Now I've given him a son . . .'

The darkness in her expression sent sudden panic into my throat. What she was saying sounded fantastical, insane. I have seen the portrait – I know there is nothing so sinister in it.

'Let me go, ma'am.'

I wrenched my hands from her grasp and staggered backwards, sitting down abruptly on the bed. There was a moment neither of us moved. Her breaths came in great heaves. With her hair pulled about and the fierce expression, she made me think of witch Lily. Gradually, the emotion left her. She nodded, put a hand to the front of her neck.

'Forgive me, Harriet.'

She crossed to her dressing table and began pulling out more hairpins, painfully it looked like.

'I expect you'll go home and marry William. I'm sure it's not too late.'

The bitterness in her voice took me back to our interview in the drawing room when I told her he was getting impatient. I wondered if she had started reading my diary then – I dropped it almost at her feet – but remembered my box had been disturbed before that. And I had heard her in the kitchen the time I hid in the pantry – she had been trying to open the servants' drawers in the dresser. My mouth went dry as felt.

All the pins were out, and her hair fell around her shoulders, heavy and soft. She turned in her seat to look at me.

'You have been a friend to me without knowing it.'

It was almost the same thing she had said at Mrs B's about me liking her portrait.

'You have made me understand . . . something. Something very important.'

I waited for more, but she was staring at me expectantly, as if I was supposed to know what she meant. After a moment, she lowered her gaze.

'You know about my lady's maid before you? Helene.'

I nodded.

'She . . . she became pregnant in London. Once her condition was known, I had to dismiss her. I believed it was Laurence and . . .'

Her eyes glistened and the words seemed stuck in her throat.

'She had tried to tell me, but I wouldn't listen. Not until it was too late. There was a boy, who . . .'

She stopped, swallowed.

'He ran away. And when I saw the portrait – saw what it meant – I *knew*. I made Laurence tell me the truth.'

Taken by a sudden thought, she stood up and went to the fireplace. Pulling out the candle from one of the candlesticks, she raised the pusher until she could pick out something from inside. Next, she went to the dresser and knelt down. She slipped what turned out to be the key into the lock of the bottom drawer and opened it. I stood up to see, half expecting a glimpse of red ribbon, but she took out a photograph.

'I want you to know why I read your diary. This was the house when I first came here.'

The picture was taken at the front and all the household was arranged there. It was clear the indoor staff was three times the number of people now with extra maids and boys in livery. The boot boy was there. Clockface was unmistakable, in pride of place next to the missus with Barrett on the other side of the master. The missus pointed at the girl next to Clockface.

'That's Helene.'

She was pretty in a clear, simple way. Like a sketch, all lines and blank spaces that add up to something pleasing. And young. Likenesses often aren't likenesses at all though from what I've seen. I remember Annie's Andrew and his friend Robert talking about police photographs in the kitchen at Gloucester Square – you'd think likenesses of criminals would mean they could always be identified, but they said it seldom works out that neatly. The missus' face alone could have been such a photograph, showing one side of herself, remote and haughty. Clockface might have been a pleasant sort if that was all there was to judge by. I'd like to be able to make a picture of them that was true. Only the master seemed to have been caught in full. The others were looking at a camera, having their picture taken one day in the past – he was looking through it, now, at me. The illusion was disturbing and made me step back.

'Wait.'

She caught my skirt with one hand and, dropping the picture, reached into the drawer again.

'Helene had her baby in London. She was reconciled with her family in the end, and she wrote to me after she returned to France. It says everything. You can read it.'

I didn't want to. Helene's story was already familiar to me. What monsters it had spawned in the mind of the missus is what concerned me now. I took the letter from her and dropped it back into the drawer.

'Please, Harriet!'

She was kneeling at my feet and clutched my skirt with both hands. I tried to raise her up.

'Ma'am . . .'

'Please don't leave us. For my son's sake.'

I paused, surprised.

'For . . . for Edward's sake.'

His name sounded unnatural in her mouth, unfamiliar, and I remembered Lizzie saying that she had never used it, that she only ever called him 'the baby'. The missus rose to her feet – awkwardly as she wouldn't take her eyes from mine.

'Please, Harriet.'

She whispered it this time, as if I was a deer that might flee.

'I know I don't deserve you. But I have not been as wicked as you think . . . No, please wait . . .'

I had opened my mouth to speak.

'Please wait until this awful party is over.'

Never in my life has anyone looked at me so desperately – not even Laurence.

'I'll tell you everything. I'll explain it all, I promise. If you want to leave, I won't try and stop you.'

I have no intention of leaving. Not then, not now. I won't abandon her to her fears, whatever they are – shadows in her mind or a real darkness in Finton Hall. Both, I think, though I suspect the worst is in her imaginings. I can't believe the master put things into a portrait to torment her, or that he means to harm her now Edward exists. What a belief to come between a mother and her child. I can believe he might have been wicked enough to protect his friend over Helene, and that knowledge has worked on the missus, alone and fretting in this house, until she can see nothing but evil at every turn. Even Clockface might seem more monstrous than she already is. Make her better, Mrs B had said, and I think I can see my way finally, now I know the thoughts that afflict her so terribly. And not only for her sake – I haven't forgotten Gertrude saying I should use my position to help the other servants. Lily is beyond me, I think – I wonder if she was a thief at all or if the missus dismissed her for more confused reasons, another strike at the master perhaps. His prediction that she will turn to life on the streets weighs heavily on me. I won't abandon Francis without a friend. Nor Edward, who won't even have Lizzie soon. I know that out in the world I am a paper lady's maid – no one else would take me on these terms with these skills. It is here that I am needed, at Finton Hall, with my mistress. I gently pulled a strand of hair away from her face and took her hands in mine.

'I won't leave you, ma'am.'

Her whole body buckled with relief. She nearly sank all the way back to the floor.

In my own room, my first impulse was to snatch this diary from under my pillow and take it down to the kitchen to burn every page, as she said. Seeing the green cloth cover pained me as much as if it was the face of a friend who had betrayed me. I made myself leaf through it, remembering the missus had read every word – wanting to feel the worst, I think. Some passages mortified me; others sent ice through my veins. I had told Laurence I would keep his secret, but it is right here waiting for anyone to chance upon it. For that alone, I should burn the book. But the more I continued reading, the more protective I began to feel of my paper self. Why should I give up something that has been counsel and friend to me? It would be like banishing a blameless part of myself. If the missus read about what I saw in the carriage house, she has shown no sign of it. I shall simply be more careful in future about what I say in these pages. I changed into my black cotton dress that has the big pockets, and this fits in snugly with a pencil – it won't leave my person again.

Saturday, 27th April

There is so much bustle and excitement in the house now the day of the party has arrived, I can't keep still. I keep wandering about and getting in the way. The only guests staying at the hall are friends of Mr Gethin from London – single gentlemen or here without their wives. The Hill Court party is larger though, bringing guests of their own, and I'm full of nerves that I will be needed by the ladies in ways I'm not ready for. I heard two gentlemen arrive together. Mary let them in. Very loud and full of good spirits they were. I was lingering in the back hall and caught a glimpse of a tall, lean figure with sparse hair on his head and a strangely sagging face for one so young, about thirty. The other I only saw the back of, but he is broader with a mess of dark hair. I heard Mary giggle at something, and the portly one laughed – a surprisingly high cackle – and spoke to his friend.

'Steady, old man. Remember your manners.'

He dropped his voice a notch and said something about rules I didn't quite catch. There was more high-pitched laughter, and they moved to the drawing room.

The saggy-faced one has brought his valet with him. He and Laurence hauled luggage up to the guest rooms, and I got caught behind them going up the stairs. They were competing over who was the strongest – all that liveried muscle crouching and heaving and taking twice the time needed to get the job done. Laurence saw me first and nearly dropped his end of a trunk. They hurried to move out of my way, but I retreated back down the stairs. There was nowhere in particular I was going anyway. If the missus wants my help, I don't know what with; she wouldn't even let me do her hair after Mrs Murray saw the style on Lily. Every corner of the hall is busy with people. Downstairs is a storm with Clockface at the centre, and there are servants from Hill Court helping prepare and serve. Francis runs about like a little steam engine. The hall was probably always meant to be like this – alive with people and activity upstairs and down.

With nothing to do, I finally let myself be drawn to the library again to write this. No one seems to have been in here. I'm at the table by the unlit fire, and the door is shut so I will have fair warning of anyone entering.

I left my seat and drifted about a little. The flint mill is still in its place, and I ran my finger over the cold metal discs and frame, then picked it up and with a bit of effort turned the handle. No sparks without the flint, only the whir of the spinning wheel. I tried to imagine being the miner lighting up the dark space for his fellow worker and then – what? Did he see the sparks change colour but had no time to act? I pulled on the handle to bring the disc to a stop and hurriedly put the mill back down again – feeling as if I was about to spark a deadly explosion myself.

My room

It is as if the walls are closing in on me. This house is built more from secrets than stone. I was feeling restless in the library still and wandered along the shelves again, enjoying the orderly rows and straight spines. The steps had been pushed underneath some mighty-looking tomes that caught my eye. When I climbed up, I found they were agricultural magazines bound together, going back to the last century. It seemed strange to keep such enormous, outdated papers. I thought they must be valuable and pulled one forward. The pages snaked heavily, resisting. A strong smell of old matter lifted off the paper, as if it carried something of the sod and animals in the words. I flicked the edges with my thumb and there was a flip of the paper – something had been wedged in. Feeling for the break, I heaved the book open. A photograph had been slipped inside.

As soon as I understood what I was looking at, I clawed the pages back over, tearing and creasing the edges. I stood the book back up, pushing it into place, and turned to look at the room. No one was there, the door was still shut, but I felt as if every object, book and piece of furniture was watching me. Heat moved around my body – throat, cheeks, chest, belly. I felt a flicker through my middle. The picture was of a man, dressed only above the waist, everything below on show and standing up. And a woman not dressed at all with her hand on it, lying open to view between her legs as I've never seen anyone, not even myself.

My fingers reached for another tome and battled it open. A wide strip of card was inside this one with a series of similar painted pictures all along it – a zoetrope card. Spinning, it would have shown a woman bouncing up and down on a man – his bright prick flashing in and out of view. I feel warm just writing about it. Beneath that, the magazines had been turned into a box – a rectangle cut out and the pages pasted down. Another book nestled inside, a novel – I read scenes at random that were alike to the pictures until I heard my own breath getting short. Between the pages were photographs of a black man and a white woman joined in different poses. And not just photographs; loose, hand-drawn sketches showed men and women and sometimes men and men in amazing detail stuck onto each other in every way possible. I put everything back and got off the stepladder. Small wonder we weren't allowed to touch the books.

I stood still for a moment, feeling like a wind had ripped through the room, whirled me about and then set me back down in sudden quiet. The books seemed less homely now, less honest in their neat rows. I looked at them as at troubling strangers – strangers I couldn't help seeking out. The shelves below the agricultural magazines are full of foreign books with titles in languages I don't know. My eye was caught by an English title, *The Complete Grazier*. It was so out of place, I stared at it for long moments before my hand reached up and pulled it free. It fell open where a photograph had been placed between the pages. A woman leaning over another woman with a lash raised. The lady lying down was reading a newspaper as if unconcerned, and I saw with a sort of jolt that it was the *New York Times*. American photographs.

I remembered the book on pig breeding, misplaced, as I had thought, near the Milton. My legs walked me over to the poetry books, heart clattering like a cart over cobbles. There was no need to climb up – at waist height a volume of *Stephens' Book of the Farm* was tucked between volumes of Shakespeare. There was a small photograph of a man seated and a woman astride him but facing the same way, both naked. She was leaning back, turning her head so they could smile at each other. They looked so happy, so *free*.

I snatched my diary from the table and fled to the nursery. Lizzie would listen – say something sensible, I thought. I was wrong. There's a change come over her since the missus demanded Edward be weaned. It's as if she's already half gone. It all poured out of me as I paced around the room – how the missus had read my diary and all the things she had said about the painting. I got that far before I realised she hadn't even put down her sewing.

'And there's pictures in the library, Lizzie, hidden in the books – men and women – naked and doing things.'

'What were you doing looking through the books?'

My jaw dropped, she'd missed the point so wildly.

'But what if it means the missus is right . . .'

She blew air through her nose before I could finish.

'The missus is wrong in the head, that's as clear as day. And Harriet . . .'

She softened her look a bit.

'I doubt there's a house in the country that isn't stuffed full of pictures like that.'

I looked at her and then around the nursery, half expecting to see pictures of cunnies spilling out of Edward's toy box or propped between embroidery samples on the mantelshelf.

'I'm allowed to read the books.'

'And who told you that?'

My silence was answer enough.

'Maybe she wanted you to find the pictures, since she likes playing games with you.'

Finally, she put her sewing aside.

'Another girl would have kept her head down and enjoyed her good fortune and the freedom of the position. You can't help but go looking for trouble, though, whether it's there or not. You forget what you are to them, Harriet, and what they should be to you. And before you go accusing the master of I don't know what, there are few gentlemen who pay such loving attention to their babies as he has. He's been up with gifts and kind questions more times in the last week than she has since the mite was born.'

My eye fell on Edward's zoetrope, but it prompted such troubling thoughts, I looked away again. Lizzie picked up her sewing, applying her needle with quick jerks of the thread. I made for the door and didn't look back when she called my name.

Later

It must be past one. I'm in the missus' room. She can't be long coming up now as I heard carriages leave, but I must do something other than simply wait. I've been pacing for hours, drinking the missus' sherry, and trying to capture tonight in my mind like a photograph. The ladies' dresses – some so modern, they barely had bustles at all – their jewels and hair – brushstrokes of different colours and textures; pinks, golds, ambers, greens and more, all gleaming in the lamplight. It was like a conversation between materials and light as much as between the people – and that was a thundering like I've never heard. I think it has been a while since Finton Hall heard such a range of voices all at once – a mountain range it was – from the heights of Mrs Trevelyan greeting the young ladies to the booming foothills of the visiting gentlemen paying their respects to Lady Spencer's father, and laughter tumbling like streams through all their conversations. There was a heady smell of cut flowers and perfume, musky hair oil when a gentleman leaned in close to me (as if I was a piece of furniture) to allow a lady to pass (coils upon coils of caramel hair), and the warm scent of the elder Miss Spencer's skin as I helped unhook her necklace from her lace collar (tiny blond curls at the nape of her neck).

Only the missus stood out amongst the finery and shimmer of the ladies. She was wearing her plainest black gown, not the green dress we had picked out together, and her hair was so simply done, it almost didn't look dressed at all. The only decoration was a nosegay of violets that Mrs T had sent, pinned at her breast. She might have been a governess. I felt irritated. It seemed so contrary to make so little effort, and I was conscious of how it reflected on me, her lady's maid. A surge of sympathy for the master surprised me, and I wondered if Lizzie was right at least in part. He was faultlessly dressed and moving amongst his guests like a sun; all faces turned towards his warmth. I had not seen him before with men of his own standing and was aware of an energy running through the house, powerful as a river. I caught snippets of conversation that made my mouth drop open. There was the war, of course, but the prime minister was spoken of as an intimate, his private words reported in an off-hand manner, just as I might mention something said in the kitchen. I heard other names too, familiar to me only from the cries of newsvendors or from reading them on posters outside theatres or hustings, but to this gathering, they were real people with tastes and flaws and desires. Everywhere I went, I felt as if burning fingers were beckoning me. They slipped under my ribcage, tugging me into the river.

I wasn't alone, I think. Barrett sent me to fetch extra candlesticks from the silver room, and I was surprised to see Clockface out of her kitchen and standing at the bottom of the same stairs I'd dropped the coal down. She had one hand on her hip and was laughing her dirty laugh at someone further up.

'Not on the menu tonight, sir.'

She wagged a finger. A man's deep chuckle trickled down the steps. As I drew near, I saw her reddened face was alight with a sort of frantic joy like an over-excited child. She turned almost triumphant on seeing me.

After a secretive nod to the person out of sight, she breezed past, still quivering with some horrible delight. Of course, I looked up the stairs myself to see whom she was being so familiar with and couldn't stop myself from staring openly. Mr Murray. He turned away almost as soon as our eyes met, as if he hadn't seen me at all. I was glued to the spot, feeling as if the hall itself had shifted suddenly, revealing doorways and passages I didn't recognise and was scared to go down.

As I went back up, I passed Laurence, who was flicking the bottle cloth at the legs of the valet. He held my gaze, but I didn't mind him; he was taking care of Francis as I had asked, sending private, approving nods his way when the boy took a gentleman's hat correctly or thanked another for a tip without trembling.

In the hall, guests were starting to drift towards the drawing room for the first part of the music programme. I delivered the candlesticks and was helping rearrange some of the seating so Lady Spencer's elderly father could be pushed through in his chair, when I heard the missus introduce someone as Mr Garston. It was the name the master had mentioned, the man who liked Gilbert and Sullivan. I looked around and saw the larger of the men I had heard speaking to Mary in the hallway. His face is sharper than I expected with a pointed nose and, when he laughed, curiously small teeth. I kept glancing at the missus, but her face was unreadable.

I saw her and the master together only once while I was handing out programmes to guests who had already managed to lose theirs. Conversations were naturally turning to music, and the saggy-faced man, Mr Hicks, was speaking to a group, including the master, of opera in Italy. He described how even the most celebrated singer might be booed off the stage if the crowd found her wanting.

'At the Teatro Regio di Parma, even the servants won't open the door for her on her way out!'

He laughed, enjoying himself, and everyone joined in. The missus was turning from a different conversation and smiled coldly.

'That is because the Italians go to the theatre to hear music, not to ogle each other.'

There was an awkward moment of half-laughs. The master gave her a slight smile.

'Perhaps tonight we should embrace the spirit of the Teatro Regio. Lest our appreciation be held in any doubt. Hm?'

He beamed suddenly, making what had nearly started out as a threat into a joke, and slapped Mr Hicks on the shoulder. He whirled away from the renewed laughter and clapped his hands.

'Friends! Dear guests!'

Leaping to the front, he ran his fingers quickly along the piano keys. Everyone fell silent like obedient children. He smiled quietly into their expectation, letting the moment draw out, as if he knew his foot was on their attention and he could keep it there as long as he wanted. Someone giggled. He raised his hands and dropped his voice to almost a whisper.

'The magic is about to begin.'

He made a short speech, praising the missus lavishly and promising wonders. The air around him seemed to glow as he talked. His gaze found everyone, flickering over the room like a flame. People's faces caught light as it touched them; their smiles widened. I thought what a presence he must be in parliament. He didn't look at me, but a flicker ran through my middle like it had when I found the photographs, and I wondered if Lizzie was right about them – nothing to be worried about, just something to be expected in a gentleman's house, hidden away like the plate and jewels. A blush crept up my throat.

The master didn't take a seat but stood by the fire with his elbow on the mantelshelf. Ripples of conversation started up again as Mr Trevelyan took his place. The vicar didn't have the master's command of the room and looked a morose figure, slightly comic too with his beard sticking out under the violin he was about to play. I looked for Mrs T, feeling a bit embarrassed for her, and noticed that she also looked out of place in this company with her old-fashioned dress and naked face. The vicar raised his bow, and there was some half-hearted hushing. A rustle of skirts, a cough, a crackle from the fire, and then the music entered the room like a god. It was a shock, like being taken hold of by something invisible. I closed my eyes and felt each note twining around me like a ribbon. Together they lifted me up. I can't recall the tune now – it's vanished like a fairy.

I felt a jolt of nerves as the missus stepped forward. She looked smaller in her plain dress, unprotected without the swing of jewels and mass of hair. Mr Trevelyan was on the violin again and Miss Spencer the piano. I clutched the front of my dress and didn't let go, but I needn't have worried. Her first note seemed to stun the room. No one moved. It was not Orpheus as I was expecting but the song I first heard her singing when I took her tray up. I have no idea what the words were, only that it was filled with such yearning and light, my eyes filled with tears. Our stillness and silence felt devotional, and her dress and hair all at once made sense. She was there to serve the music – a nun at its altar, filled with grace.

My chest heaved with pride, and all my earlier irritation and nerves were forgotten. I glanced around the room, revelling in the spellbound expressions. Only the master seemed distracted; he looked at the door twice, as if still expecting a guest to arrive. Francis appeared instead, bearing a loaded tray and a terrified look. I frowned, though he didn't see me. The ices he was holding were supposed to be handed out between the parts, but he was early. Clockface hadn't waited for the order. I saw Barrett beckon him towards the serving table instead of sending him out and felt my heart lurch. It was a long way across the back of the room. Laurence was watching too, pinned to the wrong wall. Francis stepped forward as if onto a tightrope, and Barrett gestured again to hurry him up. I couldn't watch and turned back to the missus.

The song was rising, gathering itself. Her eyes closed and her brow furrowed as she sang a line; the words – whatever their meaning –

possessed her completely. She breathed in, and I could feel the music about to soar to a new height when a tremendous crash of glass shattered the spell instantly. It was as if the hall itself had cried out in protest. The guests turned as one with shocked faces to see where Francis had tripped and smashed the corner of his tray into the front of a display cabinet. Objects fell from the shelves as the cabinet rocked to a stand-still, joining the wreckage on the floor where dozens of moulded ices now lay ruined and laced with broken glass. Panicked, Francis tried to scoop them up with his hands until Laurence reached him and hauled him out of the way.

'I believe our refreshments have arrived.'

The missus spoke over the hubbub, drawing consoling laughter from those nearby. I didn't know whom I wanted to run to and comfort more, her or Francis. Her face was hard and bright, and she seemed to have shrunk, all her holiness fled away, so her dress was simply plain again. She looked across the room, and I followed her gaze to the master. He was still leaning against the mantelshelf and – my stomach flipped – staring at me. With a slight movement, he gestured behind me, and there was Barrett signalling to clear up the mess. It wasn't part of my duties, but I was too shaken and jostled to object. I looked at the missus again as I turned, trying to convey the tangle of awe and sympathy I felt for her, but Miss Spencer had moved between us to take her hand. I cursed Barrett under my breath.

Mary appeared with an old sheet and dustpan, and we gathered up as much glass and cream as we could, carrying the bundle down-stairs. Several Hill Court servants passed us on their way up with new, full trays of ices. I couldn't see Francis anywhere and hoped Laurence was being kind. Mary was full of questions, her eyes shining with the drama.

'Do you think she'll dismiss him?'

I hesitated, feeling a jag of doubt.

'I don't know. She dismissed Lily for less.'

We dumped the sheet in a storeroom by the kitchen to be dealt with later. Mary wasn't satisfied.

'But Lily *stole* things.'

'Like what?'

'My lip . . .'

She paused, looking self-conscious.

'Your what?'

'My lip colour went missing.'

'How do you know it was her?'

I was more interested in returning upstairs to the party and tried to push her towards the door as I spoke.

'My red ribbon went missing too. But if they were found in her things, we would have them back.'

She scratched her nose, standing stubbornly still.

'I didn't tell anyone it was gone. Aunt Sarah would have taken it off me anyway if she knew. There's a rule about servants not using paint.'

I looked at her doubtfully.

'Even in our own time?'

She shrugged.

'That's the rule.'

'Whose rule?'

I guessed Clockface, but Mary shrugged again.

'The master's, I suppose.'

I stared at her. The master? She had turned for the door, but on impulse I caught her arm.

'Do you know what's in the library, Mary? Hidden in the books?'

She shook her head. I felt a quickening at the thought of talking about the photos.

'In any book that's about farming, livestock management, anything like that, there's pictures . . .'

A shape loomed in the doorway. Mary started like a frightened leveret.

'Coming, Mr Barrett.'

He looked as if he was about to give us the talking to of our lives but turned instead to let us out. Mary scurried past like a mouse. I followed her through the heaving kitchen to fetch water and cloths. When we were back on the stairs, she slowed, snout twitching.

'Tell me about the books.'

A servant was rushing down the stairs, and I shook my head.

'Not now. I can show you later.'

The thought of going back to the library made my heart thump.

'I'll come and find you when I'm finished with the missus. It will be late.'

Mary hesitated. I don't know what Clockface would do to her if she was caught, but Clockface will be in bed herself first chance she gets, leaving Bridie with the hard, late work.

'It won't take long.'

A gleam came into her eye, and she nodded. We shared a nervous laugh. Like friends.

Barrett appeared again like a bad penny at the top of the stairs, service-side. He made Mary take the cleaning things and waved her through. The door opened onto the chatter of guests; they had spilled into the hall. I caught Mr Garston laughing and raising his glass to someone, a lady arching her elegant neck to fan it, a whiff of perfume, and the door shut again.

'You may return to your room now, Watkins.'

'What?'

I stared at him in horror. Not to re-join that realm of shining people, not to return to the missus and hear her sing again was unthinkable.

'But Mrs Gethin asked for me to be on hand to help, Mr Barrett.'

His eyes closed slowly, and he breathed in, long and noisily through his nose. I couldn't think why I was being banished – unless he had overheard me starting to tell Mary about the photographs. I had no choice but to carry on down the passage to the servants' stairs. He didn't move until I had walked up them, could be there still for all I know, keeping guard like a malevolent, overfed lizard. I came up here and ripped open a perfectly good bit of mending I'd been working on. It maddens me not to know what is happening downstairs, or how the missus is. Wait until the party is over, she said, and she will tell me everything.

I roamed about her room like a caged animal until my eye fell on the bottom drawer of the cabinet. With a start, I remembered the candlestick on the mantelshelf and darted over. Blowing out the flame, I removed the candle and worked the pusher as I had seen her do. The key was there. I moved to the dresser and knelt down, turned the lock. Inside was a jumble of things, but the letter from the French maid was on top – the missus' name spelled out in a beautifully even, flowing hand that gave me a pang of envy. I took it out and, still kneeling, opened it up. It took me a moment to understand why I couldn't make sense of it. *French* – the whole thing, and there are several pages of it, all tightly packed with the same gorgeous and completely mystifying letters. I threw it back into the drawer and started looking through the other papers and trinkets massed together. There is a small leather dog collar with a brass plate engraved 'George Frederick', a large iron key, masses of sheet music written by her, bills for music concerts, and a bottle of dry sherry on its side.

Then, in a cloth bag underneath it all – *money*. More than I've ever seen in my life. Coins and bundles of five-pound notes – first time I've laid eyes on paper money. I stared at it for ages as if it was only a painting of treasure. Then I pushed my fingers into it – I swear the furs in the missus' wardrobe are not so good to touch. I imagined what it would feel like if it was mine and a fire lit up in my chest. The freedom of it. The choices. Even a handful of that wealth. It made me feel reckless, as if I might push back the limits of my life, break them even. I groped for the sherry bottle, pulled out the stopper and swallowed down a great mouthful. The liquid sang down my throat and roared fire through my nose. I swigged the sherry and held the money under my hands as if it might leap away from me until my legs went numb from kneeling, and I had to pace again. All I have seen and heard tonight, the photographs and music, the beautiful guests and dizzying riches swirl around my head, around this very room. The air is alive with it. I cannot write anymore. The hall itself is spinning, faster and faster, as if it won't ever stop.

LONDON

CENTRAL CRIMINAL COURT
FIRST SESSION HELD 24TH JUNE 1878
MINUTES OF EVIDENCE

CLARA GETHIN (27), was indicted for the wilful murder of Edward Gethin.

MR FRITH *conducted the Prosecution; and* MR GILL *the Defence*.

GEORGE REED. I am a lighterman, in the employ of Mr Haynes of Paul's Wharf – On 28th May, I noticed a bag on the bank near Puddle Dock, close to Blackfriars Bridge, as the tide was going out. It was still there the next day, the 29th, so I hooked it in – it had got caught on an old anchor. It was a carpet bag. I opened it and found the body of a baby inside. I took it to Paul's Wharf and gave the information to the police. They took charge of it.

HENRY RICHARDS, I am an M.R.C.S, practising in Clerkenwell. On the evening of May 29th I was called to the City dead-house, and there saw the body of a male child of about five months – it was dressed in a nightshirt, and there was a tape tied, quite tight, around its neck. I made a *post-mortem* – strangulation was the cause of death. I formed a judgement that it had been dead about three or four days and in the water for as long.

Cross-examined. I can speak with a degree of certainty, because we have a large number of bodies our way, being near the water, and I have a good deal of experience.

Monday, 29th April

There is a table next to the window that serves as a washstand, and a chair that is at odds with the uneven floor. I have been sitting here some time. My eyes avoid themselves in the mirror, and look, if anywhere, down into the sooty yard. When anyone appears to use the privy or fetch coal, I draw back quickly, and the chair lists so, for a panicked moment I think I will fall. I can hear sounds from the street even here – horses' hooves, barrow boys calling, a bucket of water being sloshed down steps. The world feels too close. I blow my nose and already there's black in it, just from breathing. My stomach squeezes itself into a tight ball every time I think of why I am here.

I shall write myself back to her room two nights ago, and the breathless quiet after the carriages had rolled away. She arrived without warning, slipping in like a ghost, while I was sprawled on the window seat. I rose hastily and shoved the sherry bottle behind a curtain. She didn't notice that or anything else, certainly not how clumsy my hands were as I undressed her and loosened her hair. Her eyes had that faraway look. I didn't dare speak for fear of what the sherry would do to my voice. When I was done pawing at her, she sat in a chair by the fire, head back and arms and legs falling anyhow like a doll that's been played with and thrown aside. I tidied up the dressing table and pulled the corner of the covers back on the bed before bidding her goodnight. She began speaking before I reached the door.

'I sang well, did I not? Although it was only a silly party and a room full of fools?'

I remembered how her voice had taken hold of me before the crash of glass.

'You sang like an angel, ma'am. As if we were in a grand theatre.'

A smile gently lit her face. I walked over and knelt beside her.

'What was it you were singing, ma'am, before Francis dropped the tray? What did the words mean?'

Her eyes seemed to see me for the first time.

'It's by Handel. The words are Italian.'

She spoke them – the foreign sounds rich and warm on her tongue – then translated.

'*Let me weep over my cruel fate. Let me yearn for freedom.*'

After a moment, she became grave and took my hand.

'Harriet. Go straight to bed, won't you?'

The change of tone startled me, and for a moment I was certain she could see into my mind. Her look was commanding, but as I stared back at her, there was also that glimpse of something fearful and beseeching just under the surface.

'It's been a long day.'

I nodded. She didn't say anything further, nor did she drop her gaze. I bade her goodnight again and left with my heart doing odd things in my chest. I went into my room, shut the door more loudly than I needed to, and stood as still as a gatepost. No one had heard me and Mary talking on the stairs. We were alone. She couldn't know. I opened the door again as quietly as possible.

The Hill Court servants and even Bridie had all gone. Mary was sitting at the table in the servants' hall with her head resting on her arms. She jumped when I touched her shoulder and looked up, bleary and anxious, like a little animal that can't remember if it's home safe or not. I thought she'd be cross at how late I was, but she rolled her eyes once she'd woken up proper and told me how the missus had hung on even after Mrs Murray went to bed and sat at the piano, playing odd notes, as if she was settled there for the night.

'And every time I looked in, she wanted something else – a cup of tea or a fresh candle, like she was looking for ways to keep me up. I knew you'd be waiting for her upstairs. She even kept Francis up and running around with pointless jobs – he was dead on his feet.'

'Francis! How is he?'

She shifted round in her chair and leaned in.

'Laurence said he was tripped up by Barrett.'

'What?'

She nodded.

'Barrett went to take the tray off him but knocked him off balance with his foot. Blamed poor Francis, of course.'

'You mean he did it on purpose?'

She spread her hands and shrugged. I wished I had seen it for myself. It seemed unlikely – what reason could Barrett have? But a shiver ran through me when I thought of how Clockface had sent Francis up early on his own, and then had more than enough ices in reserve.

'Was the missus angry?'

'I don't think so. She wouldn't sing again though. Went all quiet and starey.'

I nodded, distracted.

'She's in one of her strange moods.'

'Does she have another kind?'

She asked it with such a straight face, I snorted. We looked at each other and smiled. It brought us back to who we were and what we were doing – two maids at Finton Hall planning a night-time raid on our employers' library.

'What's in the books then?'

She whispered it, though right then there were yawning empty rooms between us and another living soul in the house. I whispered too.

'Follow me.'

I picked up a candle and went out into the passage. Mary stopped me as I turned left.

'Let's go up the west stairs.'

It was a longer route as it had us walking underneath the library to the end of the house before going up and doubling back, but it also meant that most of the way was under cover of the servants' corridors. I assumed that was her reason and followed her along to the right. As we came nearer the stairs, she slowed down and looked back at me with a grin and a finger on her lips. I saw light coming from under the door where the silver is kept and straight away realised the real reason she had brought us this way – Laurence. She pointed, gesturing that we should go in. I shook my head and hurried forward to catch her arm.

'What are you doing?'

We had to mouth at each other. In the candlelight, her face was distorted into planes of light and shadow, so it looked more like a mask.

'Let's surprise him.'

Her eyes were bright with excitement. I shook my head again.

'What about the library?'

Mary nodded enthusiastically.

'He can come too.'

'No!'

Panic punched sound from my lungs. The word dropped like a single pebble into the darkness. Mary stood on tiptoe, waving her hand with frantic little movements to shush me. She was enjoying herself. I put my own hand up to try and calm her.

'We'll get into trouble. He'll get us into trouble.'

She started laughing feverishly – almost in silence except for little gasps, wisps of sound that floated into the passage after my pebble.

'Mary.'

She shook her head, almost choking with laughter and turned towards the door.

'Mary, don't.'

I spoke aloud, sharply, not bothering who heard. The idea of being in the same room as Laurence looking at those pictures squeezed my innards to nothing.

A sound like a bed being sat heavily upon came from inside the room. I grasped Mary's arm again to drag her back, but she threw herself at the door, pulling me with her. It took me by surprise how strong she was. I dropped the candle and had to let go as she wrenched herself free – the sudden release meant she burst through the door. It flew wide open, smashing against some piece of furniture, and she stumbled forward, falling at the foot of Laurence's cot. I saw the inside of the room for only a moment before the door swung back again, blocking my view. It was like looking at a picture – apart from Mary pitching forward, everything else was still, and like the pictures in the library, I hardly knew what I was seeing at first. A large doll's face, hovering over the end of the bed. Red lips, painted cheeks, black brows. A red ribbon around its neck and something black and lacey draped around its bare shoulders. The word 'Laurence' staggered about in my mind but refused to connect itself. And then limbs – knees in the air either side of the face and strange angles – for a moment it was a nightmare fat spider with glowing white legs. The door bounced shut, making everything vanish, then bumped off the latch and swung open again. A mop of hair beneath the doll face twisted around to show another, upside down face. Mary cried out – a strangled sound. There was a close smell of sweat and candle wax. The spider squirmed apart, separating itself into Laurence and Mr Hicks valet. Mary got to her feet, making small, keening noises and blundered back out into the passage. She charged blindly into me, then pushed me away and veered off to run up the stairs. I heard her grappling with the door to the main corridor.

Laurence called her name. He stepped unsteadily off the bed and came towards me. Apart from the ribbon and piece of lace – close up, I noticed it was the shawl the missus was wearing when I first met her – he was naked. His part was shining and heavy and bobbed as he moved. He looked for a moment as if he was going to run up the stairs after Mary, but the doorway held him. The doll face turned to me. Behind the red lips and painted-in brows, his expression was full of loathing. He must have thought I'd brought her there on purpose. I said the first thing that came to my lips.

'That's my ribbon.'

The stain was visible on the messy bow at the side of his neck. In the back of my mind a thought came about what had happened to my print dress when it went missing. Without a word, he stepped back, reached for the door and slammed it in my face.

It was almost perfectly dark without the candle. The light coming from Laurence's room didn't do much more than outline the door. I could hear muffled voices inside, low and urgent, and sounds of movement from the bed and across the floor. It seemed the only thing moving in me was my heart – it beat a strong drum that got faster as I stood there. I didn't try and find the candle but turned on my heel and groped further along the corridor to the storeroom where Francis slept. It was too dark to see inside, and I had to stumble and feel my way to his pallet. Short, steady breaths came from the warm bundle of blankets. I let out a breath of relief myself, though I don't know what fear had seized me, only the sense that something was wrong; the missus had kept him up late and wanted me to go straight to bed. He didn't wake, exhausted by the long day, and I hurried back through the dark towards the stairs. On the next floor, I found the corridor still dimly lit with lamps. Mary had left the servants' door open. I shut it with as little noise as possible.

A lighted passageway at night can be as eerie as a dark one, I found. There was a keen sense of being watched and having nowhere to hide. I knew there was no gargoyle on this floor, but I glanced about me anyway. The library was on the right, door shut. At first it seemed as quiet as the corridor, but as I drew nearer, I heard murmurs. For a moment, I trembled on the edge of flinging the door open, but then the high laugh of Mr Garston brought me back to myself. The gentlemen were still up. Mary and I couldn't have crept into the library even if we'd got this far. I wondered if the pictures were still in their books, or if this was just the sort of evening they were being kept for.

I hurried on, taking the quickest way up to the attic, the way Mary would have gone. But she wasn't in her room. A creeping dread came over me that I couldn't explain, looking at the empty little space with its meagre furniture. I started down again, meaning to look in the kitchen but first put my head around the door to the third floor. There were lamps still lit there too. The master's rooms were across the landing, the door to his sitting room open a few inches. I hesitated. He would be in the library with his guests, and Barrett would most likely be downstairs too. I stepped carefully across, wishing I had my house slippers on, and listened outside the door. Silence. I pushed it open enough to see inside.

There was no one there. All the strange devices and mysterious boxes gleamed, silent and still between the lamps. Another door at the opposite end from the portrait was also ajar. I was about to duck back out when my eye landed on the missus' portrait, proud above the fireplace. All her wild words came back to me, and I found myself drawn further into the room.

It was even more beautiful than I remembered. She looked so alive, I believed I could blow on the wisp of hair by her ear and it would move, or reach out and touch the soft fabric of the dress, feel the pleating under my fingertips as I had when I wore the real one. Her eyes stared at me, stern and, I thought, expectant. I took a breath. She had mentioned the dog and there it was, asleep at her feet. No reason to think it dead. It had a leather lead attached to its collar that disappeared where her skirt covered the stone seat. There were music sheets next to her and more that had drifted to the floor – only a vague idea of the notes sketched in. I looked at the canary fluttering in mid-air beyond the balcony. Its wings were a whir of movement and its body curved under, its tiny legs sticking out as if it was trying to stop itself mid-flight. It looked as if it was trying to hover, to keep close to the missus. I began to relax. To see what the missus saw in the painting, you had to want to see it. It was likely she had planted her own fears in it when she was pregnant and desperate about Helene. If she looked at it now, I thought, would she still see the same threats? Pretty country scenes of woods and parkland with a shooting party and pheasants breaking from undergrowth gave way to the towers and machinery of the master's mine. That was all.

'Impressive, isn't it?'

His voice rang out behind me. Turning, I reached for something, anything, to say.

'Sir, I . . .'

I could only stare at him. He raised his eyebrows and smiled good-humouredly, as he used to.

'Are you looking for something?'

He walked forward to stand beside me.

'No, sir . . .'

I fell silent again. He was looking at the portrait, his head a little to one side, and I blurted it out.

'I didn't know about the dress, sir. That I was wearing that one.'

He regarded me a moment and then nodded.

'I know, Watkins. It's all right.'

I felt ashamed, as if I was betraying the missus, but at the same time relieved to have said it. He moved to a side table and picked up a book.

'I hope you don't mind my saying it looks rather more at home on your mistress.' There was a smile in his voice. 'What do you think of it?'

He gestured to the portrait. It was like the flint mill all over again. I couldn't believe he had simply accepted my presence and picked up a conversation.

'It's very beautiful, sir.'

'Ah yes. And beautiful things hold secrets, do they not?'

He was flipping through the book he had picked up and leaning comfortably against a desk, one ankle crossed over the other.

'I enjoyed that idea immensely. It rather sums up my little collection here – I'm glad you've had the opportunity to see it.'

I glanced at what looked like a pair of ornate scissors displayed on a velvet cushion, the blades shaped into a crocodile's head, but my eye was drawn back to the portrait. There was a river flowing between the industrial and country scenes, and I followed it until I saw a figure I hadn't noticed before standing on a hillside. It was quite small, and I took a step forward to see better. I sensed the master look up.

'The detail is extraordinary, isn't it? I can look at it for hours.'

It was a man with a gun lifted to his shoulder. He was slightly apart from the shooting party and aiming a little off from the others. I followed the line of the barrel to see what the game was. It drew my eye further and further out of the background until suddenly, shockingly I was seeing the canary in the moment of being shot. I blinked at the violent jerk of perspective and followed the line again back and forth between the gun and the bird. It wasn't a mistake – the canary's mid-air flutter was no longer a pretty dance for its mistress. A small sound escaped from the back of my throat.

'Bravo, Watkins. I believe you are starting to see.'

He had moved back to my side. I followed the dog's lead up to where it disappeared under the dress and then traced the line above the balcony into the background. There was the tiniest detail in some trees, a few strokes making up a limp thing hanging from a branch and children with sticks playing and pointing.

'The artist is quite ingenious, isn't he?'

The blood seemed to freeze in my veins.

'Of course, you are already familiar with some of his more . . . playful work. Some of the sketches he kindly contributed to my collection?'

I turned and eyed him wildly. He tilted his head a fraction.

'I believe you have developed an interest in agricultural practices.'

The smile broadened.

'I am rather pleased you disobeyed the instruction not to touch the books in the library. It was there to prevent ordinary housemaids giving themselves a fright, but I don't think we can call you ordinary,

Watkins, can we? Since you are here without permission, perhaps you would also like to look at these.'

He slipped something out of the book he was holding and moved so he was between me and the door.

'They are more to the taste of a weaker sort of man – like two of my dear friends downstairs – but I always say one should indulge the foibles of guests.'

He held up a plate. It was of the same nature as the others, only in the glance I gave it before looking away, I saw that the poor, naked figure was much younger, younger even than Lily. The boot boy.

I set off without warning to skirt around a huge globe on wheels, but the master took a few unhurried steps backwards, blocking the door. He held up another picture. I veered away, crashing into a table. Something slid across the surface, and he moved swiftly to rescue it, laughing his boyish laugh.

'How perfect.'

He was close enough for me to catch a male smell of tobacco and soap – expensive, not like William's fresh dirt or Laurence's cheap scent. I backed quickly away towards the fireplace and cracked my head against the high mantelshelf. A monstrous red wave crashed through my skull. The master watched me a moment.

'I think you enjoyed our little talk about the flint mill, didn't you, Watkins?'

My eyes were swimming from the blow. I didn't trust myself to run.

'I wonder if you can guess what secret this is hiding.'

He held up the thing I had knocked across the table. There was a handle and at the end of it, a shape like a closed bell.

'Pretty, isn't it?'

I looked away. My nose was running, and I drew my sleeve across my top lip.

'You have to give it your attention, Watkins. Isn't that what you said?'

He waited. My heart thudded a painful count.

'Well, I'll tell you if you're shy.'

He turned the object so it caught the light.

'Its invention and history are rather obscure, but you can see that this part would fit very neatly into the mouth, like a pear.'

A pear. In the portrait, she wears a pear-shaped pendant. She had asked if I'd seen it, knowing what he meant by it – he must have already shown her this thing. I looked in spite of myself. The bell part – the pear – was turned towards me.

'It is enough to prevent speech by itself. No one could talk – or sing – with it in place. But also, by twisting here, the mechanism opens up, rather like the petals of a flower.'

The handle was a screw. As he turned the end of it, the pear split into sections, opening up – a metal claw – wider than any mouth could stretch.

'Of course, there is no need to go so far, but I believe the results are interesting – the jaw cannot withstand the pressure. The teeth . . .'

'Where is Mary?'

I cut across him. He stopped winding the thing and looked at me. I held his gaze.

'Where is she?'

My throat had clamped shut, and I was speaking in barely more than a whisper. His eyes narrowed.

'Mary is not in bed? I wonder . . .'

He seemed to be calculating something of consequence, something he hadn't expected, but there was also a gleam in his eye.

'Where could she be? Did you have an appointment perhaps – in the library?'

His blue eyes glittered at me. The dark unease I had felt in the attic room billowed up into a horrible understanding. It blotted out the sitting room, the pear-shaped device, the master himself, and I ducked, flung myself around an ottoman and pelted towards the open door. I crashed into an orderly bedroom that was more plainly and simply

172

furnished than the rest of the house. Using a bedpost, I swung myself around towards the door onto the landing. The master hadn't come out of the sitting room to cut me off. There was no sound of him following. With one hand holding up my skirt and the other on the banister, I flew down the main stairs, jumping several steps at a time. I don't know how I reached the ground floor without breaking my neck.

The corridor was as deserted as before. I didn't tiptoe this time but rushed straight to the library and threw the door open. It was much darker inside, only a low fire and a few candles dotted about casting warm pools of light between shadows. My eye was drawn to chance surfaces and textures – the gilt titles on book spines, the curve of a polished table leg, Mr Garston's oiled hair. He was sprawled on a chair by the centre table, a pipe in his hand that swayed about as he conducted his own slurred singing. The air was thick with tobacco smoke. As my eyes adjusted, they found Mr Murray. He was leaning against the stepladder – I saw only slices of him through the wooden bars, enough to see his shirt hanging loose and his hand fumbling underneath it around his trouser buttons. I don't know if it was an undoing or a doing-up. He was swaying off balance. Reaching out to steady himself, he knocked a garment to the floor that had been draped over a step. The way it landed like something jointed and stiff, I knew it was a corset. He didn't notice, staring slack-jawed as he was over to the left of the fireplace. The fire half lit two figures in that corner, one pale, one dark. The dark was Mr Hicks. His body and loose face folded and dripped like candle wax around Mary. I couldn't understand what he was doing at first.

I don't want to write about her here. Why record what those vile men made of her? Enough to say she seemed without feeling, no life or awareness in her expression. A slow laughter dribbled out of Mr Hicks like unguent as he tugged at the wreck of her clothing – not to remove it, as I first thought. He was playing like a little girl with a doll, arranging petticoats and torn chemise. After a moment's admiration of his work, he suddenly clapped his hands and threw his long form over her, pressing her into a grotesque embrace.

'Cunt! Cunt! Gentlemen!'

It was Mr Garston. The light from the doorway had finally drifted through his drunkenness, and whatever else fogged his mind, to a small clearing of thought, and he had swivelled around to look at me. He threw his head back and let out a halloo. With sudden energy, his large body hefted itself out of the chair and charged. I froze. The other two took up the halloo, Mr Murray swinging with one hand from the stepladder and howling at the ceiling. I snapped to my senses and took off like a leveret, circling the middle table. Mr Murray swung for me, still holding on to the ladder, and missed. I could hear Mr Garston labouring behind me, his spurt of energy slowing to a determined trudge.

'To me! To me!'

Mr Hicks held his arm out wide while still hanging onto Mary with the other, smiling like an idiot. I put my arm around Mary's waist and pulled.

'Let her go.'

She lolled between us like a drunk we were carrying home. A hot, damp hand circled the back of my neck and yanked me forward. I tried to outrun it, but Mr Garston was overbalancing himself, clutching at my dress and hair. We stumbled into the centre of the room and fell hard against a table, nearly overturning it. I was dragged down. The weight of him thumped the air from my lungs, and a high laugh wheeled into my ear. I tasted hair oil, sweat and the sickly smell of a drug. Something heavy had landed on the rug beside us. I felt blindly about while, still laughing, he leaned on my chest to bring his face level with mine. My fingers found metal teeth, a wooden handle. The first breath jagged down my throat as he wheezed above me.

'Now then, I've tasted French maid – let's see how plain English compares.'

I would not have thought a face could be used so like a weapon. For all I clenched my teeth and turned my head away, he smothered me with wet lips, hot breath and greasy skin. Impossible to breathe. His tongue was large, a strange, arching creature in itself. For a moment I could think only of pressing my head against the floor until wood or bone gave way. Then I remembered mouths also have teeth.

The creature slithered away as I bit down, but I caught the tip and held on. There was an explosion of sound, a surging taste of metal. He pulled away roaring, which gave me room to swing the flint mill. It hit the edge of his eye and temple, I believe, for he gave an abrupt squeak – almost of surprise – and rolled off me like a giant leach. I sat up, spitting his blood, fighting for air.

The door swung open, and the room became illuminated by lamps parading in. I squinted until I could make out Barrett, slick as ever, calmly placing a light on a side table. He turned and took in the carnage, marking each of us in turn. A dark displeasure stole across his face but not surprise. I looked at Mr Garston. One eye had filled with blood; the other stared straight up. His mouth was open as if shocked by what he saw, and the flesh of his chins and cheeks trembled. Barrett walked over to put a light on the table by the fire and set down a couple of books that were tucked under his arm.

'Gentlemen, Mr Gethin has retired for the evening. He sends his apologies for not joining you and hopes you will amuse yourself for as long as it pleases. He requests . . .'

A slight sourness to the word . . .

'He requests that you confine your enjoyment this evening to his cellar, tobacco and, of course, the resources of the library.'

Mr Hicks was still holding on to Mary, blinking, but seemed to have forgotten her. I scrambled to my feet. He shrank away as I advanced, alarm popping all over his face. I spat again, a red haze, and he staggered backwards as if shot. Mary was sinking to the floor. I caught her around her waist and pulled up the body of her dress, holding it in place as I walked her to the door. It was hard work – her legs moved like a foal's. Barrett was standing over Mr Garston, saying his name, and looked up as I turned. I pulled the door shut on his calculating stare.

Then it was just me and Mary in the ticking stillness of the hallway. Breaths. More breaths. The air strong-armed its way in and out of my lungs. I wanted to be sick, but knew not to, not yet. I changed my grip on Mary and set myself to the task. Twice on the stairs, I had to stop and kneel down beside her, waiting for strength. Whatever they had given her had turned her to clay – heavy and passive. It was as if she'd been shoved so far within herself, she couldn't get back out.

The attic stairs were unthinkable – my body ached with the violence done to it and my arm shook from holding her up – but I didn't even look at my own bedroom door. I hauled her straight into the missus' room, not knowing what I wanted – to beg for her help or scream at her for letting this happen. She was up, sitting in the glow of a dying fire with one candle lit. I pulled Mary to the bed and almost collapsed on top of her. Her eyes were still dull, but she moved her head as if some part of her was trying to surface. I lifted her legs onto the bed and smoothed the hair away from her face. The room grew lighter around us – the missus was lighting lamps and candles. She stopped on the other side of the bed and looked across at me, her face drawn tight and pale. After several long moments, she spoke.

'What happened?'

'She was in the library. With them.'

She started slightly as if an insect had bitten her and looked down. 'Did they . . .?'

Her question boomed around the room.

'I don't know. I don't think . . . there wasn't time.'

I walked over to the chest to pull out one of the missus' clean nightgowns. The mirror caught my reflection. Wild hair, wild eyes. Blood in my teeth. I stumbled across to the washstand and poured water from the jug, doused myself with it. My mouth wouldn't come clean. I leaned over the basin, hands shaking.

'I've hurt Mr Garston.' I watched the red of his blood swirl in the water. 'Badly, I think.'

The missus was silent a moment.

'Come here and help me.'

We set to work, removing Mary's boots and stockings and peeling off her dress. Her hands pushed at us weakly – I don't know if she was trying to stop us or fighting something in a dream. We managed to get the nightgown over her head and her arms into the sleeves. The missus took hold of one of her hands and rubbed it between her own. She gently placed it on the cover and stroked her arm, talking softly. Anger began to bloom in the pit of my stomach. We had to turn her on her side to undo her petticoat and pull off the torn chemise. The missus undid her drawers and pulled them down. She paused, nodded and drew the nightgown over her legs.

'It proves nothing, I suppose.'

Once Mary was settled with half the cover pulled over her, her eyes began to close. The missus went back to sit by the fire. It was now barely an ember, but she still gazed into it. I felt pain throbbing and singing all over my body – like someone playing the devil's music with my bones. The anger erupted.

'You *knew*. You knew what was going to happen.'

My voice was hoarse.

'You did nothing to stop it.'

The missus shook her head.

'I told you what he was. I told you about Helene and the letter she wrote.'

She was so calm I wanted to strike her. I wanted to hit her harder than I had hit Mr Garston, watch her smooth skin swell up and turn lurid.

'Helene? Helene's French. That letter's in *French*.' I pointed at the bottom drawer. 'You told me nothing. And what you did say was . . .'

177

She looked up sharply and finished for me.

'Insane? Hysterical?'

We glared at each other. It was true. A low burbling came from the canary's cage. It was that dead hour of night, stranded between two shores. There seemed no certainty of reaching morning.

'I . . . had not thought about the letter being in French.'

She laughed suddenly.

'Perhaps I am a little mad.'

My hands were still shaking.

'You must be, ma'am, to stay in this house and do nothing but take singing lessons and hold parties and play spiteful games with your maid.'

She reared out of her chair.

'Nothing, Harriet?'

Her gaze shifted quickly over my shoulder, but I had heard the door this time and was already turning. The master shut it quietly. I moved, putting myself between him and Mary. He noticed and put on a look of mild disappointment.

'Good evening. I hope there is nothing the matter? I heard voices.'

Fear ruffled through me as if I was made of feathers. He looked down at a box in his hands, rubbed his thumbs over the top of it.

'I wanted to congratulate you, my dear, on a mostly successful evening.'

I eyed the box and felt my pulse quicken. The missus' face was a white mask.

'What have you allowed to happen, Ralph?'

The master threw a look at the bed.

'Ah, well, if you're looking for someone to blame . . .'

He spoke wearily, as if he was being forced against his will to talk of unpleasant things.

'Remember, my dear, it is you who insists on dismissing servants faster than they can be replaced. And it was your own ill-advised choice of maid who led Mary to the library in the middle of the night when she should have been in bed.'

The missus' eyes flicked to mine. The master watched us.

'It appears she has an interest in the contents of some of the books
– books which, I believe, she was clearly instructed not to touch. I am
afraid she has also just now seriously injured one of our guests. The
doctor has been sent for. I am afraid the constable may have to be
raised too.'

She started to speak, but he put his hand up.

'It is my fault, my dear.'

Each word landed distinctly, as if he meant it.

'I have been away too long. Now sit down, I have something for
you.'

The missus glanced at the box with as much suspicion as I had.

'No.'

'A simple gift.'

Her head went up like a horse about to bolt.

'My dear . . .'

She darted away from the fireplace to the cabinet. He folded his
arms and tapped the box against his lips – that look of mild disappointment again. Walking away from her, he made for the window and pulled
the curtain back a few inches. Dropped it again.

'These evenings . . .' he reflected. 'They aren't good for your nerves.'

He had his back to us still, though he might as well have been
holding a knife to our throats. After a moment, he looked to the side.
He caught the cloth of the birdcage between two fingers and lifted it
to peer in at the canary.

'The singing is making your symptoms worse. I shall talk to the
doctor while he's here.'

He threw the cloth back so half the cage was revealed. The canary
fluttered its wings and chirped again.

'The lessons must cease, of course. Your outings to the vicarage – to
our good vicar.'

He looked at her and smiled.

'I want to help you. Won't you let me look after you?'

When she didn't answer, he placed the box on the dressing table and opened the door of the birdcage.

'We shall spend some time together in London. I should not have left you here so long with only music to divert you.'

In one movement, he reached in and caught the canary in his fist. He brought it out, close to his face.

'Too much music can tire the nervous system, especially in females – it is well understood, well documented in Europe. Overstimulation of the imagination – they say it can lead to immorality, despair . . .'

He raised his other hand and wrapped it caressingly around the first, his thumb and forefinger resting either side of the bird's tiny head.

'Ralph . . .'

'Even destruction.'

A twist, and he'd done it. There was not so much as a snap. At least not outwardly – inside, I felt my guts flip over and a sickly feeling of having reached out to catch something and missed. Turning the bird over, he pinched its feet between his fingers and let it dangle limply. For a moment, he seemed absorbed by the wing feathers – they had fallen open like a fan – and the loose neck. Then with a careless flick of the wrist, he tossed it onto the bed next to Mary and stepped over to the dressing table. He tapped the box.

'You will wear this tomorrow with the blue dress. Your sackcloth and ashes performance has grown tiresome.'

He didn't look at either of us again. On his way to the door, he stopped briefly to consider the missus' portrait, the girl in green. A gentle smile crossed his face that made me want to throw my guts up. Bringing his attention back to the present, he spoke to me while looking at his pocket watch.

'We must hope Mr Garston recovers, Watkins.'

The door closed behind him as quietly as before. A terrible shaking came back into my limbs.

'What will they do to me?'

The missus crossed the room and put her arms around me. I was rigid. 'What will they do?'

She made quiet shushing noises, speaking gently as she had to Mary. 'Be calm, Harriet. Sit down with me. Here.'

We perched on the edge of the bed next to the dead bird. She smoothed my hair and rubbed the top of my arms. I looked at the little corpse, at Mary's still form. My staring eyes seemed to see everything, not just there in the room, but all the scenes I had ever witnessed in the house and vicarage. I heard again everything that had been said, all the sly comments, the rumours, the ravings. The cruelty. Words broke from me like a cry.

'It was supposed to be Lily with those men tonight, wasn't it? Not Mary. That's why she was hired. That's why you dismissed her. You were trying to protect her.'

The missus took my hands in hers, squeezed my fingers. She didn't speak for some time.

'Barrett and Mrs Clarkson choose them. They pick out the youngest, those without families.'

My eyes felt as big as the room.

'All those other servants too? You dismissed them all to keep them away from those men?'

I had thought nothing else could shock me.

'Why haven't you told anyone?'

She gasped, almost a laugh.

'Who would believe me? My husband is the Honourable Ralph Gethin, MP. His friends – men like him, and others who choose not to see – preside over police divisions, the courts, government itself. Should I tell them? He has several doctors who wouldn't hesitate to say I am out of my mind. They have all the evidence they need. But what can be said of Ralph? He does nothing directly himself; his own hands are clean. There are servants who believe him to be the kindest of employers – Duncan, Lizzie – and those who know the truth are controlled by Barrett.'

'Like Laurence.'

She nodded. My mind reeled.

'Laurence knows about these evenings? He knows what happens?'

I remembered his desperation in the yard after I caught him with the garden hand. He had been unwilling to explain what bound him to the hall. The full truth of it grew luridly clear in my mind. The missus paused as if trying to find the words.

'Laurence was controlled and blackmailed by Barrett and Ralph from a young age. They crawled under his skin until he couldn't tell where they ended and he began. If he betrays them, he betrays himself – they never let him forget that. To object, to walk away – it is not so simple. Not for anyone.'

I tried to read her face. Did she *pity* him? She put a hand on Mary's arm, changing the subject.

'Mary is Ralph's first mistake. She was always left alone – Mrs Clarkson is her aunt – but he lost control when he brought those men here.'

She suddenly reached for my hand, holding on to both myself and Mary as if she could save us from a disaster already visited.

'I convinced myself you would be safe. You are different – stronger – and older than the others.'

And a lot plainer, I thought. I felt Mr Garston's weight on me again and felt sick. She continued, speaking almost to herself.

'I never thought he would let me keep you. You intrigued him, I think. There must be something about you he thinks worth corrupting.'

I shivered. The room grew smaller and colder.

'But he couldn't risk hurting you in any obvious way, not with your family and your ties to the Stanworths.'

I remembered the interest he had taken in my family – finding out if anyone cared for me, anyone with enough influence to cause trouble. Panic was rising at the thought of the constable. With Mr Garston, the master had something to use against me, and it didn't matter who my friends were. Would people believe me? I tried to sound brave though my voice was thin.

'That's me and Mary and Helene then – three of us to speak out with you.'

The missus looked at me as if I'd suggested jumping out of the window. She leaned in, fierce suddenly.

'Helene would never be believed now, nor Laurence, even if he changed his story. And Sarah Clarkson would denounce her own niece before breaking ranks with her master.'

It was true. Clockface was in it up to her neck. I remembered her familiarity with Mr Murray – 'Not on the menu tonight, sir' – perhaps she found children for many an upstanding gentleman. The missus was still speaking fiercely.

'You don't know how they can twist the truth. They will turn whatever happened with Mr Garston against you. All anyone will see is his blood on your hands.'

I thought of Mother's letter.

'But there are already rumours . . .'

'Of course, there are rumours.'

She shook it away as if it was too plain to mention.

'There are always rumours and people who suspect, but what has happened? Ever?'

I started to protest more, but she cut across me again in a voice that almost begged.

'He will take my son. He will corrupt him.'

She searched my face.

'Do you not see? Do you not know what he will do? It will be his way of punishing me for the rest of my life.'

I did and didn't see. She was punished anyway, her movements controlled, and worse – I caught a fleeting sense of what her life must be and clutched her hands.

'But I saw the portrait, I saw everything in it, like you said – I believe you! And he has things – awful things. He showed me the . . . the pear with the screw that opens up – it breaks your teeth, your jaw. He told me . . .'

'Shh.'

She lifted her hands to my face.

'I know. It's all right. It's time.'

I didn't know what she meant, but I clung on to her as if she was a lifeboat, swirling us into the dark. She turned to look at the bird.

'Look, a dead canary.'

Freeing one hand, she gently touched the feathers.

'The sign to flee, remember? When the air is poisoned.'

To flee. How easy that sounded. To turn back the way you had come, run along familiar passages to fresh air, light, life. But where could we run back to? The ceilings and walls had caved in behind us. I didn't expect an answer, but I asked anyway.

'Where would we go?'

She paused for a second, staring straight at me as if she was trying to work out who I was. Then she said it. One word.

'Italy.'

A place. A journey's end.

I blinked at her. There was none of the madness I had seen before, no black wells hiding secrets in their depths. Only a plea, naked now and in the open. She turned quickly to look at Mary, whose face was slack still, and drew me over to the chairs in front of the hearth. We leaned towards the dead fire, clasping each other's hands as she spoke. The plan itself was simple, as simple as a child dropping one game to begin another. For the missus I could see it was already real. She had taken the steps a hundred times in her head, from leaving Finton Hall all the way to her first appearance on the professional stage in Italy. She knew which theatres to try first. I listened in growing amazement, thinking how she had been planning this, working out details, no doubt scribbling them down and then burning them to ash, right under my nose. And I had thought her weak in the head. I had come to see her as a kind of invalid, and all the time she had never needed me really, not in the way I imagined. She needed me now though, as an assistant, a companion – I would no longer be merely a lady's maid. My life could become something new, unimagined even in the yearnings of this diary. Would I do it? Would I take the risk?

I watched her. There are so many questions still, so much I still don't understand about her behaviour or her plan, but I have been wrong about too many things. I imagined going home, looking for another position, all the while knowing what was happening at Finton Hall, knowing that she was fleeing alone and unaided, waiting every day for news that she had been caught. My heart found the courage.

'I shall go with you.'

Tears flowed from us both. She hurried on as if our weeping was only a vagary of the weather, telling me it was necessary I should hide myself first. Something was in motion, and I must go to London ahead of her and wait.

'No.'

I shook my head.

'I can't leave you, ma'am. Not with him.'

'You have to go.'

Her hands gripped mine so hard it hurt.

'You know everything now, and after Mr Garston, you're not safe. Ralph will use it to crush you.'

I tried to think of another argument, but the truth was my hair stood on end at the thought of Garston. She leaned in closer.

'It is only for a few weeks. He will do nothing to me in that time. It may even work to our advantage that you are not with me. I have prepared for this for so long, Harriet, I can't risk leaving before everything is in place.'

'But can't I help? What will you do?'

She shook her head.

'Keep yourself quietly – see no one – and wait for my instructions. The less you know beforehand, the safer it is for both of us. Do you understand?'

I did, though I was loath to leave her. Edward too.

'I will look after the baby for you, ma'am, when we go.'

Her eyes turned oddly flat. For a horrible moment, I pictured her face collapsing inwards. Doubt stopped my heart.

'You *are* bringing him?'

She gave a slight nod.

'Of course. I won't let Ralph keep him.'

Her response was strangely weak after all she had just said, but then, in a moment of revelation, I remembered she had wanted him weaned early. This was why. My thoughts rushed on.

'What about Francis? I can't leave him here.'

She shook her head again.

'You must go and quickly, without provoking Ralph further. I can keep Francis safe for now.'

'Safe?'

I looked at Mary.

'Why didn't you dismiss him, ma'am, like the others?'

She raised her hands and let them fall.

'I can't dismiss everyone. The housemaids are within my reach, but Francis belongs to Ralph. He dazzles him with gifts and attention – you've seen it. He is weakening all other ties. Francis will soon doubt himself, and anyone else, before he ever doubts Ralph.'

I watched her face, waiting to see evidence that she would never let that happen, but outside two horses galloped up to the front of the house – the doctor. Morning was coming after all. The missus rose and eyed me fearfully.

'You mustn't be here.'

Details. They had to be decided quickly.

'Call yourself Helene – or Helen – Helen Dubois.'

She started opening drawers, pulling out items of clothing, chemises and stockings, discarding some and throwing others on the bed. My mind raced. I couldn't pull Francis from his bed and drag him into hiding with me, but I couldn't consent to leaving him in this house either. I remembered how Mr Murray had stared at him. The missus was speaking in an urgent whisper.

'I'll give you money to sew these now and send more when we remove to London.'

I caught up with what she was saying.

'Helen Dubois? Your maid?'

'A French name will serve you. If you need further work, it will attract ladies who think French girls make finer seamstresses.'

She abandoned the clothes and opened a drawer for writing paper.

'You will need a character . . .'

The old fear crept into my belly.

'But I'm not French – I don't speak . . .'

'Say you grew up here, your mother is English and your father died when you were young. That is more or less Helene's story, only the opposite – she was raised in Lombardy. A real person's life – adapted – will sound more truthful.'

I didn't say that I myself knew very little about her last lady's maid. There was no time to argue.

'It is only for a few weeks. Then you can be whomever you wish.'

A sudden smile hit her face as if thrown from that future time. It vanished as quickly as it had come.

'Don't tell anyone where you are besides me. Send me your address as soon as you find a lodging. No . . .'

She looked up from her desk, thinking.

'Address it to me but send it to the vicarage through Mrs Trevelyan. That is safest. She will neither read it nor put it into anyone's hands but my own.'

187

I nodded. My eyes turned to the portrait and the girl in green. Her captivated expression seemed to shimmer more brightly than ever. I won't see her again. From now on, I shall think of the scene as empty, sunlight on an abandoned chair.

A faint gasp came from the missus. I waited while she stared, almost without expression, into the box the master had left. After a moment, she held it up. Nestled against velvet was the choker from the portrait. A plain band with a pear-shaped pendant, catching blue and green in the lamplight – opal, I think. Its stalk and leaves were made up of tiny diamonds. She shut the box and cleared her throat. Our eyes met.

In my own room, I changed into my print dress, packed my box and bundled the clothes the missus wanted – or pretended to want – sewing into my carpet bag. She ran down to the stables herself to order the cart. I dragged my things down the servants' stairs and through to the boot room without a light, terrified of meeting Barrett or Laurence at every corner and landing. The house was quiet except for my breathing and the blood beating in my ears. I opened the door which led into the yard and a grey dawn. The cart wasn't there yet. I listened to the silence behind me and after only a second's hesitation, turned back into it.

Francis was still fast asleep. I shook him until he was blinking at me in something like terror.

'What time is it, miss? Am I in trouble?'

I cupped his face in my hands.

'Francis, listen. I have to go away.'

His eyes widened.

'I wish I could take you with me, but I can't. Work hard, be good, and I will write to your parents. They will call you home, and when they do, you must go.'

'Home? Did I do something wrong, miss?'

He looked like he might cry.

'No, nothing wrong. It's . . .'

I heard the missus in my voice.

'It's better this way. But you must leave when they come for you and not argue. One day I'll tell you everything.'

I hugged him to me, feeling as if my heart might burst, and got myself out of the room before I started crying myself. There was little time but, hardly knowing why, I turned further into the house and climbed the servants' stairs. The library was empty and untouched. A cold, sickly smell lingered. There were bottles and glasses on their sides, books strewn on the floor, some of their insides too. Mary's stays were still crumpled under the stepladder. Dark stains flecked the wood and rug near the table – Mr Garston's blood. The taste of it filled my mouth again, and I gagged, holding onto the back of a chair until I remembered it was the one he had been sitting in. As I turned to leave, my eye fell on the flint mill on its side on the floor. I picked it up, tucked it under my shawl and hurried back to open the door – where my luck ran out. Laurence was standing there. His eyes were bloodshot, and I could see the redness of his skin where the paint had been scrubbed away.

'Where is Mary?'

He snarled it. The strange doll and fat spider came back to me – the close air, the valet's upside-down face, Mary's keening. My hand clutched the mill out of sight.

'Why do you care?'

It didn't even matter about the boys anymore. He must have guessed what was going to happen after the party, knowing already how wicked the master and his friends are. I couldn't forgive him for that or explain it away like the missus. Revulsion made me push past him into the passageway. He caught hold of my arm, twisting it.

'Why did you bring her to my room?'

I tried to wrench free. There was a sound – someone coming down the main stairs. Laurence's grip tightened as time pulled taut; the steps drew closer. Mrs Murray reached the hall, turned and saw us. I thought

Laurence would back away but instead he dropped my arm and walked towards her, marching down the hallway and seemingly growing taller and larger with every step. I saw shock and then fear rising in her eyes. There was a moment I wasn't sure what was going to happen. He bore down on her as if he would trample her into the ground. And maybe he would have, except she cowered to the side with a frightened little squeal, stumbling against a table. Laurence bared his teeth and darted his head at her as he passed, making her squeal again. Then he was gone. Mrs Murray straightened a little, clutching the throat of her dress. I don't know what I expected her to do, but not what she did. After a few moments, in which she drew herself up and nearly commanded the twitching in her face, she glared at me.

'Girl! No one has brought hot water or tea.'

I stared, heart beating so loud I thought she'd hear. My reply came as clockwork.

'I'll bring it up now, ma'am.'

'Too late. What time is breakfast?'

'Nine o'clock, ma'am.'

It wasn't yet six. Her pale eyes gleamed at me like bones. She was the only wife staying at the hall – it must have been because of her that the Murrays were given the room furthest from the library. I wondered if Mr Murray's return to bed had driven her up early, what horrible things this horrible woman knew. Perhaps this was how she bore it, pretending not to see anything but the trivial and petty, clinging to a sense of herself through meanness and vanity.

'I'll have tea in the drawing room. Immediately, mind.'

'Of course, ma'am.'

I curtsied, thinking she would be a long time waiting. She stalked away, a little unsteadily, and I followed her as far as the hall. Before taking the stairs down, I hesitated, as if something had whispered my name, and looked around. The eye in the cabinet was peering out, burning with hate and wickedness, as if it was the eye of Finton

Hall itself. I could leave, it seemed to say, but that didn't mean it was finished with me.

The missus was waiting in the yard, hands clenched so her knuckles were white. I climbed into the dogcart while the stable lad went to pick up my box and bundle. My eyes felt scratched on with a stick.

'I have told him to take you to the next station, in case anyone looks for you in the village.'

The missus reached over to squeeze my arm, but her eyes were full of fear.

'The doctor is still with Mr Garston.'

I nodded and took her hand.

'Come with me, ma'am. Come now.'

'No, no.'

She shook her head.

'I have to stay here.'

There was decision in her voice.

'We shall see each other again soon.'

The boy was returning with my things. I whispered.

'Tell Mary I'm sorry.'

She nodded.

'I'll do everything I can for her.'

She had to step back to let the boy heave the box in. There was nothing else we could say then. The cart jogged forward, and I was being carried away.

I looked up at the house before we drove under the trees, as Lily had done. The last time I had seen it so clearly from the outside and not as a pressing series of rooms, things to clean and faces to avoid was the day I arrived. All the gables and turrets made it look like a small castle – I had thought it enchanted. My dearest wish on leaving was that I should never see it again, but I clutched the flint mill to me as if I'd traded it for a piece of myself.

It's in my box now, jumbled with my possessions. My clothes are strewn over the floor where I dropped them last night. I am too tired and sore to cast this itchy blanket off and dress. The only comfort of London I've discovered this time around is that names come last – who you are doesn't matter so much as your coin. I chose one of the cheaper boarding houses on Warren Street in Islington and offered to pay a month up front. Mrs Cole's pocket swallowed my money quicker than a dog gobbling a biscuit. It wasn't until I was hefting my box towards the stairs that she asked my name.

'Helen Dubois.'

I said it too loud, half expecting her to call for the law, but she only nodded without interest. As soon as my door was shut, I sat with my back against it, arms hugging my knees. I haven't opened it since.

MAY

Thursday, 2nd May

Nothing from the missus. I keep to my room, only going out for meals and newspapers, and once to send my address to the vicarage. The other boarders are all young women, mostly maids who don't want to live in, one with clerical work who looks so young she reminds me of Lily. Helen Dubois is a quiet girl, keeps to her room, likes to eat alone. Not very interesting.

In the mornings, I scour the papers for news of Mr Garston, for my own name as someone wanted. London is busy with other outrages – bank robberies, dead babies pulled from the Thames, the brink of war. It is an effort to stop myself from walking to Gloucester Square, to see if they have arrived, if only for a glimpse of her, to reassure myself all is well. I try to sew or write, hoping to recapture the stitch-by-stitch, word-by-word ordering of my mind. If I sit by the window there is enough light for most of the day, but I often find myself staring into the dingy yard, my mind growing thick with fears. It mithers me that she is so trusting of Laurence when she knows he is controlled by the master. What if she lets something slip? I write the letter to Francis's parents over and over, begging them to remove him from the house – everything I have seen and know about the master goes into it. The more I remember, the more worried I am for the missus. At the same time my words seem unbelievable. I worry Francis's parents will think me a liar, a wicked servant with a grudge, trying to cause trouble. I worry it won't be enough.

Friday, 3rd May

I cannot do nothing; the waiting is torture. Instead of walking to Gloucester Square, I wrote to the Girls Friendly Society, asking about Lily. I don't know which charitable organisation Clockface hauled her out of, but there can't be that many for girls. Then I walked to all the servants' registry offices I could find, especially the lower sort. I visited four in the hope that if she hasn't returned to the charity place, she is at least trying to find domestic work. The master's words haunt me – that she will be selling herself on the street by now.

Saturday, 4th May

Four more registry offices. Nothing.

Monday, 6th May

The Girls Friendly Society replied to say they don't know her, but to try the association that befriends young servants. I walked to the address they gave, and from there was redirected to a different office. The woman in charge seemed very surprised that I'd come looking. She blinked a lot and asked me several times who I was. My heart leapt. Lily had indeed come back the day she left Finton Hall, but then vanished again after only one night. None of the other girls knew where she had gone, or so they said. The woman's expression told me she had her own grim ideas but was keeping them to herself. I begged that she would write to me if Lily ever came back, and she softened slightly, seeing my concern, and said she would. I could see she held out little hope.

I tried two more registry offices, but my heart had gone out of it and my feet were sore. It seems unlikely now that Lily is looking for domestic work. Her cruel dismissal from Finton Hall might have put her off service for good, and where else would she go? The master and charity woman had already made their opinions plain, and I could think of nothing better. I walked nearly as far as Stepney in low spirits and would have carried on right up to the door of Francis's parents if it wasn't for the missus' warning not to show myself to anyone. A dream woke me in the night, making me sit bolt upright. Something about Laurence moving the portrait of the little black child at Finton Hall and refusing to tell me where he was taking it. Sweating in the darkness, I remembered the painting is over a hundred years old. The silver circlet around the boy's neck isn't just a pretty part of his livery – it's a slave collar. I believe the master enjoys hiding his wickedness in plain sight, just as in the portrait of the missus.

She has told me to visit no one, but I fear my letter to Francis's parents will miscarry, and once we have left for Italy, I can do no more for him than I have for Lily. *If* we leave. The doubts come when my feet and fingers are stilled. I lie on the bed staring at cracks and stains in the ceiling. Italy feels unreal, a place in a dream, impossible. I imagine the missus has been found out by Laurence or changed her mind, that police will be sent to my door about Mr Garston. I think of Mary and the boot boy, and it hurts my stomach to know Francis and Edward are still there. Tomorrow, I—

Mrs Cole's maid Betsy frightened me witless by knocking on my door. A message has arrived at last, unsigned.

Tomorrow, Tuesday, 3 p.m. Mrs B. St J.

Tuesday, 7th May

St James' was Mrs B's favourite church, the one she took us to most Sundays even though there were several nearer the house. 'High church,' she'd whisper and squint happily like a cat. It was a long walk. When the familiar tower came into view, I was surprised to feel a rush of grief. I kept my head down and shawl across my face.

It was empty except for a figure at the back moving about on some business. I sat down near the front at the far end of a pew to wait. A picture of Christ on the cross hung on the wall. It made me think of Gertrude at the vicarage and her good Christian words. Likely, she will never know the truth about the master. What will she think if it gets out I have gone with the missus? If we are caught? And Mrs Trevelyan, my parents, William? I may never see my family again. Fear made me sick suddenly. Taking Edward is breaking the law, a terrible crime. My eyes turned towards the painting, but I couldn't look straight at His face, frightened of what I might see in its expression. The background to the cross showed Jerusalem in the distance and I thought of the missus' portrait and all the sinister things in it. Her face had looked expectant. Slowly, I brought my gaze to the foreground. This Christ stares down at his grieving Marys. His expression is sad, tired and helpless. Defeated. It seemed odd to me to have painted him that way. A cloth is draped over his hips, and it brought back a vision of my Mary in the library, undressed and helpless in the hands of that man. Anger returned, and I noticed suddenly the most obvious thing about the crucifixion. It had never crossed my mind before. You have to break some very important laws to get nailed to a cross.

'I was unsure if you would come.'

I turned quickly. She was in the pew behind me over to the right, wearing a light blue cloak and a straw bonnet, which hid her face. He has made her dress as he wishes. At her throat was the pear-shaped choker.

'Keep looking forward.'

I did as she said, feeling elated that she was near me and real after I'd spent so many days with my own thoughts.

'Are you well?'

I smiled, though she couldn't see it.

'I am, ma'am. I hope you are?'

She gave one of her huff-laughs.

'Much the better for seeing you. I have very little time. You haven't changed your mind?'

I shook my head.

'What do you want me to do?'

I heard the pew creak as she shifted in her seat, perhaps looking around to make sure we were alone.

'I need you to be ready. When the time comes, we will need to move quickly. I'll send pieces of sewing regularly – try to send them back without the delivery boy seeing you to be safe. You will know it's time when I send a red petticoat.'

She carried on talking, low and fast. I learned that Lizzie had left, and a new nursemaid and lady's maid had been appointed. They both treated the missus with distrust, no doubt fed stories by Barrett and Clockface. I listened so hard, I don't think I even drew breath. When she finished, the empty church seemed to ring with her words as if she had shouted them.

'Do you understand?'

I nodded. Except I didn't, not everything.

'Why do we have to wait? Why not choose a day?'

She paused.

'There are things I have to do. It's better if I don't tell you everything. Will you be able to keep yourself?'

She sounded hesitant.

'Do you need money?'

I heard in her voice how unschooled she is about the cost of things. Money is an unknown language to her. It sank an unpleasant feeling into the pit of my belly about the future.

'No, thank you, ma'am. But when we get there . . .?'

It seemed bad luck even to mention it, but I knew I wouldn't see her again until we were past the point of turning back.

'I . . . I am sure I can keep us until I find an engagement.'

It was the first time, to my ears, she had sounded wholly unsure. If it comes to it, I can only suppose they need maids in houses over there as much as in London.

'Mr Garston, ma'am?'

She paused again.

'He has lost the sight in one eye.'

The hairs on my arms and the back of my neck stood on end. With the fear came a kind of awe that my own hands could have brought about such a calamity in another.

'Are they looking for me?'

I heard her picking her words carefully.

'Not publicly. Ralph told a story to the doctor about you being inebriated and hysterical.'

'Won't Mr Garston go to the police himself?'

'He knows Ralph could destroy his life with one word – he will do as he is told. But you are not safe. Ralph is working to find out where you are. He has written to your parents – he told me that. He wants me to know he is in control still. I was worried you might have gone home.'

I felt a hand circling my throat and squeezing.

'Written what?'

'Oh, it will be all concern for your welfare after your unfortunate . . . loss of control, perhaps – he will have found a way to hint at Garston's injuries. He – we – will be eager to know you are safe if you return home or write to them. He is sowing the seeds to undermine you.'

I was silent. The floor seemed to have fallen away from under me. The worst is I don't know what my mother would believe if it comes to it.

'I must go.'

Hearing her start to rise, I spoke quickly.

'And Mary, ma'am?'

She sat down again.

'Isabel is taking care of her at the vicarage. She will recover.'

Something not terrible at last.

'Ma'am.'

I turned my head.

'Is it very difficult . . . with him?'

There was a silence.

'It isn't for much longer.'

She rested her hand briefly on my shoulder.

'God keep you, Harriet. Remember – a red petticoat.'

I've never heard her mention God's name before except for that one time in the library when she caught me singing Milton's poem and asked if I thought it was true – that they also serve Him who only stand and wait. My eyes turned to Christ on his cross again and the pain daubed into his mother's face as she watches him suffer. I suppose it all depends on where you are standing and waiting.

—

I have burned the letters I wrote to Francis's parents and written another. It gives no detail; it is a warning only to remove him from the house, that he is not safe there. I must trust it is enough. It may be weeks before the missus sends her sign – I won't wait, nor will I leave it to the post. I must take the risk of delivering it myself.

Later

Francis's family live in rooms above a corset-maker's off the Mile End Road. The street is short but busy as nearly every house has a shop of some kind at the bottom with wares spilling onto the pavement. I edged past an old couple inspecting second-hand furniture and hesitated in the corset-maker's doorway, clutching my letter and getting in the way of customers. My palms were damp with nerves and the clammy air – it was still drizzly but sticky this morning. The shouts of costermongers pummelled my ears, and the smouldering of a tinker's coal pot caught in my throat. I held the edges of the envelope with the tips of my fingers so as not to mark it and wondered how to deliver it into their hands without showing myself. A messenger boy seemed safest, then I could watch from across the street. I looked around, searching for someone suitable, and saw a fruit seller over the road. His boy was crying out about slices of pineapple. Before I could move towards them, I felt a hand take hold of my elbow.

'Are you looking for my husband, dear?'

I turned and knew her at once for Francis's mother. She was spotlessly dressed in a dark red wool dress and straw bonnet and carried a basket heaving with packages. The troubling, almost-blood smell of fish drifted up. She looked down at the envelope in my hands, which clearly showed the name Bowman, and back to me. There was a directness in her expression as firm as the grip on my elbow. I imagine she keeps her household of men in the strictest order. But there was also a sparkle in her eye that was all Francis.

'Yes, I . . . this is for you.'

I held it awkwardly towards her. She studied my face without hurry and seemed to find something in it – something not altogether welcome, I thought, but then a smile spread easily across her features.

'You are Francis's friend, Harriet.'

The urge to run seized me. I felt as exposed and raw as the fish, but she was laughing.

'That is your handwriting?'

She nodded at the envelope and chuckled again at my scared expression. Instead of taking the letter though, she pushed me towards her door.

'Come, my husband will be very pleased to meet you.'

She made a sort of humming noise over my excuses and laughed to herself some more. The stairs were steep, and she followed slowly behind me, each step an effort as if her joints ached. I ran back down to take her basket. At the top, she pointed into a tidy front parlour and called names into the back of the house.

'Sit.'

She gestured to a chair in a corner. A wooden cross hung on the wall, and there were neat rows of pamphlets stacked on a sideboard. I was up again as soon as Francis's father entered – a tall man, as neat as his wife, looking a little befuddled at the summons. Mrs Bowman introduced me as 'Francis's friend', and her husband threw off the befuddled look at once and peered at me with the same intent look she had.

Another figure had come in behind him, a boy of about sixteen. Mrs Bowman handed him the basket and nodded. The boy glanced at me and left again – I heard him thundering down the stairs a moment later. Then they were all kindness, making me sit and thanking me for visiting. Mr Bowman pulled his chair a little nearer and leaned his forearms on his knees. His long hands hung loosely. They had the marks of physical work from some time past, and ink stains on the pads of his fingers. I felt comfortable with him, unashamed of my own hands. He enquired about my health and journey, where I had travelled from – I lied. Mrs Bowman drew back a little, near the window. Neither of them mentioned the envelope I still held in my hands. At the first break in his pleasantries, I held it out to him.

'This is for you. I'm sorry for coming to your house, but I'm worried for Francis.'

He didn't take the letter, and I was struck that neither of them showed any sign of surprise or alarm. Mr Bowman merely raised his eyebrows and spoke kindly.

'It's very kind of you to come all this way for Francis's sake. We know you were a friend to him when he was alone and frightened in a new place.'

201

He stopped there without asking why I had come. His silence flustered me, and I answered the question I had been expecting.

'Finton Hall is a terrible place. Mr Gethin isn't the man everyone thinks he is, and some of the servants are just as bad.'

He listened thoughtfully, nodding, then smiled at me almost apologetically.

'Francis writes that Mr Gethin is very kind to him.'

Mrs Bowman spoke from the window.

'He is teaching him about art; Francis is allowed to study and learn from his collections.'

I stared helplessly into the man's face.

'Francis doesn't know what is happening to the other servants.'

'I see.'

He nodded again and looked at me more closely.

'So, it is not Francis who is in trouble?'

I felt I was drowning.

'No one is safe in that house, Mr Bowman. Mr Gethin . . .'

I stopped talking. Mrs Bowman had made the smallest movement. I caught it in the corner of my eye – a tiny jump of attention. She looked away from the window as I turned my head to her, but it brought me to my feet. I should have known from the beginning – the way she had looked at me in the doorway. They knew I was coming; they even knew what I was going to say. My words had been untoothed before I set out. Mr Bowman rose too.

'Child, don't be frightened.'

I couldn't think in that moment what had happened. Francis must have told someone what I'd said to him – Laurence, of course – and the master or Barrett had written to these good people of the deranged servant coming their way telling terrible lies. The Bowmans' soft voices and careful gentleness were all to keep the mad girl calmly in their parlour. Keep her for what? I snatched one of Mr Bowman's hands and pressed the letter into it, speaking rapidly.

'His valet and housekeeper find friendless children to employ, and then Gethin gives them to his friends – powerful men, Mr Bowman – to use as they wish. They hold parties. I know a girl . . .'

I faltered slightly.

'She was abused, sir. And another I think is now on the streets. It's always the young servants, sir. Francis is not safe.'

Mr Bowman's kindly expression had dropped when I took hold of him. He was hearing me now, and I saw doubt – the beginnings of it – flicker in his eyes. Mrs Bowman had stepped closer, listening, and they exchanged a look. I yanked on Mr Bowman's arm and shouted into his face.

'Why will no one believe it?'

I sounded hysterical, but he didn't flinch. He looked me full in the eye, a wondering dread spreading over his features, as if I was changing shape in front of him.

'A policeman . . .'

Mrs Bowman had hurried to the window again. I don't know if it was said in warning or relief. Mr Bowman was still staring at me, a thousand thoughts rising behind his eyes. He opened his mouth, but there was no time, and we both knew it. I looked desperately into his eyes one moment more and then ran for the stairs. He let me go.

My heart hammered so hard and fast it hurt. I was about to be caught. My diary was still in my pocket – the missus would be undone too. In the street, I saw a constable's helmet bobbing behind a delivery cart coming from the Mile End Road. Francis's brother came into sight beside him. A shout went up as I reached the other end of the street and rounded the corner.

It was a narrow lane of terraced houses, unswept. A child asleep in a doorway stuck his leg out as I ran by, nearly sending me headlong. Gleeful laughter followed me around the next corner into a wider street. A totter's cart was just moving off from outside a tailor's. As I reached it, the footsteps behind me were cut short; angry curses followed. I looked back to see the boy dart into the road in such a rush he knocked into a woman crossing with a child. I hopped onto the back of the cart. There were heaped sacks, broken things, old clothes bundled together. The smell of filth was overpowering. I buried myself amongst it all and pulled a stinking greatcoat over me. Through a rent in the material, I watched the policeman hobble into view and pick up pace when he saw the boy. They ran towards the cart, and I held my breath until they were past. Francis's brother also appeared but stopped at the corner, looking both ways – he wasn't interested in the policeman's wounded pride. I hid myself completely, wishing the pony would go faster than its rickety plod, and was relieved after a few moments to feel it turn into a side street. The totter called out for people's rags for what seemed half the length of London. Then we turned again, ambling down a new street before coming to a stop. I scrambled out, gulping for air, and surprised a man smoking in a doorway. He leaned over and slapped his knees in amusement as I scurried away.

I walked quickly, deeper into Stepney. My bearings were sound enough to know I was heading south towards the river and that seemed good enough. Anywhere the master's web hadn't reached. Invisible threads were spinning out towards me and everyone I knew, I could feel them, holding me fast, blocking up the eyes and ears of friends. Had I saved Francis? I don't know. I wanted to break into a run, as if I hadn't been overtaken already – false versions of myself racing through the world now, fleeter footed than I could ever be. Nowhere felt safe. I drifted west, keeping clear of the clamour of the docks. The river rose to meet me at London Bridge, and I crossed it. My path should have been north, but I didn't want to return to my lodgings even if – as common sense told me – the master knew nothing of them yet. I carried on south and west. Perhaps some part of me did know where I was going. There was one friend the master didn't know about. At least, I prayed so. Annie wouldn't be told what to think anyway.

The first blood-thumping fright had left me by the time I reached Lambeth, and in its place came a weariness that dragged at my bones. Doubts came too when I finally found her street amongst the unending terraces, dredging her address from memory. She was married to a policeman. Andrew's division was far from Stepney, and the missus said the police hadn't been told of Mr Garston's injury, but when a washer-woman pointed me to number twelve, I lingered on the pavement as I had outside the Bowmans'. In the end, I was too tired to argue with myself and knocked. No one came. Somehow that was the last thing I expected, and I sat down on the step to lean against the doorjamb and close my eyes.

'Har!'

I started out of my doze like a gun had gone off. Even now I don't know how long I had been slumped there for every neighbour and passer-by to see. The woman in front of me was wearing a plain, shabby dress with a dirty shawl draped over her head. It was so unlike Annie, I could only stare at her, blinking, until she flung off the shawl and pulled me to my feet for a hug. We peered into each other's faces.

'Har, what are you doing here? Have you come to see me?'

I nodded. Why else would I be in Lambeth at her door? She rapped my forehead with a knuckle.

'Well, you're at the wrong house. We're number twenty-one.'

I looked groggily around at the door behind me.

'Are you back in London now?'

'I . . .'

I realised with a shock that I had a story for Helen Dubois, but nothing for Harriet Watkins. All I had decided was that Annie must know nothing of my plans with the missus.

'I'm . . . taking a short holiday – with a bit of sewing on the side – and then I'll go home.'

Her face lit up.

'To marry William?'

205

'Oh . . . no.'

I had brushed over that point in my letter.

'I broke it off.'

Her face became very intent, and then a wicked smile spread over it.

'Even better. Come on, let's go home and talk.'

I let myself be swept along, feeling the sweet comfort of a good friend's arm in mine. Annie was full of chatter about nothing very much. She wasn't really interested in why I had left Finton Hall, too busy watching passers-by on the street while pretending not to, like an expert pickpocket – or policeman, as I found out. In her parlour, she threw clothes and bits of sewing off a chair to make space for me and skipped off to make tea. I picked a postcard from the floor of Margate where she had said they honeymooned and placed it on the crammed and dusty mantelshelf.

Over tea, she told me she had been posing as a desperate unmarried mother hoping to send her baby out for adoption. Her clothes were a costume. The woman she had been visiting was suspected of taking in nurse children without being registered.

'Guilty as sin.'

She grinned and swirled her tea.

'She's expecting me back tomorrow morning with the baby and ten bloody quid. But she'll find a detective at her door instead.'

She hooted. I must have looked as confused as I felt.

'Andrew's friend, Robert – you met him, remember, the one who's sergeant now' – she winked – 'he's taken it on himself to rid the world of murderous baby farmers, the kind that promise to foster children or find new parents for them, but put an end to the poor things instead and pocket the money. It happens more often than you'd think. I *told* you in my letter.'

'But why are you . . .'

'Well, there aren't any police *women*, are there, more's the pity.'

She shook her head.

'So, it comes down to the wives of policemen to do their dirty work for them, like everything else. And it had to be me because Detective Sergeant Robert doesn't have a wife . . .'

She leaned forward with that wicked smile.

'Which is why I think it's a particular stroke of good fortune that you turn up today, *not* Mrs William.'

I fell back in my chair.

'Annie!'

'What? He liked you, remember? Why don't you come and . . .'

'No! That's not what I'm here for.'

She pulled a face.

'What *are* you here for? Where are you staying?'

'Just . . . a room.'

I clutched at a lie, an area I'd passed through on the way.

'In Aldgate.'

'Don't sound like much of a holiday.'

'It's not really.'

I was floundering. Annie frowned at me.

'Are you well, Har? You look tired and . . .'

I nodded quickly.

'Too much walking. I felt like seeing London again, that's all, and thought I'd look around for a new position. I'll go home in a bit when the needlework runs out.'

'Well, thanks for telling us you were coming. Your last letter had less to say than that chair you're sat in. Too grand for us since you were made lady's maid?'

I picked up a bit of buttered bread and threw it in her face. Annie always loved a fight – best way to distract her. She pressed her lips together and lifted the teapot as if she might chuck it. Laughter spilled from both of us.

'I'm here, aren't I?'

'Visit *properly* when I don't have washing to do. Sunday.'

'I will, but just you and Andrew.'

'Have it your way. You're a strange one, Harriet Watkins.'

I walked home even though I was tired and it had started to drizzle, glowing from spending a simple hour in a friend's company. It's taken some of the terror of Stepney off. I still shiver, thinking of what might have happened. The master's name is weighty enough for the constable to have held me until word could be sent to Gloucester Square. Then all would have been lost. As it is, he knows now I'm in London, that I haven't gone quietly away. I can feel the web all around me, finding me out.

Sunday, 12th May

Wild horses couldn't have kept me away from Annie this morning. Not after the last three days. I think I was already starting to sicken on Wednesday night. On Thursday, I woke with a head buzzing like a beehive, and a throat like I'd swallowed half the bees. Walking home in the rain must have done it. I got no work done and kept to my bed, relying on Betsy to fetch me broth. Three days with nothing to do but worry. By the time I could get myself out of bed, I needed a friend even more than on Wednesday. I had a powerful urge to spill everything out. The old Annie would have taken it to her grave, probably. But she's gone and married a bloody policeman.

'Christ, you're white as a sheet.'

She pulled me into the parlour and hollered to Andrew. I took in the room, clean and tidy for guests this time with dusted ornaments and a spread of food on a sideboard. She fussed about with shawls and blankets for me and then cutlery and napkins. At Mrs B's she had clattered around the kitchen and thrown dishes of food about like a clumsy, bad-tempered bear. It was lucky Mrs B's eyesight hadn't been good enough to notice the ironing.

'What are you grinning about?'

'You. And your starched doilies.'

She looked both cross and sheepish at the same time, which made me laugh out loud. Her face recovered itself, and she tapped my head with her fingers.

'You're still in there then. You looked like a hounded rabbit on Tuesday and one caught in a snare today.'

She offered me devilled eggs and searching looks.

'What did they do to you in Hertfordshire?'

I was ready with Harriet Watkins today.

'It was a bad place in the end. Mean.'

She nodded knowingly. I shrugged.

'And I have a fancy to see somewhere else. Scotland maybe, or France.'

'France? Harriet's going to France!'

She said it to Andrew, who walked in looking freshly scrubbed. Happy.

'Is she?'

Happy and uninterested. Marriage suits him as well as it does Annie. Being master in his own house has dulled the world outside for him.

We had a sort of picnic in front of the fire despite the warmer weather. It was the most comfortable I've been since before Finton Hall, except for Annie's questions. Every lie hurt. I watched them, secretly wondering at their unthinking confidence in the next day and what it would hold. As if it was more normal to live life on a knife's edge. They spoke of his work, visits to family, neighbours' gossip, and I had to push away thoughts of what might have been. Even more so when Andrew said something coy about extra mouths to feed and Annie looked at me with a soft expression and rubbed a hand over her middle. I put down my plate and pushed away blankets so I could get up and hug her – praying to God she hadn't seen the truth in my face. Her news shouldn't have come as a shock; it shouldn't have stabbed me in the heart so hard I felt sick.

We made a happy group from the outside, laughing about the hours in Mrs B's kitchen, chatting about the future. Annie kept looking at the clock, I noticed, and when I said I should get back, she launched into another story about Gloucester Square. It was twenty minutes before there was space enough in her flurry of words to plonk down my cup and saucer like a full stop. Someone knocked at the door.

She leapt up.

'I'll get that.'

I looked at Andrew. He knitted his brows and looked at his empty plate.

'Robert's here, Andy.'

Annie drew the sergeant into the room, avoiding my glare. I remembered him very well. Lively grey eyes that you don't notice at first because of the birthmark – a dull red island on his right cheek that draws the eye all around its bays and spits until you feel him looking at you. Andrew rose to shake his hand. They met as people do who see each other often but are always glad.

'You remember my friend, Harriet, don't you?'

Annie was shrill with treachery. Robert looked at me. I nodded quickly.

'Hello.'

No smile – he looks first and looks hard. He made me nervous when he visited Gloucester Square – I think because he's with the detective lot rather than an ordinary bobby like Andrew. He's got a proper schooling and a soft voice.

'Hello. I'm interrupting.'

'I was about to leave.'

Annie piped over us insisting on tea, and we both said we had to be going, which threw me into a panic about leaving at the same time. Robert said he just needed a moment with them. Andrew dragged a chair across.

'Have something to eat first. How's your housekeeper? Still laid up?'

Robert looked at the meat pie.

'She is.'

'Your housekeeper's ill?'

Annie sounded too concerned. Robert scratched his chin.

'She's broken her arm.'

'Oh! How are you managing? Do you need anything doing for you?'

Anyone would think it was both his arms broken.

'Harriet is the best seamstress in London.'

My back went cold.

'She does fine work for the gentry. Darns faster than I can snag my stockings and look at that detail.'

She reached out to touch the stitching on my collar. I flinched.

'Annie . . .'

'You said you were looking for more work while you're in London.'

We stared at each other. I hadn't.

'I do have trousers that need a few stitches. I need a new set of shirts, for that matter.'

Robert spoke into the silence. He gave the first hint of a smile.

'Settled!'

Annie clapped her hands together. I was forced to smile back. At least, my lips made a shape.

'Give him your address.'

Robert immediately took out a small book and pencil from his pocket. Snared rabbit was about right – I felt the wire tightening.

'I'll come for it. My landlady doesn't allow . . .'

Everyone waited for me to finish.

'She doesn't allow deliveries?'

His eyes were like lead shot.

'I'm . . . She gets annoyed with all the parcels. I pick up work myself now.'

I pushed my nails into my palms. Annie tutted.

'Strange woman. You should move. Come closer to us.'

She spoke cheerfully, but I'd made the room feel odd. Robert looked at me a moment longer, then wrote in his book and neatly tore out the page. He offered it to me.

'It's not far from here.'

'Not far?'

Annie threw her hands in the air.

'It's three steps around the corner; you might as well take it home with you now. You can wait five minutes for him to have a mouthful, can't you?'

So we sat down again. Robert brought out an envelope and handed it to Annie. He glanced at me.

'Everything's in there.'

She turned to place it on a dresser, winking at me as she did so. Another baby farmer appointment. Robert ate a plateful and the three of them spoke about the reorganising of the detective department. I listened and looked interested and heard nothing. The sergeant's eyes kept turning towards me, watchful. Then that was over, and it was time to leave. Annie hugged me and whispered a false 'sorry' in my ear.

Outside, Robert smiled with the clear half of his face, as if the other half wasn't interested, and gestured down the street.

'It's . . .'

We started walking, and I felt tiredness cloak me. The illness had been short, but I should have been in bed. I felt his attention on me and heard him take in a breath. More questions were unbearable.

'Is it usual for you to work on a Sunday?'

It came out so sharp, there was an awkward pause. I realised it sounded like a rebuke and felt a wild laugh bubbling up. To cover it, I put a hand over my mouth.

'Quite often, yes.'

I was grateful at least not to get a lecture about criminals not resting on the Lord's day. He was about to say something else, so I cut in again.

'You're a sergeant now?'

'Yes. Detective sergeant.'

Another awkward pause and then my too-late-remembered congratulations.

'You're the darling of Scotland Yard, Annie says.'

I sounded sarcastic, but he laughed.

'Annie should be running the place with her instincts. I wish I could use them both full time – Andrew is like a terrier when he's onto something.'

There was a silence.

'Annie told *me* you were lady's maid at your last place.'

Bloody Annie.

'Yes.'

'Mr Gethin's house, wasn't it?'

I looked straight ahead, unspeaking. He continued.

'I hope when the Liberals are back in, they put him in the cabinet. We could use more men like him.'

I couldn't have said anything to that if I'd tried. Robert waited a moment and then carried on.

'I keep an eye on politicians, you see. In the force we can bring criminals to justice and the rest, but it's the politicians who change the game. If the law doesn't adapt to what's happening down here' – he pointed at the pavement – 'we're just going to go on uncovering the same old crimes and not be able to do anything about it.'

He spoke with warmth, losing the watchfulness. Probably bored of trying to get anything out of this odd friend of Annie's. I made an effort.

'I hadn't thought of it like that. I thought the law was the law, and then there were people who broke it.'

'It's a dance between law and crime. My work should have been helped by an Act passed in seventy-two, but it doesn't come close to dealing with the problem. I have to prove the scale of it, the numbers of infants involved – I don't know if you've read about the bodies in the Thames – so the people at the top can't pretend any longer it isn't happening. That's half the trouble – people don't like to admit what's going on. They look the other way.'

'You should be an MP yourself.'

He laughed.

'I don't think they'd have me. I wouldn't want it anyway – I like it down here where I'm free to get my hands dirty. And be invisible if the work calls for it. I don't want to be well known.'

He tapped his birthmark.

'This already makes me stand out too much.'

'Invisible?'

'Sometimes. We have to fade into the background to see what's going on. Pretend to be something we're not to get at the truth. It's part of the job. But there's little point to it if the people in charge don't listen.'

'And you think Mr Gethin would listen?'

Robert lifted his hands briefly as if they were holding a tray of delights.

'He wasn't born into his position, he knows what it is to adapt, and he often speaks for reform – he's willing to look at what's in front of him. He's popular too – he spoke in favour of going to war, but he's willing to support outsider causes like the repeal of the Contagious Diseases Act. They say he personally involved himself in improving the safety of his miners. I hear he employs injured miners as well as abandoned children on his domestic staff?'

I thought of the flint mill and didn't trust myself to speak. It wasn't their safety that interested him, Detective Sergeant. My chest had tightened and that now familiar burn of anger threatened to break into flame. So, the master is a saint in the eyes of the world, not just the vicarage kitchen – he even champions women's causes. I thought of the missus with that choker around her neck. The world will not forgive her. Or me, lying to my friends and the police. For the first time, I welcomed it, the anger. I could feel it pushing aside the doubts and showing me where my path lay. It was stronger even than the fear. I nursed it in silence.

'Was it a good place – working for Mr Gethin?'

Poor Robert. What an awkward companion I made. He must have been wishing Annie had minded her own business as much as I did.

'He was hardly there. I didn't see him much.'

It would have been obvious to anyone, never mind a detective, that I was holding something back. I felt him look at me, that watchfulness again, but he left it alone. The rest of our talk was of shirts and patterns and material. I waited in the hallway of the building where he has his rooms, weathering the lingering stare of a passing neighbour – mutton chops and wet lips. I stared back with as much contempt as I could muster. He wasn't used to that and looked away. Robert turned up again with the items of mending and an old shirt to copy bundled up very neatly and tied with cord. He wanted to pay for a cab.

'I'd rather walk and take an omnibus. But thank you.'

His eyes were serious. I could see him looking for a way to insist, so with a nod, I headed for the door.

'Don't you mind it? Going about by yourself?'

His voice told me he didn't approve. I stopped at the door.

'I like it.'

I was going to say more, but then thought I don't have to explain myself to him or anyone else. Walking quickly down the street, I felt the cloak of tiredness lift a bit. Somehow, I'd avoided giving my address to a policeman (and Annie for that matter) and was getting a few bob off him too.

Wednesday, 15th May

A bundle of sewing arrived from the missus. I opened it with heart thumping. Her green silk gown, very fine, with a request for a balayeuse to be added to the train – the slip of paper pinned to it said 'not urgent'.

Wrapped up in it were lengths of cotton. 'Servant's dress – urgent'. The time must be getting close. Robert's shirts aren't finished yet though I've been busy with them since Monday – I went out and bought the fabric first thing that morning. I don't want to attract attention by disappearing with them not done. But the dress has to be ready in time. She even put in some plain handkerchiefs with instructions to embroider the initials of her new name in the corners. It seems a bit much, but perhaps she is right. Details could save us or be our undoing.

Friday, 17th May

I found a half sovereign in the pocket of Robert's trousers – I wonder if it is a test. Not left the house. All I do is cut and sew. I have barely slept. The stitches are like laying train tracks – all the time I feel a thundering engine bearing down on me and I can't get them in fast enough. The dress is done.

Sunday, 19th May

I finished Robert's sewing this morning and borrowed the iron to get everything as pristine as possible. A cab would have made the journey easier with keeping the shirts unrumpled, but I didn't dare spend the money. All I could think about was dropping them off at Annie's, having a cup of tea and coming back home to my bed. She greeted me as warmly as before and without a hint of shame – even when she ushered me into the parlour and there was Robert, sitting awkwardly on the edge of his chair in his shirt and waistcoat. He stood up and gave me that half smile. I dumped his clothes on the table with a lot less care than I had shown them on the jolting and crowded omnibuses. Annie was relentless.

'Try them on in the other room, Robert – see if they need any alterations while Harriet's here.'

I think he saw my face.

'I'm sure they're perfect.'

'Well, sit down, sit down, have some tea.'

The idea of turning around and trudging all the way back again without even resting my bones forced me into the nearest chair.

'Where's Andrew?'

'On his beat.'

She poured drinks and then said something about a piece of washing that she had to see to in the yard and disappeared. I don't know if she expected us to fall into each other's arms. After last week, I didn't believe Robert was there to court me. It put me on edge that he was there at all. His lead-shot eyes were aimed at me, but he didn't seem about to speak. I ran my eyes over the ornaments and postcards on the mantelshelf.

'What you said before – about law and crime being a dance.'

I glanced at him. He looked slightly startled.

'Yes?'

'What if a law *makes* people criminal, so they don't have a choice. If a law is wrong . . .'

'I didn't say laws are wrong. Only that they need to keep in step with what's going on for justice to be done.'

He eyed me.

'There will always be criminals who bend current laws to their advantage. They are still criminals.'

'What about . . .'

I don't know what I thought I was doing. Perhaps it was the long journey or having no one to talk to except myself all week but seeing him again seemed to take the lid off a pot I hadn't known was boiling. I should have been able to tell everything to this detective, offer up every damning detail that I had witnessed at Finton Hall and be heard. The missus should have seen the master hauled in front of a court of law. Instead, we were running like fugitives, while this policeman sipped tea and spoke of justice. I thought of the missus stealing her own child away, and Helene, raped and forced onto the street. The French maid had become a real presence for me after what happened in the library. Her handwriting was etched into my memory, all those words offering up the truth to the missus. I had become an echo of her, living alone in London with a clouded future as she had done before her baby came. The course of her life decided by the same men who had forced mine. I'd even taken a version of her name. But I couldn't speak – I couldn't say any of that to this grey-eyed man of the law.

'What if . . . what if someone can't afford to eat because they can't find work, and you saw them take a bit of bread without paying for it? I saw that only today coming down Gray's Inn Road on the omnibus – a man took a loaf from a baker's van. What if he had children to feed?'

Every nerve told me to stop my mouth, but it shot open again.

'Or the women who have to give up their babies to these baby farmers you're going after. What choice do they have if they can't get work with a bastard child in tow?'

He was still looking startled.

'It's not our job to arrest innocent mothers.'

'They are still being punished though, aren't they? No one thinks they are innocent really. There's no law good enough to protect them or their children – you said so yourself.'

'Not . . .' His eyebrows went higher. 'At least . . . there are several more societies now that help women and girls . . . I know Mr Gethin is a patron of—'

I made a sound like a cow in labour. He stopped and looked at me intently. I noticed the grey of his eyes could be stony or, as it was then, deep and dark as velvet.

'Do you know someone who needs help?'

Detective Devious. I ignored the question.

'Don't you ever feel guilty about sneaking around and spying on people?'

'No. Not when a common good comes out of it. It's never without good reason.'

He was so ready with his answer, I thought he must have been asked the same thing many times before.

'It's just a matter of paying attention.'

'Pretending to be something you're not is more than paying attention.'

'We have to be able to *see*, so we can give evidence.' He sounded impatient for the first time. 'Most people make terrible eye-witnesses – they don't remember or understand what they've seen. Their account can easily be taken apart in the witness box by a good lawyer. It's difficult enough for a trained policeman to sound credible.'

He paused and then continued, as if it was part of the same thought, 'Annie's worried about you.'

I gave him what must have been a sullen look. 'It's time I went home.'

He stood up at the same time.

'I'm not your enemy, Harriet.'

'Who said you was?'

'You're angry at the police.'

'No.'

'You think because we have a job to do, we can't see the difference between a hardened criminal and someone swiping scraps to feed their family.'

'I don't know anything about it. Say goodbye to Annie for me.'

I was almost at the door when I remembered. It slapped me in the face and spun me on my heel.

'Your bloody half sovereign.'

I glared at him.

'You did that on purpose, didn't you? To see if I'd take it?'

'What?'

'It's on my windowsill. I'll send it here.'

He ran after me – went every bit as far as overtaking me on the street. I tried to walk around him, but he stood in the way.

'I promise you I didn't plant it.'

I looked up and was amazed to see laughter jumping around his face. His birthmark crinkled at the edges near his mouth.

'It was a mistake. I had forgotten about it too. I'm always losing my own things.'

He lifted his hands in the same manner as he had the week before and shrugged.

'I'm a detective sergeant who struggles to find his own socks sometimes. It's embarrassing.'

The charm was unsettling. I looked at him as at a magpie that had suddenly burst into song.

'Believe me, I have enough to do without laying traps for Annie's friends. But listen, I'll be near Aldgate on Friday.'

I immediately shook my head, but he raised a hand.

'I won't bother your landlady. Why don't you meet me at the Fenchurch Street tearooms and give it back to me there? Or even better, use it to buy us both a slice of cake?'

He smiled. Both sides of his face. I stared at him 'til I realised my mouth was hanging open – to think Annie might have been right after all. I agreed to meet him to give him his money back. After that I'll keep away from Lambeth and write to Annie that I've gone home – I'll be in Italy before she learns otherwise. It pulls at my heart something dreadful to lie.

Wednesday, 22nd May

The missus has sent me the choker, wrapped up in a short cape to go with the green dress. I hadn't seen it so close up before. The pendant is heavy and sparkles – with ill wishes, I fancy. She sent no instructions. It seems a strange thing to want to keep. I didn't want to look at it and sewed it into my own petticoat.

I have written to Mother to say I am going abroad with a new family and will write again from France (in case she writes to tell the master). It is in the other direction from Italy, I believe. I didn't put my London address, of course, and said nothing about leaving Finton Hall. Harriet Watkins is being swept away. Soon she will be less real than Helen Dubois.

Friday, 24th May

I made sure I was early, so Robert wouldn't see the direction I came from. The tearooms looked intimidating – dark and thronging inside. I waited outside for more than half an hour, watching the traffic and passers-by and feeling the heat pricking under my arms. There was a thin, yellow haze over the city today – the sun and clouds seemed caught in it, their edges fuzzed as if they were being eaten away. People look at you more if you're standing still. I felt a sitting duck for stares – from men mostly. They took aim, so to speak, and then lowered their eyes like gun barrels. Not worth the shot. A young man rushing by in a butcher's apron winked at me. I started walking up and down, trying to be invisible – I envy Robert that – pretending interest in a tobacconist's window. That was where he found me.

'Do you smoke?'

He was wearing a blindingly white necktie and looked fresh from the barbers.

'I tried a pipe once. It was like breathing in dirty wool.'

William had chased me about the paddock with it, trying to put it in my mouth. Robert nodded.

'I agree. I prefer cigarettes.'

We stood in silence a moment, which felt more awkward than usual in the midst of the street's bustle. Then I remembered what we were there for.

'Here.'

I'd wrapped the money in a spare piece of material from his shirts. He took it and rubbed it between his fingers as if it might magic a genie.

'Thank you. You'll let me buy you some tea by way of an apology for Sunday?'

'An apology?'

'I was ill mannered. Bad policeman's habit of asking too many questions.'

I looked at him and realised that I wanted to. A few moments of cake and his company. It seemed easier to say yes. I added that I couldn't stay long. The air was close and sticky in the tearoom. Robert bought us tea and slices of sponge cake, and we sat at a table near a window, although the daylight seemed reluctant to venture in even that far.

'I'm sorry it's not a prettier place. I don't know this part of the city very well.'

'I don't mind it.'

'You must be familiar with the area, staying here?'

I felt the air pressing even closer.

'Not very. A little.'

I was looking out of the window but turned before he could ask anything further.

'Why are you here?'

To my surprise, he answered frankly.

'There's a network of baby farmers in Lambeth passing children between them and I think there's a woman near London Bridge involved too. An inspector here is helping.'

'What do they do to the children?'

'It varies. Some are neglected. Some are deliberately harmed.'

'You mean murdered?'

His eyes turned stony. He didn't like the question.

'It's not a pleasant subject . . .'

'I don't mind. I'd rather know what's going on than walk around with my eyes shut.'

222

He studied me for a few seconds.

'Yes. Another body was found this end of the river. I believe far more infants are being murdered than anyone is willing to admit. The worst offenders move often and change their names, but I think I'm getting close to one.'

An uneasy feeling billowed in my stomach. Changing names and moving around was what criminals did, murderers. Robert was no longer looking at me though, caught up in his own thoughts.

'What . . . astonishes me, is how convincing they are as loving and affectionate mothers. Not just to the women wanting to adopt out their babies, but to people in their own household. I interviewed a seven-year-old girl last year who loved her foster mother as dearly as you could wish – she *felt* loved. The same woman had let at least two babies starve to death in the same room.'

'Why had the girl survived?'

'Probably as a front to make the nurse look legitimate. If a child's death comes to light, it seems less suspicious when there are healthy, surviving children.'

I thought painfully of Francis. The master must mean to keep him as a front, overwhelming him with kindness, like the missus said, before trapping him as he had Laurence. A fierce gladness seized my heart that we would be raising Edward far from Finton Hall. I shook my head.

'Clever.'

'Sorry?'

'To make yourself look respectable – likable even – and no one will be able to believe . . . No, worse than that – no one will *want* to believe what you're capable of.'

I looked at him properly for the first time, seeing him for himself rather than worrying about how he was seeing me.

'As a detective, you must have to be suspicious of everyone you meet. Even if you like them.'

'Well . . .'

He gave a laugh. 'When investigating.'

'In a way, you must have to be as callous as the criminals.'

The startled look came back.

'We have to look at every possibility.'

He stared at me a moment and then leaned forward slightly.

'I shouldn't have said anything. Most people are as good as they seem. They aren't hiding terrible secrets.'

'How do you know?'

His eyes seemed to flicker between stone and velvet. I think he was both annoyed and curious. For my part, I was enraged again. I don't know if it was him, or the thought of the master still, believed by all to be a saint. The slightest touch and fury boils up as quick as silt kicked up from a riverbed. I took a breath and looked out of the window again. The stuffy air and sweetness of the cake were making me feel sick. I glanced at him.

'Sorry.'

He shook his head.

'It's a miserable subject. Perhaps we should think of better examples. Are your mother and father . . .?'

I hooted a laugh before he could finish his question and spoke without thinking.

'My mother would gladly drown me in a washtub.'

He didn't smile, which I don't blame him for.

'Why?'

'Because I didn't go home and marry a person.'

His eyes turned to slate, and I looked down, suddenly self-conscious. When he spoke, he chose a light-hearted tone.

'I think my mother wishes she had left me on the steps of a church.'

I looked sideways at him. He pointed to his cheek.

'She never reconciled herself to this. She thinks the stain goes right through. My untainted brother gets all her affection.'

He was smiling, but still, I wasn't sure what to say.

'We haven't come up with very good examples.'

'True.'

He laughed. 'At least we know Annie will be an excellent mother.'

I thought about it. Yes. Fierce and demanding, probably, but she will cloak them in love.

'Was she angry that I left so sudden on Sunday?'

He raised his eyebrows.

'No. She was . . . concerned.'

I lifted my own eyebrows in return. A smile flickered around his eyes, and we laughed at the same time.

'I expect she blamed you.'

'I expect I deserved it.'

We held each other's gaze. His eyes had turned a lighter grey, and he was looking at me with all the interest the master had – only, as if I was a person rather than a curiosity to be trapped in a box. In spite of myself, I didn't want to look away. It was only a moment, but in it I imagined what it might be like to see him differently, not as a stranger but as a man I had something to do with. I remembered how Mary had kissed Laurence, the way she had embraced him, and felt my face grow warm.

Robert's hands were resting on the table, the fingers loosely interlaced. They were like a gentleman's hands – like the master's – smooth and unblemished. Aware I was staring, I looked down at mine and saw the thickened skin, the trace of ingrained black down the side of one thumbnail. They called me back to myself like a slap. I saw what should have been obvious from the first. Detective Sergeant Robert Ansell is ten years older than me, educated, ambitious. Meeting him at Annie's had cheated the distance between us. The interest he was showing in me, an unemployed maid, wasn't natural.

'She thinks a lot of you.'

I put my hands under the table.

'We got close at our old place. It was just the two of us and the mistress had some funny ways – but it was a good time.'

225

'Not like at Finton Hall.'

He knew the name of Mr Gethin's house. I ran my hands over my skirt. They were clammy.

'Annie said you called it a mean place to work.'

I tried to keep my voice light.

'Yes, but also I want to see somewhere new.'

'I'm curious. It's strange that a man who looks after his workers so well would be master of an unhappy house.'

I didn't respond.

'But you said he was seldom there. Was it Mrs Gethin? I saw her once last year in the gallery when he was speaking in the Commons. She—'

'He killed the canary.'

'I'm sorry?'

'Snapped its neck in front of us.'

There was a pause.

'Ralph Gethin . . .?'

'Thank you for the tea. I should go.'

I stood up. The room was still filled with people, all with their backs to me. I pushed between them, knocking a shoulder and then an elbow that sent something smashing to the floor. On the street, I walked quickly, glad of the crowd to weave through, skirting shoeblacks and barrow boys before pausing at a corner to look back. I caught a glimpse of him outside the tearooms, a stranger again, looking in the other direction, and hurried down the side street.

Winding a way back to the main road, I jumped on the first omnibus going west. At Charing Cross I changed again. I don't know what had made me blurt out about the canary, as if that was the worst of it. Perhaps because it's the one nasty thing I've seen the master do with his own hands. A lady opposite kept looking at me in a concerned way which made me want to cry. I kept my head down until it was time to get off again and walked as fast as I could back to my lodgings.

Betsy was in the hall when I got in. It was unusual to see her standing still – almost as if she'd been waiting for me.

'Evening, miss. Another parcel for you.'

She held out a package that was wrapped as the missus' sewing always was.

'Thank you, Betsy.'

She nodded and didn't move. At the bottom of the stairs, I looked back. She dropped her eyes and ducked away down the kitchen stairs.

In my room, I threw the parcel on the bed and myself beside it and waited for the tears that had been bubbling the whole way back – opened the door to them. But in their place a weary impatience loomed. It made me sit up again, hunch-shouldered and dry-eyed, staring at the floor. I have sentenced myself to this. There is no comfort to be had in crying. I turned my eyes to the parcel. It was lighter than the others. I drew it to me and held it in my lap a moment before tearing it open. A red petticoat. I held it up and a large key dropped to the floor. The slip of paper gave a street address near the law courts, of all places, and today's date. Then 'TONIGHT' in capitals, as if the date wasn't enough. My heart seemed to grow louder with every beat like approaching footsteps. There was a bang on the door, twice.

I leapt up and tried to think two hundred things at once. Ripping the paper from the pin, I threw the petticoat under the bed and tore the note across twice, throwing the bits in the fireplace. I snatched the key from the floor and slipped it into my pocket. The rapping came again.

'Miss Doobah . . .'

Mrs Cole.

I set my face and opened the door to her. She had prepared a face of her own – righteousness rubbed with vinegar.

'I have told you I don't allow gentlemen callers.'

'I know, Mrs Cole. I haven't had any.'

Her eyebrows drew themselves up. I imagined twin archers readying to loose their arrows.

'Then why was there one here this morning? I turned a blind eye last time, but I will tolerate it no further.'

'I'm sorry?'

'I made the rules very clear when you arrived.'

The word 'TONIGHT' was still banging against my chest. I concentrated hard on a blemish on Mrs Cole's forehead.

'Someone called for me?'

It sank in.

'For Helen?'

'And not for the first time, as I said. Betsy even let him in.'

We stared at each other. I began closing the door.

'I've very sorry, Mrs Cole, it won't happen again.'

'Mind that it doesn't. I won't have my house talked about . . .'

The rest of her words were shut out, although they continued a while. I kept my hand on the doorknob until she retreated down the passage. Turning, I took two steps towards my box, then halted and went for the carpet bag on the chair instead. I stopped short of that too and finally headed back to the door and hurried downstairs to the kitchen. Betsy was on her own, preparing a chop for someone's dinner. She started when she saw me.

'Mrs Cole says a man called for me today, Betsy?'

She dropped the chop into a pan on the range. It sizzled fiercely and spat fat. Some must have hit her arm because she jumped again and rubbed it.

'Betsy?'

'That's right, miss.'

'Why didn't you say when I came in?'

'I forgot, miss, sorry.'

I watched her for a moment.

'What was his name?'

'Oh, he didn't say, miss.'

She looked relieved – no doubt a question she could answer honestly.

'Well, what did he want then?'

'He didn't say, miss.'

She turned to the pan, putting her back to me. I marched around the table and pushed the chop to the side, so it wouldn't burn. Betsy backed off, wild eyes and fidgety fingers. I tried to sound kind. I tried not to knock off her cap and drag her by the hair into the yard.

'Betsy, Mrs Cole says she's seen him before and that you let him in.'

The grimace came back, except this time it creased up her whole face. It stayed fixed that way, turned up to mine like a child's before a flood of tears. I put my hands out to her.

'Betsy, you have to tell me.'

I had to reach down to take her arms that were hanging by her sides. They were solid muscle from all the work. Finally, her face quivered into tears. She took a breath.

'I'm sorry, miss, please don't tell them, please don't.'

I pulled her over to a chair and sat down next to her, holding her hands.

'Tell who?'

'The police.'

She whispered it. Something horrible ran up my spine. By degrees, I got it out of her, though it wasn't easy making sense of her words through the sobbing.

'There was a man, miss. He said he was your friend and there was a letter coming for you, but that you mustn't see it. For your own good. He seemed ever so kind, miss.'

'A letter, Betsy?'

She nodded miserably.

'I was to put a dried posy in the window when it came, so he'd know.'

'And then?'

'And then . . .'

Her voice rose to a distressed squeak.

'And then when he called, I was to put the letter on the hall table and pretend to see if you was home, and that way, it would be his fault for taking it and not mine for giving it him, and I couldn't get in trouble with the police that way, he said.'

She turned terrified eyes on me.

'He said he was your friend and it was for your own good and he had to do it.'

Her nose was running. I asked if he had offered her money, and she burst out crying afresh. I didn't trouble asking again. There was a cloth draped over a cupboard door. I reached for it, offering her the cleanest corner. She blew her nose and looked at me pleadingly, her eyes still welling over.

'I wasn't going to do it though, miss, I swear. The letter came on Wednesday and I told myself I wouldn't, but then I thought, what if he's right and I'd be doing you wrong by not doing what he said, and then I saw him coming past to look every day, and I'd already said I would so I knew I'd be in trouble with *him*, and I put the posy out last night.'

It was difficult to stop her once she'd started. I took hold of her hands again.

'What did he look like, Betsy?'

Her eyes went wide as if the question was unanswerable.

'How tall was he?'

She raised her gaze and looked uncertainly at the top shelf above the sideboard. About seven feet up.

'He couldn't have been that tall, Betsy.'

'Well, he was taller than me.'

I remembered Robert's words about most people not knowing how to look, his frustration with witnesses.

'There must be something you can tell me. Young, old? Fair, dark?'

'Oh, fair, miss.'

She jumped on the word and moved her hand in front of her face, eyes even wider.

'Very fair. His eyelashes, miss . . .'

My heart clutched itself. She swallowed and looked to the side, suddenly breathless.

'And ever so good looking, miss.'

Laurence.

Betsy's memory was almost squeezed dry. The letter was thin and light; she was sure it was addressed to Helen Dubois; no, she hadn't noticed the postmark. When I was sure there would be nothing more, I stood up.

'I'm not in trouble, am I? You won't tell them?'

'No, Betsy.'

I stopped at the door.

'Don't you tell anyone either.'

Running back upstairs, I felt as if an invisible claw was dragging me to the edge of a cliff. Laurence must have found out the missus was writing to me, and the master or Barrett had sent him to steal the letters – he had said himself he did everything they told him to. What had she written? The master's web had finally reached my door.

The money I had hidden in the mattress went half into the purse tied to my petticoat and half into my small bag along with the flint mill, some powdered milk I had bought for Edward, and smaller items. I bundled up my black dress and the pieces I had sewn for the missus in the carpet bag. Much more, and I wouldn't be able to carry Edward as well. This diary stayed safe in my pocket. Everything else was abandoned as it had fallen, box open, stockings over the back of the chair. There wasn't time to make up a story for Mrs Cole.

I ran for it, leaning an elbow on the banister and sliding down to the hall. I was through the front door and onto the pavement in a heartbeat, walking quickly with my head down until I was on a main thoroughfare. It was a good half hour to the address the missus had sent. I hurried along, watchful as a bird hopping towards her nest. The river was out of sight, but I thought I could smell it as I got nearer, a shift in the air. Serle Place is close to the Inns of Court. I felt as if I was walking into the lion's den. Each time I asked the way, people seemed to look at me too curiously.

Eventually, I found it – a short passage with a dead end. It looked as if it should have gone on for longer but the buildings on the other side had all rushed forward and got wedged. I paused, staring for long moments down both ends of the cramped street. The houses and shop fronts looked shut up. There were few people about, but they all looked as if they belonged there. I don't think I was followed. With the last of the light, I slipped into the passage and found the right door. The key turned reluctantly. It felt as if the whole place had been abandoned years ago.

The first room was an empty shopfront or office with a dusty counter and a chair on its side. I stood still, trying to hear past the thud of blood in my ears. Nothing stirred. Locking the door behind me, I waited for my eyes to adjust to the gloom. I hadn't thought to bring a light. At the back behind the counter was another door, just visible. I groped my way towards it, frightening myself with every scuff of my shoes on the bare boards. The room behind was even darker and smelt musty. If I hadn't turned the key to the place myself, I would have sworn it was all wrong. This wasn't what I had pictured for the missus.

Eyes don't put any faith in darkness; if there's nothing to see, they paint things in – other eyes staring back, hands reaching out. A rising army of murderers and ghouls threatened to rob me of my will and send me back out into the street, so I lunged forward and smacked my knee against a table leg. It shunted the furniture inches across the floor and set something on top rocking to and fro. I dropped what I was carrying and caught the lamp before it toppled. Pain unleashes anger, which, I now know, burns away fear. I swore like one of the stable lads, and the shadows shrank back into emptiness. More groping about revealed matches.

I shut the door to hide the light and inspected the room. There's a jug of water and remains of a meal on the table – a hunk of bread and greasy bones. As well as the table, there is a chair and a pallet bed, a few bits of old plate and a chamber pot. Blankets heaped on the bed look much cleaner than the mattress. Everything else is coated in thick dust, sooty rags in the fireplace. There is a door and window onto blackness – a yard, maybe. I hung the servant's dress I made for the missus against the dirty glass. It feels more like an end place than a beginning. I have thought so much of the red petticoat, of getting here, what comes next seems unreal, a thing of mist and mystery. Even now it is beyond belief – impossible that the missus will ever come, despite the petticoat and the key and the slip of paper.

My fingers ache from writing. There is nothing to do now but wait. I have to push Laurence from my mind or the fear threatens to over-whelm me. She will come. She will succeed. Only my heart keeps jumping suddenly in my chest, as if it has private thoughts of its own and knows better.

Saturday, 25th May

Dear God, she is gone. She was right here. Edward was right here – I held him in my arms. But they are gone. I think we have been found out – what else? She would not leave without me. I have been waiting here more than an hour in the feeble light that reaches the window, unable to sit or stand for more than a minute. I cannot think. I cannot think what to do.

I fell asleep sometime in the night, and the banging on the door terrified me out of my dreams. My fingers were still curled around the key, and I was up from the pallet and into the front room before my eyes had fully opened. She pushed into the room as soon as I started to open the door and told me to close it quickly. Her face was a white blur in the dark; a black cloak and bonnet did away with the rest of her. I was so relieved she was here but found I didn't know what to say, how to address her – our relations have been thrown clear of the bounds that shaped them.

'Come into the back. Ma'am.'

I had turned the lamp down low to save oil. Once the door was shut and I brightened the light, we could look at each other. She was holding a Gladstone bag and soft leather satchel in one hand. Her other arm clutched a large bundle under the cloak. She took in the room as if she wasn't sure what it had to do with her.

'Let me, ma'am.'

I held out my hands. For a moment she looked at a loss but then dropped the bags and pushed back the cloak. Edward was wrapped up in a blanket, fast asleep, and clutching his favourite cloth with the embroidered rabbits. It was strange to see her holding him again. The picture of a mother – the circling, protective arm, the face turned to his. That tilt of the head is reserved only for babies, a special gesture of devotion. Her expression, though, was blank. She shifted to pass him over to me, and when I folded his warm and weighty little life into my arms, my heart felt like it was swallowing him up. All the fear and doubt fell away. This was right. This was why. We were making him safe.

The missus sat down on a chair. Neither of us spoke except for my soft cluckings to Edward. He didn't stir at all. I lowered us down onto the pallet and looked at the missus.

'Are you well, ma'am? Did you get away safely?'

She turned her head towards me and nodded faintly without meeting my eyes. It began to dawn on me that there was no mistress here. Both of us were now far out of our depth. I wanted to tell her about Laurence and the letter but was scared of pushing her deeper into the black wells. After a moment, she cleared her throat and something like animation came back into her face.

'We were given so little time. I gave Esther the night free and tomorrow morning, but I will still be missed . . .'

'The new nursemaid?'

'One day more and I could have kept us safe for the morning.'

'But how are we travelling, ma'am? If we leave early, we'll still be away before—'

'No.'

She shook her head and moved over to sit next to me on the pallet. Her tongue moved over her bottom lip.

'Trust me, Harriet. It's better this way – I can't tell you everything.'

I remembered how I hadn't understood her dismissal of Lily. She couldn't tell me then either. But I had said the same thing to Francis, and now I may never know if he is safe, if his father chose to believe me.

'You don't have to protect me.'

'Yes, I do.'

'I would rather know . . .'

She took hold of my arm and locked her eyes on mine.

'It's not only you I'm trying to protect. If we're caught . . .'

We searched each other's faces. I didn't dare tell her I had gone to the Bowmans'.

'It's safer if you simply don't know. I have said too much already.'

I didn't speak, and eventually she lowered her eyes, drew away. Her words were almost too soft to hear.

'I know I am asking for more than I may be forgiven.'

She placed a hand on the blanket I had laid over the awful mattress.

'We should try and rest.'

It would have been strange enough lying down next to the missus on a normal day in a normal bed. I was conscious of breathing, of every movement, of the rank smell of the mattress that must have invaded her senses too. It was, at least, warm. She had shown no sign of disgust as we arranged a bedding of blankets and her cloak. Settling down as comfortably as if she was in her four-poster, she drew her hair over her shoulder and plaited it herself. Her matter-of-factness reassured me. I asked if I could know what place this was, and she almost smiled.

'Lady Berrington owned the building. I inherited her property although naturally my husband controls it.'

She didn't even take the trouble to sound bitter.

'But she sent all the keys directly to me with some money in cash. I thought it was out of the weakness and confusion of her mind. Now, I wonder.'

'Won't . . . he look here?'

'I think not. I handed the keys to him. I thought he might find out about the money otherwise. But I kept this one. All the buildings in this passage are to be destroyed to make way for a new street.'

I looked at her in alarm.

'When?'

'Not tonight.'

She sounded amused.

'We'll be gone before he or the barrels of gunpowder arrive.'

She lay down on her back. I thought she was going to sleep, but before I could dim the lamp she spoke again.

'I wasn't kind to Lady Berrington.'

I had thought as much but couldn't say so.

'She spoke very fondly of you, ma'am.'

There was a silence. I'm not sure she believed me.

'I thought she was against my marriage because she wanted to keep me trapped in Gloucester Square with her. But perhaps it was more than that. She can't have known what Ralph is, but she didn't like him.'

I remembered the marmalade smeared on Lord Berrington's portrait.

'I don't think her own marriage was happy, ma'am.'

There was a pause as she thought about it.

'Marriage devours women. It gnaws and gnaws until there are only a few scattered pieces left.'

I had a vision of Mrs B in fragments – her hard jewels, the failing body parts, a need for gossip. All the indigestible bits. I felt a bleakness descend on me and wondered what would have survived of me with William. The missus continued.

'She was a good friend to me. And wiser than I ever gave her credit for. I was too proud to see it.'

She shifted on the mattress.

'You have been a friend to me too, Harriet. Not many servants would pity their mistress or notice how little freedom most ladies have.'

I realised she was talking about reading my diary.

'I watched you cleaning the chiffonier once. You were absorbed in the work. I felt envious of that.'

It almost sprang from my lips that some help with the furniture would have been welcome, especially that chiffonier with its intricate carvings and fussy gilt mounts. I thought what Clockface would have made of it – her mistress with her sleeves rolled up and dirty wax under her fingernails. But the missus wasn't really after the life of a housemaid. She spoke again as if she'd heard my thoughts.

'I don't mean the – what did you call it? – the drudgery of it, only the satisfaction you found in your work. I have so wanted to walk out in the world with my own banner to unfurl. To risk standing before people on my own terms – to sing, freely, as I sang in the vicarage. In that way, I have always believed I might do some small good with this life. I envied you your freedom to leave if you wished, to find another place to . . .'

She paused, searching.

'. . . to be the high priestess of the objects in your care.'

I felt my cheeks flush, hearing my own words repeated back to me, and started fussing with the blanket.

'You will be the high priestess of the theatre, ma'am.'

She was watching me.

'I understand why you chose not to marry William, Harriet. It was brave all the same. I think we have both been governed by a desire for more, to live our lives for ourselves.'

I looked at Edward lying on the mattress between us and thought to myself, not entirely – I do not wish to live entirely for myself.

He was sleeping on so soundly I put my lips to his head, worried about fever.

'His breathing is very short, ma'am.'

She looked away.

'He's just sleeping.'

He wasn't. When I woke from a fitful half-slumber a few hours later, he still hadn't moved. In my dreams, the building was being pulled down on top of us and I was smothered by dust and falling masonry. I found the corner of the blanket had rucked up and my face was pressed to the foul mattress. Wiping my mouth, I sat up. A very dim light was coming from the shrouded window. The missus was lying straight and flat on her back, staring at the ceiling – like a corpse laid out, came the unwelcome thought. Edward was very still between us. With sudden terrible misgivings, I leaned down to his face. He was warm, his breathing shallow. I scooped him up.

'There's something wrong with him, ma'am.'

The missus slowly raised herself into a sitting position.

'He's perfectly all right.'

I jogged him gently, but he was floppy in my arms.

'I can't wake him.'

'Then don't.'

Her manner was cold again. She drew her knees up and leaned her forehead against them. I scrambled to my feet, still holding him, and tried to open the door at the back. After a few shoves with my shoulder, it scraped open onto a tiny yard. The daylight was a shock.

'What are you doing?'

'Giving him some air.'

'Come inside now.'

She was there, pulling me back in and heaving the door shut as she spoke.

'There's nothing wrong with him. He's sleeping it off.'

'Sleeping what off?'

She had walked away again, unplaiting her hair.

'What did you give him, ma'am?'

'You must stop calling me ma'am.'

She snapped it.

'It's called Mother's Friend. Is that the dress against the window?'

'You gave him *laudanum*?'

I stared at her through the gloom. It was even darker since my eyes had been flashed with daylight.

'How much, ma'am?'

She turned suddenly.

'Stop questioning me. And stop calling me ma'am.'

Giving laudanum to a baby. I've heard of mothers accidentally quieting their babies forever with the likes of Mother's Friend. She took down the dress and shook it out.

'I couldn't risk him crying and alerting the servants.'

She hung the dress I'd sewn over the chair and seemed to be looking about her. I was too alarmed to answer. Laying Edward back down on the bed, I made sure there was nothing too tight around his throat and chest, and pushed the door open again.

'You need light.'

She didn't protest this time but found the chamber pot and pushed it with her toe into a space. I put my boots on and went out into the yard. There is a ruined privy in the corner, and I relieved myself there as best I could amongst broken boards, sticking-out nails, and spiders' webs. It's odd to think that as a servant I've seen my employers in their most personal moments but pissing in front of the missus myself would feel shocking. It's true, I must stop calling her ma'am.

The dress fitted her well. I went to help her with her hair, but she shrugged me off.

'Do as you would if I were another maid.'

With her bonnet on, she looked like a domestic servant in Sunday clothes – except for her face and hands. I worry she will stand out more as such a refined-looking maid than she would as a lady. It looked like dressing up. Laurence's face with the lace and rouge rose unbidden in my mind.

She was irritable and withdrawn and sent me out shortly after for water and bread for the journey. I wonder if it was to be rid of me. For all she said in the night, it seemed hard to be left in the dark about what so nearly concerns me. I studied Edward again before I left and gave him a kiss.

Walking abroad, I felt certain every passer-by must know my guilt by my face. Every glance seemed suspicious. My hands and voice shook as I handed over money for bread and asked for the jug to be filled. I also bought a pie, thinking we could mash some up for Edward since it seems unlikely the missus has brought anything with her, and a bottle of beer. Turning from the bar in the public house, I caught a movement too quick amongst the slow stares and pressing bodies of early drinkers and market workers already halfway through their day. When I turned a corner, I fancied I caught it again – a ducking away out of sight. I stopped so suddenly, thinking it might be Laurence, a woman with a great basket on her shoulders ran into the back of me, making me drop the beer. She scolded at the top of her voice, and I hurried away, too frightened even to try and save the bottle, which had rolled into the gutter. When I arrived back at the passage, I had a sense that I had been gone too long. The street door was unlocked. My eyes searched the gloom and scanned the yard; everywhere was as quiet as the grave.

I will wait until dark, and then I will go and hide myself outside the master's house. There must be a way of discovering if they were found out and returned there. What he would do to her! I don't know if I am safe here or not.

Later

The front door opened. I heard its scrape and rattle, and all my fretting and scheming fell away in a rush of relief. She had returned.

They were safe. I jumped up and hurried through to greet them. Already, I could feel the words of outrage billowing up like storm clouds. They began spilling out of my mouth in a wail, and then died utterly. The only person in the front room was Laurence.

There was a moment neither of us moved, and then I opened my mouth to scream. I couldn't have stopped myself if I'd tried. Next thing, he was on me with his hand over my mouth – his ring dug into my jaw – and pushing me through to the back room. Every part of me that Mr Garston had touched felt him again. I was stricken somehow, unable to move. It was as if I was both in my body and outside it at the same time, watching. Laurence was telling me to shut my mouth. He let go when he saw I wasn't struggling and started saying something else. The jug of water was on the table. With both my insides and out in sudden harmony, I picked it up and threw it at his head. He ducked, and it clonked the wall before falling and breaking in a splosh of pottery. I went at him, raking and snarling, but he was both stronger than Mr Garston and sober. He bound me with an iron hug. I'd have used my teeth again except I finally heard what he was saying.

'I'm here to take you to her, you mad bitch.'

I stared into his face.

'She's waiting in the cab for you.'

He stared back.

'Do you understand?'

I didn't. He let me go anyway, swearing under his breath, and bent down for his cap that had been knocked off.

'What are we taking?'

I watched him pick up the Gladstone bag and, looking around, realised my carpet bag was missing. Alarm hammered in my chest. I snatched up my small bag, which still had my money and the rest in it, and then stumbled across to the satchel. My black dress that had been in the carpet bag was inside on top of her things.

'Bring that blanket. And the food.'

I stared at him and then at the things he had pointed out. He waited, his own arms full.

'Or be hungry and cold, it's up to you.'

Shaking, I wrapped up the food and fetched the blanket, then followed him out into the passage and the street. He whistled cheerfully. There was a cab, waiting by the kerb, and when he opened the door, there was the missus. I wanted to sit down and cry.

'Up you go.'

He got in with us, sitting opposite, and we rolled off. I looked at the missus for an explanation, but her face was mostly hidden by the bonnet. Her hands lay loosely in her lap, not neatly brought together like a lady's. They seemed abandoned somehow. Empty. I jerked as if someone had pinched me and foolishly looked about the cab, as if the baby might have been stuffed under a seat.

'Where is he? Where's Edward?'

The missus turned. She looked awful, pinched and grey. Her eyes seemed to have retreated into her head.

'He's safe.'

'Safe? What do you mean?'

'Don't make a fuss. It's better . . .'

'No!'

I looked between them as if I'd woken up to find myself amongst thieves and murderers.

'You can't leave him.'

'I have no choice.'

Speaking seemed an effort, as if she was reading something out while her mind was elsewhere.

'Use your wits, Harriet. It is too dangerous. Ralph will know we have fled by now, and he will do anything to find his son. The police will be looking for a woman with a baby. Every station, every port – there won't be a mother or nurse left unmolested. There is a much greater chance of escaping notice without him. We are already late – they will be looking now.'

I was shaking my head, sudden tears making everything lose shape and swim into chaos.

'You can't.'

She tried to take hold of my hands, but I pulled away.

'I won't go without him.'

'Listen to me.'

'No.'

'Laurence will write . . .'

I gave a mad sort of laugh.

'You think your child is safe with him?'

'He will keep watch on where he is, that's all . . .'

'He stole a letter.' I pointed at him, almost shrieking. 'He bribed the maid at my boarding house and took a letter sent to Helen Dubois.'

The faintest surprise passed over his face.

'Stop shouting, Harriet.'

The missus made an impatient, near frantic movement with her hand and turned her head away. I peered at her.

'You know?'

She didn't answer. I looked from one to the other.

'What are you hiding from me? Why didn't you tell me?'

'You know why. It's safer . . .'

'Stop saying that! What have you done? I won't go until you tell me. I won't leave Edward.'

One of them must have signalled the driver as the cab jolted to a stop. I blinked past tears. The missus' face swam back into sight – it was hard, black-eyed.

'Leave, then. I won't stop you.'

I stared at her, unable to move.

'You presume much, Harriet.'

I felt ill with rage. My voice rose to a wail.

'What choice do I have? You have told me nothing. I am giving up *everything* for you and all you do is lie to me. You never meant to take Edward with you – you just don't want the master to have him . . .'

'Quiet!'

I don't know if you can say something glowed black, but that's how her eyes looked. Her face terrified me. No one spoke. After a moment, she gathered herself.

'There is also yourself to consider, isn't there, Harriet? You never truly wanted the things you are making such a fuss about giving up. Marriage, domestic service – I thought you wanted more from your life? Or was that only idle dreaming for your diary?'

She glared at me.

'It is not too late. You can get down here.'

We both knew what she was doing, goading me into place. But it was true what she said. The thought of stepping down from the cab, from the chance of this new and unknown life, from *her*, would be like stepping into grey cloud. Laurence leaned forward.

'You need to be on that train, missus.'

She put a hand up to him and continued to watch me. I wiped my eyes.

'But I thought we would have Edward . . .'

Turning awkwardly, she touched the edge of my skirt.

'We will come back for him when it's safe to do so.'

'How long will that be?'

I felt like a child whining to its mother.

'A year perhaps.'

'A year?'

'Six months then.'

She wasn't looking quite at me.

'As soon as we are settled, and I am . . . working.'

The word sounded strange in her mouth. It must have felt strange to her too, the way she hesitated.

'You are telling the truth?'

She turned to wipe the tears from my cheek, not gently, and nodded.

We made the rest of the journey in silence. I was sick with misery and doubt. Edward's absence pained me keenly – both there in the cab and looking forward through all the travels ahead. We are going so far, so very far away. He was the one certainty I had been clinging to, the only thing my imagination could reliably work upon. I had seen myself holding him while trains rocked and the missus slept; we were to discover all the new things on the ship together; later, as a treat, we would stand at the side of the stage so he could watch his mother sing. I wanted to be his nursemaid, in short, but much more than that. As long as he needed me, I would have something more important than myself to care for. Now he had been robbed even from my imaginings.

Laurence saw to our tickets at Euston. The missus clutched his arm for a long moment and looked at him without speaking. Their manner in the carriage, their secrets, sent dread spiralling through me. How could she trust him? I wanted to leave him behind as quickly as possible. He caught my elbow as I was about to step onto the train and held something out.

'Thank you.'

It was the red ribbon, neatly rolled and secured with a pin. He placed it in my palm. I looked at his face, unsure what it meant, and he winked. Then he turned on his heel and jogged away down the platform.

We have been on the train for two or three hours and have the carriage to ourselves. Now we are on our way, I feel the weight of my failures. I never found Lily. I can only hope Francis's parents believed me. Edward, I try not to think about at all. I must look forward now and help the missus. She is asleep opposite as she has been for most of the journey. One of the folded-up blankets cushions her head against the side. Exhaustion and perhaps grief have disguised her face better than any dress and bonnet. The movement of the train rocks her, sometimes perilously – it seems the blanket will slip. I keep thinking of the canary fluttering into the trees after she freed it from its cage, how small and fragile and doomed it looked. But then its cage was no protection either. I tried sketching her at the back of this book earlier but haven't the skill – I wish I could make a photograph. Or perhaps, as Mrs B would have said, the words in this diary will make the best portrait. Nobody has watched the missus as I have or sees her as I do. Perhaps I shall read my words back one day and understand clearly everything that has surprised or hurt me about her. One thing is certain – I have no one else now.

Wednesday, 29th May

We board tomorrow. Our tickets are secured, and home for our last night in England is a dirty hotel near the docks. Liverpool clatters and clunks and chokes – at least where we are. I can see the steelworks from our window, the mighty smokestacks. It dawned on me earlier that the iron ore clawed out of the hills at home is meant for such places, just like the master's coal. Father's poor lungs and Duncan's twisted leg are linked to these huge buildings, the rail tracks and steamships carting us about. It all exists because of what is hidden out of sight beneath our feet and the great efforts to dig it up. A sense of dread filled me which had no certain origin or outline. I wonder if Mother is right, and we should simply have left the stones where they were.

We change lodgings every night, and our names change every time we are compelled to give them. For fear of slipping, we no longer call each other anything but 'my dear'. At night, she whispers to me about the great singers she has seen perform, the theatres and costumes, her favourite composers. It is as if she is letting her inner world, the place she truly inhabits, finally reach the surface now we are away from London. She speaks much of the building we shall pass through as immigrants when we first arrive. It was a theatre at one time, and her beloved Jenny Lind sang Italian operas there. This strange coincidence burns with meaning for her; she repeats the fact, clinging to it as if it is a talisman against failure.

The future is becoming real, pushing the past from her thoughts, I think. We had one last conversation about what we are leaving behind. She woke on the train as I was still writing the last entry. Watched me for some time, I think.

'If someone had read your diary, what would it have told them about where we are going?'

'No one read it.'

I shut the book in a way that shut down any more questions. Meeting her eyes, though, I saw curiosity rather than criticism. I shrugged.

'I was careful.'

'I have no doubt.'

I traced the edge of the book's cover with a finger.

'Anyone reading it before now would think we are on our way to Italy. They would be looking for a red petticoat.' It was a feeble attempt to cover our tracks and sounded as much. I became defensive.

'You think I shouldn't have written anything at all. If they found me first . . .'

She shook her head and laughed.

'If they had found you, the game would have been lost already. I only meant what would they have learned about your hopes for the future. And you are right, I have asked you to give up so much else, even the comfort of your friends. It would be monstrous to deny you the consolations of a diary.'

I must have looked uncomfortable, but she had turned to the window. Rain marched across farmland, trampling crops.

'You were lucky at the Bowmans'.'

I stared at her with my mouth open. She glanced at me and leaned forward to touch my knee, a reassurance.

'Ralph enjoyed telling me, that's all.'

'I had to do something about Francis . . .'

247

'I know.'

My doubts about Laurence surfaced.

'How did they know I would go there? Only if Francis told Laurence that I . . .'

She cut me off with a wave of her hand.

'Barrett made Francis talk. He can make any servant say anything.' She sighed.

'I don't believe Francis's parents will keep him at Finton Hall much longer. Ralph can only smile away so much eccentricity in his own house.'

I remembered the flicker of doubt in Mr Bowman's eyes.

'I hope so.'

She nodded.

'And remember, no one knows we are together. Not even Ralph. He thinks we are enemies.'

Her eyes narrowed with pleasure.

'The argument he overheard between us in my room was real, after all. I did just enough to leave no doubt, speaking unkindly about you to the Trevelyans when I knew he would be listening.'

My heart ached at that. I am leaving behind so many false selves. What Lizzie must think of me – I never said sorry or goodbye. It came to me for the first time that I shall never see Mrs T's starry smiles or Tabby's deft movements again.

'You will miss the vicarage?'

I wanted for comfort's sake to speak about them, but she looked at me quite sharply and her question was weighted.

'You mean the vicar?'

I was too surprised to answer. She saw the confusion in my face and softened a little.

'I know what people say about my visits to the vicarage.'

'I never listened to them, ma'am.'

It must have been thinking myself back into Finton Hall that made me reply like the loyal housemaid. I caught myself, annoyed. She gave a scornful laugh.

'Why not? They are half right. I would have gladly followed him into hell for those hours of happiness.'

Scenes from the vicarage flashed through my mind. That dour man. But there was no use staring at her like an astonished child. She was putting us on a different footing, an honest one finally.

'But couldn't he have helped you?'

'Why would he help me?'

'If you love each other . . .'

She looked genuinely shocked.

'My dear, he loves his wife.'

Her chin lifted as she recalculated.

'No. He loves music. Then God. Then Isabel. Music is his true religion, that's where he worships. Christianity is how he deals with the tedium of the rest of life. It simplifies things by having rules. About wives deserting their husbands, for instance.'

'But if music means so much to him, your singing . . .'

'Makes me useful, a conduit, not the thing itself. He certainly has never confused it with the mistress of Finton Hall. That's what I am so grateful for. We weren't lovers, as people think. What he offered me was far greater. In the music room, I escaped myself and became something . . . weightless. But outside of it, I am as tedious to him as the rest of his parishioners.'

Her eyes glinted. The tears hardened rather than softened her expression, like a polished surface. I tried to say I couldn't believe it, but a lie would have curdled the intimacy of our talk. What she said next shocked me more than anything.

'Only Ralph really knew me.'

'The master?'

She spoke quickly.

'Never call him that again. Call him anything else in the world.'

Then she nodded.

'It's strange, isn't it? He sees more clearly than anyone. There isn't a corner of my soul he didn't pry into. I am not sure he is human.'

I remembered how he had looked like Milton's Satan in the light from the flint mill.

'He's a fiend, you mean?'

'Something like that. A very devil, although not a fallen angel. I am not sure he was ever beautiful.'

She nodded in agreement with herself.

'Beauty hurts him, and I think that is why. He desires it, but he doesn't trust it. He has to pit himself against it. He has to win.'

Her brow furrowed slightly. Mine did too.

'Hurts him?'

She thought for a moment.

'You know his father was a miner? He was in an accident underground when Ralph was very young. His injuries were terrible, but he didn't die immediately. Ralph remembers the smell of the sick room – the dressings needed changing faster than they could be washed. He told me how he had looked at his father's face and didn't recognise it as a face at all – the most awful sounds, dreadful groans came from it.

'The mine's childless owners adopted Ralph soon after. His life became one of comfort and refinement overnight, but I am not sure he ever really left that sick room. Another man might have turned such suffering to good and felt pity for his fellow men, but for Ralph, it poisoned everything that came after. He has worked hard to leave the ugliness behind, to live in beauty, but he doesn't believe in it; he certainly can't create it. So, he destroys it. He collects men like Murray and Hicks and delights in throwing them innocent children. Each child sacrificed is proof that he survived. Destruction and chaos define him now, and power, of course. He does it because he can. He fills his house with precious and beautiful things, people amongst them, so he can control them. It gives him power over what otherwise torments him – the beauty he sees but cannot have. It is his way of winning. He always wins.'

She paused and said it again to herself.

'Always.'

Her gaze fell on the diary in my lap.

'No one looks at a thing like he does – he feeds on it. It's cannibalistic. He did it to you.'

It irks me how she brings up without shame things I have written, as if I shared them willingly. I feel the intrusion more keenly now I know she is as sane as I am. She continued.

'You were half in love with him after he showed you the flint and steel mill.'

'I was not.'

She smiled again, almost apologetically.

'He made you feel beautiful, didn't he? We all love the devil until he shows us his true face.'

I was nettled. It wasn't me that had married the monster.

'If that's true, why are you so sure Laurence isn't a devil?'

She looked at me sharply.

'Without Laurence, we wouldn't be here. He has sacrificed as much as you have. More.'

'Why?' I glared back at her. 'Why would he help you?'

She turned her head away impatiently for a second. When she turned back, she looked me full in the eye.

'Mary. He would have taken her from there long ago if he could have found a way to escape Ralph. It will haunt him for the rest of his life that he didn't act sooner, before Mary was hurt. That is what gives him the strength now.'

I couldn't find a word to say. She continued.

'Laurence has never been allowed to live openly, as his soul dictates, to wear his heart on his sleeve. His affections . . .'

'We saw him with Mr Hicks's valet. Mary and me.'

I blurted it out, cutting her off. She looked at me with real interest.
'What do you mean?'

'Together. In his bed. And I caught him with the garden lad too.'

I burned hotter and grew fierce.

'But then you likely know that already from my diary.'

'Why were you in his room?'

It was like talking to Lizzie about the pictures – they both took hold of the wrong thing on purpose.

'What does that matter? Mary ran away, that's how she ended up in the library with those men. They must have seen her or heard her in the passageway.'

'Oh . . .'

She looked to the side, remembering.

'The library. You were going to look at the photographs. Ralph would have enjoyed that. He enjoys leaving his special collections about. There's always the chance a servant or guest might stumble upon them.'

I thought about it. Perhaps that was why he let me stay on at Finton Hall – his need for an audience, a witness. He wanted me to see the truth in the paintings, the books, the flint mill, knowing it would hurt me and that I could do nothing about it. 'Behold!' he had urged when we first met. But it was the missus, not the master, that insisted I should use the library. I spoke pointedly.

'Is that why you urged me so strongly to read the books?'

She held my eye for a moment.

'Yes. I suppose I hoped if you did see them, it would make you think differently about him.'

I huffed and repeated Lizzie's words, claiming her worldliness for my own.

'I imagine every gentleman's house in the country is stuffed full of pictures like that.'

The missus tilted her head and frowned at me.

'Some, yes. But the pictures of children?'

I remembered the photograph of Joe, the boot boy – the master had held it out to me – and felt sickened. I changed the subject.

'Laurence was wearing your lace, and my ribbon and Mary's rouge. He was the thief. He must have stolen the ring he gave to Mary too.'

She sighed.

'I gave him that ring and the lace. And a few other things.'

It was a detail she threw off before fixing me with a look.

'Do you know what is going to happen next? He is going to marry Mary.'

I let out a laugh of disbelief.

'She'll never have him.'

'Then she's a fool. He loves her. You have a lot to learn, Harriet.'

We were both silent and angry for a moment. She spoke first.

'I see it is difficult for you to understand. But if Laurence is a devil, he is a lesser one than I. Ralph picked him to be an ornament, another pretty thing to add to his collection. He might as well have been shipped over from the colonies with the other curiosities.'

Her expression turned bullish.

'Being prized for how you look can be as great a misfortune as being hated for it. Laurence has known no other life, but it doesn't mean he wanted this one. When Ralph understood what he was, where he went for company, he and Barrett used it to bind him even more tightly to them. His very life is in their hands. They could have him jailed, or worse.'

She eyed me.

'Not every secret in Finton Hall is wicked – do not mistake the servant for the master. The theft of your ribbon is the greatest harm Laurence has done you.'

I became aware of the tidy roll I had put in my pocket with the diary.

'Why would he betray Mary, if he cares for her so much?'

She sat back a little.

'He isn't an angel. But wouldn't you take what happiness you could find in that house? Share light and warmth where it was offered?'

I looked away, thinking of something I had taken from the library besides the flint mill. The missus continued.

'But Mary – what happened to her. Laurence loves her deeply. He's willing even to risk defying Ralph.'

I remembered Mary's face as she fled Laurence's room.

'I can't think she will forgive him.'

She sighed again.

'They mean much to each other. You saw that; you wrote about it.'

I turned my head quickly to the window.

'Please don't talk about my diary.'

There was a silence, though I could tell she was studying me.

'I only read your diary to see the house through your eyes. I needed to know if you were in any danger from Ralph. But it became about more than that, I confess. I couldn't give it up. You helped me see more than I expected. And I became . . . I became reliant on it.'

It wasn't a good enough reason to my mind, and I didn't reply. She sighed.

'I understand. One word more. Clockface.'

I glanced sideways. Her face broke into its wide smile.

'Oh, what else was she? Ding Dong?'

She laughed with real mirth, throwing her head back. I was in no mood to be mollified and refused to smile.

'We should have been friends sooner, Harriet.'

It was a deliberate appeal to my affections, using my name and all. As I watched her, I began to doubt if I could ever create a true portrait through my words. She is no longer the pale lady I met at Mrs B's, or the unhappy wife pushed to the edge of reason by Gethin. I am still becoming acquainted with this iron-willed woman who refuses to be trapped and silenced, who must have schemed for months to leave her husband and never lost her nerve. A goddess after all, perhaps, but one without a heaven, stumbling over the same sharp stones as the rest of us. Her eyes were still shining at me, an invitation. I remembered where we were going, and why – how the impossible had, within a matter of weeks, come within touching distance, all because of her. I leaned forward and took her hand. She placed her other one on top and gently rested her forehead against mine. It doesn't matter anymore who reads this diary. We are past the point of returning. The only thing in front of us now is America.

VOYAGES

Saturday, 1st June 1878

The Graphic

BABY FARMING

Every now and then a corner of the curtain is lifted which veils the iniquities of baby-farming from the public gaze, as in the shocking cases now being investigated in Lambeth and the City of London. Our readers are, no doubt, sufficiently familiar with the dreadful revelations that have been made public. The remedies adopted hitherto are very inadequate to guard against this evil. Registration and inspection of houses where young children are taken in to nurse may do something; but where, on the one hand, there are parents who wish to get rid of their children, there are sure to be found, on the other hand, hardened wretches who will accept the charge upon the tacit understanding that the baby is to be allowed to die as soon as is decently possible.

JUNE

Monday, 17th June

I cannot think how to begin. The words won't come. They are pushed
out by other words, not my own – words I first read on a park bench
in New York ten days ago, and which have rung in my head ever since.
I have tried to write that I don't believe it, that I will not believe it.
Then I try to write that I am afraid. My hand and pencil are like stone.
When I last wrote in these pages, there were few enough certainties,
but now even they are fractured, grown dark. The seasickness left me
this morning, and I have been trying to begin, encased in this little
cabin – a tiny seed floating towards rocks, back towards England. We
are only a few hours away now. Sometimes it feels like a coffin, but I
have no wish to go on deck. There is little sense of movement in these
waters, just the rhythmic thud of the engine and the occasional pounding
of children's feet along the passageway outside. They make my heart
pitch each time they come by, and I think with failing courage of that
sea-faring superstition – children are a sign of good fortune.

We learned that and many such beliefs on the journey out. Sneeze
to the left for luck, a shark following means death, whistling raises a
wind. In steerage, these sailors' myths hung in the air like the stench
of unwashed bodies and rotting food. It was impossible to write. I
suppose being nearer to the water, we felt more keenly how our lives
depended on the whim of the gods. It was in every violent creak of
wood and thump of wave, each roll and lurch, as if we were in the
belly of a whale rather than aboard a steamship. I wish now there really
were such easy signs to point to and say, 'This is a warning; this the

signal to go back; here is where the darkness seeps in.' There is little mention of sailors' lore in cabin class, but then there is no one here I wish to talk to. I am alone.

Or perhaps the signs were always there – if I had known how to look. Her uneasy sleep, the dreams that furrowed her brow and made her cry out. I put it down to the strain of leaving, the discomfort and shock of steerage. We were a long way from Finton Hall where each pleat and fold of the laundry is scoured for bedbugs before being allowed upstairs. Onboard, we slept side by side with strangers, women who farted and snored and sang and moaned. Our low dormitory with its rows of bunks made me yearn even for the little attic room I shared with Mary. We took one walk together after we had laid out our beds, but the missus refused to linger, even when a fiddler started up and drew a crowd. The dirt, the coarse voices and language, the lack of privacy – she can't ever have been in the middle of such life before. The number of languages spoken, the different smells and clothing made me feel we were in a miniature, floating world. It is a collection I think Mr Gethin would covet. I was shocked myself by the noise and crush of it, but I saw it all the more keenly through her eyes. There was nowhere to wash, the drinking water tasted dank, we all had iden-tical bowls and spoons like orphans or prisoners. The food at least was not awful, but I could barely bring her to touch it. Many had brought their own, and the air became thick with wafts of fermented goods, cured meats, onions, cabbage, and cheese turning rancid. When we looked into a family room where a group of women were feeding their babies, she turned swiftly on her heel and hurried back to our bunks. I thought she must regret leaving Edward.

Seasickness found me quickly. The port floating away so determinedly once we set off gave my stomach a turn in itself. I watched the land as if simply keeping my eyes on it would keep it from disappearing. Some part of me believed we would always be able to see one shore or the other, that the sea couldn't be so big. The water swirled greenish close to the sides – sometimes pond dark, sometimes light as a spring leaf. I remember staring at the unending churn of it until I frightened myself with the thought of falling – the desire, almost, to fall. After that I could only sit miserably on the deck while my stomach churned in kind, unable to think properly, never mind write. I thought the missus must feel the same, lying under her blanket so long, but when the storm hit a few days later, it was she who tended to me. While every part of my body was swimming or squirming about like maggots in a bucket, she found a large tin bowl from somewhere. Keeping it steady enough to contain the vomit was impossible – the stink was just another feature of the unendurable but unending misery. When I finally woke to a calm ship and sore stomach, she was motionless under her blanket again.

Two days after the storm, things happened that even I could recognise for the bad omens they were. I was feeling well enough to return to the deck for fresh air – cold, restless air by then, the hoary breath of the ocean. The ship had become another big house I was trapped in, with first-class passengers above us in every sense. I heard there was even a library on the upper deck, which gave me a feeling of foreboding, as if we had never truly left Finton Hall at all. I could hear a band playing on the saloon deck, and was thinking I might be able to persuade the missus—

It has become harder and stranger to call her that. So much has changed besides our names since we left England. We are not the people we were, or thought we were. Mrs Gethin – no, that is worse. Clara then.

Clara.

I had hoped she might come out from the unhealthy fug of steerage if she knew there was music playing, but when I went below she was up for once, kneeling on the bunk and surrounded by the contents of her bag – shawls, music sheets, writing materials, bottles from her toilet. As I arrived, she had just started on mine.

'It's gone.'

She meant her money. All of it. It had been in a pouch she kept close under the blanket, but she had forgotten to take it with her to the water closet. She spoke in violent gasps, and her hands shook as she pawed at my belongings. Third class had taught her the meaning of money at least. The loss of so much of it – our security vanished in a moment – made me lightheaded with disaster. Fresh waves of nausea rolled through me. There would be no time to get our bearings – finding work would be urgent from the moment we stepped off the ship. Service, of course, for me. And for the first time since I left Finton Hall, the question came about Clara – what if she was not successful as a singer? The possibility had never crossed my mind in England. To me, she sings like an angel, but what do I know of the professional theatre, of its demands and expectations? What would become of us if she failed?

My own savings were still hidden under my petticoat. It would be enough perhaps to put a roof over our heads for the first night in New York, buy us food for a few days. I gathered myself and was leaning in to whisper that much when she stopped suddenly and stared into the bag. My mind raced as she lifted it out, and we both looked at the flint mill and then at each other.

'You stole it?'

Absurdly, I wanted to protest. Not that I had taken it, but that it was stealing. I nodded.

'Why?'

It wasn't a question I had asked myself, even when I packed it in place of lighter, more useful things at Mrs Cole's.

'I wanted to take something from him. Something he cares about.'

She looked at me steadily.

'And . . . I don't want to forget what happened.'

It was too difficult to explain that I also felt the need to rescue it – that I was somehow releasing the dead miner from Gethin's grip. She weighed it in her hands, thinking, then dropped it back into the bag

264

and silently held out her arms to me. It was an awkward embrace, twisting towards each other on the bunk, not a word spoken. She retreated into herself again soon after. Nothing more was said about the money, but I felt the loss of it lodge in my gut like a needle.

What more to say of our passage? What else was there to warn me? The sickness never fully left me. To distract myself from the awful rolling sensation, I trespassed one day, opening doors I shouldn't. Ladders reached down. I had thought we were already in the 'downstairs' of the ship, crammed as it was with servants and labourers, all rushing to the land of freedom to find themselves new masters. But I found a world below that. I heard and felt the boiler room before I saw it – a clanging and raging that shivered my skin and rattled my skull. When I finally stood on the threshold, I thought I was looking into hell. Heat and flame and flesh. Men shovelling and shovelling, load after load of coal into the furnace, then raking out the ashes in a ferocious cycle, their streaming backs and huge arms glowing in the burning light. They looked like punished gods. I remembered Gethin's face lit up in the same way by the sparks of the flint mill, his gleeful laughter, and felt sweat break out on my brow. He was still with us, even there. It was coal from mines such as his – perhaps even his own – powering the very means of our escape. The creeping dread I had felt in Liverpool returned. I watched the stokers, toiling dangerously below the surface out of sight, just like their brothers digging themselves to death in the mines – the end the same as the beginning – and for a moment I was in Clara's bedroom again, watching helplessly as Gethin snapped the canary's neck.

America finally appeared as promised, a new world, safe and solid and thrilling. Passengers grinned at each other in the sunshine and sweet-smelling wind, their faces drawn and pale from the journey – I expect mine was the same. I ran back downstairs and dragged the blanket off the missus.

'We are here. There is to be an inspection and then they are putting us onto barges.'

She looked at me from somewhere very far away and shrank back. I took hold of her hand and whispered the name she had chosen for her new life.

'We are here. Remember who you are.'

The inspection passed in no time – they barely looked at us – and we were herded onto barges and steamboats like frightened cattle. The missus held onto me and followed like a silent, scared child. Her other hand covered her eyes – the sudden sky-wide glare after so long must have hurt.

Gulls flew overhead, crying out harshly. Cormorants perched on boat masts with their wings spread out to the sun like sentinels. The bay was as unreal as a picture – all the boats and ships were clean and colourful, brightly painted in whites, reds and blues. There was none of the smoky grime of the Thames traffic or that hazy pall hanging in the air.

I pushed forward to the front of the steamboat so Clara could see better. At first, she seemed unable to make sense of the view, as if it was all just shape and colour and no meaning. But as we drew nearer, her eyes fixed on a huge round building surrounded by a mighty wooden fence at the edge of the island, and emotions moved over her face like reflections on water.

'It is Castle Garden, Harriet.'

Her fingers grasped mine tightly. I glanced at the people closest to us. Hearing my real name spoken out loud was like looking down to find my skirt and petticoat missing. She took a breath in and then let out what might equally have been a cry or a laugh.

'It's where Jenny Lind sang. The first time she came to America.'

I smiled at her as I would at a child or an invalid.

'I know, my dear.'

She never took her eyes off it, even when we were right underneath and being called to disembark – I had a job getting her to move. We shuffled quietly from sea to land, clutching bags and blankets. After a final medical inspection, during which my hands wouldn't stop shaking, Clara walked into Castle Garden with her back straight and her chin up as if she was walking onto a stage. Her eyes lifted above the mass of bedraggled and anxious immigrants to the rafters. They call the main bit the rotunda, and it's enormous. All signs of the theatre have gone, but I still think she was seeing an enraptured audience rather than crowds of tired travellers, perhaps even hearing applause in the great hum of hundreds being examined and registered and sent on their way under one roof. I wished she would stop acting so queenly and look more like the rest of us. We gave the names we had used on the ship to a clerk. Clara had sense enough to play the part of a domestic servant, talking in a voice that mimicked mine so well I almost laughed with nerves. We were asked if we were staying in New York and then pointed past the ticket desks towards the exit. I almost hesitated, as if it might be a trick. But we were through. The rotunda swarmed in front of us in all its busy-ness and purpose, and we were free to join the other immigrants, free on American soil. I gripped Clara's hand and pulled her into the crowd.

People were clustering around food stands – the smell of fresh bread nearly made my knees give way – or hurrying to make use of the luggage delivery depot, letter-writing departments, exchange brokers and a hundred other welcoming services it seemed. I crouched behind some-one's trunk to delve into my skirts and untie the purse from my petticoat, then led Clara to the right queue. While waiting to change our paltry fortune into American coins, I overheard two men agreeing they would go back to the labour exchange next. I asked them where it was, and they said a different building outside the rotunda.

'They got jobs need filling all over the country. We're cabinet-makers, heading west.'

The one who spoke had an open face, and I felt my shoulders relaxing. If there was plenty of work, we could make a beginning – or I could. Clara didn't look like she was going to be any help, standing by my side with that faraway look – the men kept flicking glances at her. But I felt my courage returning. It was good to be able to look at two friendly faces and smile into another's relief. The other man was slower to talk, but I caught him eyeing me with interest more than once and had a sudden, unexpected, sense of Robert – a flash of grey eyes. It was the first I'd thought of him. The talker asked about us, and I answered as we'd rehearsed.

'Housemaids. And I'm a seamstress.'

'That's right.'

Clara spoke up suddenly, snapping into life beside me.

'Maids of all work really.'

I looked at her in surprise. She gave them and then me a wicked grin.

'For our sins.'

The men laughed, and I stared with my mouth open, flummoxed by this strange new companion. She began talking in her new voice as naturally as if she'd been gossiping with tradesmen her whole life. They recounted funny stories about the voyage to each other, as if it had all been a merry escapade, and then the men reached the front of the queue and bade us goodbye.

When our turn came, I collected our strange American coins with a lighter heart and tucked them away in my bag. Clara stood to one side, studying her hands and turning them over curiously. She spoke softly in her normal voice.

'I fear I have been neglected by my lady's maid. Look at these nails.'

They were cracked and dirty. I also noticed the streaks inside her collar, the greasy hairline, and we all still carried the stench of steerage with us, filling the rotunda with its rotten air. Picking up her bag and moving her on, I told her she was a thorough disgrace.

She gasped and looked delighted.

'Filthy. Like a chimney sweep.'

I don't know why our grimy state made us weak with laughter, but we were brought to a standstill, bags and blankets dropping at our feet.

Other immigrants passed with wondering glances as we doubled over, speechless. Clara straightened finally, one hand on hip, the other on the front of her dress, feet set wide, and let out a great sigh. It was not the posture or bearing of a lady – far too natural and carefree for that.

'Did I hear one of the clerks say there was a washroom?'

We gathered our belongings, and this time it was she who took my hand and near danced us through the crowd, humming something spritely. I had a job to keep from knocking into people and was laughing and scattering apologies in our wake when she came to a sudden stop. Her grip on my hand tightened. I looked up at a row of tall boards giving the names of boarding houses and lists of prices in different currencies. Beside them, runners called to the crowd and handed out cards. I saw the sign she was looking at. The Miner's Arms. An ordinary enough name for a public house, but I felt a cold breath on the back of my neck. The runner saw us looking and rushed forward, offering to take us there at once. Clara took his card wordlessly and turned to me, eyes wide. Then she laughed again, too loud, too hard. The wild look returned that I had seen so often in the mirror at Finton Hall. I pulled her away.

'Let's wash first.'

As we weaved between people, we came across a monkey sitting on a man's shoulder, baring its teeth at us. Clara stopped and chattered to it in her maid's voice, laughing with real delight when it reached out and tugged a lock of her hair loose. Looking wilder than ever, she announced a pet monkey would be her first purchase. Monkeys alarm me even more than horses and, anyway, we had no money, but I noticed the card for the Miner's Arms had slipped from her hand to be trodden underfoot, so I agreed – as long as we could call it William.

We found a washroom, where I half stripped to soap the most offensive parts of myself but didn't change into my clean dress. Saving it for when it mattered, I reasoned. Clara scrubbed at herself until her skin turned red, all the while singing a bawdy song at the top of her voice.

I don't know where she'd learned such a tune, perhaps listening under her blanket in steerage. She flicked water at my astonished face, and leaned down, laughing again and half-naked, to pull out the skirt of the green dress I had added the balayeuse to at Mrs Cole's. I touched her arm.

'Not here?'

The excitement was carrying her too far, I thought, but she firmly removed my hand. Her eyes were dark.

'I didn't come all this way to creep in like a criminal, unseen.'

Doubt must have shown in my face because her expression changed to mischief, and she prodded me in my stays.

'Such worry, Harriet! Find us something to eat and wait for me outside.'

There were long queues for the bread stands in the rotunda. I stood in one for ten minutes before I remembered my purse was no longer under my skirt but in the bag I had left with Clara. On my way back, I could see the thickness of the castle's brown, stone walls in the gateway – as wide as a man is tall. On impulse, I walked between them, as if they were no more than cobwebs, and into the sunshine of the yard. The warmth of it hit my freshly washed face, and I felt the lightness of having nothing to carry and no one to attend to. It was in that moment, I think, that I truly understood I was free, the moment it settled in my bones as a certainty. I caught the shouts of street hawkers outside the gates, a whiff of a cigar, another of baked apple, and heard my stomach growl.

Clara still wasn't outside the washroom when I returned – I remember thinking I would have to learn great patience – but then I couldn't see her inside either. Bags vanished too. A nasty memory of finding her and Edward gone from Serle Place flashed into my mind. The same knot tied itself tightly in my belly. Walking back out, I got the sense that something was wrong. There was a shift in atmosphere, a dip in the hubbub, as if Castle Garden had slowed suddenly and caught its breath. And then a pinprick of sound. It seemed at the centre of the change, pulling everything towards it. I hurried back into the rotunda. Some people were still bustling out, dragging children and belongings; others had paused and turned their heads, catching the same shift I had. The sound continued, growing louder, and then floated out into what was clearly a musical note, a voice singing. It filled the building, reaching up to the very dome.

I rushed forward and stopped again just as abruptly next to an old man in dirty corduroy trousers. He was staring open-mouthed at the singer. Clara was high up on a bread stand above the crowd. The dress made her a silken green vision amongst the coarse wools and dirty cottons clustering around her feet. Her hair was caught back, bare except for a ribbon woven through it. She was the girl in green from the portrait, only matured and in the full bloom of her beauty.

But the sight of her was nothing to how she sounded. I recognised the song from the musical evening – the one by Handel. In the drawing room it had given me goosebumps; there, in the cavernous space of the rotunda, it was frightening. The words came back to me – *let me weep over my cruel fate, let me yearn for freedom*. I clutched the sleeve of my neighbour's coat, but he didn't notice. Her voice was enormous, like nothing I had heard before. It was the sky, and we willingly lifted our hearts to its unearthly light, its velvet darkness. I was *hearing* the sunshine and storms I had seen sweeping across the landscape when I met her for the first time in the hall. Back then, it had been a strange and troubled mistress I greeted. I had wanted only for her to notice me so I might be of service. God, if I'd known. I watched her giving herself, every bit of herself to the music and knew I had done the right thing by coming with her. Even without Edward. My doubts about the professional theatre turned to dust. I believe there were many in that room who felt their burdens were lifted clean off them, even if just for that moment.

The emigration depot had come to a standstill, so it was easy to spot the handful of figures pushing their way through the crowd. Two of them were already close to the stand. I came to my senses. Officials of the depot, maybe police, on their way to put an end to this distraction from business, to save the foolish woman from breaking her neck, no doubt. My heart stumbled, sick suddenly with fear. I let go of my old friend – his mouth was still open but he had shut his eyes – and started weaving towards her.

Clara lifted a hand to her throat. She was delivering the final note into the spellbound room, and even as I ran towards her, I felt a kind of exultation that Gethin had not been able to silence her after all. In spite of all his power, she was finishing her song before an audience of hundreds. When the note ended, she lowered her head. There were still sounds drifting in from outside, bangs and shouts from the baggage department, but the silence that descended over the rotunda was a physical thing. It was as if a mighty cannon full of streamers had been fired out over the crowd and everyone was now waiting for each individual piece to float down and settle on them. When the last of it had come to rest, the place shattered into a thousand different responses – clapping, laughing, yelling in different languages, caps thrown in the air. Clara opened her eyes again and looked around. I could see her letting it come to her, drinking it in, her voice reflected back in the beating of all those glad hearts. Then her expression changed. It was as if the theatre was falling away in front of her eyes, while the tired and stinking reality of the immigration depot reasserted itself. She looked with confusion down to one side. Hands reached up; someone in a blue uniform and cap was climbing up beside her. I started pushing through more forcefully. A dense crowd had formed. When I looked up again, she was down from the stand and disappearing into a press of bodies. I tried to squeeze between, but it was impossible. The crowd was being pushed back, people knocking into others and treading on feet.

They were bringing her through. The man in blue uniform led the way while reaching back to keep a hold on her arm. Another followed.

The crowd renewed its applause as she passed. She kept her eyes cast down. When a fresh round of cheering broke out, I saw a small smile form itself, hovering over her lips. Her fear and confusion seemed to melt away. I was pushed back as others were forced to make way for the party, but I saw her look up. For a moment, I couldn't remember her name, her American name. My mind scrabbled about in a panic and caught it by the neck. I shouted it twice, flinging it over the crowd. She turned a fraction and our eyes met. I beckoned and pointed to myself.

'Tell them!'

The smile vanished. She shook her head in tight movements, eyes black and fierce, mouth a hard line. I was being commanded. My voice failed, and I was knocked back again.

I kept up with the party as the crush loosened and saw another two men carrying our bags. They took her to a door near the wash-rooms where they were met by two more. There was some discussion, and she was taken through along with our luggage and the door shut. I didn't understand where they were taking her, or why. Three of the men were still outside. I tried to get close enough to hear their conversation, standing as if I belonged to a family huddled by the wall, but I was still too far away, and the child had started to cry. The father tapped my arm and held out a loaf of bread. I shook my head, distracted. Finally, one of the men by the door broke away. As he started to run off, another called something, and he turned for it to be repeated. His colleague bellowed.

'It's Gethin. G-E-T-H-I-N.'

The ground rocked under me as if I was back on the ship. With a nod, the man set off again at a run, and I realised the one who had bellowed was looking at me. Frowning, he said something to the other, who turned. I jerked to life, blinked and tottered towards them before I even knew what I meant to do. They watched me approach.

'Beg your pardon, sirs. What's happened to that lady that sang?'

I made myself into Betsy, wide-eyed and worried. The frowner, who was older, cut off his companion who seemed about to talk.

'Why?'

'Oh, she sang so beautiful, didn't she, sir? I hope she's not in any trouble for it.'

'Not for singing, no.'

'Oh.'

I looked confused. His stare was as unflinching as a bull's.

'Do you know her?'

'Know the lady? No, sir.'

'Did you come off the *City of Brussels*?'

'That's right, sir.'

'Did you see her on board?'

'Oh no. Not 'til she got up there the way she did.'

He didn't blink once.

'So you weren't travelling together?'

I let my face fall open, and then laughed as if he'd just paid me an outrageous compliment.

'With a lady like that, sir?'

I giggled again and could see his interest start to drain. The younger one was trying to weigh down his expression with the same authority.

'She's wanted in England.'

'Oh!'

I put everything into it I thought Mary would – shock and a gleam of excitement.

'What for?'

'What's your name?'

The bull had swung his attention back. I gave the name I had registered with, trying to look pleased to be asked.

'Who are you travelling with?'

'My family, sir.'

He looked over my shoulder at the family by the wall.

274

'And you're sure you haven't seen her before?'

I nodded and gave an apologetic smile. After another pause, during which his frown deepened, I stammered that I should go. Only the younger one said goodbye. Forcing myself not to look back, I walked straight up to the little family as if I belonged to them. The father smiled and – thank God – held out the loaf again. I took it this time and tore off a chunk, though nearly choked trying to swallow a bite, and then made a fuss of the still-sobbing little girl. Her mother was more than happy to pass her over to a stranger. I prayed silently and desperately that the policemen couldn't see or hear that they were French.

There were no shouts, no running footsteps, no hands taking hold of me. Not as I dried the little girl's tears or thanked the man for his bread. I needed to go somewhere quiet to think, somewhere I wouldn't be discovered. Walking as if to return to the washrooms, I carried on between the great walls, past the labour exchange and found myself joining the stream of people flowing out of the landing depot.

She had shaken her head at me, not wanting them to see me, but what was I to do? I couldn't just leave her to be dragged back to Gethin. The smells and cries I had caught snatches of inside the depot burst into colour and life as I left it. Hawkers with food – most of it foul-looking when I saw it close up – and tobacco stands, runners hassling newcomers with offers of lodgings or work, red-faced men shouting about conveyances and hotels. I dodged anyone who came near me, though it seemed to be families that were most under attack – a man with wild whiskers swept a baby right out of its mother's arms, so the rest of the family had no choice but to follow. I followed too. We headed towards the city through a park that was so beautiful and perfumed after the stink of Castle Garden, it didn't seem real.

I struggled to understand how we had been discovered. The shortest way to find out would be to go to the police myself and explain – surely they had no right to make her go back; deserting a husband wasn't a matter for the law. I came to a sudden stop. Edward. She had kidnapped his son. Fear sapped the strength from my limbs. Were they looking for me too? They had my bag; the flint mill was in it and all of our money.

There were benches along the avenue. A man was sitting on one, smoking a pipe and reading a newspaper. Smart shoes and groomed moustaches, clearly not an immigrant. I sat down next to him. The quiver of his moustache showed me the odour from my dress had reached him. He glanced sideways, folded his paper and stood up.

'Excuse me, sir? Have you finished with your newspaper?'

He looked at me doubtfully. It was bewildering to think that for some people this was an ordinary day, an ordinary park, and for others the very hinge on which their lives were turning. After a moment's hesitation, he held out the treasure. My thanks didn't touch him.

I wasn't hopeful, but I needed to find out if Edward had been discovered too. Perhaps they would release her if she told them where he was. My breath caught at the thought. If Edward was returned to Gethin it would be worse for him than if he'd never been taken. But I also knew in my heart that even if Clara gave up her son, Gethin would never let her go so easily. My eyes darted about the tightly packed columns of print. I couldn't guess if a wife deserting an MP in London and stealing his son would hold any interest for people in New York, even if it was known she was fleeing this way. The pages were full of news about electoral fraud. There was an article about an asylum. Weddings, obituaries, weather.

The weather yesterday in London and neighbourhood was fair.

That's what it said at the bottom of a column. I felt on the wrong end of a horrible joke. We had left London nearly two weeks ago and had been travelling further away every day since. It was terrible to be able to read in black and white what the weather was doing there *yesterday*, as if we had been tricked into a circle or come no distance at all.

When I found it, I didn't know it at first. TELEGRAPHIC NEWS. Large print at the top of the page. My chest tightened. Beneath the headline, a list of the main stories from around the world: an assassination attempt, a massacre, a New York rowing team in England, and amongst them:

Murdered baby is MP's missing child

Not the right MP, not with murder in the sentence. But my back had turned cold. Something dark was twisting in my bowel. My stomach started to revolt, and I had to lean over the back of the bench as it tried to rid itself of the morsel of bread I'd eaten.

Missing child.

Her face in the cab in London, the things she had said, her nightmares. My own sense of foreboding. I wiped my mouth, hands shaking, and forced myself to seek out the story.

In a shocking turn to an already extremely painful case, the body of a baby found in the River Thames was last week identified by its own father, Mr Gethin MP of Finton Hall, Hertfordshire. The body of the five-month-old boy was discovered by a lighterman close to Blackfriars Bridge in London on May 29th. It had been placed in a large carpet bag and there was cord wrapped around its neck. Chief Inspector Vince of the Metropolitan police said Mr Gethin had been anxious for the safety of his wife and son since they went missing on May 25th. The police have been working tirelessly to find Mrs Gethin and believe she may have left the country.

Details slotted into place – the date, the place in the river, the carpet bag. My body twisted so I could retch again. I spat and rested my forehead against the back of the bench, eyes closed. Waves of nausea and horror washed over me, one after the other. I don't know how long I sat like that. The very discomfort of the position somehow kept my mind from plunging into total darkness. A bruise formed on my forehead, and it helped to press it. Without warning, tears came. Gouts of burning grief for Edward that I thought would smother me. People tried to talk to me, some with the best, others the worst intentions, but I was too fiercely elsewhere in my head. After a long while – hours, I think – it dawned on me that I was not in the hands of the police, and God knows, if they had been looking, they would have found me by then. I became aware of New York, a few hundred yards away, tall and solid and clanking with cranes and traffic and rough beginnings. Thoughts drifted towards me. Unthinkable thoughts, but they came anyway. What if I kept walking? Disappeared into America? What if I carried this burden silently into a new life?

A woman walked past me pushing a pram. She was looking into it and speaking to the baby with such love in her eyes, I was nearly sick again. My mind rebelled at the thought of returning to so much loss. What could I possibly do for Clara with Edward gone, if it was by her own hand? She didn't want me to show myself – perhaps she was trying to save me from the consequences of her own madness. It chilled me to think of her smile as the police led her away, as if a part of her had known all along this was as far as she could run, that she would never escape Gethin.

Let me weep over my cruel fate.

America yawned to my left. I could feel its energy, its newness. Freedom was a stone's throw. I stood up, but in standing, remembered another burden. I felt it as my skirt shifted, a weight I had been carrying without noticing for weeks. The pear-shaped choker, sewn into the hem. It stopped me as sure as if a hand had taken hold of my dress. I remembered the master placing it on her dressing table. I remembered the portrait, the canary, the cruelty. What if the newspaper account was untrue? What if I was seeing what someone else wanted me to see? Question marks are cannily shaped. They caught me with their hooks.

I am tired of writing. The hooks, the not knowing, have not let me go, pulling me back almost as far across the ocean. I am scared of arriving, and I am also desperate for this journey to be over. There are thumps and voices from the other cabins, passengers preparing to leave. The children have returned, pounding down the corridor as if they are not children at all but a terrible reckoning bearing down on me. I brace myself every time they pass my door, and my mind instantly, against my will, returns to the last time I saw Edward, drugged but alive still in Serle Place. Could I have known? Could I have saved him then? The questions tear at my heart. I cannot even answer for myself.

Tuesday, 18th June

There is a narrow alley behind Annie's house. The wall is high, but there is a wooden door, rotten enough for a person on the outside to see into the yard. I waited, feeling out of place in my new cloak and gloves, but also hopeful – it was early evening, threatening rain, and the washing was out. My guess was right. After less than half an hour, Anhie appeared, humming in that leisurely way of hers and hauling a basket. I felt my heart start to pound and doubts surfacing again that I had spent days arguing down.

'Annie.'

I knocked softly on the wood, and then again, harder.

'Annie.'

She peered at the door.

'Who is it?'

'Harriet.'

I had left without a word, after all her kindnesses. After a long pause, she put the basket down and walked towards me. The door shook as the bolt was pulled free. It opened a few inches, and we stared at each other.

'Sweet Jesus.'

She threw it wide and reached out an arm to pull me through, but I held back.

'Wait. Is Andrew home?'

'Not yet.'

I tried to read in her face what she knew, but there was only shock and puzzlement.

'Am I in trouble, Annie?'

Her mouth fell open slightly. She leaned in closer, whispered.

'Christ, Har, we've been worried out of our minds about you. Come in, for God's sake; it's not Andrew you need to fret about.'

Her words didn't hold much comfort, but I let myself be drawn into the yard. She bolted the door again and, turning, looked me up and down. I saw her take in my new clothes, the good quality chip bonnet with its ribbons and feathers, my pristine travelling bag. She was kind enough to look beyond them, put her curiosity aside.

'Are you hungry?'

I was starving. Standing on the upper deck as the ship slid into port yesterday, I wondered if I had eaten my last meal as a free woman. In my lodgings and on the train, I was too anxious to eat at all.

Annie fed me cold potatoes and beef. Her kitchen was warm and smelled faintly of lye. The plain food cooked by a good friend tasted so good, I couldn't speak. She waited until I was finished and then silently slid a newspaper across the table. I had already seen it. News was the first thing I looked for after safely and freely setting foot on the docks. I had hoped to hear Clara herself through the reports – an explanation or even confession, but she has not spoken since her arrest. She is a sensation all the same. The story has been talked inside out by the newspapers, taking up more space than the war congress in Berlin. I have arrived in the middle of a national obsession. Her trial is to begin in a few days, but her guilt is already decided.

'Have they written anything about me?'

Annie was watching me carefully, as if I was a barrel of gunpowder someone had set down in her house. She shook her head. I lowered my fork, glanced from the paper back to her.

'How do you know then?'

Her head shook again faintly.

'We only know you went with her to Liverpool and probably to America. Is that where you've been?'

I stared at her.

'How do you know we went to Liverpool?'

She ran her tongue over her top lip.

'Robert saw you. He . . .'

I stood up, knife and fork clattering on the plate, and turned away to lean against the sideboard. It was my fault then. He'd found me again somehow. Annie rose as I did and followed, standing close but not touching.

'Did she do it?'

I turned to look at her.

'I don't know.'

She searched my face. I didn't want to tell her about the carpet bag or how she had drugged Edward or any of the damning details that had crushed me into my berth the whole way from New York.

'She promised me we'd come back for him. She said he was some-where safe.'

Annie lifted a hand to the front of her dress protectively. I felt the unspeakable thought writhing to the surface. The muscles in my face screwed tight.

'She took him while I was buying food. What if . . . what if she didn't go somewhere safe? What if she really drowned him, and I . . . I did nothing?'

Annie put her arms around me and held on while the wave of horror crashed through me again. When I was washed up on the other side of it, she drew back.

'Come into the parlour. Tell me everything.'

I have been so long used to hiding the truth, to keeping my heart shut and bolted against discovery, I found at first the lock had rusted. Turns out simple truth-telling takes as much practice and care as lying. It came out in awkward bursts and disjointed thoughts, but as I talked my way back into Finton Hall, the memories and words began to flow together until I was being carried along on a torrent of confession, it felt like. An unburdening finally. Annie listened to it all in silence. She looked more thoughtful than horrified when I described the master and his friends. Difficult to shock a policeman's wife, I suppose. My doubts about Clara came out in spite of myself, but also my yearnings for a different life, for a different reason to live. My true mistress wasn't the wretched woman in Newgate who had lied to me; it was the miracle she turned into when she sang. I don't know what to call it – a state of grace, the purest part of herself revealed. What difference does it make if it's divine or human, if it redeems just the same? But that was before Edward – before the newspaper that tore up the past and the future and shattered my heart.

I told Annie everything, how sitting on the bench outside Castle Garden I had all but chosen to step into a new life until I felt the weight in my petticoat and remembered what I had sewn in there.

'Where is the choker now?'

Annie's eyes flicked about my new dress as she asked it, making me smile for the first time.

'I pawned it.'

She hooted.

'They must have thought you stole it.'

I suppose I had. It took a few tries to find the right broker, one whose customers pawned gems and silks rather than ragged bedding and children's boots. I learned to play the proud and tight-lipped lady's maid, hinting just enough at an abandoned mistress. I out-performed the musty stink of my dress, and the broker pretended to believe me. All I know is that the master must have spent a fortune on that necklace.

I was richer than years in service could have made me and that was just the pawnbroker's sum. Walking out into the New York evening, I knew I wasn't going to spend the night in an immigrant boarding house.

'Do you have much left?'

I shook my head.

'Not after the ship. Dollars aren't worth much here.'

It doesn't matter, though I didn't know how to explain that to Annie. The money itself isn't important. I chose a ready-made dress in a department store and had it altered there too. They have great tall mirrors so you can look at yourself from head to toe. It was like seeing myself for the first time – free of roles, free of place, neither a maid nor an immigrant. Or rather, I could be those things if need be, but I was this woman in the mirror first. New York showed me to myself.

It showed me other things too. Walking the streets, I saw new kinds of camera for sale that anyone could use, portable and, while my purse was full, affordable. A different life had beckoned, shadowy, difficult, independent, and I thought of Milton's poem and the 'talent' – the money that was meant to be used by the servant to make something more, something bigger. But it was a dream of another life, one I might have known if my path had been different. The woman I saw reflected in the mirror was always going back to Clara. She was stitched into me. Edward too. He died the very day I thought I was running with him to freedom – I couldn't leave even his ghost behind.

Then in the telegraphic news, it was reported that two hundred miners had been killed in a pit explosion in the north. It was nothing to do with Gethin, but it made me think of the flint mill and how he had loved it for its deadly light. He would have it back now. I recalled Clara's expression when I tried to explain why I had taken it, and the way she held out her arms. I walked to the booking office and spent the money on my ticket home.

Annie was looking at me a little wonderingly.

'What will you do?'

She sounded as if nothing I said would surprise her.

'I have to see her.'

'Har, you can't.'

'What did I come back for then?'

'It's not safe.'

'No one's looking for me, are they?'

She stood up abruptly and walked to the mantelshelf. Pulling something out from under the clock, she returned and handed me an envelope. It had my name on it.

'Robert thought you might write to me. He asked me to send you this if you gave an address.'

I took it from her, turned it over in my hands.

'He's the reason we were caught, isn't he? He told the police.'

Annie cleared her throat and clasped her hands together.

'He also saw the baby they pulled out of the river.'

I felt my face and throat tightening again. She carried on.

'He's not . . . You have to . . .'

She sighed impatiently.

'Oh, just read it, Har. It explains everything.'

Dear Harriet,

It is my dearest hope that if this letter is in your hands, it means you are far away from London. You may not yet know the role I played in Mrs Gethin's arrest, and I do not write this in expectation of your forgiveness. My only hope is that, knowing the facts, you will understand the importance of keeping away from your mistress and will not be tempted to show yourself. That I was acting firstly out of concern for you and later in the service of my profession is of no comfort to me. I will not urge my motives on you but simply set down what happened.

I followed you to your lodgings in Warren Street after you delivered my shirts to Annie and Andrew's house. They were worried about you, and it was clear to me from our conversation that you were hiding your real address. You spoke of seeing a man steal bread on Gray's Inn Road. No omnibus route from Aldgate would take you through that part of town. I hoped to speak with you about it when we met again at the tearooms. When you left in distress, I chose to look for you at your lodgings later that evening. The maid became nearly hysterical when I said I was a policeman, but I learned eventually there was no resident with your name. A room had been let to a seamstress calling herself Helen D – she could not properly recall the surname. She allowed me into your room where I found scraps of paper in the fireplace. Put together, they showed that day's date and an address in Serle Place.

I went there and watched from a doorway in the street opposite. At around three o'clock in the morning, a hackney cab stopped at the entrance to the court. When it pulled away, I saw a cloaked and laden figure let into the abandoned shop, which I later understood to be Mrs Gethin. A few hours after, you came out and I followed you to the market and back. When you left the address once more with a man and luggage, I was able to follow you to Euston Station in another cab. There, I recognised Mrs Gethin, though she was dressed as a working woman. I learned from the clerk that your tickets were for Liverpool. The man returned to Serle Place, and there I stopped following him.

You had already hinted at cruel behaviour from Mr Gethin. Your secrecy and Mrs Gethin's disguise painted a clear enough picture. As no crime had been committed and I had followed you for personal rather than professional reasons, I resolved not to interfere. I heard nothing about it from any quarter for several days and began to think I had misinterpreted the situation. My own work occupied me fully as the body of another baby was recovered from the Thames, which I am sure is the victim of the baby farmer I spoke to you about. The child had the same material wound around his neck as her other victims, and he matched a description given by a mother in Sheffield whose letters were discovered in my suspect's house.

Two days later, I was summoned by my chief inspector, who told me Mr Gethin had alerted the police about his wife's disappearance and had voiced concerns for the safety of his son. A discreet investigation was underway, and I had been informed because of my specialist work. I think you will understand that with a child missing, I was obliged to tell him I had seen Mrs Gethin at Euston Station with a tall young man and a maid. Against my better judgement at the time, I didn't name you. I now bitterly regret mentioning you at all.

The next afternoon I tried to escort the mother who had arrived from Sheffield into the mortuary to identify the baby. I was prevented and told the child had already been identified and the case was out of my hands. I applied to my superiors without success. Next day, it was in the papers. Mr Gethin had identified the child himself. His wife was now at the centre of a major hunt. Liverpool was mentioned. I have tried to argue that the child could be both Mr Gethin's son and also the most recent victim of my suspect. They tell me the evidence contradicts that, but when I push for details, I am warned off. There is increasing pressure on me to stop asking questions, and I believe it comes from high up, above my immediate superiors.

Even without Annie's (vehement) testament to your character, I do not believe you would ever knowingly be involved in the harming of a child. Mrs Gethin's innocence or guilt is beyond my knowledge – I don't know how she was employed while I followed you in the market – but I believe there are powerful forces working to bring about her conviction. I have no right to ask for your trust, but please be careful, Harriet. By leading them to Liverpool, I may have cost an innocent woman her freedom, and I do not begin to calculate the injury I have done to you. I pray that you are still unknown to them. If it is in my power to assist you in any way, I hope you can believe that I remain,

Your humblest servant,

Robert Ansell

The mother from Sheffield. She filled my imagination like an angel of mercy. I confess in that moment I was little able to consider her own dreadful plight. All I could think was – is it true? Is there even the smallest chance that the dead baby isn't Edward? I re-read the letter three times, thoughts spitting like hot fat, until Annie couldn't wait any longer.

'Well? What do you think?'

I couldn't tell her. There was so much that was painful rubbing alongside the desperately thin hope, jostling for space. If I had never gone to Annie's, I would never have met Robert again, and I would now be in America with Clara, forging a new life. We would have walked through Castle Garden's gates together, felt the energy of New York calling us both, begun what we had come to do. Robert's determination to know my business was calamitous – a reckless and powerful beast, springing into my life from nowhere. It had ripped our careful plans to shreds with one swipe of its claws even as we thought ourselves safe. I could not have known the lengths he would go to. The man had stood outside Serle Place *all night*.

'Fuck . . .'

I leaned my head in my palm, went to stand up, sat down again, hands in fists either side of the letter in my lap. It was also true that I might not have heard the news so soon. And what would I have done if I had seen the newspaper article – what would Clara have done? Or would we have returned in ignorance in six months or a year like she said and not been able to find him? Because there was something else in Robert's letter that offered a different glimmer of possibility. If the baby was Edward, nothing would bring him back, but perhaps the worst had not happened. I smoothed the letter out. What if Clara gave Edward in good faith to a baby farmer? I turned to Annie.

'The safe place she told me about. She could have paid this woman to look after Edward. It might be she never meant him to come to harm.'

Annie pursed her lips.

'Why isn't she saying that then? She's not said a word to defend herself.'

'I don't know. But she read my diary with your letter in it – it might have given her the idea to send Edward to a foster mother.'

It had plagued me relentlessly that my own diary might have prompted the missus to go down that path. Annie looked grim.

'If she read my letter, she'd also know it's an easy way to be rid of a child for good. Plenty of mothers know what they're paying for when they hand their babies over.'

Such a possibility existed – of course I knew that too, but all the same I wanted to stop Annie's mouth.

'Why are they covering it up then, not letting Robert find out if the baby farmer was part of it?'

She leaned forward, softer.

'It's likely they have good reason, Har, or it might be some daft politics between the City boys and the Met – it's not Robert's patch. But he's beside himself, you know. He looks like a ghost.'

'So he should.' My voice rose. 'He's right not to expect my forgiveness. Who does he think he is following me and going into my lodgings?'

'A worried friend?'

I all but spat. She sighed.

'He couldn't have known it would lead to this, Har.'

I didn't answer, and she continued.

'You don't know that she isn't where she deserves to be – you admitted it yourself. What matters is that you mustn't try and see her. What if they put you in the dock too?'

I nodded to stop her fixing me with her warning stare. The door rattled soon after and delivered Andrew into the room. I couldn't help but feel alarmed at the sight of his uniform – guilty even – though I know he'd disobey twenty chief inspectors before crossing Annie. We talked it all through again over tea – his pink cheeks and wide, astonished eyes make me wonder how he commands respect on the streets. I reluctantly agreed to them letting Robert know, but not to meeting him myself. Somehow, if we were both in the same room, I don't know whom I'd hate more. I'm bedding down in the parlour. Annie hugged me goodnight and made me promise I would keep clear of the Old Bailey. Seems I must turn the lock on my heart again.

Wednesday, 19th June

I gave the name I used in America. Walking through the passages and gates of Newgate with the other visitors, my heart in my mouth, I was reminded strangely of Castle Garden. The prison is a square rather than a rotunda, but it shares the same slab-walled authority, designed to hold humanity at will or at bay. Its very sheerness is frightening. I felt a familiar sense of stepping onto a different shore with an unknown country ahead of me, but this was a darker place – a land of endings not beginnings.

There was a walkway separating us, lined by two rows of bars and iron grating. A warder patrolled between the shouted conversations of prisoners and their friends. I don't know what I thought our meeting would be like in such a place. My mouth was dry. I realised I was scared of meeting her eyes. And then she was in front of me, wearing a clean gown, her hair dressed much as it had been when she sang in Castle Garden. I would have said she looked unexpectedly well if she hadn't been staring at me in horror. Her fingers gripped the bars.

'Why are you here?'

I stuttered, my mouth working without sound. She shook her head.

'You must go. Go far away from here. You should not have come back.'

'I can't. They are covering up the truth. The police and Mr Gethin.'

I mouthed it at her. She shook her head again, and I shouted over the hubbub.

'Tell them everything, ma'am. Who did you give him to? Did you pay for him to be fostered?'

She frowned, not answering.

'I know someone who can help. But you have to tell the truth, tell them where you took him.'

The warder was close by. Clara glanced at him and brought her face right up to the bars.

'He's safe.'

An icy hand ran down my back. I couldn't believe it. She was smiling.

'Ralph will never have him.'

'But . . .'

I stared across at her, terrified that the real distance between us was greater even than the guarded passageway. For the first time, I wondered what exactly she meant by 'safe'. Perhaps she hadn't lied. She saved the servants at Finton Hall by dismissing them. What if she believed she was saving Edward by destroying him?

'What do you mean Ralph will never have him?'

A kind of panic seized me.

'Where is he?'

She continued smiling, as if I was the one who couldn't see straight.

'They will find you guilty, Clara.'

I was suddenly angry.

'I'll tell them what happened. I'll get up in court and tell them everything.'

Her face changed, swift as a cut, from gentle to savage.

'You must go. Don't let them see you. Please.'

Her voice faltered on the last word. She dropped her hands from the bars and stepped back.

'Wait.'

I shouted it so loudly the warder turned towards me, but Clara had gone. Shaking, I staggered back between the looming walls and heavy gates and into the street. It had all happened in an agonising rush, more like having dust kicked in my face than a conversation. I came away less certain about what I think than before.

Annie was furious. There wasn't any good pretending I'd been three hours fetching a bottle of beer for our tea. I forgot to pick it up anyway. She slammed the lid on the copper and threw wet linen about with the same reckless energy as she had at Mrs B's. Finally, she kicked a bundle out of the way that was waiting on the floor and sat down opposite me, red hands flat against the wood.

'What's the hold she has on you? You jilt William, leave all your friends for America, and now you're risking your own neck when she's as good as hanged already.'

I flinched. She'd been tiptoeing around me so far, but I'd made her as mad as Clara had made me.

'You think they'll hang her?'

I heard how small my voice sounded. Annie made an exasperated noise and scraped her chair back. We didn't talk about it for the rest of the evening or mention it to Andrew, who bore our uncomfortable silence without comment, nursing it carefully as if we'd placed a sleeping wild cat in his arms. It's awake now though – I can hear them above me, Annie's barely suppressed outbursts. Strange how I was less lonely and more certain of my own edges in New York where there wasn't a single soul who knew me.

Friday, 21st June

My medicine – or punishment – was Robert.

'Someone has to talk sense into you.'

Annie led him into the kitchen where I was mending a bobby's shirt for her and then stood by the back door as if to stop me from bolting. Which was as well – I had an impulse to flee the way I had arrived. The paleness of his skin made the birthmark more vivid. His eyes were flinty, but there was a hesitancy that hadn't been there before. He stood in the doorway, holding his hat out slightly as if it was a gift he was worried might offend.

'I'm glad to see you, Harriet.'

I bit down on telling him I couldn't say the same. Snapped off a piece of thread before answering.

'Thank you for your letter.'

He nodded, gestured at a chair.

'May I?'

I shrugged.

'I won't be stopped from going to the court, so you can save your breath.'

He paused in the middle of sitting down and then lowered himself slowly.

'I could go for you.'

'What good would that do?'

He put his unblemished hands on the table.

'What if you're seen?'

I didn't speak.

'You're very loyal to her.'

Loyal is a difficult word. It sounds so like a good thing. Every way of answering I could think of balled in my throat. After a moment he carried on.

'You don't believe she is guilty?'

'Mostly, no.'

'But you are not sure?'

I looked up, ready to tell him I was done with his questions and that he'd caused enough trouble with his meddling but was silenced by the emotion in his face. His eyes had turned dark velvet and there was something like recognition in them. I found myself simply answering instead.

'At the gaol, I wondered if she believed she had saved him from his father, that she had done the right thing by killing him. If it *was* her that did it. I don't know.'

Robert leaned forward with an earnestness that made me uncomfortable. That beast with all its power and determination to know the truth was still stalking about.

'Why do you think that?'

'She said Mr Gethin would never have him – she honestly wanted me to believe that. It was the way she was smiling.'

Annie blew air through her lips. Robert kept staring at me as if my face was covered in fine print that he had to squint at to read.

'Do you remember the clothes the baby was wearing before she took him away?'

It wasn't the question I was expecting, though I could answer easy enough. I had changed Edward, straightened his bonnet, loosened his collar so he could breathe.

'A white dress, buttoned at the top, with a knitted blue jacket and bonnet.'

'Good quality?'

'Yes.'

Annie cut in.

'The baby farmer would have taken them if they were worth something.'

One of Robert's fingers tapped soundlessly against the table.

'The body in the Thames was wearing an old nightshirt.'

'There you are.'

'If it's the same baby.'

We both looked at him. Annie put a hand on her hip.

'Why would Mr Gethin say the baby was his if it isn't? And if Edward is alive, whoever's got him would come forward surely, or leave him somewhere – they must know what's going on.'

Laurence.

'I need to find Laurence.'

Robert lifted his chin.

'The man at Serle Place, who took you to the station?'

'Yes, he was the footman at Finton Hall. He helped Clara – I don't know how much, or what he knows.'

'You said he was a brute.'

Annie was doing well to keep her voice down. I could see how she saw it: an unnatural woman, a depraved servant. Her arguments were straight and sharp as a blade.

'He's not come to save her, has he? They most likely did it together. He's the last person you want to run into.'

I watched the muscles working in Robert's face. It wasn't until he had said that about the baby not being Edward that I understood the catastrophe happening in his own life – his beloved police force turned rotten again, his very career threatened. He had worked hard to catch that baby farmer; he *wanted* the baby to belong to the woman from Sheffield. In the kitchen he turned back to me, eyes a perfect storm.

'You should be at the trial.'

I think my mouth fell open.

'No one else knows the details of their lives like you do. You'll see what I can't.'

It was the answer I hadn't been able to find for Annie. I nodded, feeling relieved, and at the same time very frightened.

Monday, 24th June

I knew there would be a crowd. They had been queueing up since dawn to see the upper-class baby murderer, eager to know if she was as beautiful as the newspapers said. Beauty and horror together make for a special fascination. Robert policed us a path to the door and with a word to the man there, got us up to the public gallery. We could have sat at the front, but we had already decided neither of us should make ourselves too obvious. Mr Gethin was almost out of view in a seat on the right. The sight of him stabbed fear into my heart. Quiet, reserved, serious. Unremarkable in a sea of other men. To look at him – and he would have known people were doing little else – one would think he couldn't hurt a fly. But on the same side in a different row was Mrs Trevelyan. Pale and patient with her hands folded in her lap. I could have sobbed to see her.

The judge was announced first. I would never have thought watching a man walk into a room and sit down could have such a violent effect on my guts. Then Clara's name was called. The dock is below and just in front of the gallery, so when it came to it, I could hardly see her at all. Once people had sat back from craning to look, I saw the top of her head, her hat placed forward with a single feather, a style that suits her well. I wondered if it was Mrs T that was bringing her clothes.

I hate the courtroom. It's a pit of life – as if a giant child has been out creature-collecting with a wooden bucket. I felt at any moment the wigged specimens bunched together on the right might start crawling all over the plainer bodies in the lower section (many bald pates on show), or the fidgety public would finally spill over and drop from the balcony on silk threads. The jury in banked seats opposite the wigs, on the other hand, looked pinned in place, two orderly rows of waiting grubs.

When the court was settled and the jury sworn, a clerk read out the charge. Hearing Edward's name spoken, I was crushed again by the weight of loss and had to fight hard against tears. Clara was asked for her plea. She didn't speak. Her silence stopped everyone's breath; the whole courtroom was suspended without movement like dead things pickled, until the judge lowered his head and ordered a plea of not guilty to be entered.

From then on, I felt it was all running away from me. The lawyer employed against her, a Mr Frith, began a speech that made my hands go clammy where they clutched the edge of the bench. Robert looked at me several times as facts rang around the court – Clara's violence towards her own portrait, her coldness as a mother, her harsh treatment of servants. The prosecutor's voice was as sure and firm as the wooden panelling running around the room. It straightened the jury's spines and gave the gallery a platform on which to build their prejudices. There was tutting and shaking of heads all around me, gathering blood lust.

'But what reason could there be for Mrs Gethin's behaviour?'

The prosecutor paused as if genuinely mystified and let the question flutter about the court.

'A woman with youth and beauty, marrying into a life of luxury her own family could no longer provide, all the comfort and splendour of Finton Hall, a baby. A *beautiful* son.'

He stopped again, letting us all think about that beautiful son.

'Was it the Honourable Mr Gethin?'

He spun around suddenly and pointed.

'Was he a terrible husband? This man who campaigns ceaselessly for the rights of fallen women? Was he so tyrannical and cruel, so brutal in his treatment of his own wife that she was driven to acts of violence? And did this cruelty all take place in the same home that he also opens to society's most desperate, the lame and the friendless, providing employment and shelter for those who can find it nowhere else?'

His head turned back to the jury, a smile of disbelief flickering around his mouth. Several of the grubs actually smiled back.

'Well, let's say that he was – a brute, a wolf in sheep's clothing. Why then should the servants be made to suffer? Why then would a mother turn from her innocent child, a child in need of her protection? And why later would she strangle that same innocent and throw his body into the Thames?'

There was a flinching intake of breath in the gallery as if that was the first they had ever heard of it.

'No.'

The lawyer became grim, almost angry.

'Today you will hear what sort of a woman Mrs Gethin is. You will hear it from those closest to the family, those who witnessed – and suffered – her behaviour for years. A resentful, implacable, grasping woman, whose unfounded malice towards her husband was based on sheer vanity.'

He produced a piece of paper.

'A husband who offered her everything that was good.' He held the paper up and shook his head.

'But she didn't want what was *good*.'

Lowering it, he began to read. It was the police account of her singing in Castle Garden. The official wording made her performance sound both vulgar and ridiculous, and he put on the apish expression of a music hall comedian to describe her climbing the bread stand. Titters of laughter went around the crowd.

'And for this . . .' He held the paper high again, a torch of truth. 'For *this* she murdered her own baby son.'

I don't know how I didn't stand up and start screaming. He went on to speak about the recent spate of murdered infants found in the river. Robert kept wiping a hand across his mouth, as if to make sure it stayed shut, especially when it was claimed that Edward's murder had been designed to look like a baby farmer crime. My stomach writhed so terribly, I thought I would bring up my guts onto the floor of the gallery.

Witnesses came to a stand between the jury and judges' bench: a lighterman who had found the baby in the Thames near Blackfriars Bridge, not very far from Serle Place; the doctor who performed the post-mortem; the constable who had first been called – Robert leaned forward in his seat. It wasn't easy to hear up in the gallery – or see. A carpet bag was shown to the jury, and I strained my eyes trying to make out if it was mine. I had to look away from the length of fabric and the baby's soiled nightshirt.

Then it was the new nursemaid that I hadn't seen before. Her words were particularly hard to catch. Pretty and young – one of Clockface's – but stiff as a peg doll.

'She's terrified.'

I would have been too with the whole court staring at me, but I saw what Robert meant. She looked as if her eyes might roll into the back of her head. The lawyer led her through her time as Edward's nursemaid, how Clara had wanted to keep Edward in her room the night they disappeared. Then he pointed to the nightshirt and asked if she recognised it. Even from the gallery, we could see she was shaking. She began to say something, but the judge cut across to tell her to speak up.

'It might . . . it might be Edward's.'

'Might?'

She jerked her head back as if the word was a slap.

'He . . . had one very like that.'

'She's lying.'

Robert whispered it urgently in my ear.

'With the stains, it's difficult . . .'

'Take a closer look.'

The lawyer gestured for it to be taken over to her, but she shrank back.

'No, I'm sure. I'm sure he had one like that.'

There was a break soon after, and everyone shuffled out, discussing Clara's certain guilt. We stayed on the street nearby, too restless to find somewhere to sit or eat. The air was close. I pawed at a dropped playbill with my boot.

'Why didn't Clara's lawyer question her? No one even asked if Edward's nightshirt was missing.'

Robert was smoking a cigarette, head down, other hand jammed in his trouser pocket. He rubbed his forehead with his wrist. Smoke hung in the muggy air.

'No one is trying to prove the baby isn't Edward.'

I wanted so much for it to be true, what he had said at Annie's. Or perhaps I just wanted him to carry on believing it, even if I couldn't.

'Do you really think it isn't him?'

He blinked as if his eyes were tired.

'Annie's right – there is too much against it. But something's off or they wouldn't have shut me out.'

'Why don't you tell her lawyer about your baby farmer?'

'There's no evidence now.'

'But the material you said he was strangled with?'

'Too common to mean anything on its own, and anyone could have read about it in the papers from the other murders.'

I could feel the claw around my chest again, dragging me to the edge.

'But her lawyer must . . .'

'Her lawyer is there for form's sake because it's a murder trial. The judge has to appoint one if the accused won't or can't pay.'

I thought of the choker, my second-class cabin and new clothes. Robert carried on grimly.

'If she won't speak and the evidence is against her . . . All he has that I can see is that there are no witnesses who actually saw her with the carpet bag.'

I swallowed with difficulty. If I told him she had taken mine when she took Edward, would he stop doubting she was guilty? If I said it out loud, would I?

'Is that enough to stop her being convicted?'

'Unlikely.'

He stamped on the cigarette.

'Do you want to go back in?'

There was still a big crowd waiting for their turn in the gallery. Robert looked down the line, which started just behind me, and then sharply over my shoulder. He put out a hand to take my arm, and I spun around, expecting all kinds of horrors. It was Mary. She stood a little apart from the crowd, staring hard.

'I thought it was you.'

The last time I had seen her she was lying unconscious on Clara's bed in Finton Hall. I stepped forward, but she retreated as far, stumbling as her foot slipped off the kerb. There was something bruised about her. The brightness had gone, though the determined little animal was still there.

'I'm looking for Laurence.'

She didn't meet my eye as she said it. I remembered the keening noise she had made at the foot of his bed that night.

'We want to find him too.'

She flashed me a look and another at Robert.

'He was meant to come back.'

More people were joining the queue. She glanced furtively amongst them.

'When?'

'After he helped *her*.'

She tossed her head towards the court.

'He was supposed to come back two weeks ago.'

I stared at her.

'You knew he was helping the missus escape?'

She didn't answer but carried on darting looks at everyone and everything in sight.

'I'm not supposed to be here. Mrs Trevelyan said not to. But I don't know where else to look.'

'Mrs Trevelyan?'

She sniffed.

'I'm at the vicarage now. I took the train this morning.'

Robert stepped into the road and threw up his arm, hailing a cab.

'We shouldn't be talking out here.'

Mary regarded him blankly. I introduced him as a friend of mine, but she hardly seemed to listen. He fixed her with one of his flinty looks as a growler rolled up.

'Let us take you to the station. Harriet will write with any news.'

He seemed in a hurry. Mary hesitated. Her hand moved across the front of her dress in a familiar gesture.

'You will?'

I nodded. We found each other, I think, in the look we shared. It was as if we were back in Finton Hall, still haunted by a place we shall never set foot in again. As she turned to the cab, I thought I saw a new fullness to her body in the way her skirts swung and felt a horrible misgiving. The journey was strangely silent. Questions screamed in my head that I couldn't ask in front of Robert, but when the carriage jerked to a stop, he didn't move.

'Stay where there are people at all times. I'll meet you at Annie's later.'

'Are you going back to the trial?'

His eyes flicked to Mary and away again.

'There is something I need to do.'

He paused and put a hand on my arm.

'Go straight back to Annie's. Don't go to the trial by yourself.'

We found a table in the refreshment room while we waited for her train. I watched her over scalding cups of tea neither of us touched.

'Mrs Trevelyan has been looking after you?'

Mary nodded faintly.

'She looks after everyone. Even her.'

'What did Laurence tell you?'

She gave me a quick look on the slant and didn't answer.

'Did Mrs Trevelyan know what Laurence was doing?'

She shrugged. 'A bit. He wouldn't say much about it.'

'About the missus?'

Tears glistened in her eyes, and she wrapped her arms around her middle.

'I don't care about her.'

She meant it. Her voice was low and hard.

'We're getting married.'

It came out like a challenge, or even a threat. Again, she wouldn't meet my eye. I tried to smile my way back into her sight.

'You're going to have a family?'

She took a deep breath and nodded, held herself tighter. Of course, the father was Laurence. My first awful thought was foolish – the soirée was too recent for her to show.

'What will you do?'

'I can stay at the vicarage until my time. Laurence will have found a place . . .'

She was forced to stop, lips clenching together to keep from trembling.

On the platform, I took her hands in mine; they were limp and cold.

'I'm happy for you, Mary, I really am.'

She looked up uncertainly. The old twitching whiskers, working me out. Tears pricked my own eyes as I smiled at her. I waited until she seemed to accept it and kissed her cheek.

'Robert will find him. I'll write when there's any news at all.'

It wasn't going to be good news, and I could see she knew it too. Rattling back to South London on the omnibus, all I could think was that if Laurence was coming back, he would have written himself.

Annie all but jumped on me when I returned, pulling me into the parlour and locking the door behind us as if an army of murderers was at my back.

'Robert sent a message. You mustn't go out again.'

She was bunching her apron up in both hands. I thought how it made her look like a child.

'He spoke to someone from the City police. They found a body in the rubble where the street's been knocked down. He thinks it's your footman.'

302

Later

Robert came back just after six, asking if I was home before Annie had the door half open. The sight of me seemed to take the strength from his limbs. He collapsed into a chair without even a greeting and stared into the unlit fire. I sat down opposite.

'Is it him?'

He ran a hand through his hair, then fumbled in the pocket of his waistcoat.

'Do you recognise this?'

He passed me a man's ring.

'From the little finger of the right hand.'

It was heavier than I expected and horribly real. I felt my heart grow sick under the weight.

'Mary would know for sure. But, yes, I think so.'

I looked at him and my voice collapsed to a reluctant whisper.

'Did you see him?'

He nodded.

'The body was still at the mortuary. It looked like him. What was left.'

I sat up so I could take a deeper breath and glanced at the kitchen door, ready to run if I had to retch.

'What happened?'

He shook his head.

'They can't tell how he died. His injuries are great, but they might be from the wall falling in. There was certainly a fight, though, marks on his hands . . .'

He rubbed the knuckles of one of his.

'But he's been dead at least two weeks.'

'Two weeks?'

'At least.'

I saw Laurence's wink as he turned away from me on the platform, how he had jogged back towards the street. He might have been dead before we even left England. Annie was standing back a little, like a spectator.

'What does it mean then? Was he murdered?'

Robert shifted so his elbows rested on his knees. He rubbed his forehead.

'Unknown, at the moment. But the body must have been hidden by someone. Unless they were outrageously careless about searching the buildings before knocking them down.'

I asked what had made him go back there.

'A feeling. Your friend – Mary – said she hadn't heard from him for a fortnight. That's not very long after you left Serle Place.'

He slapped both hands hard and flat against his thighs and stood up, turning to face the mantelshelf. His body was strung rigid. Annie glanced at me.

'You couldn't have stopped it, Robert.'

He spoke to the wall, one hand over his mouth.

'I gave my chief inspector the address. He passed on everything I said to Mr Gethin. I suspect he's in his pay.'

I barely caught his next words.

'I might as well have been working for him myself.'

He turned again, arms hanging by his sides.

'I'll try and find out more tomorrow.'

His eyes found mine. It was like looking into a bruise.

'Leave London. Go to your parents, anywhere, at least until the trial's over and everything's calmed down.'

Annie nodded, stepping forward.

'I'll have Andrew go with you to the station when he comes off his round in the morning.'

I became aware of the cosy parlour, the polished furniture, the postcards above the fireplace. It's better that I don't stay here. I don't want to bring any more trouble. They both looked relieved. I didn't tell them that I can't go home though, that I don't trust my mother not to write to Gethin. At the door, Robert turned to say goodbye (in the corner of my eye I saw Annie slip into the kitchen). I don't blame him anymore. I don't even blame myself. Neither of us ever held enough of the pieces – we were always going to be looking at the wrong picture. I spoke first.

'Thank you.'

He winced. Silence tightened between us. The furrows in his brow deepened.

'You know, Harriet, I don't know who's guilty. I don't even know how many crimes have been committed.'

For a moment, he looked like a bewildered child.

'But they are going to get away with it.'

I lifted my hand and very lightly touched his birthmark. It wasn't the sweetheart or even motherly gesture it sounds like. I think I wanted to touch him in the way one wants to touch a struck tuning fork. He took my hand in his and ran his thumb once over the rutted skin down the side of my finger. I thought I'd mind, but I didn't. When he'd gone I found I was still holding Laurence's ring in my other hand.

———

What do I know? What do I want? The truth? I think I am blind to it. I keep looking for what isn't there. Scratching at these pages in snatched hours, borrowed corners – who is it for? If words are like stitches, I have been pushing the needle too far all this time – catching at myself with the thread without realising. If I try to stand and lay it aside, I can't – it is stitched into me now. I turn Laurence's ring over and over between my fingers in the candlelight. He risked everything to save us, and he didn't run. I don't know what else he did, but he didn't run. It is enough – leaving London and Clara now is no more possible than stepping out of my own skin.

Tuesday, 25th June

Andrew escorted me all the way to the station and, maddeningly, into
the carriage – I discovered the persistence in him that Robert so
admires. I was able to slip out again while he was distracted by a
talkative lady on the platform and made it to the Old Bailey in time
to sit in the second row against the wall. It was a different crowd of
spectators from yesterday, newly eager. I wondered if Clara could hear
the whispers and rustlings above her, a gentle, deadly hissing. A newspaper I picked up on the way to the court reassured me I had missed
nothing decisive from yesterday afternoon – more laying out of facts
about the murder and Clara's whereabouts. Today the lawyer was
moving on to Clara's character, calling witnesses to support his earlier
conjuring of an unnatural witch.

I slapped a hand to my mouth, dread worming through my guts as
Clockface stepped up. To my mind, she was sewn firmly into the fabric
of Finton Hall like a monster in a nightmare – she should have melted
into air beyond the gates. But there she was, looking as real and self-
assured in front of the court as she ever had wielding a carving knife at
the head of the servants' table. I watched helplessly, swallowing down
panic – a rabbit tricked by a stoat. No trace of the spitefulness and hate
that laced every encounter with the missus. Not a word of French. Only
a trustworthy servant and helpless looker-on to her master's misfortune.

The truth, nothing but the truth. Cook and housekeeper to Mr
Gethin for fifteen uneventful years before his marriage. A new mistress
– difficult, peculiar even, but Sarah Clarkson had known worse. Until
it *was* worse. Cruel and frequent dismissal of staff without notice – a
lady's maid, housemaids, parlour maids, pageboys. Managing the household had become impossible. Violent outbursts against everyone,
particularly Mr Gethin – in front of the servants, no less – and damage
done or threatened to his priceless collection. Her own portrait, a gift
from him, she tried to stab and rend with a knife. Yes, a knife.

The lawyer took his time. Mrs Clarkson – the respectable upper servant, both remote and intimate in the lives of her betters – would linger in the minds of the jury, her words recalled as gospel. There was shifting about in the gallery as people left for fresher air or to reclaim their own lives and dramas; others took their place, whispering, rustling. I leaned forward to hear better.

'Oh, everyone loved little Edward. He was a delightful baby . . .'

Clockface tried to smile but cut her voice off as if with emotion. The lawyer smiled in sympathy.

'Everyone?'

She nodded.

'The whole household . . .'

She hesitated, as if reluctant to say it.

'All except his mother, Mrs Gethin. She wouldn't have him with her.'

She delivered at least half her answers directly to the judge, drawn as always, I realised, to the most powerful man in the room. What she wouldn't do for them, these untouchable gentlemen, to win their attention, their approval. Gethin must have seen that, her great need to feel raised up, but also her desire to smite those beneath – he had watched her bullying the knife-cleaner. She might have stumbled on his secrets as I had, or it's possible he chose her because he sensed they were cut from the same cloth. Instead of shrinking in horror from the truth, she had readily embraced it, feeding her own lust for power from the source. Abominable kin, Clara had called them. The lawyer narrowed his eyes.

'It is usual, is it not, for a lady of Mrs Gethin's position to leave much of the care of her child to a nurse?'

Clockface looked troubled.

'But she almost never saw him, nor entered the nursery and . . . well, we all thought that was for the best, to be truthful.'

'Why is that, Mrs Clarkson?'

She turned again to the judge.

'The times she did go up, she was violent. Frightened the wet nurse half out of her wits by throwing things about and smashing them. Gifts for the baby.'

There were gasps and mumblings in the gallery. My veins ran with ice. Lizzie must be waiting to come out and say it was all true. She wouldn't even have to dissemble like the bitch in the dock. The lawyer raised his eyebrows, but Clockface continued unprompted.

'She seemed to detest the child.'

'Detest is a strong word.'

She nodded sadly.

'We believed it was on account of her feelings for the poor mite's father. I heard her say that any child of his would be a curse or cursed itself.'

There was more unrest in the gallery – someone tutted right next to me – and the judge called for quiet. I tried to imagine Clara saying that – was it possible she could have said that? Then a familiar, hated voice in my ear, like an echo.

'Do you think that is true, Watkins?'

I started and went to jump up – even before turning to look at him – but Barrett grasped my wrist, hiding the movement by leaning into me.

'Sit down.'

I pressed myself into the wall, head turned away.

'You have a choice, Watkins.'

I don't know how he made me hear him. He was stealthy as a spider in the corner of a web, wrapping its victim in invisible threads. His words, barely more than air, bound like iron.

'Child stealing and murder.'

He tutted again.

'The court won't be merciful.'

My skin was clammy and cold at once. He cleared his throat softly.

'Not with your history of violent acts.'

I jerked in my seat, but he leaned closer against me, breathing stuffily through his nose.

'Nobody wants to believe a lady would kill her own child, do they, Watkins? But a servant?'

He breathed in as if considering possibilities.

'A criminal character who savagely attacked a gentleman, half blinding him – who took advantage of her master's absence and tricked her way into a position above her station, one who could manipulate a weak-minded mistress . . .'

Sweat pricked my upper lip. I couldn't move.

'Do you see, Watkins? Your policeman can be made to testify that he saw you. The landlady in Liverpool will be able to identify you.'

Clockface had disappeared from the court below, and I heard Lizzie being called. I knew she would innocently condemn me too, simply by telling the truth as she saw it. The door opened, but it wasn't her that stepped through. A child I thought at first, and then the net that had been thrown over me cinched tight. Not 'Lizzie', of course. *Lily*. She was neatly and fashionably dressed – the clothes looked too new – her head held high. A boldness showed in her face, but there was a hardness there as well, a worn look. Barrett shifted his position slightly and nodded towards her.

'Your fellow servants in particular remember the influence you enjoyed.'

Her voice was as deep as ever. She answered questions readily, with a note of insolence. I could feel the gallery liked her – a tiny queen holding court, conscious of her power. The story went the same way as before – a hard mistress, a lovely baby, disturbing behaviour. My voice trembled.

'Why are you doing this?'

Barrett's reply, when it came, was dry and flat.

'You know why.'

309

Lily was doing everything she'd been told to – paid to, no doubt, though I could see that avenging herself on her former mistress was wages enough. It was all about Clara and Edward – she told the lawyer she'd heard things that froze her blood.

'Such as?'

She looked straight at the dock, at Clara.

'I heard her tell the master that she wished his son was born dead.'

The gallery gasped as one. Lily's eyes flickered around the court. She was enjoying herself. In her own mind, she was beyond harm, making her own choices, but I knew that no matter whose clutches she had fallen into since leaving the charity, she was still as much Gethin's victim as if she had stayed at Finton Hall. She would never know how Clara had tried to save her. Barrett's voice was soft as silk.

'I'm sure you value your life, Watkins. Why should you throw it away for a mistress who would happily watch you hang? Do you think she'd speak up to save you?'

Lily's small chin lifted.

'And I heard her telling her lady's maid who she was very thick with that she'd as soon dash his brains out as own him for any of hers.'

The public broke into voice with chatter and outrage. Irritable calls for quiet came from the judges' bench. I couldn't breathe. Barrett leaned into me.

'You have more sense than that, Watkins. Certainly more sense than that rutting dog of a footman.'

A coldness I've never felt before ran down my spine. Laurence. Signs of a fight, Robert had said, injuries that might have been caused by falling masonry – or not. Barrett was so close it was as if he was talking in my head. His next words chiselled themselves into my skull.

'As I said, you have a choice. All you have to do is tell me, and I'll let you walk away. Tell me where she's hidden Edward Gethin.'

The court lurched sideways. I felt as if I was falling against the wall. My head whipped around to look at him. His eyes had narrowed so, they were all but shut. I could feel his will pressing against my mind, his certainty that I would answer. That I *could* answer. Something like laughter boiled up under my ribcage, hard and frantic. Clara was innocent. I turned front again. There were still shouts for calm. Lily was smiling to herself. The air couldn't get into my lungs. Clara was innocent, and Gethin had lied about the dead baby being Edward. He didn't know where Edward was. Barrett was still looking at me, eyes beginning to widen. My evident shock had tripped him. He could see in my face that I knew less about it than he did. But I was over the edge – nothing below me – and starting to fall. Gethin's monstrous lie had conjured this courtroom, this crushing machinery of the law, the noose threatening Clara's neck. Robert's words rang through my head. They're going to get away with it.

'It's not Edward! They're lying!'

I was on my feet. The room swirled around me – faces turned my way, a mass of searching eyes from every direction.

'It's not Edward!'

I kept shouting it. The court had turned silent at first, but then voices from the bench started barking orders and the fuss around me started up again, louder than before. There were jeers to shut my mouth and counter cries to let me speak. Barrett had quickly stopped trying to tug me back down. Two constables were fighting their way across the gallery. I was yelling again that the baby wasn't Edward when Clara stood up and turned to look at me. She had to arch her back slightly over the rail of the dock. Our eyes met and my words cut off as sure as if her hands were squeezing my throat. She looked at my frantic face with something like wonder, but it was her calmness that shut my mouth. It seemed to make its own space in the press of the court, as if we had fallen into a quiet spot. Her eyes were clear.

A constable reached me and began hauling me along the narrow space between benches.

'You fool.'

Barrett hissed it at my feet, his sleek face roughed out of shape for the first time. Hands clutched at me as I stumbled along, some helping, some pawing at my body. I began to understand what I had done. Terror flew at me in black flurries, dreadful wings beating. The master would never let me walk away now. *He always wins.* Everyone in the gallery was staring at me, and every single eye seemed changed at once to the lover's eye in the cabinet at Finton Hall – a hundred of them, brimming with hate and now also triumph, and all reflecting the image of a gallows. Barrett was right – they would not hesitate to hang a servant.

I thought my legs were going to give way beneath me when there was another shift in the attention of the court. A different voice had spoken that caused an instant hush below. The gallery caught it and leaned forward. Even the constable paused. Clara was still standing, facing the bench with her hands on the rail. Everyone was now staring at her. A judge ordered her to repeat what she had said.

'I plead guilty.'

Her voice commanded the stunned court, as if a sentence was being passed on us. She spoke steadily and without emotion.

'I killed my son. I put him in that carpet bag and threw it into the Thames.'

The silence continued for a beat, and then the gallery burst into an uproar. It was impossible to hear anything being said below, but I saw a figure rise slowly from the seats on the right. The master stood with one hand on the back of the bench in front of him, the other half raised towards the dock. To the rest of the court, his expression must have been exactly that of a man hearing such awful words from his wife. Shock, amazement, horror. But I saw what was rippling beneath it – rage. It writhed up from the depths of him. He had thought he could predict what Clara would do, but he was wrong. With her false confession, she was condemning herself, but she was also defeating him.

To the world, Edward was now officially dead, forever out of his reach. I watched fury filling his eyes like blood, hot and blinding, and understood that Clara had won.

Wednesday, 26th June

She has escaped hanging. Mrs T returned to the court to hear the sentence this morning while I waited in her hotel room. Yesterday, she was already in the street when the constables dragged me down from the gallery. News of what was happening inside had spilled out of the building already, and the pavement was full of people pushing towards the door. Somehow, she pulled me free and into a cab.

At her hotel, I sat on a dusty chaise longue and told her about Barrett, about the night in Serle Place and how I hadn't known for certain the baby wasn't Edward until now. She kept saying, 'Oh my dear,' and the stars creased around her eyes. I am glad Clara has her for a friend.

'Do you know where Edward is? Did she tell you?'

She shook her head and picked at the fingers of her glove.

'Clara wouldn't tell me her plans. She thought it safer. I . . .'

She stopped playing and yanked the glove off, finger by finger.

'I couldn't believe what I was reading in the newspapers.'

I saw she had also been forced to ask herself terrible questions. She had seen Edward's blood on her own hands too. I leaned forward.

'She has put him somewhere. I think only Laurence knew.'

She looked up, abruptly eager.

'Mary has been beside herself about him. Where is he?'

I told her what Robert had told me. Afterwards, she was quiet for a long time. I took Laurence's ring from my pocket and held it out to her.

'Mary should have this.'

She took it without speaking. Every now and then she gave a little shake of her head and a corner of her mouth twitched.

'That dreadful man. To think he is an MP.'

I needed her to come back to me. I wanted her to have all the answers.

'Why did he say the murdered baby was Edward?'

She shook her head again.

'I can only imagine to force Clara's hand, so she would have to give up the child, and he could say he was mistaken in his grief. Who knows what depths such a man may sink to? He must never have believed she would let it go to trial, that she would sacrifice herself like this to keep the child safe from him. He underestimated her.'

She smoothed her skirt over her knees in a deliberate, careful movement. Her voice seemed trapped in her throat.

'As did I.'

She sent for Tabby, who arrived this morning and waited with me through the terrible hours Mrs T was in court. I wrote to Annie and Robert, but otherwise sat without employment, unable to speak. Tabby sewed and filled the silence with nothing very much, trivial news from the vicarage. She was full of scorn for Mr Trevelyan.

'He pretends he can't see what's right in front of him. Won't read the papers, won't look at Mary, who's clearly growing a child right under his roof, and he acts as if his wife has come to London for the shops. He complained that Gertrude's jam was too sweet though – we had to scrape her off the kitchen floor.'

Mrs T's knock came just then. After all the waiting, my courage failed at the last moment. It was Tabby who trampled over her dropped sewing and grappled with the lock. Mrs T was talking before the door even opened. Clara's lawyer had marshalled doctors and pushed for the court to find her insane. She was found guilty of murder but escaped the noose. As Mrs T said, a woman killing her baby is shocking, but putting a noose around a lady's neck is an even greater affront to the natural order of things. The judge, at least, couldn't stomach it. He has sentenced her to be locked up in an asylum.

Thursday, 27th June

We were allowed to see her in her cell this morning before she was moved. I was frightened of how she might be, imagining dark wells of fury or despair, but she rose to greet us in the stony, narrow room as if we were old friends entering the drawing room of Finton Hall. I was the one who fell into a passion, throwing my arms around her and sobbing. She pressed me to her until I had recovered, then made me sit with a handkerchief on the hard platform that served as a bed. It was the handkerchief I had embroidered with her fake initials for America. Mrs T told her about Barrett threatening me in court (but not about Laurence). She did her best to make Clara change her mind and tell the truth about Edward.

'Don't call him that.'

It was the only sharp word I heard from her. She quickly softened and smiled.

'Edward is a Gethin name.'

They regarded each other silently for a moment, and then Mrs T nodded faintly. She pressed her lips to Clara's cheek and stepped as far away as the cell would allow. Clara sat down next to me and took my hands.

'If I told them where he is, it wouldn't save me from the asylum. Do you understand that?'

I nodded, sickened. It was true. She had done enough to be considered dangerous and unnatural by every innocent and blinkered looker-on. I hated everyone then. Not just the guilty – the master and his lot – but every Gertrude and Mr Trevelyan who sat so complacently on their sluggish morals.

'It will be my consolation that Ralph will never know where he is.'

Her eyes bored into mine, burning away my thoughts and making me sit up. She held my gaze.

'I don't mind what he becomes, rich or poor, so long as he is free of his parentage.'

My heart started to quicken, already beginning to understand. Clara leaned forward and whispered in my ear. It took few words, less than a minute to say. She drew back enough to watch my face.

'Do you understand?'

My hands gripped hers so tightly it must have hurt. She was staring at me intently.

'Will you do this for me?'

I nodded. The enormity of it rolled out, vast, a new landscape.

'But you . . . You can't spend your life in an asylum.'

I was fighting to breathe again. The lines and planes of her face seemed to grow sharper, as if a mental struggle – an act of will – had brought her more into being.

'Why not? When I can do no more, and my son is safe? I shall always have that.'

I saw a thought hesitate behind her eyes. When she spoke, her words faltered.

'It is true, Harriet, that I found him – I found his existence – difficult. After he came, I was ill – I have never known such darkness. I knew by then what kind of man his father is. To have brought another life into that hell was more than I could look at. I saw only that my own life was over. Ralph would take the music from me somehow, and I knew I wouldn't survive it. When I decided to escape, it was blindly, as a creature simply fighting to save itself. I would have left my child behind. I would. But Harriet . . .'

It was her hands gripping mine now.

'That would have killed me too in the end. There is no doubt. It wouldn't have mattered if I were singing in the finest theatres in the world. You made me see that. Reading your diary, I knew I would never have any life at all if I left him for that monster to corrupt. That's why I kept reading your diary; it was my guiding light.'

Her eyes filled with tears and something desperate.

'I never *wanted* to be a mother. I didn't *want* a child with us in America.'

It was as if she was pleading with me to believe her.

'But I love him. I love my son.'

She paused. The words seemed to summon strength, renewed certainty.

'I do this for him willingly.'

It was clear that she had decided, but I still couldn't let it go.

'What about your life now, and everything you planned for? To be shut up and locked away . . .'

My voice broke off. She smiled, squeezed my fingers.

'But don't you remember, Harriet? They also serve who only stand and wait.'

I saw she was beyond me. There was only one question left, and the words came thick on my tongue.

'His name, Clara? What do you call him?'

She hesitated, then touched my cheek gently with her fingers.

'You decide. I know you will choose well.'

I don't know how I took my leave of her. When I was at the door, she called me back, almost timidly. Her expression had changed. It was trembling, full of light.

'I sang well? Did I not?'

There were tears in her eyes. She smiled hopefully, like a nervous child. I remembered seeing the heavens and mountaintops when I first heard her, the way she had flung her voice over fields and hedgerows on the way to the vicarage like springtime itself, the thousands in Castle Garden whose arrival in a new land would forever ring with the beauty of her song. I told her all this in whispers, holding her close to me, until the warder shouted, and we had to go.

1879

Wednesday, 2nd April

I had decided not to write another word. The course of more than one person's life depends on my silence, and what shouts louder than a diary in the wrong hands? It will be destroyed today – I should have burned it long ago. That being so, there is little danger in writing out an ending – and there is an ending to this. I had not realised all those nights straining my eyes and cramping my body that it was not my story I was recording. My role has been handmaid and midwife. I was the miner working the flint mill, labouring to throw light on the scene – but when the explosion came, it was not my life blasted. I am the one walking away. Which is why I cannot throw this book to the waves without scratching out what happened last. It seems to me its loss will not matter, so long as it is written – the writing itself will stitch it into me. Her story will be a part of me, more alive than memory, beating in my blood.

I went back to Annie's to wait. We knew Gethin would be searching still, even if he could never claim his son publicly, but I didn't fear another trial. My outburst in the gallery proved I was ignorant of Edward's whereabouts; Barrett had seen it in my face. Mr Gethin is on his own now in his search – he has played his card with the police and the newspapers and lost. I think of his lie, and even now it gives me a thrill of fear. Robert believes he pretended the dead child was his to make the police work faster. A murder investigation demands more time and effort than a runaway wife. It's true, I believe it too – he would have risked more than any ordinary man to crush Clara, to make her give up her son, to win. I believe he so loves destruction, he is willing to court even his own.

Barrett found me one more time, dropping into step beside me as I walked home from a charring job. The streets were still full of people celebrating the prime minister's return from Berlin. The Russians had been chopped down with words, and we didn't go to war after all. Peace with honour, they called it, as if to console themselves. I imagine Mr Gethin was looking forward to reading reports of atrocities.

Barrett pretended to escort me past a group of men roaring with song and drink. He was smooth, sleek as ever, as if nothing else had passed between us, assuring me of generous sums should I come to hear of any news, even a hint of where Edward might be. I bit my lip until I tasted blood. It was too much to bear – that he could talk to me in the street like that with no fear for his freedom, no chance of the police bearing down and dragging him away. I try not to dwell on it, nor think of my own silence while Gethin carries on preying on the innocent, unseen and unchecked. The newspapers pour pity and praise on him in equal measure. I never bothered with them before, but now I cannot stop myself from reading every mention – it is like scratching a wound. Come the next election, it is said the Liberals will most likely win, and he will rise like a star in the cabinet. Perhaps to the very top. If nothing stops him – and why should it? – he will be remembered as one of those unquestionable persons I have also read much about: a Great Man. Nothing can be said against him then; they may as well make him a saint and be done with it. I shall follow him though, wherever I am; I shall always be watching for a misstep, for the day he brushes too close to chaos. I never said a word to Barrett. When he left me, I ducked into an ally to be sick into a gutter and spill burning tears for Laurence.

After that, I was even more careful. A dozen times I visited St James' before going near the painting. If anyone was watching, there was nothing to see but a devout woman praying twice a week in her favourite church.

'Behind the cross,' Clara had whispered, 'the painting you were staring at when I came in.'

I studied it again, waiting for the verger to finish clearing the hymn board. The exhausted Christ, the grieving women – they were my allies now, harbouring a secret hope. Their pained expressions seemed to me exaggerated, a performance to hoodwink the unknowing. The verger walked down the aisle, shoes clapping the stone floor like a loud clock ticking, and went out. I moved quickly, every footstep and rustle of my clothes barking into the silence. Up close, the paint itself was all I could see, ridges and lines from the brush, colours separating out that from a distance blended to skin and desert. I tucked my hand carefully behind the frame. My fingers bumped and teased. They found it wedged into the back edge and pulled it out – a soft tube of rolled-up leather. Slipping it into my pocket, I walked unhurriedly out of the church.

I opened it at Annie's, locked in the privy in the yard. Inside were papers. Copies of letters with a petition and a receipt from the Foundling Hospital.

The 25th Day of May 1878
RECEIVED a Male Child

Memories: finding bills for concerts at the Hospital on her desk in the morning room at Finton Hall and in the locked bottom drawer; she had even spoken of it. I felt a shudder, though it was a warm day. My idea of a foundling hospital, for all its high-placed patrons, brought with it the chill wind of the workhouse. It seemed unthinkable that she had delivered her son into the hands of strangers, abandoned him to the hard grind of an institution. I turned to the petition and letters, copied out in Clara's beautiful hand.

To the Governors and Guardians of the Hospital for the Maintenance and Education of Exposed and Deserted Young Children

THE PETITION of Helen Dubois

of 23 Warren Street

HUMBLY SHEWETH

That your petitioner is unmarried, 19 Years of Age and was on the 15th Day of December 1877 delivered of a male Child which is wholly dependent on your Petitioner for support, being deserted by the Father.

She had given my false name, my address at Mrs Cole's, but everything else belonged to the real Helene Dubois and her son, a baby only a few weeks older. The Hospital guardians demand references and proof before they accept a child. They wrote to the lying-in hospital in west London where Helene had given birth, and the matron confirmed the girl's character and situation. They asked Mr Trevelyan for a reference, and he had written to praise her attendance at church. This was why Clara had made us wait. She was fashioning a safe passage for her son out of the cobwebs of her former maid's life. No one would know his true identity, and 'Helen' could reclaim him later while Helene herself was safely in France with her own child. I remembered the end of that long and awful night at Finton Hall when Clara told me to take Helene's name, as if she had only that moment thought of it. 'A real person's life will sound more truthful'.

It was only later I understood the strange drama with Betsy and the stolen letter at Mrs Cole's. The Hospital would have written to that address to say 'my' baby had been accepted. Laurence made sure I never saw the letter. Other things fell into place over time – memories that caught me unawares while I was cleaning furniture or threading a needle, locking me into stillness like a statue. It might have been Laurence who took my print dress from the drawer the time it went missing, but it would have been for the missus to wear in London. She would have had to petition the Hospital in person as Helen. I dare say she mimicked my voice then too. How long she had planned all this and at what point she chose to include me, I will never know.

I kept the secret as close and guarded as she and Laurence had before me. It was a butterfly in my cupped hands. I understood now why she hadn't told me – or anyone except Laurence. All those years silenced and cowed by Finton Hall, and he had chosen the most dangerous road in the end for another's sake. He must have known the risks better than anyone. A fierce, grief-stricken urge to speak to him seized me, to set things right between us. I was very alone in the weeks after the church, more alone than I needed to be. My friends lived with a sliver of myself. I acted as if nothing had happened, taking work as a char and sewing, helping Annie with the washing, saving as much as I could. I watched my hands become coarse again.

My business with Finton Hall wasn't finished though – there was one thing I couldn't leave alone. I walked all the way to Stepney one Saturday and knocked on the Bowmans' door without hesitation. If they called the constable again, so be it; Gethin already knew where to find me. A maid answered, and I was shown into the tidy parlour. Francis's parents stood before me like startled horses until Mrs Bowman stepped forward and undid me completely by taking my face in her hands.

'We have prayed every day for your safety.'

I spent most of my visit sobbing. They told me how they had decided to bring Francis home, but as it turned out, Laurence brought him back before they could act. He pushed him into their arms and told them Finton Hall was no place for a child. It must have been the day Clara and I left London – perhaps the last thing he ever did. My tears only stopped streaming when they told me about Francis himself. He is apprenticed to a glassblower. The news struck me between the eyes, and even as I write this, I can't keep from smiling. No more trying to capture gleaming things with slate or pencil. From now on he will make his very own – shiny, beautiful, glass vessels to hold up to the light. I remembered him blowing soap bubbles from his clay pipe in the boot room, and the thought of it set me off. I giggled until I couldn't stop, until the tears were running down my face again, and Mr and Mrs Bowman were laughing too without knowing why.

It wasn't the only house where Gethin's web had broken – or failed to stick. One day I boarded a train for home and found Mother still deeply indignant about the letter he had sent. Turns out my fears were unfounded – she can't abide anyone criticising me but herself.

'Such nonsense he wrote, as if I wouldn't know if my own daughter's head was straight on her shoulders. I knew there was something peculiar about that household. Just look at his wife! And then you wrote – cool as a cucumber – that you were going to France.'

No one was interested in my time in 'France'. I was a puzzle not worth the trouble of solving. The great family hope now lay in my sister who was courting the under butler at Beechwood. Everyone looked older, especially Father, but otherwise I spent four days wondering how a place could look so the same when I had changed so much. I saw little of William – Dorcas no doubt saw to that. Coming out of church, I heard her bark two words at him, and he followed like a smacked puppy. But I felt little curiosity about them or what their life might be. In spare moments, I stole away to walk the lanes of my childhood – a stranger who somehow knew every turn, gate and blasted stump by heart.

In the end, it was Robert. He wasn't the policeman I had met months earlier, unbending in his zeal for the law. I am sure that man would have felt it his duty to restore 'Edward' to his father. We started taking walks together, often without talking, two washed-up survivors pacing the shoreline. His career, at least in his eyes, was over. He had made too much trouble about the drowned child and then Laurence's body; they took him off the baby farmer investigations. When he did speak, it was in vague circles about going abroad, starting again, until one day I began telling him about New York and how I'd felt right on the cusp, a new life pulling at me. I told him about the money and the new clothes, the camera I had itched to possess and the misty yearnings it had prompted.

'It was loyal of you to come back.'

He had called me that before. This time he spoke as if it had little to recommend it. Such virtues had lost their lustre.

'I had to know the truth about Clara's child and what the newspapers were saying.'

We walked on a few paces before he spoke again.

'I wonder what she did with him.'

I didn't speak – it wasn't a question after all – but Robert can weigh silences like stolen goods. He kept looking at me and finally came to a halt.

'You know.'

The light was fading, and we had wandered into a quiet street without lamps. I couldn't see his face very clearly, which is why I think I came out with it.

'I'm going to raise him. When I'm ready.'

He didn't say anything for the longest time, not until we'd started walking again, and then it was only to make another observation.

'You will need help.'

I let go the details one by one in similar shadowy moments. It was an agony of wanting to and fearing to at the same time. He never pressed me. I wrote to the Hospital as Helen, asking after the baby's health, and when the reply came back, I found I couldn't open it. I took it to Robert. 'Alive and well,' he said promptly after a glance and waited in silence as I wept my relief against the trunk of a plane tree.

Then he invited me out one Sunday for a 'surprise'. We travelled into north London and walked through Bloomsbury. He led me towards a building that commanded three sides of a large square. Carriages clustered along the roadway. The Foundling Hospital. I drew back, horrified, but he pointed to a place where people were streaming in. We joined them, walking into the high-ceilinged chapel, which smelled faintly of linen and polish. Box pews lined the walls, facing centre. In the balcony behind a dizzyingly tall pulpit were rows and rows of neatly dressed children, the Hospital choir. As the service unfolded, I began to understand what Clara had done. Music is the very heart of the Hospital. The foundlings are steeped in it, drilled in it. If she was never able to return for her son, if he was never to learn who she was, he would at least grow up bathed in song. Their voices caught me off guard. I wasn't prepared to be shaken in my seat, the music settling on me like a blessing. Robert took my hand. I laced my fingers through his and held on.

This isn't the place for an account of our courtship, if that's the right word for it. It happened without fuss, like a change of season. I looked at other men and they started to seem incomplete, strangely blanched, without a birthmark. If eyes didn't bruise like shifting skies, they were cold as marbles to me. There was him, and then there was only him. The fleeting sense I had once felt that he might be something to do with me, that he was mine to know, returned. I noticed his knuckles, the slope of his shoulder, the width of his mouth. His body seemed the natural outward form of his courage and intelligence, his quiet humour. All the yearnings I had felt seeing Mary and Laurence together, the confused desires prompted by the books, found an answer and continuation in him. I showed him one day what I had taken from the library the night of the soirée. He was kissing the freckles on my face and neck at the time – he said it was like following clues, one led to the other, and he never knew where they would lead. I pushed off his lap and fished this diary out of my pocket. The photograph of the woman and man smiling into each other's faces as she sits astride him – naked and open and unashamed – had been hiding in these pages since that night. Until now, I never even dared write that I had taken it. Robert studied it silently as if it was a weighty piece of evidence. Then he drew me back onto his lap, eyes like storm clouds, and continued his pursuit of clues. Turns out I have freckles in places I never suspected.

We were married on a foggy day in November with Annie and Andrew as witnesses – their tiny son slept all the way through it, swaddled against Annie's chest. Mrs Trevelyan was the only other wedding guest. Afterwards, we ate stewed oysters and made toasts. We were happy. I linked arms with Mrs T as we walked her back to her hotel. She was reluctant to speak of Clara on such a day, but it was rare that I was able to see her, and our letters had to be so guarded.

'How is she?'

She sighed and pressed her lips together.

'She asked about Laurence. I am not sure I chose wisely in telling her. She took it hard.'

I was silent a moment. His death weighed heavily. The verdict said it was accidental, sweeping away any possibility of bringing Gethin to account. Mary and Mrs T at least saved him from a nameless, pauper's grave. His daughter will be raised knowing only that her father was a fine man, a defender of women and children.

'Better than her thinking he left her to face trial alone.'

'I don't know. She blames herself. That is a hard thing to carry with you in such a place, year in, year out.'

'Your letters made me think the asylum is a good one?'

Her head tipped from side to side. A good asylum is still an asylum.

'She told me she feels freer there than she did at Finton Hall.'

'You don't believe her?'

'Oh, I do. Only that isn't saying terribly much, is it? She is comfortable at least. Gethin has spared no expense – he wants to appear noble. She writes music, and they let her sing. Her doctors are . . . progressive.'

The word was suffocating.

'I should visit. Barrett hasn't come near me again.'

'No.'

She shook her head.

'I think not. She refuses visitors. It is too painful. She is used to me, but I don't go often.'

I remembered buttoning her cuff at Mrs B's, that first feeling of grace in her service. The bitter helplessness of mourning a living person made me breathe in sharply. Mrs T looked sideways at me.

'It would help, I think, if I were able to take her some good news.'

I considered a moment, choosing my words carefully.

'Tell her we are going away when we have enough saved . . . *far* away. And I shall do as she asked; all is . . . *well*, and there is nothing to fear. Also, tell her . . .'

I dropped my voice lower.

'Tell her that Laurence has a new namesake.'

Mrs T gave a little gasp and squeezed my arm.

'I shall tell her. She will like that.'

After a moment, she couldn't help herself.

'May I ask – at least – in which direction you are going?'

I took a deep breath in, filling my lungs as if the foggy air was as soft and perfumed as May. The future shimmered like the light on New York Harbour. I closed my eyes to see it better.

'West. To America.'

My pen is reluctant to rest. Perhaps all stories resist their endings. Although this, after all, is a false end – Clara continues to breathe; her child sleeps beside me in our tiny lamp-lit cabin, rocked by the ocean, unaware even of who he is; Gethin searches on, though we have done everything we can to avoid discovery, snatching little Laurence away from the Hospital at the last possible moment. I have taken his likeness a few times, though I am still learning how to use Robert's wedding gift to me. The camera is as pristine and frightening as this book was when it was new and blank. I think when I have succeeded in making a good photograph, I will have it delivered by hand to the asylum. No message. She will know.

We are paused between selves now, between lifetimes. None of us shall ever again answer to the names we were christened with. When Laurence's nurse mother placed him in my arms at the Hospital – so grown he was, it made my heart ache – she kissed his forehead and murmured her goodbyes to little Thomas. He has had more names in his short life than he has had years. It makes me think of a housemaid I knew who had to answer to a different name in three different situations, one after the other. The world is quick to stamp us for its own convenience. Perhaps that is why I linger, putting off an ending. The truth recorded in these pages is dangerous, but it is hard to let it go. My lovely gift from Mrs B is battered now, the cover scuffed all over, the paper fattened with writing. I should tie it shut with Laurence's ribbon and drop it overboard. Perhaps water will seep in, washing away the words – just as my spilled tea dissolved William's handwriting in Finton Hall. I wonder if it is enough simply to carry the truth silently within me, if the world should be allowed to tell a person's story any way it wishes.

Laurence just stirred. As I straightened his blanket and stroked his cheek, I noticed the roughness of my hands again. It doesn't trouble me now. I like to see the history written there, and Robert kisses them as well as if they were a lady's. He will be back soon, and I shall take my turn in the salty air, look towards our future as if land is already in sight. Perhaps I shall take this book with me, drop it safely into the darkness and let my own story begin.

There is time here, in the middle of the ocean. I do not need to decide yet.

Acknowledgements

Debut novels aren't always the same thing as first novels, and this book owes much to its two predecessors and the encouragement I received from friends and family from the start. I am forever grateful to Rob Curling for his unbounded enthusiasm and gleeful grammar corrections, for the Path to Joy as pondered over and pursued with Lauren Pett, and for pebble-hunting with Skye Loneragan. My cousin Fern Wells cheerleads as if it's her job and once swerved off the road to impress upon me a better definition of success. Rebekah Lattin-Rawstrone and Tom Collinson have become my treasured go-to writer-readers; their feedback on early drafts is always hugely helpful and generous, and I can't now imagine finishing a book without them.

For several years now, I have enjoyed the support of my extraordinary agent, Juliet Mushens, whose commitment, passion and insight are always startling and inspiring. You are the good writing-angel on my shoulder. Thanks also to Rachel Neely, who stepped in so brilliantly, Liza DeBlock, Kiya Evans and the whole wonderful team at Mushens Entertainment.

I have been just as fortunate in my editor, Katie Bowden, at 4th Estate. I had not expected the editorial process to feel so genuinely collaborative and exciting – there is something magical in the way you see into a story. I am also extremely grateful to work with a team at Harper Collins that includes Katy Archer, Matt Clacher, Michelle Kane, Paul Erdpresser, Emma Pidsley, Lola Downes, and (briefly but excellently) Sadé Omeje. Huge thanks to Andrew Davis for the inspired and spectacular final cover.

My thanks to everyone who offered a bed or meal or listening ear over the years while I wandered about, especially Elaine Cowin.

Thanks also to other friends and readers, who perhaps don't always know how helpful they've been – to Book Grubbers past and present, the beloved MDra gang, my whole Tynemouth Road family, Sam Birkett, Anna Madeleine, John Berry, and my glorious, new-found friends in Scotland who so readily celebrated with me. Finally, thanks to my family for always, always asking how the writing's going, to Dad for his support and wildlife stories from the cabin, and to Mum, whose love of words and literature infused my world from childhood and helped make this possible.